Praise for *Darkroom*

"*Darkroom* comes complete with a great m~~~~ ~~~~ ~~~~ts, and beguiling adventure. Josl ~~~~ ~~~~al landscape through an entourage ~~~~ ~~~~ ~~~~is one—and take a walk on the pe~~~~ ~~~~

—Steve Berry, *New York Times* ~~~~ ~~~~ ~~~~y

"Mixing the end of the Vietnam War with a young woman's paranormal visions of a murder in today's New York, Graham has created a modern political thriller wrapped in a historical puzzle inside a tale of redemption. The short chapters, told from the point of view of the various characters, give it a cinematic feel and a breakneck pace."

—*Author Magazine*

"Bravo! Graham takes characters and puts them inside each other's lives in such a way that it's impossible to put his book down until the last word is read. . . . [His] power with words is absolutely incredible and paints one of the most powerful pictures I've ever seen, anywhere."

—*Suspense Magazine*

"A vivid retelling of historic events [that] bring the Vietnam War to life in alarming detail. If you like thrillers . . . then grab this book when it's released. You'll enjoy every minute of it."

—*Rhodes Review*

"A spellbinding and riveting tale of suspense with international flavor . . . Wrapped in authentic history, but woven into a tale of mystery and intrigue . . . full of twists and turns . . . this riveting tale will keep readers on edge. A book that I highly recommend."

—*East County Magazine*

"Graham takes us on a ride full of twists and turns in this emotionally charged quest to find the truth. . . . I actually found myself holding my breath at times and sympathizing with the characters, feeling outrage when they were wronged, hating the villains or even forgiving them. When it was all said and done, I didn't feel like I had finished a book; I felt like I had been on a journey."

—*The Top Shelf Book Reviews*

"*Darkroom* is a twisted tale of conspiracies [that] moves at a frantic and suspenseful pace. . . . Mr. Graham immediately grabs hold of the reader with the tenacity of a pit bull and will not let go until you have read every last page and emerge exhausted and happily satiated from this astonishing ride. . . . I would not hesitate to recommend *Darkroom*. . . . You won't be disappointed."

—PsychoticState.net Book Reviews

"The intensity and heart-pounding thrills you'll feel as you read each page [of *Darkroom*] will leave you breathless. Blending history with current events, Mr. Graham is a talented author who can wrap the reader in a cocoon of emotions, from bitterness to redemption, and leave the reader feeling as if they were in the story, as if they were the ones plotted against. A fantastic job!"

—Partners in Crime Book Reviews

Darkroom

Joshua Graham

HOWARD BOOKS
A Division of Simon & Schuster, Inc.
New York Nashville London Toronto Sydney New Delhi

Howard Books
A Division of Simon & Schuster, Inc.
1230 Avenue of the Americas
New York, NY 10020

This book is a work of fiction. Names, characters, places, and incidents either are products of the author's imagination or are used fictitiously. Any resemblance to actual events or locales or persons, living or dead, is entirely coincidental.

First Howard Books trade paperback edition May 2012

HOWARD and colophon are trademarks of Simon & Schuster, Inc.

For information about special discounts for bulk purchases,
please contact Simon & Schuster Special Sales at 1-866-506-1949
or business@simonandschuster.com.

The Simon & Schuster Speakers Bureau can bring authors to your live event.
For more information or to book an event contact the Simon & Schuster
Speakers Bureau at 1-866-248-3049 or visit our website at www.simonspeakers.com.

Designed by Davina Mock-Maniscalco

Manufactured in the United States of America

10   9   8   7   6   5   4   3   2   1

Library of Congress Cataloging-in-Publication Data
Graham, Joshua.
    Darkroom / Joshua Graham.
        p. cm.
    1. Photojournalists—Fiction.   2. Women journalists—Fiction.   3. Vietnam
War, 1961–1975—Fiction.   4. War crimes—Fiction.   I. Title.
    PS3607.R3385D37 2012
    813'.6—dc22   2011020222

ISBN 978-1-4516-5469-1
ISBN 978-1-4516-5477-6 (ebook)

Scripture quotations are taken from the King James Version of the Bible, public domain; the New King James Version, Copyright © 1979, 1980, 1982 by Thomas Nelson, Inc. Used by permission. All rights reserved; and THE HOLY BIBLE, NEW INTERNATIONAL VERSION®, NIV®, Copyright © 1973, 1978, 1984 by Biblica US, Inc.®. Used by permission.

For Katie, my bride, my muse,
the mother of my children, and my best friend.
On countless levels, this book would not exist without you.

The general killed the Viet Cong; I killed the general with my camera. Still photographs are the most powerful weapon in the world. People believe them, but photographs do lie, even without manipulation. They are only half-truths . . .

—Eddie Adams, Pulitzer Prize–winning photographer of General Nguyễn Ngọc Loan executing Nguyễn Văn Lém, a Vietcong officer, with a pistol to the head

Prologue

IAN MORTIMER

Making people disappear isn't quite as easy as I remember. Of course, I'm not as young as I used to be. Rigor mortis will soon set in, and I've got to dispose of this poor lass's body straightaway. How can I possibly be doing this again?

Thankfully, no one's around this time of night. And with her limbs properly weighed down, she'll stay under until . . . Bugger! Only three bags in the trunk. I shall have to improvise.

Right. Everything is ready. I cross myself and pull her ever-stiffening body from the trunk. She's slight—just shy of forty-five kilos, I'd venture—but quite muscular in the limbs.

A heavy duvet of clouds obscures the moon. It's beastly cold out. Here on the remote side of the pond, far off the path, the row-boat is hidden behind the thicket of reeds, exactly where I left it last night. My headlights are off and I'm parked close enough to lower the body into the boat and row out.

As I lower her into the inky water, I'm careful not to splash. Her sweatshirt balloons, and bubbles surround her. A mane of flaxen hair spreads on the water's surface.

Bollocks, she's not sinking!

With my oar, I nudge her down. Even though her hands and feet have submerged, her hair still floats. A halo around the back of her head.

In the distance, a pair of headlights looms. It's a blooming patrol car. No choice, I've got to row back and get away from here. But look at her—the back of her sweatshirt and her head are still bobbing at the surface.

Back in my car now. Slowly making my way back to the main road, I steal another glimpse. She's still just beneath the surface, her blond hair a clear marker.

The patrol car's headlights vanish behind a bunch of trees. If they turn left, they'll be here in less than a minute.

I'm about to crawl clear out of my skin.

And then it happens.

Two large bubbles pop out from under the sweatshirt, just at the nape of her neck, and the weights do their trick. The lass's body sinks to the bottom of the pond.

That was too close.

With all lights off, I drive off. A minute later, I can see in my rearview mirror that the squad car has just passed the pond. Didn't even slow down. I'm well on my way home now. Into the warmth of Nicole's embrace, and to kiss Bobby as he dreams of ponies and puppies.

Good Lord, what have I done?

1

XANDRA CARRICK

Bình Sơn, Vietnam: October 2008

This was her wish. Dad kept saying that from the moment we boarded our flight at JFK to our first step onto the fertile soil of *Bình Sơn*, which in English means "peaceful mountain."

En route to our penultimate destination, Tran, our middle-aged guide, tells us all about the scenery through lively gesticulations and nasal broken English.

"This place all rice field now." He lifts both hands and spreads them wide. Enthralled by the verdant fronds and the sound of exotic fauna, I hardly notice the weight of my backpack. "But during war, *Việt Nam Cộng Sản* come here in Bình Sơn."

Perhaps it's because I appear more Vietnamese than American that he breaks into the native tongue. Ironically, Dad, an American, knows more about this country than I do. He's quiet and has been holding the urn under his arm, staring out at the hills.

Out in the lush green paddy fields, a boy prods his water buffalo with a bamboo stick, distracting me from Tran's narrative. "Viet . . . what?" I've had enough years in weekend Vietnamese language classes to read and write. But this term escapes me.

"*Việt Nam Cộng Sản*. V.C." Tran laughs. "You know, Vietcong? Charlie?"

I glance over to Dad, to whom this would hold more meaning. He shrugs.

That same emptiness in his eyes, which have grown darker and more profound since I was a child, evokes a blunt pang. It's been over a year. Rather than drawing closer, he's grown more distant.

Of course, Tran has no idea that he's hiking with Peter Carrick, Pulitzer Prize-winning photojournalist who earned coveted accolades for his on-the-spot photos of the massacre at Huế. Nor does Tran realize that his daughter, Xandra Carrick, is a respected photojournalist in her own right. I may not have won a Pulitzer—not yet, anyway—but at twenty-seven, working for the *New York Times* is not too shabby.

"Vietcong fight American soldier here," Tran explains, stopping to catch his breath.

I can take some pictures, which I do more out of responsibility to my craft than anything. "Now just rice farm family and water buffalo. Even water buffalo part of family. You know, *Chống cảy, vở cấy, con trâu đi bừa.*" Which means, The husband plows, the wife sows, water buffalos draw the rake. A proverb Mom taught me years ago, but it's lost on Dad, who keeps staring at the hills.

"You okay, Dad?"

"I'm fine."

The boy driving the long-horned beast is at most twelve years old. His loose pants are rolled up past his calves and his feet are submerged in ankle-deep water.

Narrow, peaked hills stand over the horizon, Titans guarding this remote village nestled in the manifold waterways of the Mekong. Palms sway in the earthy breeze blowing through the window and brushing through my now unruly hair.

I reach for Dad's hand. One can only speculate on the reason for his reluctance to make this trip. As for me, this is my first time in Vietnam and I'm taken by its overwhelming beauty. "Was it like this when—?"

"Xandra, please. Don't."

"But there's so much I want to know about this place, about you and Mom."

"You know my answer." The same for years, from the moment I first developed an interest in his career and experiences during the war.

"Even now?"

"Your mother would understand." Dad's gaze returns to the hills. "She knew how I felt about coming back here, but . . ." His gaze wanders off, draws him away to a time, a place, far off and forbidden. I know that look.

"Never mind, then." I kiss his hand, lean into his chest.

For the next fifteen minutes, we continue quietly along the trail. Finally, Tran turns around and smiles, a gold tooth glinting in the setting sun. "Okay, we here."

Still in awe of the breathtaking landscape, I set my pack down, and stretch. The ground is soft and moist, but at the same time it's as solid as the sidewalk outside my apartment on Central Park West.

Beyond the hilltops, the sun falls to rest in a poignant wash of amber. The *chrink-chrink* of Rain Quails rings out invisibly behind an emerald veil of bamboo in the distance. Every thought arrested, every word, no one speaks.

The light is perfect, though it won't last much longer. And despite the somber occasion, I simply cannot forsake the scenery. These shots will help me to remember.

The shutter sounds from my Nikon ripple the silence like a stone tossed into a glassy pond. Still transfixed on that same spot up in the hills, Dad lets out a pointed breath. "Probably not the best time."

"Just a couple more. For Mom." A twinge works its way up and lodges in my throat. As Charles Kuralt so aptly put it: "There is melancholy in the wind and sorrow in the grass."

"Make it quick, will you?" He pads over to Tran and hands him a roll of greenbacks. "*Cám ỏn nhiêu lˆâm.*"

With both hands, Tran receives his payment and bows. He waves and returns to the trail from whence we came.

All is tranquil as the sun passes her mantle to the rising moon. We are serenaded not only by the Rain Quails' ditty but by a chorus of frogs and crickets as well. Farmers and their water buffalo slosh back to their huts about half a mile downstream of us. Yet they can be heard as though a mere stone's throw away.

For the first time in this journey, Dad puts his arm around my shoulders, warming my heart as nothing else can. He points to a vacant hut, with a kerosene lamp glowing in the window. Leaning into the security of his strong shoulder, I nod and take a moment to consider the significance of this place. Both to him and Mom.

"We start at daybreak." He takes our bags and approaches the hut. "Let's settle in."

As I follow him into the hut, an unexpected irony arises: I've never traveled so far just to say good-bye. But I am glad to have made the trip. Mom would be pleased.

This was her wish.

2

GRACE TH'AM AI LE

Thirty-Five Years Ago
Binh Son, Vietnam: January 7, 1973

I always knew the war would come to the South. Before the Communists sent the Vietcong back down the Ho Chi Minh trail, before the Spring Festival attacks during *Tết Nguyên Đán*, I knew. I had seen it all in my dreams. I even foresaw my parents' deaths, which left me and my brother orphans, forcing us to flee to the village of my aunt and uncle.

Some of the boys in Bình Sơn, on this side of the Mekong Delta, had expressed interest in joining the Vietcong, my brother included. Everyone else feared this would eventually draw a confrontation to our otherwise untouched hamlets.

And so it had.

The trip back from Saigon was only 120 kilometers, but it was like going from one world to another. At first glance, you would not imagine a war was taking place. Abundant green mountains, flowing waters of the Mekong, all resting under cotton clouds and sunlit skies.

Amongst the countless generations of farming families, I was the first girl, if not the first person, to leave and go to university. Now, upon my return, my entire life had changed.

At the bottom of the dusty road, where the foot of Bình Sơn touches the water, all that remained of the huts in the neighboring village were charred embers. Not a soul stirred. I could only hope that everyone had escaped.

Higher up, I looked to the hills where once I lived. Where Huynh Tho still lived. Perhaps, because it was hidden behind bamboo and palms, it had been spared. So quiet were the mountains. But for the whispering wind, nothing stirred. Not even a bird.

Off the road's side, I walked under the shade of the trees. I had to find my brother and quietly bring him back to Saigon before it was too late.

Quietly. How do you take an angry young idealist who espouses the goals of the Vietcong away from his village quietly? The thought of an argument with Huynh Tho made me as anxious as did the war itself.

I stepped toward the path leading to our village. Each snap of a twig jolted me, as if it were a gunshot. But there was no one in sight. The utter quiet unsettled me.

Without warning, less than ten meters from the path, a terrifying explosion threw me to the ground. Through the ringing in my ears and the clouds of dust and smoke, I could tell. A battle had just erupted all around me.

"Huynh Tho!" Disembodied and hollow, my voice sounded as though I were underwater. Flashes of light, thumping explosions reverberating in my chest, the *tat-tat-tat-tat* of gunfire. Too frightened was I to lift my face from the dirt.

But that is what I had to do. For if I remained, I would surely die. And Huynh Tho, who was only sixteen, would be left alone with nowhere to go. Disregarding the fear that clutched my heart, I crawled to the most remote part of the woods.

This proved a terrible mistake.

In hopes of hiding behind the trunk of a tree, I got up to run. Someone began shouting. My English was not so good at the time, but the little I had learned at university sufficed.

"Get down!" cried the American, from somewhere I could not see. "Lady, get down!"

I spun around, seeking the direction from which the desperate voice called. In that instant, a whisking sound rushed toward me. A sharp twinge knocked me back, as if struck by a stone.

Then came the searing sensation below my collarbone, which I shall never forget. A spot of blood spread on my shirt. My head grew faint. My body became too heavy for my legs. Down I went.

The world around me blurred.

I began to shake.

So cold . . .

3

SUZANNE COLBERT-COLSON

Colbert Estate
Napa Valley, California: October 2008

Until recently, I had never cared for his line of work, or his career aspirations. Politics was never my cup of tea. But one thing I'll say for my husband: if there's anyone who can do the job right and get this country back on track, it's him.

In his first term as one of California's senators, Rick had been widely acclaimed as a no-nonsense, tell-it-like-it-is legislator who produces results, not just talk. It's a testament to his worthiness of the US presidency.

And, yes, he's an independent. How about that? Not since Ross Perot has the nation perked up its ears and listened like this. When my husband looks the nation in the eye and promises change, they believe him.

And they ought to.

I know better than anyone that Rick is a man who never accepts defeat, who always keeps his word. Just look at his service record. He doesn't like my bragging on him like I do, but I am proud of him. He's a decorated hero who saved many lives during the Vietnam War.

I'm sure whatever shred of privacy we've enjoyed will soon be obliterated when Rick wins the election. But that loss of privacy doesn't frighten me in the least. We've lived a very open life for the whole world to see. No secrets, unlike our opponents whose pasts keep coming back to haunt them.

Despite the efforts of those slimy politicians to defame him—both Republicans and Democrats—no one has ever been able to dig up any dirt on Rick. You know why? Because there isn't any. So what will the public find when they scrutinize the life of President Colson?

They'll find a loving father who never missed a game his star quarterback son played before going off to Princeton. They'll find a devoted husband who stood by me for three decades, even after I became wheelchair bound with MS. I can count on the fingers of one hand how many times he couldn't come with me to doctors' visits and PT sessions. He always kept family a priority, wasn't afraid to say no to his career. I think it's his integrity and unwavering principles that have garnered him the reputation and respect he now enjoys.

I'll never forget the day I found out I had MS. Jack was eight months old and learning to walk. The news caught me by surprise. Besides fatigue, which all new mothers experience, I thought I was fine. But when I got the call to see my doctor as soon as possible, Rick made the appointment. You see, he had noticed the symptoms before I ever did. From the day I got pregnant, he always had his nose in medical books and journals, researching and monitoring my health.

When we got the news, I broke down and cried. It was supposed to be the happiest time of our lives. Jack was our pride and joy, Rick had just been elected deputy district attorney, and his political career was taking off like a rocket.

Rick took me in his arms and just held me for the longest time. When I calmed down, he said, "We're going to beat this, Suzie. Don't you worry. I promise, I will do everything in my power."

I wanted to say, "*Who are you? God?*" But he was so sincere, I didn't have the heart to suggest he was just saying things to make me feel better. Well, I was wrong. He wasn't just saying it. Did I mention that one of Rick's greatest strengths is that he can look tough decisions in the eye and face them down?

He took a sabbatical to take care of me and Jack. A year out of his career at its height. And whatever free time he had, he spent talking to medical experts, going to the library, you name it.

Sure, there were some rough days where I wished I could just curl up and die. But I have to say, because of the love of this beautiful man, every day of my life has been worth living. None of the billions of dollars I've inherited could ever make me feel this way. Because in the end, what do you take with you? Not the money, the houses, or yachts; not the fame of being the heiress of the Colbert Media empire. Judging by the way Rick's lived, he never cared for those things anyway. No, what you take with you into eternity is the love of those who've sacrificed themselves for you.

We now have two beautiful boys, Jack and Gary. I call them boys, but they're really fine young men, both attending Ivy League schools on full scholarships. Rick is on his way to the White House, and I, though frail, am the luckiest, most blessed woman on the face of this planet.

Lest you roll your eyes or gag from the sweetness of it all, I'll confess Rick isn't perfect. In fact, he'd be the first to admit it. There are times he gets so involved with his responsibilities that he'll allow himself to get overwhelmed. And those are the times he just sort of vanishes for a few hours. Okay, sometimes it's a day or two. But when he comes home, he's left it all at the office and it's as if nothing's happened. He's able to give us his full attention again.

Sure, I'm biased. I haven't got even a fraction of the knowledge of pundits. But no one knows this man as I do. And I'll put whatever days I have left into supporting him.

I believe in him.

4

XANDRA CARRICK

Binh Son, Vietnam

If for most of your life morning begins with the din of car horns and garbage trucks, bucolic quietude comes as something of a surprise.

Across the room, Dad's empty cot lies bathed in golden sunlight pouring through the open window. Perched on the wicker nightstand, a salamander tilts its head. I reach out and let the little guy crawl onto my hand and up my arm.

It lingers for a moment, then climbs down the bridge of my fingers back to the table. Dad stands outside by the edge of the river, gazing at the hills. The urn in his hands seems heavier than it ought to.

"Dad!" I wave at him through the open window.

He turns and nods. So severe, yet dignified in a way that projects strength and constancy. Good to see that again.

I haven't adjusted my watch, but judging by the angle of the sun, it's probably near eight thirty.

It's time.

After washing up, I go out to join my father by the river. I've prepared my backpack with everything I'll need. Dad is not aware of the fact that I've brought the Graflex Speed Graphic along. Considering his reluctance to talk about his past—especially his Vietnam days—I have a feeling he might be less than pleased.

But it seems only right that I brought the very camera that helped make his career back to the place where it all began. And besides, it's been mine ever since I left for college.

"In my day," he had told me, "it was the camera of choice for the press. You just don't get the subtlety, the finesse, those infinite shades of gray, with all the bells and whistles of these digital doo-hickeys these days. It's more work, for sure, developing film and enlarging photos in the darkroom. Large format is old-school even for analog photographers. But greatness is not a thing to be had instantly, like microwave popcorn."

Indeed. And if this Graflex could talk, oh, the stories. He'll forgive me for bringing it when he sees the amazing pictures I take of this day, a day we'll never forget.

Dad paddles our boat, glancing every now and then down at the urn. He whispers silently, his eyes ever returning to the hills. I must have taken twenty shots of the fishermen wearing cone hats and mending their nets.

A river dolphin follows us and peeks up with curiosity. Vibrant white-tailed douc langurs call down from tree branches. The earthy scent of life clings to the warming air. Everything Mom described and more.

We've stopped. Clutching the backpack with the Graflex, I'm excited about using it here. But how will Dad react when he sees it? He pulls the boat ashore, and for a moment, sitting here as his strong arms pull the rope, I'm five years old again. And he's still my superman. If he only knew.

Tears welling up, his eyes are fixed on the urn. He doesn't see me. My loss is twofold, shifting between each rueful prong: the loss of my mother and the loss of the father I once knew. My own tears begin.

It's been just over thirteen months now. Haven't I already traversed the steps of grief? I've watched Dad fall apart and pull himself back together, but never quite back to his original self. Now, it's all coming back to me. As if this entire year never happened. The grief, the void—it's all coming back. I realize now that it's never really left.

If he only knew.

Dad chokes, sniffs, and points to the urn. "Would you?"

"Of course." Shaking with emotion, I'm afraid if I don't hold on strong enough, I might . . .

With a deep, wet breath, I clutch the urn to my heart. "Mom . . . you're finally home."

5

Mom had suffered from chronic headaches. She finally went to the doctor, expecting to find nothing more than lack of sleep, poor diet, and poor exercise habits as the cause. Instead, she left his office with a death sentence.

From the day she'd been diagnosed with a malignant primary brain tumor to the day she died, she remained cheerful, though more pensive than usual. Even though she outlived the doctors' predictions, her passing blindsided us emotionally.

Then came the funeral, the relatives, all the official business with lawyers and insurance companies. During the entire time, Dad withdrew into a shell of silence. It was a few days after the funeral before he could even speak to anyone.

The presence of relatives, especially my cousin Janine and my favorite nephew and niece, brought some degree of comfort. But the truth is, with all the logistics that fell upon me alone, there was hardly any time for me to cry.

Eventually, everyone went home. For the next eight weeks, I lived with Dad in Del Mar. The emptiness of his house resounded like a phantasmal void.

A week after the funeral, the duty of retrieving Mom's ashes fell upon me. Dad had accompanied me, but it was I who handled the entire transaction, while his vacant gaze hovered. For most of my time with him this past year, I had to lead him by the hand like a child.

That my own life required attention escaped me. I had just returned from Iraq, having completed an assignment covering the families most likely to be targeted for female suicide-bomber recruits. The assignment had been cut short by Mom's diagnosis, and, needless to say, I never completed it.

But the time away afforded me opportunities to reconnect with Dad.

Somewhat.

We had always been close when I was younger. And according to Mom, my following in his footsteps had made him proud. But things started to change when I became an adolescent.

I must have been twelve when I first begged him to teach me photography. My first camera was a Pentax K1000, a beginner's 35mm single-lens reflex, which was not too shabby if you knew what you were doing. So, I persisted with determination that I apparently inherited from Mom.

Instead of endearing me to him, it seemed to make him uneasy. "You really don't want to do this," he'd say. "Photojournalism isn't the glamorous profession you think."

"I don't care, Daddy, I'm going to be just like you. Oh, and I love pretty pictures." At twelve years old, you haven't got all your priorities straight. Nor do you notice or properly interpret the gravity of your parent's tone. Not when dreams of becoming like your hero fill your head.

Never one to be discouraged, I simply taught myself whatever Dad didn't have the time to. Lots of mistakes, spilled chemicals, and broken equipment. What can I say? Dad and pretty pictures. It was a no-brainer.

In retrospect, I suppose it was more of a calculated fiscal decision for Dad to start teaching me. My mistakes were costing him too much.

Mom would gently guilt Dad into taking me out to the beach,

into the city, and, when I was older, out on assignments when he traveled on the weekends. "You're a Pulitzer Prize winner, and you won't teach your own daughter?"

That was the kind of all-expenses-paid-round-trip-first-class guilt trip she'd send him on. I, none the wiser, only smiled as he relented and got over himself.

Even now, standing next to him, holding the ashes of his departed wife, I struggle to understand his misgivings toward my emulating him.

A warm breeze brushes through my hair like Mom's fingers whenever she spoke of Vietnam's beauty. Dad lifts the urn from my hands and points his chin up the hill. "Up that path, behind that stand of bamboo trees." He puts one hand behind the small of my back, gently urging me. But it's the warm, maternal breeze whispering against my neck that compels me forward.

To my surprise, when we pass the wall of trees, the ground is level and clear. Charred black, the skeletal frames of several farmhouses shudder, as though one strong gust could blow them away like dandelion spores. The rest are simply dirt pads where other homes once stood.

"Before the war, hardly anyone knew this place existed." Dad sets the urn on a rock and removes his courier bag. He sits on a fallen tree trunk, wipes his nose, and sniffs.

"So this is where Mom grew up."

Dad nods and heaves a weighty sigh. He's fatigued but not from the climb. It's a weariness from bearing the weight of unspoken burdens. And he's worn this look for as long as I can remember. Over the years, it has etched lines into his forehead, turned his chestnut hair silver.

Sitting next to him, I lean my face into the crook of his neck. His bristly jawbone tickles me. "You okay?"

Why doesn't he answer? How I wish he'd just tell me what's troubling him. Maybe it's more than just letting go. But of what? I have to ask. "Dad, is there anything you want to talk about?"

"Why do you ask?"

"You seem—I don't know—distracted." I didn't want to say

it, but he almost seemed afraid. "Like there's something out there."

"You're seeing things that aren't there. Did it as a kid, doing it now."

"And you're shifting everything over to me when, really, this is about you. You've been doing that since I was a child. Mom always—"

"Xandra, can we please do what we came to do and leave?"

Well, that didn't go well. I give him an appeasing kiss on the cheek. "Of course, Daddy. I'm sorry." He's not angry with me, just a bit on edge. It's all right; I'll get it out of him one day. But not today.

"Your mother made me promise to bring her back to her birthplace and scatter her ashes. Returning her to the soil of her home."

He picks up the urn, cradles it in one hand, and pulls a piece of paper from his pocket. He looks at it, shakes his head, and blows out a terse breath. "Dammit, why did she have to . . ."

"What is it?"

He turns to me, his eyes softened with a look of solidarity. "I mean, she knew that I never believed."

"Is that what's been bothering you?"

"I've got nothing against religion." Which was exactly what he kept yelling in one of their biggest fights. Mom wanted to take me to Sunday school when I was about seven or eight. But Dad had planned to take me to the zoo. It ended up with angry words and tears.

"Church was never your thing, I know." I'm hugging him sideways now, trying to get my arms up and around him.

"Yeah, well. Some sins are unforgivable anyway," Dad murmurs, barely audible.

"What?"

"Nothing." He wipes his brow. "Mom wanted me to read this, and I'm going to do it."

So that was it. Unresolved differences. His reaction was a bit out of proportion, but I suppose it makes sense. "Wait, Daddy.

Can we just take a minute and recall a thing or two about her? Happy things. Wouldn't that be better?"

After a thoughtful moment, he turns to me, slips the paper back in his pocket, and wraps an arm around me. "You're right, Xandi. You're right."

We spend the next ten or fifteen minutes recalling some of our favorite stories.

"Like the time Mom had a dream about fishing and insisted we go out to Montauk." I wrap my arm around Dad's. "You thought she was just being superstitious."

"No, I'd come to trust her intuition, especially when she had those dreams." He blinks and wipes his eye. "It was like a sixth sense with her."

"How many did we catch, four?"

"Baker's dozen."

"Or the time she threw a surprise fortieth birthday party for you and you came downstairs in your boxers."

"Oh yeah. Surprise!"

Our laughter is like dark chocolate. He dabs his eyes with his sleeve. "Can't believe it's been an entire year."

"I can still hear her calling us for dinner."

"She was an incredible woman, Xandi. Full of love and wisdom. No one ever loved so unselfishly, so unconditionally. I think it's because for her whole life, she was . . ." Searching, I gaze deeply into his visage. "She was . . . grateful."

We're facing the narrow river at the bottom of the hill now. Tied to a bamboo tree, our flatboat bobs in the current. Dad looks at me. I give him a nod. Ready.

A rush of cool wind that causes the palms to dance embraces us. Cicadas crescendo and join in the chorale as Dad opens the lid of the urn and tilts it into the breeze. He crumples the paper from which he was going to read and lets it fly into the gust along with the ashes.

"Dad!" How could he do that? It may not have been his belief, but it was Mom's dying request. It was her wish.

And then, as the ashes flow down into the trees and over the river, he smiles, with tears in his eyes, and recites the verse. I remember now. Yes. His photographic memory.

"For all flesh is as grass, and all the glory of man as the flower of grass. The grass withereth, and the flower thereof falleth away: But the word of the Lord endureth for ever."

6

I thought I'd be filled with joy, seeing Mom's final wishes carried out. But before I know it, tears blur my vision. Words catch in my throat.

"Daddy . . . ?"

For a long time, we're silent.

The urn is empty, the verses recited. It's all we can do to hold on to each other and say good-bye to the woman who gave me life, and, according to Dad, the woman who saved his, though she insisted it had been the other way around.

This was their happy dispute that lasted for the entire thirty-three years of their marriage. Seven months after she left us, over-looking the waves of Del Mar, Dad said, "She was the only light in the darkest days of my life."

We don't say a word for God knows how long. Motionless, we remain in each other's arms until it feels right to let go. Once again, Dad is anxious to leave. But tears notwithstanding, I can't let this moment go undocumented. As a photojournalist of his stature, he's got to understand this. Especially with the Graflex. It's so fitting. I can just hear Mom say, *"It's so pretty, Xandi. Take a picture of that! You're the next Ansel Adams."* To which I'd say, *"No, I'm the next Peter Carrick."*

I reach into my backpack and pull out the camera as he walks off to stow the urn. "Give me a minute, Dad." While he fixes the straps, I snap off about three photos of the ruins, the rock, the remains of the decades-long uninhabited village. This is, after all, Mom's final resting place.

At the sound of the Graflex's shutter and film winder, he stiffens. Without turning around he says in a controlled voice, "Xandra, what are you . . . ?"

A dizzying dread fills me, but I continue taking photos all around the area. From my head to my feet, a tingling sensation numbs my extremities. Dad's footsteps approach slowly as I lower the viewfinder. Instead of pleasant surprise, his countenance blanches with outrage.

"Dad, what's the matter?"

His mouth is moving, but the words don't form. He's pointing at the camera and his expression wavers between anger, betrayal, and panic. What demons have I conjured?

"Why did you bring that?"

"I don't know, I just thought—"

"Put that away, right now!" The harshness in his voice, the anger in his eyes, and I'm that four-year-old girl who had run out into the middle of the street, only to get yanked back and scolded.

"Why, what's wrong?"

Rather than repeat himself, he snatches both camera and backpack out of my hands, stuffs it, zips it, and thrusts it back at me. "We're leaving today!"

"But what about—?"

"Dammit, child! Why don't you ever listen!"

"Dad!"

He takes me by the elbow, and we trudge down to the river. "Should never have given that camera to you!"

7

GRACE TH'AM AI LE

I must be dead.

From the noise around me, the heat, the tormented cries in both English and Vietnamese, I wondered if perhaps I was in hell.

"Miss, are you okay?" The voice of that American was now directly above me. I opened my eyes and, through the blur, saw the outline of a white man, the color of his clothing resembling that of a soldier. By his tone, however, he did not seem very much like one.

I do not think he understood me, because I answered in Vietnamese. "My brother . . ."

"Come on," he said. "We've got to get you out of here."

"Yes." This time I spoke in English. He reached under my arms and lifted me with little effort.

"Can you walk?"

I was about to say yes, but my knees buckled and my head fell back onto his shoulder.

"All right, then." He lifted me into his arms and carried me. My eyes were shut, but I could feel that he was running. Breathing frantically.

"My brother!" I tried to speak, but only the sound of air came leaking out. This man must have been quite strong to have carried me in his arms and run as far as he did. Again, I tried to tell him that I needed to go back to get my little brother.

But this time, I lost consciousness.

I have vague memories of the time between getting shot and waking up in a medical tent, where I lay alongside injured soldiers. One of them was screaming in pain, which jolted me to consciousness.

It took me a moment to realize where I was. Tubes went through my arm; a mask covered my face. In that brief moment, I began to panic. I wanted to let out a scream, but the very effort brought a sharp jab to my chest.

"Whoa, take it easy there." It was the man who carried me out of the battlefield. "We thought for sure you were a goner. But the doc says you're going to make it. Isn't that right, Doc?" He called this into the tent, but there was no one in sight at the moment.

Again, I wanted to speak. This time I also attempted to sit up. The pain was twice as bad, and it must have shown on my face. My kind rescuer stood from his chair. "Don't try to get up just yet. They're going to airlift you to a hospital back in the city. Bullet passed clean through you. Damned near hit an artery."

I motioned for him to remove my mask. With strained effort, I managed a whisper. "Thank you."

"It's nothing, Miss. Couldn't just leave you there." He had a camera strapped around his neck, and it dangled precariously over my head.

"I think you are not a soldier?"

"No. I'm an independent photojournalist traveling with Echo Company." He extended a hand to shake. "Name's Peter Carrick."

All I could muster was the strength to extend my fingertips. "I am Th'am Ai Le." He took them and gave a gentle squeeze.

"Pleasure to meet you, Tham . . . Tha . . ."

"Call me Grace, okay?"

"That's not Vietnamese."

"My father gave me an English name because of Jesuit missionaries . . . So thirsty." Peter reached for a pitcher of ice water and poured a cup for me. "Thank you."

"You've lost a lot of blood. But they'll get you all fixed up in the hospital."

At that very moment, I remembered the entire reason I had come back to Bình Sơn. "No, I cannot go."

"Why not?"

"My brother, Huynh Tho. I must get him!"

"Where is he?"

"The village in the hills overlooking the water."

At this his countenance dimmed. His brow furrowed, and he began to speak but stopped himself. "You can't go back there. It's too dangerous."

"I must."

"You're badly hurt. If you don't—"

"He is the only family I have left. Please, I promised my parents I would look after him."

Even as I spoke, two American soldiers came into the tent and gestured outside. "We've got a small window here. It's now or never."

With urgent eyes, Peter gripped my hand. "If you don't get to the hospital, you'll bleed to death. Grace, please. Go with these men."

"But my brother—"

"I'll look for him." He leaned in so close I could sense the intensity of his concern. "Now, go on." The moment lasted no more than a few seconds, but it seemed as if time stood still. This man, this American stranger, had just risked his life to save mine. There was a familiar, yet dreamlike feeling about him. For some reason, I felt I could trust him.

"His name is Huynh Tho." A sudden wave of nausea overwhelmed me. The saline solution flowing through intravenous tubes into my bloodstream caused me to shiver. "He's wearing a gold crucifix . . . it was my father's. To keep him safe."

"All right. I'll find him, Grace. I promise."

"How will I find you?"

He looked over to the medics. "Where're you taking her?"

"Grall, in Saigon."

Then he took my hand and patted it. "I'll see you there."

"With my brother?"

"With your brother."

Tears filled my eyes. I thought, *He must be an angel.* "Thank you, Mr. Carrick."

A moment later, and without a proper opportunity to say good-bye, the soldiers rushed me into a helicopter and it lifted out of the fields. Explosions continued to echo through the hills like peals of thunder. Black smoke arose from beneath the trees. The villages of Bình Sơn were gone. And though in body I soared above the mountains, my spirit sank.

Grall Hospital: Recovery 2
Saigon: January 13, 1973

I have made an exceptional recovery from a near-fatal gunshot wound and consider myself blessed that the Christian name Father chose for me held a prophetic meaning. For the past week, since they brought me to Grall Hospital, I have been told a hundred times what a lucky girl I am.

I don't feel so lucky. I cannot help but worry about Huynh Tho.

Each day as my strength returns, I sit up in my bed and hope that Mr. Peter Carrick will come to the door with my little brother standing next to him. He will say something like, *"Here is your brother, Miss."* And I will try my best not to weep. It will be a joyous reunion. And hopefully, after he has seen the ruthless horrors of war, my brother will put down his gun and pick up a pen, despite Uncle Viyh's insistence he remain with the Vietcong.

I must admit, a part of my heart wishes to see Peter again, if for nothing else but to properly express gratitude for saving my life. And my brother's as well.

Grall Hospital: Recovery 2
Saigon: January 25, 1973

It has been almost three weeks since I returned from Bình Sơn and still no word from Peter. Nobody seems to know how I can contact him either. This is so frustrating! I am still holding onto hope that he will return with Huynh Tho, but hope without evidence can only last for so long.

I have even begun to pray to the God of the Jesuits, as they taught my father. Everything now, I ask in Jesus' name. What a peculiar way to make a wish.

Grall Hospital: Recovery 2
Saigon: January 27, 1973

Today it seemed my prayers were answered. After breakfast and a walk with Miss Janet, my physical therapist, one of the hospital administrators found me and said, "You have a visitor in the atrium, Grace."

"Who is it?"

"His name is Peter Carrick. He says that—"

I never heard the rest of his sentence because I rushed out of Janet's grip and went straight to the atrium. "Please, Grace," she called out after me, "you mustn't run!" But I had never felt better. How could I just walk?

When I arrived, his back was turned to me, his hands in his jacket pockets. He faced the dark corridor toward the lobby as if waiting. But my brother was not with him.

"Peter?"

He turned and walked toward me. With an awkward kind of smile that did not match the rest of his demeanor, he said, "Grace. How are you?"

I bowed my head slightly. "Thanks to you, alive and well."

"Yes, well. You're looking just fine. Do you have any idea how hard it was to find you?"

"I apologize for the inconvenience."

"Oh, no. That's not what I meant." A wide smile brightened his face. "I just meant that I didn't have a translator and my Vietnamese is so poor that—"

"Forgive me, but did you find Huynh Tho?"

His smile evaporated like steam from a pot of rice. His hands went back into his pockets and he let out a slow breath. "Yes. I did."

The words caused my heart to leap. "That's wonderful! Thank you, Peter." Though it was inappropriate for a woman to touch a man other than her husband, I could not contain myself. I jumped up and put my arms around him, embracing his neck. Tears of relief streamed from my eyes onto his lapels.

But his countenance seemed incongruous. "Grace, listen . . ."

I pushed away. As quickly as my hopes had arisen, they began to sink. My stomach cramped, my breath grew hesitant. "Where is Huynh Tho?"

"That's what I'm trying to tell you."

"You said you found him. Where is he?"

"I found him, yes, but—"

"Why are you being so unkind? Please, tell me!"

Now holding both of my arms, as though I might run, or hit him, or hurt myself, Peter turned his gaze down toward me, an unspoken apology brimming from his eyes. "Grace . . ."

Oh, why couldn't he just speak without this infuriating pausing? "Please, where?"

From the breast pocket in his jacket, he reached in and pulled something out. "Grace, I'm so sorry." He placed it in my hand. Without even looking, because my eyes were squeezed shut, trying to hold back a deluge, I knew.

"Oh, Huynh Tho!"

"There just wasn't enough time." He wrapped his arms around me to comfort me. But I stiffened my arms and pushed him away.

"Don't touch me!"

"Your brother was fighting for the Vietcong. They engaged Echo Company in a firefight."

"He wasn't old enough to shave!"

"I'm sorry."

"It cannot be! It cannot!"

"Grace." Again, he tried to hold me. I responded by shouting, crying out in Vietnamese and pounding his chest with my fists. Huynh Tho, my little brother, my only family, was dead.

I kept wailing and hitting Peter's chest, but he remained there quietly until at last I grew too weary to continue and fell into his arms, weeping.

The hospital staff was now looking at us. In the back of my mind, the thought arose that they would think it improper for a young woman like me to be in the embrace of a man. A white man! But my entire world had collapsed; who cared what they thought!

I wrapped my arms around Peter and pressed my hands against his back. As I did, the gold crucifix that Peter had retrieved from Huynh Tho and placed in my hand dangled by the chain from my fingers.

8

RICHARD COLSON

Waldorf Astoria, New York City

Things don't always go as planned. That's one of those golden nuggets my mother passed on to me early in life. Still carry it around in my pocket. I had, however, planned on victory at every turn and, as a result, emerged victorious after last night's debate at Loyola with James Remington, much to the DNC's chagrin.

"Five minutes, Rick." Karen Lassiter, my chief of staff, takes my coat, my briefcase, and sets them down in the living room of my suite in the Waldorf Astoria. "Can I get you anything?"

"I'm good, thanks. Wasn't it only supposed to be four hours from Baltimore?" Day twenty-eight on my East Coast campaign tour, and the only thing worse than a five-and-a-half-hour battle on the I-95 was the traffic coming into Manhattan, even at 11:00 a.m.

"Construction in the Lincoln Tunnel, rain. You scheduled things a bit too close. But I'm not one to say I told you so." She just did. But she's right about these things. That's why I hired her.

"Just give me a couple of minutes to freshen up, okay? Make yourselves at home, help yourself to the wet bar. Just don't get too comfortable, the reception is being filmed."

Karen grins and gets right on her cell phone, while the Secret Service men step outside. I walk into the bedroom and make my way past the marble columns of the bathroom. I splash cool water on my face and take a deep breath. *Was it all worth it?*

After toweling off, I unzip my black leather toiletry bag, fish past the toothpaste and Tylenol, then put the Norelco to my five o' clock shadow, whisking away hundreds of miles and pages upon pages of speeches. Tonight, I'll deliver one of my best to my supporters from the Coalition of International Business Ventures. Topic: Transforming the Global Economy, One Commodity at a Time.

A major supporter, the CIBV pushed the legal envelope with contributions and promotions. There is no way I can give them anything less than my best tonight.

Karen knocks gently on the bedroom door. "Two minutes, Rick. Everything all right?"

"Be right out." One final pass over my salt and pepper with a comb, and I'm ready. The cell phone on the granite countertop displays 5:50 p.m. Given that I'm about to step up to the dais before cameras and hundreds of the world's most powerful CEOs in less than ten minutes, Karen's patience surprises me.

But not as much as the buzzing of my cell phone, just as I pluck it off the counter. Nearly dropped it. As soon as I see the caller ID, however, I grip it tighter. My heart races. "What is it?"

It's Cecilia, Suzanne's home attendant. "Senator Colson, I'm sorry to bother you right now, but—"

Karen knocks a bit more urgently now. "Rick?"

"Just a minute!"

"You're going to be late."

"I said, in a minute! Cecilia, what's wrong?"

The nurse's tone is even but anxious. "It's Mrs. Colson, sir. She's had a massive flare-up. We're taking her to the ER right now."

"Which one?"

"Mercy Hospital."

"Tell her I'll be there soon."

"But—"

"Just tell her, Cecilia. Thank you." I end the call before she can offer another question. When I open the door, Karen and the two Secret Service men stand waiting in the living area.

"They're expecting you in the ballroom, sir." She helps me into my jacket and fixes my tie. "You're going to miss your sound check."

"There's a problem." I push her hands away and step back. "Suzanne's had an episode."

Karen opens her mouth, then stops herself. Then, "Sir, I'm sorry to hear that. But the CIBV members paid five hundred dollars a head to be here tonight."

"It's an important appearance, I know. But not as important to me as Suzanne."

"Of course not." She glances at her watch. "But remember, public perception."

"We can work the media, Karen." *I control it more powerfully than anyone in the public could ever imagine.* "I can make Hitler look like a saint and Mother Teresa as wholesome as Madonna."

"If you miss this speech, you'll take a direct hit. No amount of media spin mitigates snubbing this group. You can't risk that now. Not when we're this close." Again, she's right. If I'm perceived as unable to keep my personal life from affecting my official life even before I am elected, what would that do to my supporters' confidence?

A few more of the event staff arrive at the door. Karen reaches up and puts a hand on my shoulder. "You're going to be late."

9

XANDRA CARRICK

New York City

The human body wasn't designed to traverse continents in so short a time span. All the great explorers—Vasco de Gama, Ferdinand Magellan, Christopher Columbus—sailed for months. My journey back from Vietnam took a day. I've yet to reacclimate to Eastern time.

It's 10:30 a.m., which for Dad is 7:30 in San Diego. An early riser, he will have been awake for a couple of hours by now. I reach over, pick up the phone, and call him. From the moment he answers, it's apparent something's amiss.

"How are you doing, Dad?"

"Better. You?"

"Unseasonably cold today." As I speak, my eyes linger on the Graflex, perched on my desk. Beside it, my cello sits entombed in its case. How long has it been there, untouched, its voice forgotten?

Dad clears this throat. "Listen, Xandi. I never got a chance to apologize."

"It's all right, I should have said something about it before blindsiding you." Once again I'm making excuses for him. Truth be told, I'd prefer an explanation over an apology for his tantrum in Bình Sơn. He'll never talk about it, though. Anything related to his war experience, from which I suspect that outburst stemmed, is off-limits. It's always been.

"So we're okay?"

"Dad, I could never stay mad at you."

"You were mad?"

"I just meant . . . never mind."

"What are your plans, now that you're home?"

"Don't know. I was thinking about submitting an entry for the Marbury."

Dad pauses. "Hmm."

"What do you mean, *hmm*?"

"The Marbury's huge. Makes the Pulitzer look like a local contest."

"You don't think I can win?"

"Not what I meant."

"No, go on and say it. I can take it."

"Xandi, I didn't mean it like that."

"You don't think I can make it in photography any more than I could in music." Propped up against the wall, my neglected cello silently affirms this.

"You gave up, even though you had everything going for you. Excellence requires more than talent, Xandi. You need dedication."

"You of all people should not lecture about dedication." As far as memory serves, he'd become an absentee dad, even when he was home. I had no siblings with whom he had to divide his attention. Mom honored and protected his right to "privacy," trained me to be devoted to him. Unfortunately, those sentiments were not reciprocated.

Dad huffs. "Why'd you call, anyway? To argue about the past?"

"What could ever possess me to imagine you'd open up about the past?"

"This conversation is over. Call me after you've cooled down."

"Call me when you get a clue!" I slam down the receiver, but I think he beat me to it. My hands are shaking and I'm breathing heavily. The Graflex and my cello stare at me, witnesses testifying against me in this mockery of a trial called "My Life."

"You've got such a gift," Mom had said backstage, the day before my graduation recital at Juilliard Pre-College. "Don't keep it to yourself. It's meant to bless others."

"I don't feel so gifted. Karina's the one who won the Avery Fisher prize, she's the one who signed with Yo-Yo Ma's manager, and she's the one that Sony Classical—"

Mom cupped my face and kissed my head. "*You're* just as good. Maybe if you were more willing to share."

"Karina doesn't share; she shows off."

"Think of all the people you have touched with your music. The senior citizens in the nursing homes, people in church. Hmm?"

"How about Dad?"

"He loves your cello playing."

"Then why isn't he here?"

"It was a last-minute assignment; he had to go."

"That's what happened last year, and the year before. He doesn't care."

"You know that's not true. He's very proud of you."

I went on stage and, according to my teacher Ardyth Alton, gave the best performance of any concert I'd ever played. But somehow, despite three encores and four curtain calls, Dad's absence hollowed out any of the joy I might otherwise have derived.

That was my last public appearance.

From then on, it was college, photography, and the hollow pursuit of winning his approval. There are fringe benefits to such pursuits, though. My current work with the *New York Times* is among them, and I can always fall back on that when I'm feeling the need for validation.

Or so I hope.

My leave of absence from the *Times* began with Mom's passing and lasted nearly a year. I'm having difficulty finding the motivation to return to my photographic endeavors. This concerns me, though Doug, my supervisor, hasn't made an issue of it. "Take all the time you need," he always tells me. "Your job will be here waiting, when you come home."

It's not so much the job as it is about my drive. What will impel me to get out of bed every day now? The thrill of capturing moments in the temporal existence of human beings from all walks of society just doesn't hold the same appeal now as it did, say, two years ago, when I thought there was still a chance Dad would one day say, "Xandra, I'm so proud of you." What am I doing it for now? Prestige, self-fulfillment? Perhaps when the money runs out, I'll gain a new perspective.

On the way to the kitchen, I pass by my poster of Senator Richard Colson. In bold blue letters, the slogan reads: Vote Colson, Vote Change.

Perhaps the new president will bring a new hope. Thank God Colson is taking the lead in the polls. Nobody wants another four years of Republican rule. On the other hand, many fear Remington's extreme views on the Democratic ticket. Colson is not the lesser of two evils, but the sensible balance. He's socially responsible, well balanced, strong on foreign policy. And he's got my vote.

Two more weeks.

Change.

That's the word that fills my head as I pour myself a bowl of Kellogg's Frosted Flakes. While I partake, Tony the Tiger reminds me of how his sugar-frosted flakes are like Colson's reform plans: "they're grrrreat!"

In this historic election year, Washington's talking about bailouts, corporations are laying off employees by the tens of thousands, and people are committing suicide because they've lost jobs, homes, face. But I'm emotionally disconnected from these troubled economic times. Mom's death has eclipsed it all.

For now, the only thing I can focus on is getting my inspiration back. Something I had hoped would happen back in Bình Sơn. While Mom's ashes had remained in Dad's house in Del Mar, I held on to her presence, if only spiritually. Now that they've been scattered, it feels like she's truly gone. I never expected to feel so empty.

Even here in my apartment, the slightest hint puts me in tears—a framed picture, the gold cross that once belonged to her brother, a chipped coffee mug she gave me three years ago for Christmas that reads, FAITH: THE EVIDENCE OF THINGS NOT SEEN.

Bình Sơn was supposed to bring me closure. But closure is a process, not an event. Perhaps the few photos I took there will help me to connect with my inner feelings. I'll develop them after breakfast.

There's great comfort in routine. A bowl of cereal, a hot cup of coffee, checking my email as I turn on the radio and read the headlines on my laptop: Colson Crosses Party Lines, Gains Ground in Swing States. Vietnam Vet Dies After Falling Asleep at the Wheel in Boston. Foreclosures Scale Record Heights.

The radio announcer reports that a dance student from Juilliard has been reported missing for three days. "Dellafina was last seen wearing faded jeans and a white sweatshirt. Authorities are asking anyone with information on her last known whereabouts to contact the Missing Persons Squad, or the 20th Precinct at . . ."

With a sigh, I shut off the radio. Bình Sơn and New York: both jungles, one of bamboo and earth, the other of asphalt and concrete. Manhattan is where a wide range of humanity, eight million plus, compresses into thirty square miles. These are the harsh realities to which I've returned. I feel as though I've left part of my soul behind under the emerald palms of Vietnam.

My Outlook inbox bulges with months-neglected messages. Reflexively, I delete all the spam and junk mail that has accumulated.

Then, without even looking at the subject line, I notice the sender's name on the next email. My innards knot up. I'm tempted to delete the message without even looking.

It's from Ethan.

He only emails me for a couple of reasons: to borrow money or to brag about the new girl he's dating. *I really don't need this now.*

Never before had I given my heart to anyone. And the first one I felt safe enough to do so with breaks up with me because I wasn't ready to sleep with him.

In retrospect, the signs were painfully obvious—his wandering eyes, hopeless flirting, and vehement denial thereof. He'd been cheating on me from the start. Mom had a feeling about him and was right. She was always right, when it mattered. If only I'd listened.

But I really loved him. And that is perhaps what made the pain so acute.

I suppose I'll open the message. Curiosity, it's a masochistic habit I must break. This time, however, the entire look of the email is different. It's formal, not filled with 'netisms.

In the spirit of decency, I'd like to call a truce and share some good news. On December 25, 2009, I'm going to marry Felicia, the love of my life. And I'd love for you to be there.

The pen I forgot I'm holding drops to the floor.

Why would he do this? No, I'm not upset. I'm really quite over him now. Yet the walls are closing in around me and the air is being sucked out of my apartment. I've got to get out. Walk it off. Take some pictures.

I throw all my gear into my backpack. The Graflex is coming along, too, because I'm going to show the world that it's the photographer, not the equipment, that matters.

As usual, Frank, the doorman, tips his hat. "Lovely morning, Ms. Carrick." I walk right past him. "Have a great day, ma'am." Rudeness isn't my way and I regret it. I'll apologize later.

While crossing Central Park West, I nearly walk into a moving bus. The driver leans on the horn. I don't even flinch. He's got his destination and I've got mine: the old bench by the pond.

The sun doesn't even attempt to peek through the clouds, which cast sackcloth and ash over the city. Thick morning air fills my lungs as I jog over puddles from last night's thunderstorm.

Out of breath and with my thinking bench in sight, I'm doubled over, resting my hands on my knees, backpack hanging from my elbow.

Breathe.

I straighten up, and a boy on a bike speeds by, splashing frigid water all over me. "Hey!"

He doesn't even turn around.

Dripping and cold, I am nevertheless determined. Not even this shall deter me from the sanctuary. I wring out my sleeves and take my place before the pond.

Denn alles Fleisch from Brahms' *Ein Deutsches Requiem* flows through my iPod. A bit too brooding for me, so I shuffle the tracks, and in a moment I'm listening to the latest NPR podcast.

"... are aware of the fact that Senator Colson is a twice-honored veteran of the Vietnam War. He's no stranger to the difficult choices and the importance of strategy. This seems to engender a sense of trust with the conservatives in regards to his foreign-policy plans. But at the same time, his plans for middle-class tax breaks resonate with liberals and those who make less than two hundred thousand dollars a year.

"Experts predict a huge upset on November fourth. Both the Democratic and Republican parties have expressed concern because they are so polarized on the issues and have taken such a hard line in order to maintain a distinctive platform. Now, Independent Colson is poised to snatch the election from under them.

"Reporting from Independent Richard Colson's campaign headquarters in Sacramento, this is Joshua Sanford, NPR News."

Unlike his opponents, Colson's got his finger on the nation's pulse and is ready to jump-start it back to life. If only I could do the same with my own life. For the past year, my entire existence revolved around Dad. Seeing to it his bills were paid, calling the insurance company to file death-benefit claims, making sure he was eating. Depression struck him hard, and for the first five months, he could barely get out of bed. Thank God he's better now. Maybe now that he's fulfilled Mom's final wishes, he'll be able to move on.

I, however, have grown acclimated to a life where my own needs are so foreign, it requires a passport to even think about them. It's time to get back into photography. If what Doug and the critics say is true, I'm closer now than ever to reaching my lifelong goal. Even Dad had once alluded to it, especially with my work in Fallujah. I can just feel it. That's why I'm aiming for the Marbury Award for Outstanding Photojournalism. The fifteen thousand dollars is nice, but really, it's the prestige and the doors this prize will open that motivate me.

But can I even approach Dad's level of achievement? If I could just prove myself, exceed his expectations . . . It all comes back to him, doesn't it?

Enough.

Time to take some pictures. Visual free association: I aim Dad's Graflex at the first thing I see—a gray-brown mallard waddling through a puddle and into the pond, three yellow ducklings in tow. Dad's Graflex has traveled the world and captured events of historic significance.

Now I'm using it for ducks.

At the most inopportune moment, my cell phone rings. Quacking in surprise, the web-footed entourage scampers away. It's Doug, likely calling to beg me to return to work. Eschewing the appearance of desperation, I let it ring a couple more times before answering.

"Doug who?"

"Very funny. How are you, Xandra?"

"Tired."

"Things go well in Vietnam?"

Filial piety precludes me from regaling him with the eminent Peter Carrick's capricious antics. "Smashingly."

"Wonderful, wonderful." A strange pause. "Look, Xandra, there's something I need to talk to you about. Is this a good time?"

"For you, Douglas, any time is."

"Okay then." He lets out a tense breath. "You know how much I love your work, don't you? And beyond that, my admiration for you personally?"

"Yes, yes. You worship the ground on which I walk."

He chuckles dryly and draws a long hissing breath through

his teeth. "Look, I don't know how to tell you this. It's the last thing I would have imagined, though I guess I should have seen—"

"Why don't you just come out and say it?"

"Right. Of course." A pause, a sigh, it's taking every bit of patience to conceal my annoyance. "Xandra, management has been forced to make some changes due to the recession. They've cut over fifty percent of middle-management positions globally. The budget for our department has been impacted severely."

"But we're okay, right? Our positions are secure."

"I'm sorry, Xandra." Reading from a canned script: "I regret to inform you that due to corporate restructuring, effective immediately, your position has been terminated."

It's unreal. Like watching myself from outside of my body. "I . . . I've been laid off?"

"Stinks to high heaven, I know. It's hell for me too—I had to let Greg and Martin go as well, and they're not exactly spring chickens. They've got families and—"

"Oh my—" After a yearlong sabbatical, I was so looking forward to getting my life back on track.

"I feel like crap. We all should've seen this coming. That's what happens when they turn the reins over to the freakin' bean counters. Nothing matters but the metrics, the bottom line. Wasn't always like this, you know."

"What am I going to do?" And the more ominous question, what will I tell Dad?

"You'll be getting a decent severance package. But you need to sign and return a form with an NDA—boilerplate, of course. Any questions, I'm here."

"Oh, sure. You're there." A wave of bitterness crashes down over me. "Good to know you're sitting there, in your corner office, feet up on your desk, while people like me, Greg, and Marty—"

"They're letting me go too. A week after you guys, after I've cleaned up the carnage. Handed me an ax, and then a shovel to dig my own grave."

I swear silently. "Doug, I'm sorry."

"It's okay. Should have heard what I said to *my* boss. Lucky for me he's a forgiving man."

"Yeah. Lucky."

"Anyway, like I said, call me if you need anything. Really, anything at all. Carol and I are here for you."

"Thanks. I appreciate that."

"Good luck, Xandra."

10

RICHARD COLSON

Was it worth it? After all the sacrifices we've made, is this what it all boils down to? I take a deep breath and enter the room. "Suzanne! Oh, you poor thing."

IV drips connected to her arms, she turns her head, winces, and opens her eyes. "There you are."

"I'm so sorry. The flight got delayed, ice in Chicago."

"It's all right, honey. You're here now."

"I wanted to call off the—"

"No. That would have been—" She grimaces and sucks in a thin breath. "Can I have some ice?"

I reach over to the beige plastic tumbler, place a chip between her lips, and kiss her on the head. "One to ten."

"Better now." She kisses my cheek. "Before the morphine, it was a twelve."

It kills me that I wasn't here for her. "You're more important to me than any blasted speech, than this whole campaign. You know that?"

"Come on, how much time would you have saved? An hour?"

"That's not the point. When it comes to priorities, I don't flounder. But this time, I did."

"You made the right choice." A weak slap on my hand. She

smiles. "But you know, Rick, if you'd dropped the ball in New York on my account, I'd have to kill you."

"I left Karen behind at the Waldorf Astoria to field residual questions with the CIBV and the press. As soon as I stepped off the stage, I rushed to Newark and took the first flight to Sacramento. Would have been a lot quicker if I'd taken one of those CEOs' corporate jets."

"And violate your own travel policy? What are you thinking, sweetie?"

"When it comes to you, all bets are off."

Suzanne tries to turn on her side, but it's too painful. Instead, she points to the control dangling from the bed. "Sit me up?"

"How's the pain right now?"

"Comes and goes. I'm at a steady six or seven. Sit down, Rick. You look tense."

Obedient as a school boy, I pull up a padded chair and lean my elbows on the edge of her bed. "Suzie, I'd never have made it this far without you."

"Same here." She gives my hand a loving squeeze.

"But seeing you like this, I have to wonder. How am I going to take care of you if I get elected and—"

"*When* you get elected. Honey, listen. I don't know how much longer I have. Sometimes it gets so bad, I just want to give up."

"Don't ever talk like that."

"But I go on because of you. You're what this country needs right now. What the world needs. Don't you see? The role you're going to play is historic. It's much more important than either of us individually."

"But—"

"Don't throw it all away because you're afraid of what might happen to me."

These are the times—those rare times—that truly bring me to my knees. I gather up her cool, dry hands and press them to my lips. "I don't deserve you."

She laughs, coughs a little, then sighs. "For better or worse . . . we deserve each other." Her voice trails off and she shuts her eyes. The monitor's continual beeping fades. Exhausted, I put my head down on the bed. I could use some rest as well.

This lasts for all of thirty seconds.

A knock on the door, and the doctor comes in carrying a clipboard. "Oh, excuse me, Senator."

"Quite all right. She's asleep."

"Finally." He extends a hand. "I'm Dr. Choi. Since your wife got here, she's refused to sleep or increase her morphine drip regardless of the pain. She was waiting for you."

"Will she be all right?"

"This kind of flare-up isn't all that common for patients with MS. The degree of her pain concerned me, so I ran some more extensive blood tests."

"Did you find anything?"

Choi lowers the clipboard and holds it behind his back. "Yes."

"And?"

"Doctor-patient confidentiality prevents me from sharing this with you without Mrs. Colson's consent."

"You've got to be kidding."

"I'm bound by an ethical code."

At this, I rise to my feet. Surprised by my height, the doctor takes a step or two back. "Dr. Choi, you need to tell me what's in that report."

"I'm sorry, Mr. Colson, I—"

"My attorney will be happy to discuss the terms of Mrs. Colson's health-care power of attorney. I have a legal right to know, especially since she's incapacitated. Now, do we still have a problem, Doctor?"

Like a cornered rabbit, Choi's eyes grow wide, darting between the door and Suzanne.

"Do we have a problem!"

"N-no sir." He stutters and hands me the report. "But I'd feel more comfortable if you discuss this with my supervisor from this point on." Without mentioning who exactly that is, he steps out of the room.

But I'm already scrutinizing the report, too engrossed to notice. Struggling to decipher the cryptic medispeak, I come upon a page with the word highlighted in bold print: DIAGNOSIS . . .

The clipboard falls to the floor.

11

XANDRA CARRICK

Could this day get any worse?

Best not to ask. Not even rhetorically.

Toweling off after my second shower of the morning, I stare out over the bare tree branches in Central Park. Like mindless automatons, people walk to and fro like ant drones. But ant drones at least stop momentarily to touch antennae and communicate. Those people out there don't even seem to notice one another, though they brush up against one another frequently.

Did that kid who splashed me with his bike even know what he'd done? Too often people in this city pretend that others in close proximity don't exist. It's the only way, I suppose, to cope with being crowded next to complete strangers on the subway, the bus, or the sidewalk. We'd go insane here in Manhattan if we had any delusions of Texas-size personal space.

About the only personal space I have is my apartment. On the kitchen table sits the Graflex, its lens winking as though it knows something I don't. I exposed the remaining film on the pond and the ducks that waddled through the puddle with which I'd been baptized. At the very least, I'll be able to develop the shots from Bình Sơn.

I've converted one of my closets into a darkroom, something I would never have done had Dad not given me his Graflex. "Taking the shot is only half the game," Dad always says. "The real magic happens in the darkroom." Judging by his work, I've got to agree.

Thankful for the 70mm film-back adapter and the developing tank I got for a hundred bucks on eBay, I get right to work. The chemicals' sour smell makes my eyes water. What price, Luddism? Dad would be proud.

It's taking longer than I remember from photography lab at Stuyvesant High School. Back then, we were working with 35mm.

Finally, I've finished exposing a couple of proof sheets. Because I enjoy the thrill of watching the images come up, I've always placed the exposed sheet in the tray with the emulsion side up. Let's start with the ducks, Huey, Dewey, and Louie. Three of them in a row.

Fading into view, the waddling apparitions look as though they're smiling. I had to get down pretty close to the ground for that shot.

The next print is the pond itself. What I like most about this shot is the glassy water reflecting the trees. I tilt the tray back and forth for the proper agitation—there's a word for you—and the edges of the pond fade into view. The ripples in the developer solution almost look as if they were in the pond itself. More of the pond's reflective surface emerges.

And then, something completely unexpected happens.

Blinking incredulously under the safelight's blood-red glow, I'm tempted to flip the fluorescent light switch on to make sure I'm not just seeing things. Something appears that cannot possibly be.

Finally, after blinking twice in disbelief, the entire image comes up clear as day. My eyes confirm what my mind cannot fathom.

A scream threatens to bust from my lungs.

12

GRACE TH'AM AI LE

University of Agriculture and Forestry
Saigon: March 30, 1975

It has been over two years since I learned of Huynh Tho's death. Though I continue to grieve his loss, I have come to accept it. So much has changed. Most of the American soldiers have left Vietnam. I have completed almost all my studies and will graduate this year, if the war permits.

Peter Carrick, who travels throughout Vietnam taking pictures of the war, has come to visit periodically, checking on my well-being, seeing if I need anything.

In the past five days, both Hué and Da Nang have fallen to the Communist forces of the North. However, living in Saigon is like wearing a blindfold. If not for television and radio, you might not know our country is being torn apart. But now, with reports of the Communists approaching the South, I worry that Saigon might soon come under attack.

Peter told me about the horrible things the Americans found after they repelled the National Liberation Front from Hué seven years ago. Mass graves and evidence of unspeakable atrocities perpetrated by the Vietcong. Now they have taken Hué again.

What if the Communists come to Saigon? It is said that they target Catholics, intellectuals, and businessmen, treating them as counterrevolutionaries. Eight Americans who had been captured in Ban Me Thout were said to have been executed, perhaps by beheading.

How could this be? How could my brother have joined hands with these people?

I have fully recovered from my gunshot wound, but as for my heart and mind, I am not so sure. Some of my wealthier classmates have left the country with their families. Classes have been postponed indefinitely.

I, however, have nowhere else to go.

Whenever Peter returns, he stops by to bring me apples and oranges or whatever he finds in his travels that he thinks I might enjoy. Perhaps he feels guilty about Huynh Tho. I still wrestle with his death.

Frightful and cruel as the Vietcong may be, Huynh Tho was killed by American soldiers. I do not know who I am most angry with. I suppose I am most angry at the war itself.

Yesterday, Peter brought *Phở Ga* (noodle soup with chicken) for lunch. I was surprised when he arrived at my dormitory with most of it spilled on his clothes. "I meant for us to sit in the courtyard for a light lunch and a chat," he said.

I handed him a towel. "I think Chinese people eat those, and dogs too."

"No, that's *cat*. I said *chat*."

"How is that spelled?"

"c-h-a-t."

"*Le chat?* No, the French don't eat those."

If not for his endearing smile, I would have been mortified at my confusion. I soon learned that he meant for us to have lunch and informal conversation. This came as a welcome diversion from my depressing thoughts.

"Let's get something from the cafeteria," I said, helping him dispose of the unfortunate Phở Ga. "I know of a pleasant garden where few people go."

* * *

We arrived with our food and a blanket and settled under a *Cinnamomum loureiroi*, or a Saigon cinnamon tree, as it is commonly called. There, we lay on our bellies and for the entire time partook of our meal in silence.

There was no need to speak. The rustling leaves and birdsongs were enough to help me forget that the war that had claimed so many lives—children, mothers, brothers, fathers—raged on, not far from the haven of Saigon.

For now, I would content myself with this peace.

"Grace, what will you do when . . ." Peter struggled to fashion his thoughts into words.

"When what?" I was now lying back with my head resting on my bundled up sweater, gazing at the shapes of the clouds. "Oh, that one looks like a rabbit, don't you think?"

"I think it looks like Santa's beard."

"Whose?"

Taking his place next to me so he could see better, Peter said, "What will you do when—if the Communists come to Saigon?"

The question had remained in the back of my head, like a forgotten, half-eaten apple in a dusty corner. "I have not given it much thought." The rabbit stretched and came apart. Through its remains, a black helicopter soared westward through the sky.

"People have been evacuating. The concerns are real. If the Communists take Saigon, God only knows."

"What will *you* do, Peter?"

He pointed at another cloud. "What does that one look like to you?"

"You tell me."

He stared intently and frowned. "A shovel."

"To me, it is a sword." How odd, I never thought of such things. Small animals, trees, and flowers are what I usually saw. Not weapons. "Will you be evacuating too?"

"I'm afraid I must." He turned to face me, his eyes searching. "They're urging all Americans to leave. I've only stayed this long because . . ." He stopped and turned away.

"Why, Peter? Why have you stayed?"

Without explanation, he stood and walked ahead toward the shrubs. I sat up to see what he was doing. Every now and again, he opened his mouth, as if to speak, and gestured with his hands. But each time, the words seemed to fail him. Finally, he turned back and sat next to me. "I stayed because of something you told me when I told you Huynh Tho had died."

"I said many things."

"You said you were alone in the world, your family gone, your entire village destroyed. I didn't feel right just—"

"So it is your pity that keeps you here?"

"No, it's not that."

"Thank you for your concern, Peter Carrick." I stood up and began to march back to my room. "But you may keep your pity!"

Saigon: April 9, 1975

Since our last meeting, I have not seen Peter even once. If only I had not been so prideful. How ungrateful and unbecoming of me to treat so poorly this man who, from the day we met, only meant well.

Where is he now? Has he gone back to America? Da Nang fell last week, and thousands of people tried to evacuate before it was too late. Some three hundred of our armed soldiers tried to force their way onto a World Airways plane that landed at the Da Nang airport. Some of the people there, desperate to flee the city, actually lay down under the plane to prevent it from taking off. As many as thirty people died, some of them crushed under the wheels as the plane took off. When it landed here in Saigon, the rebellious soldiers were placed under guard.

That is how bad things are getting. What will I do?

About nine thousand evacuees from the Da Nang coast boarded an American military chartered ship that brought them to Cam Ranh Bay toward the south.

What will we here in Saigon do when the Communists come? That is what Peter had asked me before I turned my back and left him standing under the cinnamon tree.

Most of the faculty have left the city, and those who remain are quite anxious. I have nowhere to go, however. The dormitory is my only home.

Around dinnertime, as I walked toward the cafeteria, someone tapped my shoulder. It was Peter! At first I was elated. But I quickly restrained myself, lest I appear inappropriate. "I thought you had evacuated."

"I probably should have. But you know, I was feeling sorry for you." He says this with such a big smile, I know he is joking. The American way of being so forthright was jarring.

"You are teasing me."

"Of course I am. I brought you something." He held out a silk covered box. Very traditional, except for the clumsily tied ribbon and bow.

"But I have no gift for you."

"A peace offering."

"It is not necessary, Peter."

"Just open it, please. You know you want to." Again with the forthright speaking. But he was right. I was desperate to know what he considered a peace offering.

"Thank you." As soon as I opened the box, a familiar aroma rose up. In that instant, so many memories came to mind, most of them surrounding phở and family. I unwrapped the tissue paper and there lay a bundle of cinnamon bark.

"It's *Quế Thanh Hoá*. Or *Cinnamomum loureiroi*, whichever you prefer."

"Saigon cinnamon is fine." I shut the box and bowed.

"Ironic, I couldn't find it here in Saigon. Had to get it farther north. They told me it's an important ingredient in Phở Ga."

Impressed, I admired the intricate pattern of the silk outer lining. "Why?"

"To remind you of our first date."

"You mean our first fight?"

"Let's not remember that, okay?"

I brought the bark up under my nose and took a deep breath. Without warning, I became emotional. "It reminds me of home."

Later that evening, Peter took me to dinner at Pho Hai, one of his favorite restaurants. "It's not overrun with tourists, and the food is more like home cooking," he said as we ate.

"That is true. But my cooking tastes better."

"Perhaps one day, you'll prove it to me."

"You have something on your chin." Though I was pointing straight at the broken-off piece of noodle, he could not find it with his napkin. "Here, let me." With my fingertip, I wiped it off, as I would for Huynh Tho when he was a child.

Neither of us felt embarrassed. The mutual recognition of this fact caused our eyes to meet. He took my hand gently and caressed it in a way that no one had ever done before.

"Grace, listen. The Communists will be here any day. I don't have any choice but to leave Vietnam and return to the United States. You need to think of a way to leave as well."

I was not going to argue or become offended. But still, I wished to know. "You never told me why you've stayed."

Now he held both of my hands. So warm and strong was his touch that I felt it through my entire body. "I stayed because of you. Since I met you, I felt something special, something that doesn't come but once in a person's lifetime."

"What did you feel?"

"A connection. It's a sense that we share a common destiny, that I'll never be complete without you. That we should start a new life together, grow old together."

A million thoughts intermingled in my head. Never did I imagine that through this forthright manner, he would profess his feelings for me thus. "I am without words."

"Then let me tell you something else. It wasn't a coincidence that you happened to step into the woods of Bình Sơn and I was there to protect you. And it wasn't a coincidence that after three years in Vietnam, you are the only person I feel at home with. Is it any wonder I can think of no other woman but you? We share a bond, though tragic in its origins."

"Peter, if you have something more to say . . ."

He drew a long breath. "Come to America with me. Like you said, there's no more family for you here now. And your friends are leaving as well. Don't be alone. We can start a family of our own."

My breath grew short. This sensation was quite foreign to me. "But I cannot come with you to America unless—"

"I love you, Grace."

The very sound of those words sent a tingle through me. "Don't say that. Please. I am not comfortable with those words."

"How about it? We can go back to California, get a house by the beach, settle down with two children, a big yellow dog. You can do anything you like. Drive a car, go to a baseball game, eat hamburgers, get a job, anything. And we can do it all for the first time, together." Peter then did something I'd only seen in old black-and-white American movies. He took a tiny box from his pocket and opened it to reveal a diamond ring. Then he got out of his chair to kneel before me on one knee. "I guess what I'm trying to say is: Grace Th'am Ai Le, will you marry me?"

13

RICHARD COLSON

Suzanne's discharge from Mercy Hospital brought little comfort, what with her diagnosis. In two hours I'm supposed to fly back to New York, where Karen Lassiter and the rest of my staff awaits, and from there, jump right back on the campaign trail.

I haven't yet told Suzanne about her diagnosis. How can I?

She sits up in the bed, gazing out the french windows at our ten-acre property. Before we were married, she'd inherited all this from her father, the late Lawrence Colbert, billionaire media mogul with whom I'd never been all that impressed.

But this house—or mansion, rather—makes Suzie happy and that's what matters. Privet hedges, century-old flowering crab-apple trees, incense cedars and redwoods around the outskirts surround the expansive front lawn. The yard itself is Suzanne's pride and joy, which she lovingly cultivated by her own hand, until the MS struck. And even now, from her mobile throne, she directs her staff to plant and care for dozens of species of trees and Mediland roses, all framed by boxwood hedges.

"Good to see you up and alert." I place a tray with poached eggs, Earl Grey tea, and croissants with blackberry jam on the bed and kiss the tip of her nose.

She inhales deeply and beams. "Do you realize that I've only lived nine years of my life outside of this house?"

"Kind of *Wuthering Heights*, don't you think?"

"Have you even read Brontë?"

"Who?"

"Never mind, you sweet fool." She kisses me and sips her tea.

"I'm going to have to leave again."

"It was good of you to come back and see me. But promise me you won't do that again unless it's a *real* emergency."

"Real? You say tomato, I say to-mah-to." I pull up a chair, sit beside her, and make a grab for her croissant. That earns me a playful swat on the hand.

"I'm serious, Rick. Promise me. Life or death."

I can feel my smile evaporate. The test results from Dr. Choi weigh heavily on my heart. Even now, I wonder if it's in Suzanne's best interest to tell her.

She touches my arm. "You in there?"

"What? Oh, yes. I was just thinking."

"About?"

A pause, a smile, then a shrug. "How good it is to see you in good spirits again."

"Come on, I know that look. What's on your mind?"

She has a right to know. It was wrong for me to think otherwise. But is now the best time? "You know me far too well, I'm afraid."

"Is it bad?"

I nod.

"Tell me."

Just like that? Tell her things are far worse than either of us imagined? "I don't know."

"You'll have to, eventually. And in my condition, you don't want to waste any time."

"That's not funny."

"I'm serious."

"All right." I stand, walk to the window where the sun bathes the left side of my face until I commit to the words I'm about to say. "I'm calling it off."

"Calling what off?" She puts her teacup down and pulls her

robe tighter around her shoulders as if my words rode on a chilling El Niño breeze.

"My campaign. I'm not going to run."

"Oh, Rick. Why?"

"I've spent the past year living out of a suitcase, traveling all the states, gearing up for the greatest victory of my life. But you know what? That's an entire year I lived without you. And without you, it's all worthless."

"I've never complained."

"That's what makes it harder. You're the greatest thing that ever happened to me, but I've sacrificed you for my career. Why did I ever allow something like that?"

"I told you to. Rick, this isn't about me, or even about you. You're the hope of this nation, don't you see it? You're going to turn things around. That's why we've both made the personal sacrifices. It's your calling. We've been through this."

"After last night, in the hospital—"

"Just a flare-up. I told Cecilia not to bother you with it. Look, I'm all better now. See? Now get back out there and win that election."

"You don't understand."

"What do you mean?" She shudders and points to the windows. "Could you shut them, please? It's so cold in here suddenly."

As I swing the windows shut, my heart pounds. "Dr. Choi did some blood tests. And I saw the results."

"I'm getting better, right?" Her blind optimism makes this all the more difficult.

"Not really."

"Then what did it say?" She leans forward, away from the headboard, and hugs the pillow tightly to her chest. I go back and sit by her, hold both of her hands, and look her straight in the eye.

"You've got lymphoma."

Suzie sits silently, her parted lips trembling. Finally, she turns away. I press my face against hers. "I'm sorry, honey. I didn't know when I should tell you."

Sniffling, she replies, "So that explains it. The loss of appetite, the sudden weight loss, the fevers and lumps."

"None of which you told me about."

"I thought it was the MS." She turns to face me with a valiant smile. Her eyes are red, but she dabs them dry with Kleenexes. "How long?"

"It's stage four. Dr. Choi says six to eight months. Dammit, if I'd been around, I would have noticed the signs. Might have been able to treat it sooner!"

"Rick, don't!" She sobs. After a few slow breaths, she says, "Never second-guess your decisions, not the ones you tortured yourself over. You'll go crazy looking back at would-haves and should-haves."

"I don't care! I will not make any more decisions that I'll regret for the rest of my life."

"Honey, listen—"

"I'm pulling out of the race and spending all my time with you. You'll see, Suzie. I'll get you the best doctors—forget Dr. Choi, I never liked him anyway. You'll get the best treatments, and if they don't have anything adequate, I'll buy a research lab, hire the world's most brilliant scientists, and create one for you. We're not going to take this lying down. I fight to win, you know that. We're going to beat this!"

"No . . ." Tears roll down her face.

"No?"

"You don't pull out of a fight. Not when you're this close to winning. Isn't that what you always said about Vietnam, we pulled out when we could have won? You've never been a quitter, Rick. Don't start now."

"I don't want to spend another minute away from you. You've sacrificed so much for me already."

"If you quit now, it will have all been in vain."

A strong gust blows open the windows and rushes through, sending the sheer curtains up like white flags. I can't dispute her logic. The strength of reason returns to vanquish my errant emotions. Still, it goes against every fiber of my being to turn my back on her, especially now.

"The tough choices." She lies back down, curling up under the covers. "It's what brought you to where you are today. It's why the country needs you. Because you can make them."

"What good is any of that, if I have to live the rest of my life knowing I squandered these last few . . ." *Don't even think that!*

"It's all right. Like you always say: for the greater good. Sometimes you have to make sacrifices. That's what you and I have always been about. I'd be a hypocrite if I allowed you to stray from that."

"Hush, Suzie." I wrap her in my arms and hold her close, the warmth, sighs, and tears filling that small space between us. I kiss her forehead, her eyes, her lips.

"You've got a flight and another speech to prepare," she whispers, resting her icy fingertips upon my face. "And I need to rest."

"All right."

"Don't dishonor our sacrifice."

"I swear, I won't."

She drifts off. Wiping tears from my eyes, I rise and shut the windows again. Just as I return to take the tray from her bed and place it on the dumbwaiter, my cell phone buzzes.

It's Mark Collinsworth.

Quickly, I step outside and answer. "This is not a good time."

"I'm sorry, sir. But you specifically told me to update you, regardless of time or convenience. That's what you wanted from a project manager."

"Make it quick."

"We may have a containment issue at stage three."

"Which one?"

"Carrick."

I scoff. "He won't be a problem."

"Don't be so certain. I've been watching him. He just came back from Vietnam."

"To scatter his wife's ashes, that much I knew."

"Something happened, and he came back early. Do you want me to have the subcontractor cover this? Because I can easily—"

"No. Best if I handle it. Personally."

"You've got a lot on your plate. Sure you don't want me to put the sub on this?"

"Absolutely not. Now listen, I'm flying back to New York in a couple of hours. Keep tabs on the operations and contact me only if there's a credible threat. Clear?"

"As glass."

"And don't worry."

The call ends. Collinsworth seemed less than convinced. But I can't risk anything with Peter Carrick. Maintaining his position is a delicate balance, which if tipped, could make the presidential race the least of my problems.

14

XANDRA CARRICK

I've always felt that images, as they come up on the emulsified surface, are somewhat phantasmal, but this is the worst possible confirmation of that sentiment. A tingling sensation prickles my scalp, back, and fingertips.

There, shimmering in ripples of the chemicals, beneath the amber hue of the safelight, something I could not possibly have imagined arises in the photograph of the pond. A figure, face down, her golden hair radiating in all directions, floats in the water.

She's wearing a white sweatshirt with a large Greek Beta symbol emblazoned on the back. And she appears to be wearing jeans. It's that girl on the news. The dance student from Juilliard reported missing.

But she wasn't there when I took the picture!

Without hesitation, I reach back and switch the lights on. This photo has got to—

Wait.

On second glance, she's gone. Not the photo, it's all still there, the pond, the ducks, the trees reflecting in the water. Only the girl is gone.

I take the negative from the enlarger and clip it to the wall-mounted light box. Here's the shot. Identical to the printed picture.

But there is no girl.

I'm certain I saw it.

My mouth is dry, my veins are about to explode. I wasn't even thinking about her before I developed the picture. I'm choking on the fumes in here. Need some air.

For the next few minutes, I sit at my kitchen table sipping a mug of coffee and staring at the unremarkable black-and-white photo of the pond. There's got to be a scientific explanation for this. Perhaps it was a subliminal thought, some psychological occurrence where you see things planted by the subconscious.

I wasn't imagining it, the details were too clear. And yet, there's nothing in the picture that even hints at the girl now. The darkroom door is still ajar; the overhead fluorescent light flickers dimly.

Outside, clouds that earlier seemed to be thinning with the pledge of afternoon sunshine have turned charcoal. Peals of thunder rumble in the distance, sending a cold shiver through my body.

For the next two hours, pacing like a caged panther, I deliberate over going back and making another print. Finally, I decide. I *will* develop another print.

This time, nothing happens. The second one is identical. No ghostly images of dead bodies floating in the pond.

But I'm sure of what I saw.

The voice of the radio announcer resounds in my head: "... *authorities are asking anyone with information on her last known whereabouts to contact the Missing Persons Squad, or the 20th Precinct ...*"

15

"No, I don't want to give you my name . . .

"Right.

"Because I don't want to get . . . Look, I don't know what else to say; would you please just have them check the pond?" Too nervous to continue, I end the call to the 20th Precinct. The last thing I need is to be connected to this case. There'll be endless questions: "Why do you think we should trawl the pond?" "How do you know about this?" "What's your relationship to the victim?"

Great, I forgot to block the outbound caller ID. All I wanted was to alert them to a possible lead. It was the responsible thing to do. I don't need a reputation as a crazy prank caller. I should never have called. They'll surely trace the call back to me.

But how could I sleep knowing I kept silent, while even the tiniest possibility exists that there was truth in that image I saw.

It's probably best to forget it and get back to work. Ordinarily, I'd go to the park for inspiration, but considering what today's foray yielded, I'll seek an alternative.

Though I'm loathe to take on the responsibilities of a couch potato, I succumb to the lure of channel surfing with the occasional break for *The Price Is Right, Dr. Phil, Channel 9 News.* By the time I get to *Oprah,* I've had enough. I must get out of the apartment. Starbucks sounds good right about now.

On my way out of the elevator, Frank smiles and tips his hat. "Better bring an umbrella, Ms. Carrick. Looks like rain."

He's a saint. Kind of reminds me of an old uncle who pinches your cheeks and smiles all the time. "Frank, I'm sorry about this morning. I'd gotten a bad email and . . . well, then I got some even worse news after that, and . . ." He's smiling at me the way Dad used to when I was in elementary school and had a bad habit of thinking out loud. Nonstop.

"You got an umbrella, Ms. Carrick?"

"I'll have to go back up to get one."

He reaches behind the desk. "Here. People leave 'em around and never come back for 'em. I got dozens." He hands me a bright yellow number with a rubber-duckie-shaped handle. Perfect.

"Thanks." I marvel at the blinding hue. "No chance of my getting lost in a crowd with this."

"Why would you want to get lost?"

"I don't know, sometimes . . . Anyway, thanks again."

"You got it, Ms. Carrick."

"Could you please just call me Xandra? 'Ms. Carrick' makes me feel old."

He stoops down with a smile and gently pinches my cheek. "You got it, Ms. Xandra." Anyone else but Frank the doorman and he'd be on the floor, holding his privates and reeling in pain, having gotten the point of my boots. I return the smile and thank him again for the yellow-rubber-ducky 'brella.

As I step through the revolving door, that tingling feeling running from my scalp to my fingertips returns. With greater intensity. A flash of crimson and blue assaults my eyes. What I see across the street arrests my breath.

16

It never occurred to me that the police might take my tip seriously. Or that they'd respond this quickly. Parked over on the northbound side of Central Park West is a pair of squad cars, presumably from the 20th Precinct, and two black Crown Victorias.

I cross the street and shoulder through the growing crowd. An ambulance pulls up to the curb. The first person whose attention I can get is the Pakistani lady who runs the corner Hebrew National hotdog stand. "What's going on?"

"They got here an hour ago," she says. "Started talking on their walkie-talkies and then the black cars came. Now the ambulance."

Yellow crime-scene tape seals off the entrance to the park. A uniformed officer finishes speaking on his wireless and stands in front of us with his back turned. I reach out to tap his shoulder, but he's too far away. Instead, I lift the yellow tape, step under it, and call out so he can hear me above all the chatter. "Excuse me, officer."

He turns around, scanning the crowd for my voice. Cold drops of rain begin to fall, but I'm too focused to open my duck 'brella. "Ma'am, you're going to have to keep behind the tape."

"*New York Times*." I pull out my press badge, which I won't return until they ask me for it. "Can I ask you a question or two?"

"Wait for the press conference."

"I don't need a detailed statement."

"Where's your camera?"

I hadn't planned on taking any pictures, so I find myself coming up short on excuses. Thankfully, I always carry my digital point-and-shoot in my pocket. "Here."

"Ah, you ain't on the job."

"Can you just tell me what's going on?"

"It don't take a freakin' rocket scientist." He points his chin to the park entrance where a pair of officers wheel a black body bag on a gurney.

It's her. Without even seeing, I know. "Is that . . . Do you know who—?"

"Lady, you gonna take some pictures or what? 'Cause if you ain't, I need you to get behind the tape."

"Yeah . . . okay." I snap off a few, even after the news vans arrive. It's pouring now. Flashes from my Nikon Coolpix are answered by those in the sky. He's right. It *don't* take a freakin' rocket scientist to know what's happened, or who that is zipped inside the body bag.

Chilled to the marrow, I carefully open my duck 'brella and cross the street to return to my apartment. As I leave the scene, I faintly hear one of the police officers calling out to me.

17

RICHARD COLSON

The image of Suzie curled up under her sheets, pale and spectral, shrouds my thoughts like a burlap hood. I can't shake it, it's almost prophetic. And yet, despite the guilt, it's the thought of the security project unraveling that most afflicts me.

I ring for the flight attendant.

"Can I get you anything, Mr. Colson?"

"Another coffee, please."

"Black?"

"Absolutely."

I've never enjoyed the East Coast in the fall, when the air turns cold and the days short. Right now, none of my enthusiasm for public office seems to matter. As the clouds roll under the wings of this 727, I'm tempted to assess how I arrived at this incredibly tense juncture.

No. I promised her I wouldn't look back and second-guess things.

Instead, hoping to extricate myself from the dread that grips my heart, I stare out the window and drift. Daylight drains from the sky. Even before the sun falls to the moon's insurgence, white clouds turn gray. *Many shades of gray.* Like the many issues I've confronted in my troubled life. And yet, the pinnacle is in sight.

With each passing day, the polls favor me more and more. Shouldn't I be excited?

Not with all these complications.

As if waiting for just the right moment to spring, the flight attendant returns with not only my coffee but an in-flight phone. "You have a call on six."

"I left specific instructions."

"Yes, sir. But it's Mark Collinsworth."

"I see. Thank you, I'll take this in private, please." Which she understands to mean that she should wait outside the first-class cabin, with the rest of my staff.

A call from Mark can only mean further complications. He never calls outside of the scheduled intervals. "What is it now?"

"We definitely have a breach in section 3b of the execution phase."

"Are you sure?"

"Come on, sir."

I peel the tinfoil off the half-and-half container. "He was your mentor. You know better than anyone how unlikely that is."

"I'd like to remind you that I objected to hiring him for this project."

"Okay, what are we talking about here?"

"It's still several levels out of range, but there's been level two exposure."

"Then it's still containable."

"In theory. Our best bet is to terminate his contract, and let me handle his segment."

"No, I need you in the project manager role."

"With all due respect, the sub's become a major liability. I say we cut our losses. If not me, then I have a roster of suitable replacements."

"It hasn't come to that."

"You don't want to wait until it does."

"I'll let you know."

"How am I supposed to get my work done when you keep letting sentimental issues cloud your judgment at every—"

"I said, not yet! You were hired to implement and oversee this project, not to second-guess me!" My fingers are wet. I glance down to find half-and-half splashed all over my hands and tray. Barely any of it made its way into my cup.

"Sir, I only meant—"

"I know what you meant, Mark. Look, I've been more than patient with your sophomoric attitude. You're every bit as replaceable as any of the subcontractors you've been appointed to manage, is that clear?"

Silence.

Which I take as a yes. For all his swagger, Collinsworth does have a point. But it's not his call. "Your next contact had better be of the utmost importance. I haven't the time or patience to deal with anything less."

Even as I hang up, my hand continues to tremble.

18

XANDRA CARRICK

Getting drenched twice in one day, along with a gruesome discovery through what I still refuse to recognize as a precognitive vision, puts a damper on any hopes for photographic inspiration. Seeing the body bag was enough to curtail my Starbucks run, and that's a significant commentary as to its effect.

Already, the phone has rung and stopped twice. But I'm so shaken I didn't even consider picking up.

Ringing again.

If it's important, they'll leave a message.

Sitting with another cup of hot coffee and wrapped in a wool throw blanket, I'm watching the live footage on *Channel 7 News*. Brenda Woodward holds a microphone in one hand and a large red doorman's umbrella in the other as she speaks into the camera. Why isn't anyone holding the umbrella for her? On the screen, the superimposed image of a pretty blond girl in her early twenties appears next to Brenda.

"... still needs to make a definitive forensic ID of the body, but according to the police who noted the clothing the victim was wearing—a white sweatshirt with a large Beta symbol on the back—we're fairly certain that this is Stacy Dellafina, the Juilliard Dance student reported missing since—"

Click.

The remote shakes in my hand and remains suspended along with my open mouth. It's enough to send me running to the bathroom to fully express my nausea. The chill, the tingling, it seems as though time has become irrelevant.

Until a knock on the door jolts me from my stupor.

Muffled through the door: "Ms. Carrick?"

"What in the world?" Who is that, and how did she get up here without Frank's announcing her?

"NYPD. We know you're in there, Ms. Carrick. We just need to speak with you."

I go to open the door without undoing the security chain. A woman in an ebony raincoat holds up a badge confirming her identity. Beside her stands a man with a different badge. This one displays three bold letters: FBI. The female detective steps forward. "A moment of your time, please?"

Within a few seconds, I'm back on my sofa, the television is muted, and I've offered two complete strangers coffee. The police investigator introduces herself as Lieutenant Margaret Nuñez. She stands quite still, looking around my apartment for God knows what. Though she speaks with a calm voice, her tone is as cold as the rain outside. "This is Special Agent Kyle Matthews with the Bureau."

"Ms. Carrick." Agent Matthews extends a hand. It's so warm to the touch that I pull away, my cheeks burning. "I'm with the FBI. Nice to meet you." There's a kindness in his deep-set hazel eyes. But the rest of his slightly worn features suggest a life of rugged experience beyond his thirty-something years. I've seen the same look on soldiers in Iraq—young officers who've seen so much death during their first deployment. They try not to let it affect them emotionally, but you can always see it. The eyes don't lie.

Still standing at the outskirts of my living room, Detective Nuñez turns her gaze toward me. "It's come to my attention that you called in the tip that led us to the victim."

Crap. I knew this would happen. "Guilty as charged."

"Did you know that the victim was found at the bottom of the pond, weighed down with bags of rice tied to her limbs?"

"No. I . . . That's horrible." I want to appear shocked. But I'm failing miserably.

"So." Nuñez takes one step closer to the sofa on which I'm sitting. "How did you know?"

"I don't know; I just had a hunch." My hands grow cold and damp.

"Oh, come on."

"You wouldn't believe me."

This is where Agent Matthews finally says something. "Try us."

I'm trying not to shake. Is it because of the rain or the sheer absurdity of it all? "So is this a federal investigation? I thought it was a local missing-persons case."

"Once again," Nuñez says, impatience brimming, "how did you know?"

If I tell them the truth, they'll start profiling me as some kind of psycho. But if I don't come up with a plausible lie . . . I hate lying. I'm a terrible liar.

"Ms. Carrick," Nuñez says, "the truth. It can only help."

"All right." I stand and step over to the table where the Graflex sits haughtily. Apparently, it *did* know something when it winked at me this morning. About to rest my hand on it, I refrain. It was all just a coincidence. A bizarre coincidence. There must be a scientific explanation. But I'm not going to risk it. "This morning, I went down to the park to clear my head and get some inspiration for my photography. As I was taking pictures, I thought I saw something in the water." All right, a partial lie.

"Can you describe what you thought you saw?" Nuñez asks, scribbling in a notepad.

"I don't really remember, it was so brief. Maybe it was the way the light hit the water." I clear my throat. "Whatever it was, it made me think of that dance student. A long shot, but I had to try."

Nuñez's eyebrows knit tightly. "Three days, and no one saw a thing."

"Lucky I guess."

"You guess."

Matthews comes between us and hands me a business card. "Thank you, Ms. Carrick. If you can think of anything else that might be helpful."

"I hope not." I take the card. His fingertips brush against my hand. Again, the blood rushes to my face. Oh my, did he notice?

As Matthews and Nuñez leave, she mutters something to the effect of this being her case and that he's only here as a consultant. Before I can hear anything else, the elevator doors slide shut and they're gone.

This wasn't the way I envisioned my first day of freedom.

I'm going to have to have a word with Frank.

Thunderstorms make for the kind of day you just want to curl up in bed and sleep. After the bizarre events of this day, I wouldn't mind doing just that for another few weeks.

Dinner consists of sushi delivered and a Diet Coke, courtesy of Ichiro's. If I were feeling more social, I'd call Hailey, Jenn, and Tina and go out. But they're all cutting back on eating out, what with the economy and all. I end up spending more money having my dinner delivered to my apartment.

The laptop screensaver draws my eyes. Photos from childhood that I've scanned over the years fade in and out of view. There's Mom holding my hand by the rock wall at the Cloisters. The next is me and Daddy playing basketball in the driveway. Here's me sitting on his lap. I was seven years old and had just learned why birds fly south for the winter. I talked his ear off while he listened with genuine interest. Loving me unconditionally. It's been years.

I still don't know when exactly it happened, why it happened, or how. But at some point, he simply retreated into a dark cave of introspection. Dad wouldn't talk to anyone about what was troubling him. Anytime we noticed the despair on his face, he'd quickly feign happiness.

No one knew why. He had everything a man could want: fame, wealth, success, a family that adored him. Had I disappointed him somehow? Is that the reason?

I'd like to call him now. But I'm still smarting from our last conversation. He's the one who should be calling me. To apologize and make amends.

But that'll never happen. He's too proud.

Like me.

19

IAN MORTIMER

The dreaded phone call comes at the worst possible time—in the middle of a board meeting of the St. Deicolus Children's Foundation that's run overtime. In haste, Avijit gives the financial report for Q3. All eyes and ears are upon him. The incessant buzzing of my BlackBerry, however, causes them to turn toward me to see if I'll answer or dismiss it.

A quick glance at the caller ID confirms my fears. It's TR. *Bugger, not now!* With a silent apology, I excuse myself from the meeting and take the call in my office next door.

"Ian?" TR is calm. A bad sign.

"I told you never to call me at work."

"We need to talk."

"I wasn't contracted to talk!"

"You were hired because of your reputation."

"There's irony for you."

"Come now, I know your work; you're the best."

"Another time, another life, perhaps. This was a one-time service I delivered, only because—"

He scoffs. "Seems you haven't made good on your deliverables."

"What are you on about?"

"You haven't heard?"

"Heard what?"

"You're getting rusty, old friend. The police found the Della-fina girl's body in the pond."

My innards twist into so many knots. Twenty years ago, this would never have happened. "That's absurd."

"Someone phoned in a tip to the police. Which means they must have seen you."

"Bollocks! I scoped out the entire area before—"

"I'm sure you'll be more open to my suggestions next time."

"There is no next time."

"Oh, but there is."

"You listen to me, old bloke. Our business is done."

"Not when there's a big operation to clean up after your shoddy work!" TR calms himself. But the tension beneath his words seeps through nevertheless. "What's happened to you, Ian? You were a virtuoso, your reputation preceded you both domestically and abroad. It's almost like . . . like your heart's not in it anymore."

All I can think of is Bobby now. He's not quite seven and has no idea what kind of man his father really is. "Things have changed."

"And they're going to continue changing. Now listen. I'm going to send you some data my person in the Department dug up. You're going to fix this, you hear? Any of it traces back to me, you know what happens."

It's not as though he needs to reiterate his threats. I'm already beholden to him in the most perverse way, and no amount of posturing is going to change that. "You don't have to—"

"It'd be a shame if you couldn't get the Praxol for Bobby anymore. And thanks to the FDA, it's near impossible to get onto wait lists for experimental treatments these days." The doctors had given Bobby ten months to live. That was a year and a half ago, thanks to the Praxol, which by FDA regulations might take seven more years, if ever, before it becomes available.

"Stinking sonofa—! You fancy yourself God or something?"

"As far as you're concerned. And think of Nicole too—all those nights she spends alone . . ."

"I swear I'll tear your bloody—"

"Relax, Ian. I'm just saying that it'd be a shame if she were to find out about your past. Why, I don't think anyone could take that kind of betrayal. She'd take Bobby as far away from you as possible. All because you didn't have the integrity to correct a tiny mistake."

"Don't be daft, I'll fix this. But after that, we're done. Do you understand?"

"We're done when I say we are. And if you do your job right, all will be fine. Nothing would make me happier than to complete our contract amicably."

"Right."

"So Ian, are we square here?"

"Just have your man send the information."

20

XANDRA CARRICK

Last night's thunderstorm left a musty odor in the streets as the midmorning sun begins to evaporate puddles, which reflect objects around them. Still haunted by yesterday's darkroom experience, I don't dare look into any of them.

I'm taking the subway uptown to Feldman's, the only photo-supply store I trust. If I'm going to win the Marbury, nothing but the finest supplies will do. Mr. Feldman knows Dad's Graflex because they're the ones who serviced it all these years.

The best thing about riding at 11:00 a.m. is that the train isn't crowded. You can relax and read a newspaper comfortably and not worry about intruding upon another's space. Or them upon you.

Today's news source is *USA Today*. According to the front page, Citicorp plans to cut about fifty thousand jobs and Colson is ahead in the polls. He's creating a genuine sense of excitement in this election. Unlike Ross Perot, Colson poses a significant threat to both the Democratic and Republican nominees.

Headlines in the local section announce the positive identification of Stacy Dellafina's body. The report states that she was found based on an anonymous tip. The missing-persons case has become a murder case, and the authorities are trying to find the killer.

I'd best distance myself from this.

I want nothing to do with psycho killers. The details of crime investigations make my skin crawl. I could never be a forensic photographer. Better to work in the mall, taking Santa pictures.

The conductor announces, "West one hundred thirty-seventh street," and I'm off.

I step onto the platform, but as I walk toward the exit, I can't shake this odd sense that someone is following me. I glance over my shoulder. As far as I can see, I'm wrong.

On to the stairs. My own footfalls echoing against the tile walls and concrete floors make my heart race. Now, an additional set of footsteps follows.

It's nothing.

Or it could be a mugger.

In the morning?

This is New York. Stranger things have happened. I don't want to become a statistic, so I pick up the pace. By the time my fast walking turns into a jog, the footsteps behind me are matching my speed. I'm being chased. Or I'm acting like a paranoid idiot.

I rush past the exit gates and out onto the street.

And onto a crowded sidewalk.

Amidst a sea of faces, not one of them is looking at me. There probably wasn't anyone there. People jog through the subway all the time without the intent of attacking anyone.

Okay, Xandra. You're losing it. Pins and needles prickle at my skin, from my head to my extremities.

Even as I shake it off, a brief sensation floods my mind. Like being under water, bubbles rising up. Smothering any sound I try to make. I'm not able to breathe!

It's not until an old woman bumps into me that I pull myself out of this dread. "Watch it!" she grumbles and continues down the sidewalk.

Not taking my usual time to shop, I quickly find the needed chemicals and paper. Feldman's may be one of the oldest mom-

and-pop photographic-supply stores, but it's well organized. Ready to pay, I take the wallet from my bag and a business card falls to the counter. It's Agent Matthews's.

"Cash or credit?" Marty smiles at me the way he has since I was twelve, when Dad first brought me here.

"Oh, yes. Sorry. Credit." I'm still eyeing the business card when I hand Marty the Visa. For some reason I want to call Matthews. Something tells me he might actually believe me if I told him about my hallucinations.

"Sorry, kiddo, it got declined." Marty hands the credit card back to me. "Got another one?"

"Wow. That's never happened before. Maybe it's because I just came back from overseas and used it in the airport in Saigon."

"Yeah, call them. They'll straighten it out for you."

I hand him my debit card. This time it goes through. It hits me now. I've already maxed out my Visa card and planned to pay it down with my first paycheck after returning to work. Oh well.

"Here ya go." He hands me my card and bag full of supplies. "Don't be a stranger. And say hi to your dad, will ya?"

"Sure."

I step outside and realize I'm still holding Agent Matthews's business card. Maybe I should call now and set up a meeting to discuss . . .

Just what will I say to him, anyway?

There's a clear view of the subway station from outside Feldman's. Not as many people around now.

I'll take a cab back.

21

MARK COLLINSWORTH

This isn't project management in its true sense. But I recognize the parallels Colson's drawn between the traditional business model and this special security project he's appointed me to head up.

The pay scale is a major step up for me, probably because it's 75 percent travel. This is my third trip back to California in less than a week. But it's a rush. I'm the youngest member of the team, and many of my former supervisors now report to me. You know why? Because I get the job done. I'm not afraid to roll up my sleeves and get my hands dirty shutting down operations, terminating employees, cutting budgets and positions. Does that make me heartless?

I don't care. You don't climb to the top without stepping on a few heads.

The black-tinted windows of my limousine hardly block the effects of the blinding sun. For pity's sake, it's November and girls are prancing around in brightly colored bikinis. Dudes with surfboards under their arms drip seawater. I hate Southern California.

The driver cracks open the black privacy window. "We've been here for an hour, Mr. Collinsworth."

"We're early. He'll show."

"Of course." The privacy window goes back up. I've never seen so much superficiality as I do here in San Diego. With all the money spent on cosmetic surgery, it's no wonder this state is suffering from a $40 billion deficit.

At last, he's here. I open the door, invite him in, and shake his hand. "Mr. Carrick, thanks for taking the time to speak with me."

He looks around and sits. "Where's Colson?"

"He sends his regrets, but he's on the trail and can't make it back to the West Coast until next week."

"I'm out of here."

I grasp his arm and pull him back to his seat. "I won't take more than five minutes of your time. Come on, join me for a drink."

He pulls his elbow away and scowls. "Least he could do was meet me face-to-face. Who are you?"

"Mark Collinsworth, project manager." I open the wet-bar and pour myself a Jack Daniel's. "What's your poison, Pete?"

"You're wasting your five minutes. I'll give you thirty seconds to get to the point or we're done."

"Efficient, cut through the crap. I like that."

"Tick-tock, you little—"

"All right. It's simple. The senator wants to make sure that you are still in compliance with the NDA."

"As if they were just trade secrets."

"The terms are clear. Are you in compliance?"

"I've been in compliance since before you were in diapers." Carrick fixes me with a sidelong glare. He's in his late fifties but looks fit enough to prove a considerable threat. I like the poker face, though. He's the kind of guy we could use on the team. Colson doesn't agree, but given the right incentive, I think I can turn him. "Have you considered my offer, Pete?"

"Yes."

"And?"

"I only have two words for you, and they're not very nice."

"Fair enough. As long as you uphold the NDA, we'll maintain the status quo."

He lets out a sardonic huff. "That what you call it?"

"For lack of a better term."

Disdain in his every movement, Carrick slides over to the door and opens it. "Tell Rick the NDA is fine. And that he'd better uphold his end, or so help me—"

"We both know he keeps his word, Pete."

Without warning, he turns, grabs me by the shirt, and slams me back against the door. "It's Mr. Carrick to you, boy!" Baring his canines, breathing heavily, with fists trembling, he'd probably kill me on the spot, if not for the terms of the agreement. Careful to conceal my apprehension, I laugh. "I *so* wish you'd join the team."

"Don't hold your breath." He shoves me once more for good measure and opens his door. "On second thought, hold it."

22

XANDRA CARRICK

This is the first time in three days that I've gone into the darkroom. I'm now fairly certain my hallucination was just that. Face it, there are outlandish coincidences in life.

My proof sheets from Bình Sơn are still clipped up to the easel. I'll have to enlarge those next. But right now, just to prove that I only imagined it, I'm going to develop another print from the duck pond.

I rock the tray, let out a chuckle. "It'll come out just like the others. You'll see." First the water's edge, the reflected trees, the waves in . . .

"Oh no." Stacy's body is there again. And this time, there's a white, rectangular object . . . she's clutching a white laptop computer in one hand. Looks like a Mac. This time, I'm not as frightened as I am intrigued. I shake the tray, and the ripples distort the phantom image. Now everything's gone, and a faded image of a computer screen comes into view. At first, I can barely make out what it's showing. But now it's clearing up. A web browser . . . it's a blog. Her blog.

"All right. Just stay right there, okay?" As if talking to an image in developer solution made any sense. Of course, when I switch the lights on, it's gone. If this is just another coincidence, then nothing will come of it, right? It's just another hallucination.

A minute later I'm dialing Agent Kyle Matthews.

It gets dark early these days. At 4:45, the sun has already gone over the Hudson, casting its amber hues on the sides of tall apartment buildings overlooking the park.

It's best to meet with Agent Matthews here at Starbucks, rather than at my apartment. He's wearing black Levi's and a rugged denim shirt. No stranger to the gym, apparently. I like how he looks with glasses—learned. His short cropped hair reminds me of some of the brave men in Iraq who treated me like a queen when I was on the base and traveling via Humvee around Fallujah. He's as handsome as Dad was in his pictures from back in the Vietnam War.

"So, you think you might have more information about the Dellafina case?"

"I might."

"Because you didn't call me here just to have coffee."

"No." The thought makes me pause unwittingly. "No, I didn't. Have the investigators checked Stacy's laptop?"

"How do you know she has one?"

"She's a college student, isn't she?"

"Good point." Matthews leans back and takes a sip of his latte; it leaves a frothy white mustache on his upper lip. "Yes. We've checked it. Nothing unusual except—"

"Is it a MacBook?"

"Another lucky guess?" He's not as credulous this time. But it seems inevitable that the image I saw reflects reality. Hope for a scientific explanation seems more and more elusive.

"MacBooks are popular on college campuses."

"So, what's this new information?"

"I'm not sure, but I think she might have had a blog."

"Facebook, Myspace, LiveJournal, yeah. We found nothing unusual there."

"You sure that's all she had?"

"One can never be absolutely certain."

"Can't you have them check a bit deeper? Don't those people also check things like ID addresses, that sort of thing?"

"You mean IP address."

"That's what I said."

"So you have reason to believe there's more to find?" When he smiles, the white latte mustache almost makes me laugh. But I'm not going to tell him about it. Not just yet.

"I have a feeling. Yes."

With a thoughtful expression and a white frothy brim on his upper lip, he ponders. "Just what makes you think this?"

He's going to think I'm involved, I'm sure. Absently, I twist a lock of hair around my fingers—a bad habit Mom has bugged me about since childhood. "I just . . . Never mind. I knew this was stupid."

"Just relax, Ms. Carrick."

"I'd feel better if you just called me Xandra." Will inane phrases never cease to flow from my lips whenever I'm around him?

"As long as you call me Kyle." He opens his cell phone and dials. At this point, I'm eyeing the exit, seeking the clearest path to escape before he calls the police to arrest me as a suspect. He senses this and places his warm hand on mine. Then he lifts a finger and whispers, "Hold on." There's no force whatsoever, just lightly resting his hand on mine. And yet, he's holding me to my seat as if I were handcuffed.

"Glen? Kyle Matthews. Listen, I want you to run a full ISP sweep, traceroute and all, on the MAC address associated with Stacy Dellafina's laptop. Focus on social networking and blogs . . . Yeah, I know. Yeah-yeah-yeah. No, there might be something if you take it to the next level . . . Of course I'm serious. Trust me. Call me if you find anything of interest, okay?"

For once in my life, I'm speechless. Kyle smiles again, and I can't help but notice the boyish twinkle in his eye. His hand is still on mine, and I'm not sure why I haven't withdrawn yet.

"Why didn't you . . . ? Excuse me, I'm sorry." Finally, I take my hand back from the table.

"You thought I was going to have you arrested?"

"With all this information, maybe. At least taken in for questioning."

"You're not a suspect."

"What makes you so sure?"

"For one thing, you don't fit the profile." A couple of girls at an adjacent table are looking at him and giggling. He takes note of this and turns back to me. "What?"

"Don't kill me, okay?" I pull a paper napkin from the dispenser and wipe his upper lip. "You've had that there the whole time."

"And you didn't say anything?"

"It was kind of cute."

"Maybe I should have you arrested after all."

We both laugh. For a moment I forget we're talking about a murder investigation.

"Who knows what else you're not telling me." His grin begins to fade.

"Look, maybe this was a bad idea. I mean, I made a lucky guess is all. Promise me, whatever you do, you won't tell anyone about the blog thing. I probably imagined everything."

He shakes his head and exhales slowly.

"What?"

"I get it," he says. "You don't think you can trust me because you've got a secret that no one could possibly believe. You're afraid of getting entangled with something that could end up involving you—or worse—costing you."

All I can do is blink. Right now, there's nothing I would like more than to tell someone what happened in the darkroom. Because it's driving me crazy.

"I just want you to know, Xandra. You can trust me. And I don't think you're insane."

"Who said anything about—?"

"Your eyes."

"Profilers!"

"Thanks for the latte." He gets up and places his hand on my shoulder. "If you feel like talking about it, call."

23

The Marbury Award submission deadline is about a month away and without a photograph I'm confident about submitting, each day that passes makes me more anxious.

It's been a couple of days since my last darkroom episode, and to be frank, I haven't given it much thought. That's probably because of Kyle. I'm on a first-name basis with a federal agent now. Splendid.

If I think more about my visions—hallucinations, rather—I'll eventually have to talk to him about them. Part of me really wants to, but another part wants nothing to do with all this superstition. That's all it is.

For the past couple of days, I've gone to places of great human interest and taken pictures with the Graflex, despite my misgivings. The antique camera drew more than one odd look from passersby.

From Chinatown to the Village on foot, I tried to capture all walks of life, in all conditions. The grimy homeless man leaning on his shopping cart and inadvertently posed next to a slick executive with her Sergio Rossis and Prada tote, the policeman helping a lost elderly Chinese woman across Canal Street. This is New York—for all the good and bad—the city I love.

I even managed to snap a photo of an NYU student holding a

campaign sign depicting the rugged, can-do face of Richard Colson. Vote for Colson, Vote for Change!

Time away from the Stacy Dellafina case has helped clear my mind. I'm ready to go back into the darkroom now. One of two things will happen. One: I will see nothing unusual and know that everything I saw had just been a random coincidence. Strange as it was, things like that do happen.

Or two: I will see more mysterious images. If that happens, I will definitely call Kyle Matthews. Either way, I'm ready.

Everything's in place. I'm just about to shut the darkroom door when my cell phone on the coffee table outside buzzes like a nest of angry hornets. "It would ring now."

I'm going to let it roll over to voice mail.

Lights out.

Under the protection of the safelight, I begin my work. Today's shots might actually yield a Marbury winner. A minute into the process, my landline rings.

"Oh, come on. Not now." Let it ring. I'm busy getting my life back on track. It's about time for me to make a contact sheet when my answering machine starts taking a message. It's pretty loud and I can hear it through the door.

"Xandra. It's Kyle Matthews. We need to talk."

24

"Hello? You there, Xandra? If you are, please pick up."

Muttering things that Mom wouldn't be proud to hear me say, I reach for the cordless I keep in the darkroom. "Kyle?"

"Screening your calls?"

"I'm a little busy."

"Can we talk?"

"Can it wait?"

"Not really."

Does he expect me to drop everything just to talk to him? "Give me a sec, okay? I'm in the darkroom right now."

"In your apartment?"

"Yeah, what's so hard to believe about that?"

"I just didn't think anyone . . . never mind."

This contact sheet isn't going to turn out anyway. I wipe my hands, step out into my living room, and exhale. "Okay, what did you want to talk about?"

"I'd rather do this in person."

"Sure, that'd be really convenient for you. But I have things to do today and—"

"I'm not far."

"Where are you?" The answer comes with a knock on the door. "You've got to be kidding me."

"I think you're going to want to hear this."

I open the door, and there he is standing there. Tall, confident, peering at me over the rim of his glasses. "May I?"

I remove the security chain and let him in. "You're impossible."

"That's what Momma always says."

"Says?"

"I still am."

"Apparently." I motion to the living room. "Have a seat. Can I get you something to drink?"

"No lattes, thanks."

Returning with two cans of Diet Coke, I take a seat across from him and offer him one.

He gives it a queer look. "Diet?"

"Do you know how much sugar there is in regular Coke?"

"Keeps me going."

"That's the caffeine, mostly."

He takes a sip, grimaces, then smiles and tilts his can toward me. "Gotta maintain that figure of yours, I suppose."

"Not sure how that's relevant."

"It's not. But this is." From his raincoat lying across the sofa, he pulls a stack of paper and places it on the table. "Turns out you were right."

Even after two or three glances at the numbers and cryptic language on the paper, I still don't know what I'm staring at. I look up and shrug. "What is all this?"

"Stacy did have another blog."

"Really?"

"It's no longer up on the internet. When you try to go to the web address, you get 'Page could not be found.' It's been gone almost three weeks now, and the hosting service has since expunged its cache. No backups either, which is odd because—"

"Hold on! I was right?"

"You've led us to another key to this case."

"But you said the blog was taken down."

After a final sip, Kyle licks his lips in distaste and puts the can down on the table. "Google has a feature that caches defunct web-sites. I found it under a different DNS name and made copies of the entries."

At this point, I'm starting to lose that confidence that took two days to build. I'm going to have to talk about the darkroom.

"Xandra, level with me, okay? Did you know Stacy?"

"I told you before, no." Now I'm up pacing before my window looking down at Central Park. My arms are folded, and I'm twirl-ing a lock of hair between my fingers. "I've never met her. Why do you keep asking me?"

"In her last few entries, she mentioned your name."

"She what?"

"That's right, she names you."

"Well, people know me through my work. Maybe she's into photography or something."

"Read the highlighted sentences in this entry dated October 25, 2008." He flips through the printouts and pins a finger down on one of the sheets. "And quit pacing, will you? You're making me nervous."

"Hmph." I step over and take the pages. The blog reads:

I've always felt there was something missing in my life since I was a child. With my parents' divorce when I was only four, I barely remember my father. Then he died when I was eight. Never had the chance to see him— wonder if that's because he didn't want to see me, or if Mom wouldn't let him, or whatever. I've been wanting to learn as much about him as possible. Mom's impossibly tight-lipped, so I did some research on my own.

Turns out, there was this photographer in the 1970s who went with my father's platoon during the Vietnam War. His name is Peter Carrick. Did a Google on the name but got little info besides his website. But check it— his daughter, Xandra (cool name!), lives pretty close to the dorms. I'm going to see if I can meet her. Maybe she

can introduce me to her dad. He could probably tell me
things about my father. Just gotta be careful not to let
Mom find out.

I'm trying to keep my hands from shaking, but it's a bit too
much. "Was she stalking me?"

"Sure you never met?"

My fist comes to rest on my hips. "Never."

"Then I really have to ask."

"Yes, I know."

25

His eyes are lasers, boring with pinpoint precision into my mind.

"How could you possibly have known all about Stacy? Her body in the pond, her blog?"

"Whatever happens, you have to believe me. I'm not lying."

Kyle gets up and walks over and stands next to me. He's looking out the window and with all seriousness says, "I can tell when people lie. And if you were going to lie, you'd have done so already."

"Right." He reads me like a book. It makes me feel uncomfortably vulnerable around him. "And you're not going to laugh."

"Trust me."

"I don't trust people who say that."

"All right, then. Sometime this decade would be nice."

"It's not that easy. I mean, I wouldn't have given this any credence if it hadn't happened twice. And you know, there has to be a logical explanation for this. No matter how bizarre, how coincidental—"

"Do you always ramble on like this?"

"Only when I'm nervous or excited."

"Which are you now?"

"You tell me, you're the profiler."

"Both. Now get on with it, will you?"

"If you'd just stop interrupting me, I might be able to." I cross my arms. An awkward silence ensues. If he's annoyed, it's not showing. I, on the other hand, feel as if my left breast has popped out of my shirt at the Super Bowl on national television. "Anyway . . . It happened in the darkroom."

"How do you mean?"

"I saw an image of Stacy lying face down in the pond, before I called the police."

"So you have a photo of that."

"No, you don't understand. I saw the image, but it wasn't really there. I mean, when I turned on the light, the photo of the pond was there, the way I shot it. But the image was gone."

He rubs the whiskers on his chin, and it makes an abrasive sound that I find strangely irritating and comforting. "Interesting."

"You think I'm lying."

"Or crazy?"

"Take your pick."

"Neither. You're sincere. Now, was it the same with the blog? Another vision?"

"Yeah. That's why I'm sure it's real. And you confirmed it by finding the deleted blog entry. Kyle, what's going on? Am I having some kind of memory lapse? Could it be that I really did meet her and have forgotten everything?"

"I don't think so."

"Then what is it?"

He doesn't answer for a while. The question sinks in deep, and I can tell he's very careful about what he says in situations like these. Finally, he turns to face me. "Can you do it again?"

26

"Do it again? You mean, reproduce the experience?" I can't believe he's asking this.

"Can you make those images appear again?"

"I don't know. Maybe."

"Can we both fit in your darkroom?"

"It'll be tight, but yes." Actually, it would be great to have him see this. I can't bear it alone much longer.

In the narrow confines of my darkroom, Kyle has to squeeze past me to get in place. My cheeks burn as his firm musculature presses against my arm and back. But his demeanor, as far as I can tell in the dimness of the safelight, is strictly professional.

After four or five tries on the same duck-pond photo, nothing turns up. I let out a frustrated breath and try some other shots. "Oh, come on." Still nothing.

"When exactly does the special image appear?"

"After the real image comes up, like a reflection in the solution, but more real."

I try a few more negatives, but to no avail. "It's not happening."

"Maybe it's me."

"All right." I reach for the doorknob and let him out. "Give me a few."

"Take your time."

"I swear, I'm not making this up."

As the door shuts, he says in a calm voice, "I keep telling you I believe you. When are you going to believe *me*?"

Without much hope for a different outcome, I slide another negative into the enlarger, expose the print. This time I try a higher contrast filter, though there's no particular reason it should make a difference. Developer, stop bath, fix.

Kyle is right outside the door. "Anything?"

"Don't nag."

The print's image in the tray is coming up now. This one is from Bình Sơn. The remains of an abandoned hut, the open dirt area in the center of the village. To my surprise, something appears on the ground that I know hadn't been there when I took this picture. "Oh . . . Oh my—"

"Xandra?"

"Not yet! Do not come in!"

I know how this will go—the moment I turn on the lights, the image will disappear. I've got to remember what I see, though. There's an old notebook in the drawer under the enlarger that I used to use as a work journal. At least I can write it down, maybe even draw some of it.

Except there's no pen or pencil to write with! "Never one around when you need one!"

"What's going on?"

"You got a pen, Kyle?"

He does, and slides it under the door. Then I record what I see. To my utter amazement, just about every subsequent print I develop has some kind of foreign visual artifact floating about it. And they only appear once. If I try to expose another copy of that same picture, nothing.

Kyle knocks on the door. "At least tell me if you're getting anything."

I've seen about four images now. "You would not believe . . ."

"Can I see them?"

"Afraid not. Give me a few more minutes."

"You've been in there for twenty minutes."

My mouth fills with imaginary cotton as I continue to write and describe these visions. The same horrific dread I felt the first time this happened encroaches upon my mind. My scalp, spine, hands, and feet are cold and numb, as if they all fell asleep at once, but it almost hurts.

The spectral reflections have stopped. I'm not imagining it. To the best of my abilities, I've written down what I saw. When I turn the lights on, all the prints appear normal without the ghost images. I can't say the same for my mental state.

It's not much, as far as Kyle can tell, but the notebook in my hand is all I can provide. And if the visions I've just seen are anything like the previous two, there's a good chance they will have far-reaching implications.

"You okay?"

"I think so." I hand him the book. His concern is genuine, not a bit patronizing. "You're shaking."

Before his fingers even touch the notebook, a heavy knock comes on my door. A black déjà vu enshrouds my heart. Clutching the notebook to my chest, I walk to the door and peer through the eyehole.

"Lieutenant Nuñez?"

"Open the door, Ms. Carrick."

Confused and more than a little afraid, I comply. "Kyle, what's—"

"Xandra Carrick," Detective Nuñez says, a male plainclothes cop at her side. "You're under arrest for the murder of Stacy Dellafina."

27

"No, wait. This is a mistake!" I turn to Kyle, but he's equally confused. Nuñez continues to read me my rights as her partner pulls my hands behind my back and cuffs me. "Kyle, tell them! I didn't do anything."

He steps forward and protests. But Nuñez just ignores him and continues to tell me that I have a right to an attorney; if I can't afford one, the court will appoint one for me . . . all the words blur.

"This is insane!" Kyle is right in her face now. "Where's your probable cause?"

Finally, the detective snaps a cold glare at him. "You ought to know, Matthews. You handed it to me."

"He what?" I'm more addled than ever.

Kyle motions for me to keep quiet. "I'm going to take this up with your chief, the commissioner—"

"You were the one who told me to check Dellafina's missing blog entries."

The toxic sting of betrayal rises into my throat. "Kyle, how could you?"

"It's not like that!" He continues speaking to Nuñez. "That information wasn't meant to implicate her—"

"Dammit, Kyle!"

He's facing me but can't quite look me straight in the eye. "I didn't mean for—"

"I asked you not to tell anyone!"

The detective's partner urges me through the door. "This way, ma'am."

"You might want to remind your frie—the suspect—that anything she says can and will be held against her in a court of law."

28

GRACE TH'AM AI LE

Saigon: April 21, 1975

I cannot believe it. President Thieu has resigned. Whatever happened during the Paris Peace Accords two years ago seems to have failed. The Americans have withdrawn their troops and all other support. Both the North Vietnamese and the Provisional Revolutionary Government here in the South have been trying to overthrow Thieu and remove whatever is left of the government supported by the United States.

Kissinger and Nixon have abandoned us. They had promised resources to help our military hold off the North Vietnamese forces, which are now approaching and getting in position to take Saigon. I am glad Nixon has been removed. It's only fair. Look what he's done to our president and country.

I have been avoiding Peter since he proposed marriage. I could not give him a better answer than, "May I please consider your request and let you know my answer in a few days?" It has been two weeks.

He is a good man, but it is not simply the commitment that frightens me. If I marry Peter, I must leave my home for a foreign country of which I know very little, where I know nobody. It is an entirely new world, and I am uncertain.

Yet, while I deliberate, my own world unravels before me. The land of my parents is no more, I have no living relatives in Vietnam, and any day now, the Communists will overthrow the government.

At the very least, Peter offers me security and safe passage. What is the matter with me? Why is this so difficult? He is a handsome and kind man. More than capable of taking care of me. Father and Mother would approve of him, as long as he doesn't force me to relinquish my heritage. Most of all, he loves me. Which is more than my parents had in a time when marriages were arranged at a very young age, like an exchange of commodities.

What shall I do? Is it too late anyway? I only hope he has not taken my silence as a rejection and left Saigon.

Saigon: April 22, 1975

I cannot find Peter. Every time I go to the Caravelle Hotel, they say he is not there. He has not yet checked out, though. I am very concerned. I heard today that the town of Xuân Lộc has fallen to the Communists. This means they have control of the key roads to the capital. I have no doubt Saigon will come under attack. It is just a matter of time.

Saigon: April 25, 1975

There is a tension in the city that is difficult to describe. Many of our troops that fought to defend Xuân Lộc have entered Saigon. While passing through Lam Son Square, I spoke with one who could not help shouting in frustration, with embittered tears. "They have abandoned us. They have all abandoned us!"

"Who, the Americans?"

"Our leaders, our commander-in-chief!"

"President Thieu?" I was still accustomed to referring to him as president.

"General Thieu. Have you not heard?"

"Yes, a few days ago. He resigned."

"No, I am talking of the news today."

"What has happened?"

"Thieu has fled to Taiwan, and they're saying he's taken all the gold reserves of South Vietnam with him." I stood dumbfounded as the soldier spat and trudged away, cursing Thieu for inviting the Communists to help themselves to our country.

Alain at the Caravelle's front desk handed me a message today. It was from Peter, who phoned it in. He had been called out on a special assignment out at Xuân Lộc at the time of the takeover and didn't have a chance to contact me until now. He is safe and will be returning tomorrow.

Saigon: April 26, 1975

Today, with the sympathetic help of the cafeteria staff, I prepared a special meal for Peter—a Western dish that Alain said any American man would surely love. Hamburgers and french fries. The only place I could think of getting ground beef was a butchers market just outside of Cholon, the Chinese quarter.

I left a message for Peter, saying I must speak with him concerning a matter of great urgency, and could he please meet me at my dormitory room. The room gave off an exotic aroma of fried onions and deep-fried potatoes sliced into little strips. Alain wrapped a little good-luck present especially for tonight's dinner. A red bottle with the words *Heinz Tomato Ketchup*, which is supposed to go with the meal.

I chose to wear my one and only ao dai. The gold silk fit tightly around me and accentuated my figure in a way that made me blush when looking at myself in the mirror. Giselle, the resident administrator, helped me put my hair into a french braid. The entire arrangement seemed strangely decadent and in a secret way sensual.

I have overprepared, I thought. *He will think I am childish and pretentious. Perhaps I should change out of my ao dai and wear my ordinary student clothes—dungarees and a short-sleeved shirt.* All I accomplished was to pace around my room for ten minutes and then stare at the wall clock for another fifteen.

At last, at about six fifteen, a knock came at the door. Giselle checked my hair, straightened my ao dai, and beheld me with an enormous smile. "You are beautiful, Grace."

"I am afraid."

"You will charm him completely." She led me to the door. After two deep breaths, I opened it slightly and peered through the crack.

"Peter!"

"Hello, Grace. Is everything all right?"

"Yes."

"Your note said it was urgent."

"It is."

"Can I come in, or should we continue this way?"

I let out a nervous giggle. "Of course. Please, come in."

As I opened the door and let him in, Giselle rushed past him and stopped for a moment, staring up at his height.

"Hello?" Peter said, confused.

"I'm Giselle." She offered her hand.

"Peter Carrick."

"Just leaving."

Peter removed his hat and inclined his head ever so slightly. Such elegance. "A pleasure."

As Giselle left, she turned and from behind his back gave me a mischievous look, pointed at him, and shook her hand as if it were on fire. I am not certain what that gesture meant, but I think she approved of him.

"Wow, Grace." He stood back and looked at me from head to toe. "You look terrific."

I lowered my eyes to the floor, pretending to be bashful. The truth was, I rather enjoyed his attention. "It is a traditional outfit."

"Ao dai? Yes. And they are lovely." His eye wandered to the table by the window and quickly shot back to me, as if embarrassed that he noticed the meal I prepared. "What's the urgent matter?"

"Please, won't you have a seat?" I struck a match, lit the candle in the center of the table, then sat down. "First, I wish to apologize for not responding earlier—"

"Oh." Peter let out a sigh of relief. "I was worried that you might be upset with me because you thought I'd left Saigon."

"Then you are not upset?"

"Are you?"

"No." I reached out and touched his hand. At first, tentatively. But when his eyes lit up, I held it tight. "Then we are . . . okay?"

"It wasn't fair for me to propose like that, with so little preparation. And even though we've known each other for a couple of years . . . well, I hope you will forgive me if I was presumptuous."

"No, you were not." I poured him a glass of Schlitz beer, courtesy of Alain's friend at the Caravelle's bar.

"Schlitz, my favorite. How did you know?"

"I have some spies." I patted his hands and squeezed his fingers playfully. "I hope you won't mind my attempt at American food."

"It smells great."

"Then let us eat."

He reached for his hamburger with great anticipation, but as soon as I folded my hands and bowed my head to say blessing over the meal, he put it back down. "Oh."

With one eye open, I grinned and said, "My parents taught me to pray before meals." At first he seemed a bit uncomfortable. But he eventually joined me, bowing his head as I gave thanks.

After two bites, Peter held the hamburger up and looked at it with scrutiny. *It must taste terrible,* I thought. But he turned to me, pointed, and said, "That's a fine burger, Grace." Immediately he took a few more healthy bites.

In the quiet moments when we looked out the window at the streets of Saigon, the last stand of the South Vietnamese people, countless questions arose in my mind. *Will I be enough for him? And will he know and care about what is important to me?*

Annoyed at my own thoughts, I decided to draw out some of his. "American women are so beautiful."

"I guess."

"They have lovely golden hair, long legs, full and round—"

"You're describing Marilyn Monroe, aren't you?"

"I don't know. Maybe." Admittedly, the Hollywood star was my sole point of reference.

He took the last bite and then started on his french fries. "That's not true beauty."

"Oh? Then what is?"

"It's not easy to define. But I'll tell you this. When I stand on a beach at sunset and it's completely quiet, that moment when the day's final rays crest the Pacific horizon, something happens. Something that reaches inside of me and makes me aware of how incomplete I am, how much I yearn to be completed. For that short time, I wonder if there might actually be a God out there, who created all this so that for just that minute or so I get a glimpse into something eternal."

"How beautiful."

"For years I've tried with my camera to capture this feeling— no, it's so much more than a feeling. It's a recognition of my finite-ness, my longing for fulfillment, to become part of something greater than myself. But so far, I haven't been able to re-create that experience with any visual fidelity."

"You seem to do so with words."

"Don't you see, Grace?" He leaned over the table and held my hands. "That's how I feel when I'm with you."

Unwilling to release the enchantment in our eyes, I smiled and realized I was crying. *I must tell him now,* I thought, *before I allow my mind to start reasoning against my heart.* "Peter, can you do one thing for me please?"

"I would do a million things for you."

"The urgent matter."

"Yes?"

"Would you please ask me again?"

His eyes shimmered intensely in the candlelight. And as he did seventeen days ago, Peter stepped away from his chair, took my hand, and knelt. "Grace Th'am Ai Le, you are the one true beauty in my life. You're the setting sun on the horizon of my life, the warmth and light that comforts me and gives me a reason to go on. You complete me." He took out the diamond ring and placed it on my finger, this time with confidence. "Will you marry me?"

Overcome with emotion, I stepped out of my chair and joined him on the floor. We embraced. "I love you." Never in my life had I uttered these words to anyone in this way. But I meant it and wanted nothing more than for him to know, beyond any trace of a doubt.

"Grace?"

Leaning on his chest, I was basking in the warmth of our mutuality. "Yes?"

"Will you?"

"Yes, Peter Carrick. I will gladly be your wife."

29

XANDRA CARRICK

Kyle must have done something, because after the detectives brought me in for processing, they didn't do much in the way of questioning. He advises me to get an attorney.

"Leave me alone."

"All right. Just . . . don't say anything until you get a lawyer, okay?"

"As though you cared."

"I keep telling you—"

"And I keep telling you, leave me alone! Haven't you done enough harm?"

He exhales long and slow and walks away as I'm led to a door.

From across the table in the interrogation room, Detective Nuñez fastens a cold stare on me. "It'll reflect a lot better on you if you cooperate."

"I would like to make a phone call."

"That's fine. But first, just tell me this. What was it, money? Or did she threaten to expose a dirty little secret?"

"I'm not obligated to speak without legal representation."

"Of course." She steps out, and a minute later her partner, Detective Bryant, brings in a phone and plugs it into a wall jack.

"What number would you like?"

I'm still cuffed, which makes it difficult to dial. So I tell him the number and he dials it and then puts it on speaker.

After five rings I know the answering machine will pick up. "You've reached the home of Peter and [Mom's voice:] Grace Car-rick. [Together:] We can't take your call at the moment, but if you'll leave your name and number, we'll be sure to get back to you." I haven't heard Mom's voice for some time. It makes me want to cry. "Never mind." I motion for Detective Bryant to hang up. "Could I try another number?"

He's kind enough to consent and dials it for me. My heart leaps when the call is answered. "Oh, thank God!"

"What's the matter?"

"Daddy, I'm in trouble."

30

I can't describe the feeling of waking up in a holding cell, not knowing how exactly things are going to go. Thankfully, I didn't have to share it with anyone overnight.

Upon Dad's advice, I've declined a public defender. I'm now waiting for someone he's called to represent me. I'm sitting on a wooden bench in a little room on the side of the Arraignment Courtroom—Part 49, waiting to meet this attorney. The armed officer stands close enough to remind me of his presence.

On the other end of the corridor, the door opens and a woman who resembles a young Hillary Clinton approaches, stops right in front of me, and extends a hand. "Xandra Carrick? My name is Danielle Reid. I'll be representing you."

"Did my father send you?"

"He called last night."

"I'm so glad to see you."

"Let's go over the facts." Danielle takes a seat next to me and pulls out a yellow memo pad. "We're going to try to get this whole thing dropped, if possible."

"If possible?"

"I'll do my best, but there are no guarantees. The priority is to keep you out of jail if this goes to trial."

Reluctantly, I tell her about the events that led to my arrest.

When I get to the part about my visions, I pause. None of it will make sense unless I tell her.

But I don't know what else to do besides tell the truth and hope things work out.

So I do.

Her pen stops midstroke. "Excuse me, did you say visions?"

"I'm not making this up. It sounds crazy, I know. But it's because I had knowledge of things that only the killer could know that they think I did it."

"We'll have to focus on the circumstances and facts surrounding the arrest, probable cause—"

A door on the courtroom side opens and an African American court officer steps in. "Showtime."

"Docket number 08N734598." The bailiff's voice resonates in the room. "The people versus Xandra Carrick." His words impale me. I can't believe my name is being called in a murder case. This is nothing like the movies or TV. The sweat in my palms is real. Standing next to my attorney and facing the very annoyed looking judge, the Honorable Victor Calloway, my knees grow weak.

Calloway clears his throat, his eyes glued to the papers in his hand. "Would the defense like to waive reading of the charges?"

"Yes, Your Honor."

Calloway asks questions of both Danielle and the assistant district attorney. The ADA then produces a bunch of notices to which Danielle responds with a set of papers of her own. A confusing exchange of papers ensues, then Calloway asks the prosecutor to make a statement.

"Due to the nature of this crime," says the ADA, "I'm recommending that the suspect be held without bail."

"Your Honor," Danielle Reid says, "that's hardly reasonable. The arresting officer's probable cause is paper thin. None of their evidence is direct."

The ADA smirks. "The suspect was privy to information that only the killer could have known."

"Something you've inferred, at best. My client was instrumental in solving a missing-person case. At the very least, she should get ROR."

With each exchange, the perspiration rolling down my spine grows colder. This can't be happening. Danielle's voice sounds like a distant echo as she argues my complete lack of priors, my ties to the community.

Finally, the judge takes a moment to render his decision. This short silence seems to take an eternity. I am disturbingly aware of background sounds: papers ruffling, pens scribbling, my heart pounding. If I'm to be held without bail, I could be stuck at Rikers for months until my trial. Where I will probably get beaten, raped, and perhaps killed before my trial ever starts. All this because I decided not to keep this vision to myself. To share my gift, as Mom always taught. Well, perhaps these visions are not so much a gift as they are a curse!

Finally, the judge looks up. "Bail is set at one hundred and fifty thousand dollars." He raps the gavel, and the sound jolts me back into the moment. My attorney and the ADA exchange a few more arguments, and then it's over.

Danielle pats my shoulder. "I'll see you back there. Your father's already wired the money."

"Did we win?"

"This wasn't a trial. But considering the gravity of the charges, I'd say we did pretty well."

"A hundred and fifty thousand is doing well?"

"We only need a fraction of that."

The bailiff takes my arm and leads me back to the door to the holding area. I'm not processing it all. Until panic seizes me. "No, wait! I can't go to jail. The real killer's still out there. I saw—!"

"Keep quiet!" Danielle hisses. "I'm making all the arrangements. Sit tight, and I'll be back to get you as soon as possible."

The whole arraignment is over so fast I can hardly believe it. According to the clock, from the moment I stepped into the courtroom till the moment I left, a mere ten minutes have elapsed.

The court officer leads me through the corridor to the holding area where I sit at a splintered desk, the varnish of which sticks to my palms and smells like pickled cabbage. His hand rests conspicuously near his gun.

It is now that random thoughts coagulate into coherent words. They flash through my consciousness like a flickering neon sign in the dead of night.

I'm a murder suspect.

31

As soon as possible.

That's when Danielle said she'd return. But as the minute hand rakes across the face of the clock, I'm beginning to doubt. Everything has been rushed, and I barely had a chance to speak to her.

An hour has passed. Idle hands may be the tool of the devil, but idle time turns the mind into his playground.

She's not coming back.

Something's gone wrong with the bail.

Dad's probably thinking, *I always knew that girl was going to be trouble. My daughter, a murderer.* Perhaps he's changed his mind. He's not posting my bail. That's fine. If he's going to be like that, I don't want his help.

An angry tear falls from my eye and spreads on the sticky wooden table. Quickly, I wipe my face and sniff. The brawny African American guard pulls a pocket-size pack of tissues from his shirt pocket and hands it to me. His stoic expression belies his kindness. I take the tissue and wipe my eyes. "Thank you."

"You'll be okay, Miss. Have faith."

I scoff. "In what?"

Not a moment too soon, someone knocks on the door and opens it. It's Danielle.

"Finally! Where have you been?"

"There was a problem with the wire transfer. The bank used the wrong receive code and . . . anyway. We're set to go." She hands the guard a slip of paper. Like some kind of claim ticket. I'm a faux fur in the coat check room at the Met.

"That's it, it's over?"

"For now. Let's go."

Hard to believe that I am simply walking out of the court-house as though nothing happened. Harder still to accept the fact that I'm not truly free. As the elevator doors slide shut, a million thoughts afflict me—not my own.

I can almost see the faces to whom those thoughts belong. They're angry, opportunistic, curious. Not curious with a desire to learn, but morbid, like rubberneckers gawking at bloody corpses being pulled from a multivehicle crash.

Danielle catches me as I falter. "Are you all right, Xandra?"

"This can't be happening."

"Don't worry, we're going to beat this. You keep saying that to yourself. And anyone you might run into. You hear? We're going to beat this."

"What was I thinking? I should have kept my mouth shut. It wasn't any of my business." No matter how hard I resist, I can't stop from crying again.

Danielle turns to me and takes my hand. "No, listen carefully. You gave the Dellafinas something they couldn't have otherwise had."

"Someone to condemn for their daughter's murder?"

"Resolution and hope. Do you know how hard it is for fami-lies who never recover the bodies of their loved ones? You've helped them; they just don't know it yet. But they will, when I win—we win this case. When the real killer is found. And that's something that might never happen if you'd kept silent."

"As far as the State of New York is concerned, they've found their killer. Case closed."

"It's not that simple." She hands me a tissue. "Wipe your nose." The elevator bell dings; the doors begin to open. I'm completely unprepared for what I find when I step out.

32

A mass of voices crowds around me. Cameras flash, blinding video camera lights and boom mics push into my face.

"Are you maintaining your innocence?"

"Were you friends with Stacy?"

"Were you lovers?"

"How did you know where her body was?"

Danielle shields me and presses forward until she turns and confronts the army of reporters. "Let me make something abundantly clear. Ms. Carrick is innocent. She's been wrongfully arrested by detectives who were eager to close the case, albeit prematurely. The charges against her are fantastical. I will see to it that this miscarriage of justice is corrected."

A reporter comes forward. Good Lord, it's Oscar Denton, Doug's boss. How many times had Doug championed me from the day I first set foot into the *Times*? An irrational sense of shame wells up. Without much success, I avoid eye contact. Oscar averts his gaze, thank God, and turns to Danielle. "Ms. Reid, how do you explain—"

"It will all come to light during the trial. My client will be exonerated."

The throng's collective voice grows to a roar, but Danielle waves them off and we push through, down the long steps to the street level.

Just as we reach the car, a hand blocks the way. I look up, and there's Special Agent Kyle Matthews. He's displaying his badge to my bewildered attorney. "I just need a moment."

"Get away from me!"

"Xandra, listen. It wasn't supposed to—"

"You betrayed me!"

"I know, I'm sorry. But if you'd just hear me—"

"I'm done listening to you." With a huff I reach for the door handle. But he grasps my wrist firmly.

"Wait. Please. I can help."

"Last time you *helped* me, I got arrested. Now take your hand off of me before—" The altercation has caught the eyes of the buzzards. They're swooping down the steps toward us now. Pointing, I speak in a low and threatening voice. "See that? That's my life, my good name, going down the toilet." Through a tearful sob: "Thanks to you!"

"Xandra . . ."

"I never want to see you again, you hear? Anything you have to say, you tell my attorney."

Danielle stands ready and nods.

"And one more thing, Special Agent Matthews." With a swift pull, I pry free. Then with the most corrosive glower I can muster, I hold his gaze. "I hate you."

33

The red answering-machine light flashes indignantly. Calls from just about everyone I know, asking what is going on, if it's true, if I'm all right.

The Graflex sits on my kitchen table, though I'm sure it's been handled and examined. So much for the Marbury. It would, after all, be inappropriate to award such a lofty honor to a murderer.

A quick glance down the hall. The darkroom door has been left ajar. A chill runs through my core up my neck and to my head. Madness. This is all madness.

According to Danielle, Dad plans on flying out to New York soon. For now, I'll take a much-needed shower and hope that I'll wake from this nightmare.

The past two days wash away and swirl down the shower drain. I'm allowed to enjoy the hot mist and penetrating heat, aren't I? After all I've been through, I think the universe owes me one. Or two.

White shampoo suds swirl down the drain. In my mind, white turns crimson—blood. I'm in the shower at Rikers Island, beaten, raped, bleeding to death in a smelly, mildew-infested shower, a heavy female inmate or male correctional officer gloating over my pierced and broken body.

I grasp the shower fixture and shake the image out. How am I going to prove my innocence? Does New York enforce the death penalty?

With my eyes shut, they come back to me, clear as if I'm staring directly at them. The phantasmal darkroom visions. Stacy Dellafina, her body, her laptop, her blog. Then the ones that I wrote in my notebook. My notebook! What if they find it?

The notebook is superfluous now because the images won't leave me. I can't seem to forget them—they're clearer than normal memories. Is this what Dad's photographic memory is like? Eyes open or shut, I can see them, feel them. There's a dissonant quality to them—tension longing for resolution. These images described in my notebook feel like the penultimate chord of a Beethoven symphony, a knock-knock joke without the answer to that crucial question: who's there?

Dammit, who's there?

First, the face of Senator Colson. It's black and white, like one of his campaign posters. He's smiling heroically. But I feel uneasy about it. Can't say why. But I still like him. Does a murder suspect still retain the right to vote?

Another image, that of a soldier, lingers as well. This one's in color. Faded like some of Dad's old photos from the seventies. It's a *Time* magazine picture with a caption: Corporal Hank Jennings. The rest of the article is faded into a blur over the picture I took of the abandoned village in the hills of Bình Sơn.

And the last one comes up blank. I had actually turned the lights on in the darkroom before that vision came up. Never got to write it down because just as it emerged, that morbid feeling began to fill the room like thick smoke. Which the steam in my bathroom resembles, now that I've opened my eyes. Note to self: find the notebook because memory fails when you need it most.

The full-length mirror on the door is fogged. Though my body reflects ethereally, the outline of my figure is clear. I've been remiss in the way of exercise recently. Hailey says I'm crazy, but I still wish my waist was a bit thinner, my legs a little bit longer, and the twins a little fuller, maybe. Not bad, though a supermodel I'll never be. Who'd want to be a walking Q-Tip with eyes, anyway? Five-six is a reasonably decent height. I can thank Dad for that, and Mom for my mysterious eyes and uncommonly opulent hair.

Eat your heart out, Kyle Matthews.

Yet, the gloating rings hollow. I'm not as angry with him as I appear. Hurt? Yes. But he didn't deserve that degree of my wrath, which is all too easy to unleash when I know—when I *feel* I've been wronged.

Admit it. He was nice.

Yes, and while you're at it, why not say cute too? "Be quiet."

With my palm, I wipe clear a spot in the fogged mirror. Before I look, that morbid sensation returns along with the head-to-toe tingling. I'm not even in the darkroom. I glance at the mirror from the corner of my eye.

Shadows behind my reflection. I know what's there. Sure, I'll see it if I wipe off the entire mirror. But I can't. I'm trembling with fear.

With a towel wrapped around me, my hair still wet, I bolt out of the bathroom. I slam the door shut, holding the corners of my towel with one hand.

Breathing heavily, I pad down the hall and pass the darkroom. Slam that door shut too, then turn toward my bedroom. Why I'm tiptoeing, I don't quite understand.

Someone knocks on my door. I nearly jump out of my towel. With perturbed steps, I trudge over. "What now?"

"Xandra?"

Oh great. It's Kyle. "Get lost!"

"Look, would you please just—"

"I am not opening the door. Now please, go away!"

The knocking doesn't stop. I've got to end this now. With the security chain still attached, I open the door.

"Xandra, if you'd just give me a chance to—whoa!" He turns his head slightly.

In my distress, I've forgotten my current state of disattire. "You've got a lot of nerve showing up here, mister. After all you've done, after all you've put me through." I'm still running down my list of grievances . . .

And there's my towel at my ankles.

I shut the door again. "Do I need to get a restraining order?"

No answer. Only the fading sound of footsteps going down the hall. He deserved every bit of it.

On the other hand, something's nagging me. Like a pebble in my shoe. I start back for my bedroom and ponder this. Then, as I sit on the chaise and stretch out my legs, I recognize what that feeling is.

Regret.

34

GRACE TH'AM AI LE

Saigon: April 27, 1975

I was dreaming of my new life in America as Mrs. Grace Carrick. In this dream, I wore a short white dress with pink and blue polka dots, walked a white, curly-haired dog on a leash, and sipped Coca-Cola from a bottle with a straw.

I barely heard the knocking on my door.

But the knocking became more urgent. "Grace, wake up!"

Wrapped in my blanket, I got out of bed and ran to the door. The sun had not yet risen, and it was too dark to see the clock. I opened the door, and Peter came right in. "Pack your things, we have to go."

"What time is it?"

"Hurry. I'll help you."

For a moment I thought this was the Western idea of eloping. But from the gravity of his tone, it could not be. "What is happening?"

He found the lights and switched them on. "Do you have a suitcase?"

"Under the bed."

Outside, in the quiet of the predawn city, a distant storm rumbled. But the thunderclaps seemed too frequent. He found my suitcase, opened it, and filled it with clothing from my drawer.

"Peter, what are you doing?"

"We've got to get you somewhere safe."

"Why?"

"Could you please get dressed? Wear comfortable shoes, something you can run in." He was trying to keep me from becoming anxious. It had the opposite effect. I grabbed a pair of dungarees and a sweatshirt and turned away from him to put them on. "Will you please tell me?"

He pointed to the pile on my desk. "Do you want these books?"

"Will I be coming back soon?"

"No."

"Then pack only the black one." It was my father's leather-bound Bible, given to him by the Jesuit priest. "Peter, what is it?"

At last, he took a moment to catch his breath. He went to the window and pulled open the shades. Up in the charcoal sky, white flashes lit the outskirts of the city; thunderous blasts resounded. To the east, the sun began its ascent. Peter pointed to the flashing sky. "The NLF's been spotted. They're closing in."

So it had finally come to this. The entire city would soon be overrun by the Communists. Without time to ponder this, I gathered my most important belongings and squeezed them into my suitcase.

By the time we exited the building, the sun had risen. We didn't realize the full extent of the horror this new dawn would bring.

Peter carried my bag and tried hard to find a taxi, or anyone who would take us. But none of the few vehicles that passed by paid us any heed.

"Let's go." He took my hand.

We crossed through Lam Son Square, and I heard what at first sounded like an airplane flying close to the ground. Peter stopped and looked up. "Oh no."

The explosion that followed shook my bones, though it seemed quite far from us. In that very moment, I felt a twinge on that scar where I had been shot back in Bình Sơn. "What was that?"

"Rocket fire."

I turned my head. Smoke and flames billowed from the middle of Cholon. The houses in the Chinese quarter were so densely packed, it would surely spread like a wildfire.

Screams of terror rose up with the smoke into the morning air. I wanted to run back to my dormitory, but Peter said because of its size, it was a greater target. We had to go around Cholon or pass through it. Another cry went out. "Help us!" a woman pleaded. "My baby! Someone, please help!"

Peter turned to me. "Find cover, I have to go in."

"I am coming with you." My chances of survival were the same as his. He took my hand, and we rushed into the smoldering neighborhood.

Like a plow, the rocket had cut a wide furrow through the rows of houses. All that remained of the homes were shards of corrugated iron. Motionless, survivors stared at the vastness of the destruction, even as flames leaped into the air.

"Someone, please help us!" A young woman still in her nightgown came running in our direction. She grabbed my arm and spoke in Vietnamese at such a rapid pace, I had difficulty understanding.

"My husband and my baby are still inside!" She pointed to her house, the entire face of which had been ripped away. The roof fell over the new opening, and from the tiny crevices, fire and black smoke billowed out.

We dashed across the street, nearly tripping on broken glass. The fire burned so hot I had to turn my face. The mother shook Peter's arm. "I heard my baby crying inside!"

Shielding his eyes from the morning sunlight, he ran around the front of the house, looking for an entry point. "There's no way in!"

The mother fell on her knees and began to wail.

He touched her shoulder and shook his head. "I'm sorry, ma'am."

She kept calling out the names of her baby and husband as she buried her face in her hands. At that very moment, I thought I heard the voice of a child. "Mama!"

An image entered my mind. It seemed like a memory, as if I had been inside this house before. At that very moment, I knew what I must do. But in order to do it, I would have to run past the fire and in between the house and its neighbor.

"It is over! My son, my husband. Oh, they are gone now!"

Before I could reason with my instincts, I ran straight toward the house. Peter did not realize what I had done. When he did, he called out, "Grace, stop! Come back!"

For some reason, I believed that this tiny space between the houses, about a meter wide, would be safe. Sure enough, when I ran right through the thin blanket of fire at the mouth of this tiny chasm, there was a pocket of air. But it was heating up quickly.

I kept low to the ground and looked up the wall. There must be a window or some sort of opening. There was, about two meters ahead, at waist level. I crawled over, tensing as the searing air rushed into the gap. Quickly, I stood and pushed up on the window with all my might.

But it would not move. Locked! Inside, a little boy no more than a year old, ran over stretching up his hands, as little ones do when they want to be held or carried. He was too small to reach the lock. Over to the side, his father lay unconscious.

The heat on my back and hands was unbearable.

A hoarse scream in the distance made me stop. What was I doing? "GRACE!" my fiancé called out in a panicked voice. "What are you doing? Get out of there!"

The little boy was wiping his eyes and crying. I could see the smoke pouring into the room. If I ran now, I might be able to save myself. But how could I leave them?

With my elbow, I smashed the glass, cut and burned my fingers disengaging the brass lock, then opened the window and climbed in. Right away, the boy ran into my arms. But no matter how much I shouted, the father would not awaken.

The air became so hot and filled with smoke, I began to cough violently. I found a pitcher of water on the night stand and splashed it on the father's face. I did not expect it to work, but I thought I must at least try. Imagine my surprise when the boy's father blinked, shook his head, and sat up. "What—"

"The window, quickly!"

He got up, staggering slightly, and took the boy as I climbed out. Then he handed the boy to me through the window as he, too, climbed out. "Down on the ground, we must crawl. Follow me!"

The father held his son to his chest and crawled forth. Behind us, a heavy beam fell, sending sparks and embers into our safe corridor.

By the time we reached the end, the wall of flames had grown.

"We're trapped!" the boy's father said. The flames from the fallen beam had also erupted and now raged hotter on our backs than before.

"This is the only way out," I said.

"We cannot go through!"

I could not have come here with this providential knowledge only to die from indecision. "We must. We'll die if we wait in here. Follow me."

"How can I know for certain you are right?"

"You cannot. You can only believe."

For a while he didn't answer. Then finally, "Take my boy with you."

I took him in my arms, wrapped him in my sweater with my arms around him. Then before I could convince myself that I was crazy for running headlong into a path of fire, I ran.

The heat and smoke forced my eyes shut, but I knew I must not stop. Finally, a rush of cool air filled my lungs. I opened my eyes and fell to my knees.

The little boy ran into his crying mother's arms. "Mama, Mama!"

Peter rushed over to me and checked to see if any of my clothes were on fire. "Are you all right?"

"Yes, but—"

"Lanh!" The woman stood, clutching her son to her bosom, shouting for her husband.

Right away, I turned and called out to him. "We're all right! Your son is fine. Don't look at the fire. Think of your wife and child, then run!"

A wall collapsed into the chasm. Even more flames rushed out.

"Lanh!" his wife cried. "Oh please, Lanh! Hurry!

Emboldened, Peter got up and rushed toward the fire. I grasped his arm. "No. It's too late."

"But I might be able to—"

"I saw it. There's no way to get in now."

The mother must have heard me because she began to sob. "No, no! Lanh, no!"

Was this what Huynh Tho's final moments were like? But he had no family around to call for him, no one to run in after him. Holding his cross, which I now wore around my neck, I could do nothing but pray.

And while my eyes were still closed, I saw a young woman, someone who looked strangely familiar, reaching down into a dark pit.

She strains and struggles and at times is even pulled down toward the darkness. And the strangest part is that, strapped over her neck is a camera like Peter's. Finally she gives one last pull. The strap breaks, and the camera falls into the pit. But from it, she rescues a man. I can only see the back of his head and his gray hair.

"Lanh!" His wife's weeping turned to shouts of elation. I opened my eyes. From the midst of the deadly conflagration, he leapt out. His clothes were on fire as he hit the ground and rolled. Peter removed his jacket and covered him, putting out the flames.

Lanh was hurt, but alive.

I was shaken. It was not like me to act so rashly, so heedless of danger. All because I saw something in my mind and believed it to be true. I don't know what it was, but I am glad I listened to the prompting in my heart, because Lanh and his son will live to see another day.

Too many others were not so fortunate. Peter came across an Australian war correspondent and a French photographer who tried desperately to help one family whose five-year-old daughter had been burned and torn to tatters by iron shards. She was alive and in torment. A policeman held her frantic mother away. They told Peter that her head could not even be lifted from the corrugated iron that fell from the roof, because her hair had been stuck to it by mortar that had turned to wax from the heat.

We finally made it back to the Caravelle, where many non-American journalists and reporters stayed, all nervously awaiting word from the American Embassy as to evacuation instructions.

I can only imagine the totality of the destruction caused by the rocket that ripped through Cholon today. It has been more than three years since Saigon has been attacked like this. I thought I might have forgotten how terrible it was. But two more such rockets hit the city today. I am certain they won't be the last.

35

XANDRA CARRICK

Dad's flight has been delayed due to a heightened terror alert in San Diego announced just before takeoff. He's going to have to re-schedule. That was all he said on my voice mail, while I was in the shower.

Now that I've sent Kyle away, gotten dressed, and warmed up a can of Healthy Choice soup, I'm calmer. But not much. I'm still shaken by that dreadful intuition I got from the bathroom mirror experience. I know that feeling. It's from the darkroom.

There's probably no point in avoiding it. I know that it's going to nag me until I face it. It's inevitable. I have to go to the dark-room and confront the images that haunt me, even though I've not yet seen them in full.

I'm surprised to find my darkroom in good condition after the police have searched it. Thankfully, they haven't confiscated any of my negatives.

Lights out.

Let the visions begin.

Somehow, expecting that I will see something puts me at ease. So much fear comes from the unknown. For the first ten minutes, *niente*. Now, as I develop another set of prints from the aban-doned village in Bình Sơn, even before any image comes up, that familiar sense approaches. It's not so much fright as it is suspense, because I expect to see something extraordinary. Something related to truth. And if experience has taught me anything, it's an important truth that may not be widely known or understood. Such as the location of Stacy's body or the fact that she was seeking me out.

Now, it appears. Everything I remember at the site where we scattered Mom's ashes, just a week ago. But there's much more here than uncovered by a superficial glance.

As expected—and yet, not—a ghostly layer of images floats in the solution over the print, as though it were a transparent overlay. It appalls me more than anything else I've seen here in the gloom.

Where the tall grass stands, the image of a ditch, dug into the ground, comes up. Though I can perceive it with my eyes, it's more like seeing it in my mind. A memory that will be forever etched there.

And piled in that ditch . . . Oh, this is horrific . . . the bodies of villagers, too numerous to count. It's a mass grave. Corpses not only of men, but of women and children as well.

It's so inexorably vivid that I don't even need to write this down in my notebook. Yes. This is that same image that loomed behind the fogged mirror in the bathroom. I sense it. Gruesome as it is, I know I'm supposed to see this. But why?

Outrage and grief course through me. It's as though I know these people. They were innocent, helpless. And the children. Something terribly wrong with their deaths—perverse, violating, cruel!

I want to cry, and at the same time bring raging justice to the monsters who did this.

The developer solution shimmers in the tray, and in a corner, behind some of the tall blades, the most disturbing part of this image emerges.

No . . .

36

He's standing there, behind the stalks, a young man in combat fatigues, yet not a soldier. Holding the very Graflex camera that he will give me two decades later, he hides. "Dad?"

As soon as this realization hits me, the image vanishes. All that is left on the sheet is the placid hillside where we scattered Mom's ashes. I have to talk to Dad.

When I call him, I get his answering machine. "Dad? It's important. Call me." Next, Dad's cell. Voice mail. My frustration levels rise to threatening peaks.

With my mind racing at the speed of light, the logical thing to do is to assess all these things the darkroom has revealed. Straight to the laptop. I type in Google.com.

A large blue circle with the letter "i" shows up on the page and the error message:

INTERNET EXPLORER CANNOT DISPLAY THE WEBPAGE

Most likely causes:
- You are not connected to the internet.
- The website is encountering problems.
- There might be a typing error in the address.

"Oh, not again." I've seen this before. It means my cable modem service is down. The TV remote is just within reach, and I turn it on. It says, "This cable box is not authorized to view this program, please contact your cable provider." Both internet and cable have been cut off. But it makes no sense, I've paid the bill.

Now I have to go through the painfully slow process of using the web browser on my cell phone. I was never good at text messaging, which becomes painfully clear as my fingers cramp up from typing in every character of my search.

I nearly drop my phone when it buzzes in my hand with an incoming call. It's Dad.

"Dad, where are you?"

"I'm sorry, Xandra, I tried to call. Are you all right?"

"Out on bail."

"Thank God. We're going to get this straightened out. Now, what exactly are they charging you with?"

"You haven't heard?"

"I have, I just can't believe it."

"The cops, the DA, they're crazy. They're actually trying to pin the murder on me."

Dad swears quietly.

"Are you coming?"

"Yes, but there are no flights till tomorrow. Sure you're okay?"

My thoughts are too jumbled now to fully process what I'm feeling. I'm so focused on getting answers, I just come out and say it. "Dad, what really happened in Bình Sơn?"

37

"What are you talking about?" His tone is awkward. Somewhere between trying to make light of the question and trying to evade it.

"You heard me, Dad. For the longest time, I knew something was bothering you. Mom always told me not to ask about your past, because it would upset you. And the way you behaved when we were there . . ."

"Your mother was right. And you should honor her memory by heeding her advice."

"Look, I know it might be hard to talk about, but I really need to know."

"Where's all this coming from?"

"Something really bad happened during the war while you were there."

"People die in wars. That's bad." He exhales sharply. "You think you can just come out of the blue and—"

"Dad, please. It might have something to do with what's happening to me."

"It has got nothing to do with you! Now quit looking for things that aren't there."

"It's really important to me."

"Why?"

"Because . . ." Why indeed? Because I had these ghostly revelations in the darkroom? Am I going to tell him this? Would he believe me? "Because . . ."

"You've got some nerve, young lady!"

"I'm sorry, Dad." I hate that he can reduce me to a child with his words whenever I approach this dangerous topic. This is the furthest I've ever dared push it. I want to get mad at him, but . . . "I just need to—"

"This discussion is over. I'm sorry you got yourself in trouble, Xandi, and I'll do everything I can to help you. But we are not going to bring this topic up again. Is that clear?"

All I can do is let out a slow, shaky breath.

"Is it?"

"Yes." It's not. Not by a long shot. But how else can I answer him?

"I'll call you tomorrow with my itinerary." His voice softens. "Get some rest. And stay out of trouble."

38

RICHARD COLSON

"She refuses to speak with you, sir. I can't—"

"Just put the damn phone to her ear, Cecilia!" It's late, and I've been so busy I missed dinner. I feel like slamming the receiver down on the desk repeatedly to punctuate my request. After a short pause and some hand-muffled dialogue on the other end, Suzanne finally gets on the line.

"Rick?"

"Oh, thank you, your highness, for granting this lowly peasant an audience."

She laughs, and then sputters. "What time is it out there?"

"About quarter to eleven."

"This is the third time you called today! How are you going to win this election if you don't concentrate?"

"I had to find out. So?"

"I guess it wasn't as bad as I thought it'd be."

"You see? That's my girl. We're going to fight this to the bitter end. And we're going to win." I don't think it wise to mention that for many, the first wave of chemo is not so terribly unbearable compared to the subsequent treatments. Why plant anxiety in her mind?

"Well, anyway. It's done." Her voice is distant.

"What's the matter?"

"Nothing. You just concentrate on your speech tonight. New Hampshire's a key state."

"Is it about the chemo?"

"I tried it, like you asked me to."

"So you'll keep doing it, right?"

"Did you ever think about life after I'm gone, Rick?"

The question clenches my heart with jagged claws. "Of course not."

"Maybe you should."

"Never."

"Science, medication, it's all good, but when a person's time is up, it's just up."

"No, Suzanne. We make our own destiny."

"To an extent. But life and death aren't meant for our hands. We do our best to be good stewards, but in the end, they're not ours to manipulate."

"You sound like one of those pro-lifers."

"Maybe I've changed my views."

"Since when?"

"I just don't want you to put so much of yourself into things that, in the end, aren't yours to control."

But hadn't I always held life and death in my hands? Every time I picked up a freaking M-16 in Nam I was saving lives, even if it meant taking some to do so. And as a district attorney, hadn't I brought justice to those who deserved it? Healing to those victims of rapists, families of murder victims? The whole reason I went into public service was to take control of life and death.

If not my hands, then whose? And as the chairman of the Investigations Subcommittee of the Senate Committee on Homeland Security, how many terrorist attacks have I already prevented? How many do I curtail every day? How many people's lives are in my hands and they don't even know it?

"I disagree. If you don't take control of your life, you're basically handing it over to someone else."

"It's my life."

"I don't want to argue, hon. Just take your meds, and we'll talk about it next time I'm back."

"Rick, listen to yourself. Don't you see what you're doing?"

"I have no idea what you mean."

"How long are you going to blame yourself for Deanna? It wasn't your fault."

"Hon, please."

"You've skirted this for too long. It's clouding your judgment now. There was nothing you could have done."

"I panicked. I hesitated. In those ten seconds of indecision, I could have saved her."

"You were only ten."

"I was a coward." The river Deanna had dared me to steal away to with her had become white rapids. Neither I nor my twin sister had realized how dangerous it was. But she had to go and taunt me about my fear of water. In the end, I was too petrified to make the decision in time. To grab her outstretched hand. I had to run back to the campsite to tell Momma and Pa that Deanna was gone. "I will never waver on a tough decision again, no matter what."

"Even if it's not yours to make?"

"Come on, Suzie!" I want to tell her, *I'm seeing to it that all the decisions are mine to make,* but realize just how crazed that would sound coming out of my mouth.

She's quiet. She knows. We'll never see the end of this argument. After a short pause: "The boys came home early for Thanksgiving."

"A month early?"

"They're taking good care of me. You've taught them well."

"Don't tell them how proud of them their father is; it'll go to their heads."

Then, behind my back, the floorboards squeak. Someone's stepped into the office. The security guards usually knock before entering. Who can it be? "I have to go now, Suzie. Love you."

I swing my chair around and immediately make eye contact. "What are you doing here?"

"Sorry to interrupt."

"I told you, only matters of utmost importance. And you come to see me in person?"

Mark Collinsworth plows forward, leans on the desk with both hands, and looks me dead in the eye. "This *is*."

"To have you barging in like this, it better be."

"We've got serious problems."

"Is there any other kind?"

"Besides needing to get your subcontractor in line, you've got a new thread unraveling."

"What might that be?"

"Haven't you been watching the news?"

"No time. Whatever I get, I get from Lassiter. She's filtering for me."

"Carrick's daughter."

"Right. Charging her with the murder takes the heat off of the sub. That's brilliant."

"We had nothing to do with it. Worse still, she's been digging into her father's past."

"And you know this how?" I glance at my watch. It's later than I thought.

"We've been monitoring her internet usage. She's booked a flight to San Diego tomorrow morning."

Just five minutes till my scheduled conference call. My collar's shrunk two sizes. "So, she'll be treated as a fugitive."

"Sir, we need to cut this off at the source."

"Did you speak with Carrick about the NDA?"

"He says he'll uphold it, but I have my doubts."

"You're the half-empty glass, Mark; you always have doubts."

"It's different this time. I really think we need to deal with him. Especially now that his daughter—"

"Fine. I'll handle them both."

Mark lets out an exasperated breath. "You're not going with the subcontractor, are you? Not after his last failure to deliver."

Without a word, I stand and walk to the door, which I open. A gesture indicating that Collinsworth should leave. "Just go and manage your segment of this operation, all right? You worry too much."

"All the same, Xandra is a real problem."

"Leave the Carricks to me."

Mark steps out, leaving a cloud of uncertainty in his wake. With Carrick's daughter now in the public eye, anything she says could draw attention and curiosity to the very thing we're working so hard to protect.

A frigid drop of perspiration rolls down the side of my face. Friend or not, I've been too lenient with Carrick. Should have taken care of this long before it came to this.

The conference will have to wait. I'm going to have to go back to California tomorrow and oversee the Carrick problem. It's time to call the subcontractor with a new set of instructions.

"Ian, this is TR . . ."

39

XANDRA CARRICK

Rest and staying out of trouble are not my forte.

After spending the entire night getting my internet back online and researching every online reference to Dad's photo-journalism work in Vietnam—scant details, strange enough—and Corporal Henry "Hank" Jennings, I find myself at LaGuardia with a boarding pass in hand, and on my way to the West Coast.

Southwest Airlines had the best fares, but the only downside is that it's open seating. Never know who you'll be stuck with, and it's six hours to San Diego.

For now, I've got the entire row to myself. Window seat too. I place my white earbuds in and dial to my in-flight playlist. Brahms' Piano Trio in B major, played by the Stern-Rose-Istomin trio. The last chamber piece I ever performed. The adrenaline of all yesterday's events ebbs. I'm nodding off as the flight attendants give their little demonstration on emergency procedures. My seat cushion also serves as a flotation device, I know. How much will that help if we crash into the desert? I wonder if we'll pass over the Great Lakes? Hush, Xandi! Leonard Rose is playing that heavenly opening.

The cello sings. I lean my head back, shut my eyes, and drift into aural bliss. So good to have this entire row to myself, all the way to San Diego—thank God for nonstops. I might just lie across the three seats when we get up in the air.

Moments later, as the violin joins the cello, someone sinks heavily into the seat by the aisle. Great. Not going to open my eyes and try to make casual conversation. With my great fortune, it will be some old guy who wants to talk the whole trip about his dentures, his vasectomy, his flatulence issues. At least the center seat's still open. Won't have to rub elbows for the next quarter of a day.

And now we're flying.

I'm a bit disappointed that I won't get to lie down across the seats. But having pulled an all-nighter, I think I might be able to sleep the whole way in any position.

The morning sun warms my face. It's not so bright yet as to require pulling the shade down. All is well. No babies crying, no annoying loud people. It's going to be a quiet flight.

Except for the passenger next to me tapping my shoulder.

Was a couple of hours of sleep too much to ask? Grudgingly, I suck in a slow breath and open my eyes.

Only to find seated next to me, with an earnest expression in his eyes, FBI Special Agent Kyle Matthews.

40

GRACE TH'AM AI LE

Today, the National Liberation Front flew their flag on Newport Bridge, just three miles from Saigon. The three-days-new President Minh gave an address to the remainder of his republic from the presidential palace. Despite the valiant efforts of our soldiers, he called for a cease-fire and negotiations.

After everything, Saigon is going to be surrendered to the Communists!

Peter has been busy speaking with various evacuation wardens about the embassy's plans. Just yesterday, after the rocket attacks, the American ambassador, Graham Martin, appeared on television, saying, "I, the American ambassador, am not going to run away in the middle of the night. Any of you can come to my home and see for yourselves that I have not packed my bags. I give you my word."

But today, as the streets resounded with every imaginable—and unimaginable—kind of weapons fire from the outskirts of the city, the evacuations have begun. Not the official embassy evacuation, but many had prepared to flee the city.

I spent most of my day in Peter's room at the Caravelle Hotel watching the news, while he spoke on the phone and met with people planning the evacuation. At one point, he lay down on the bed beside me and covered his eyes with his hand.

"Peter?"

He didn't answer. He just lay there silent, every now and then letting out a heavy sigh. It was near midnight, and we had barely spoken the entire day. I sensed he wanted to talk about something, but he never did.

Instead, it was I who finally turned and leaned on his chest. "What's bothering you? Do you want to talk about it?"

Lifting his hand from his eyes, the redness and moist tears were apparent. "It's nothing. And . . . it's everything."

"I don't understand."

After taking a deep breath, he tried to appear as if nothing was troubling him. But something was. I could tell. Nevertheless, if he did not wish to speak about it, I would respect it.

Saigon: April 29, 1975

This day will forever remain in my memory as the end of Saigon. After a night of fitful sleep, I was awakened by weapons fire out in the street. Peter was sitting before the television shaking his head as the reporter announced that Tan Son Nhut Airport had been hit by rocket and artillery fire, shortly after four that morning.

This was the airport to which most of the evacuees from Saigon were supposed to report in order to be flown out to safety. Its runways now were rendered unfit for fixed-wing aircraft.

Another report of chaos at Tan Son Nhut Airport, where American helicopters from a U.S. Air Force base were ordered not to land: a pilot had landed a fighter jet and left the engine running. South Vietnamese soldiers were ramming one of their own transport planes as it tried to take off. There were about three thousand panicking civilians on the runway.

Peter threw a towel at the television set.

"What will we do?"

"Our safest bet is through the embassy. They'll fly people out from there."

By nine o' clock we had packed our bags, eaten breakfast, and

met with the evacuation wardens. From them we received a fif-
teen-page booklet called SAFE, short for "Standard Instruction
and Advice for Civilians in an Emergency."

They brought to our attention an insert in the booklet that
said:

Note evacuation signal. Do not disclose to other personnel.
When the evacuation is ordered, the code will be read out on
American Forces Radio. The code is: THE TEMPERATURE IN
SAIGON IS 105 DEGREES AND RISING. THIS WILL BE FOL-
LOWED BY THE PLAYING OF I'M DREAMING OF A WHITE
CHRISTMAS.

"What is 'White Christmas'?" I asked.

"A song. We'll have to listen carefully for it."

The entire city was on a twenty-four-hour curfew, but I had
no interest in going outside anyway.

We stayed in the lobby until close to 11:00 a.m., when the
code came out over the radio. The announcer said, "The temperature in Saigon is one hundred and five degrees and rising."

Peter stood up, grabbed our bags. "Time to go."

A man with a very smooth voice began to sing the song about
a white Christmas. From then on, I would always associate it with
the fear and panic of running out into the streets in order to get to
the American Embassy.

A bellman who obviously had no idea what we were doing
asked Peter if he needed help with his bags. "Would you like me to
call a cab for you?"

Peter pulled out a roll of piastres and put it in his hands.
"Thank you, but that won't be necessary." The thought occurred to
me that this courteous young man might not live long enough to
spend the money Peter had given him.

To my surprise, Lam Son Square was desolate, save for a few
South Vietnamese soldiers. They were despondent; some were
drunk and took random shots at the crowds of people running toward the embassy.

"Keep your head down!" Peter called out and put himself between me and Tu Do, the main street. I readily obeyed, feeling sorry for these soldiers who fought so hard, only to return and find everyone they fought to protect abandoning them.

When we reached the embassy, we pressed through a large crowd gathered around the gate. Some merely craned their necks in order to see better what was happening. Still others clung to the bars and begged to be let in.

An American soldier examined papers presented by those wishing to enter. Once in a while, he would nod and allow someone in. But the others he would not.

"Don't let go of me," I told Peter. But the rising din of the crowd made it difficult for him to hear.

He leaned over to me. "What did you say?"

"Don't let go of my hand!" After all, I had yet to give it to him in marriage.

This was not the way I imagined my future. Never had I dreamt that I would leave my homeland. Certainly not in this fashion. And yet, despite the circumstances, with Peter's warm hand firmly surrounding mine, I was looking forward to it. A new life awaited me in what the Chinese call "The Beautiful Country." And there I would know peace, contentment. With the man I love. This strong and handsome man would be the person with whom I'd spend the rest of my life. In English they have a saying that the bride and groom vow to each other: *Till death do us part.*

The beating blades of a helicopter filled the air as it landed on the roof of the embassy building. In reaction, the crowd's clamor rose in intensity. Peter held up his papers and shouted over to the soldier behind the gate. The marine watching the gate kept telling everyone not to panic. To stay calm.

I tugged on Peter's hand until he looked at me. Puzzled at my expression, he lowered his ear to my lips, and I said, "I love you, Peter Carrick."

His eyes responded with more emotion than words could ever convey. All at once, in the midst of the tumult, he wrapped his arms around my waist and kissed me deeply.

All time stopped. Lost in his love, his kiss, his embrace, I had touched that beauty, that sense of the eternal that he told me about on the night he proposed. *"You complete me."* And for that moment, it was all I would ever need.

When we finally made our way to the gate, Peter identified himself and introduced me as his fiancée. The marine took his papers and looked them over. "All right, you can come in. But she needs to wait out there while we take you in for verification."

"Peter?" The gate opened.

"No, wait." Peter held onto the bars, as the soldier took him by the arm. "She comes with me."

"It's just a quick debriefing," the soldier said. "If everything checks out, you can come back and bring her in."

"Go ahead," I said, a bit too trusting.

"I'll come back for you. Don't go anywhere."

As the gate slammed shut, the crowd surged forward again, some waving papers, some begging to have the soldiers take their little children. One desperate mother even threw her baby over the wall, hoping someone would catch it and take it to America. Many tried to scale the concrete wall, only to be pushed back down by marines.

After a few minutes, the helicopter that had landed earlier was now taking off. Up on the roof, people crowded around a ladder that stretched to the elevated platform on which the aircraft had rested.

One man clung to the landing skid until he realized it was too dangerous, then let go before it was too late. Five minutes stretched into ten, then fifteen. Another helicopter landed and immediately more people climbed the ladder to board it.

Growing more frantic, the crowd by the gate pressed in. We were taught to fear the Communists, and now they were in our city. How could they expect us to stay calm?

I picked up my luggage and tried to reposition myself so I could see Peter when he returned. The handle slipped and the bag landed on my toes. I wanted to cry out but felt too embarrassed.

Finally, a large group of American civilians came out of the door Peter had entered. They were followed by some Vietnamese and headed for the main building where the helicopter landed.

In the midst of this crowd, I saw him. "Peter!" Jumping and waving, I called his name over and over. He tried to push through the crowd entering the embassy building across the courtyard, but there were too many people in the way.

Just then, shots rang out all around us. Everyone dropped to the ground. I could not tell who was firing, but people on the sidewalk nearby scattered after one man fell to the ground.

"Move it!" said the same marine who told us all to stay calm. With their guns ready, the other marines herded the frenzied evacuees into the building. Peter tried to break free from the group.

I stretched my hand into the bars as he passed by. Our fingers touched for just a second. "Let me get through!" he shouted. But no one heard him. They all pushed and shoved until he was engulfed and taken with the human undertow that would let nothing and no one stand in the way of their escape from Saigon.

41

XANDRA CARRICK

"Xandra, before you do or say anything, you need to—"

"Are you stalking me? I'm fairly certain there are laws against that."

Instead of a charming quip or a witty comeback, Kyle fixes a severe gaze on me. "Are you *crazy*?"

"Excuse me?"

"You're violating the conditions of your bail."

"And you're violating my right to privacy."

"Leaving the State of New York without authorization? You made bail because your attorney said you *weren't* a flight risk."

Flight risk. I almost have to laugh at the term.

"I could put you in cuffs right now." He's whispering and leaning in close. "Now, would you like to explain to me why I shouldn't bring you in as a fugitive?"

"Would you like to explain to me how you followed me onto this flight? And why?"

"Xandra, this is serious." A crease of frustration bunches up between his eyebrows.

Again, I'm at a loss for words. It makes sense that I should not leave New York without permission. In my haste, I neglected to consider how it's going to look at my trial. "If you wanted to arrest me, why wait till we're in flight?"

"I have my reasons."

"As do I."

"We're not getting anywhere with this line of—"

"Arrest me, then."

"Ugh!" He's trying his best to contain his vexation, but slamming the seat cushion betrays him. He leans back in his seat and rubs his temples. The dark rings under his eyes testify to sleep deprivation. But I have no sympathy for him. Not after all he's done.

"It's your fault I'm being charged with"—I glance around and lower my voice—"you know."

"Believe me, I had no idea Nuñez was so desperate. She was only supposed to follow up on the leads. I promise, I never—I even reiterated that you're not under suspicion. I guess that's where she stopped believing me."

Despite his sincerity, I'm still angry. Though not so much now. "So if you're going to arrest me, what are you doing here?"

"We never concluded the business of the darkroom. I read what you wrote in your notebook, the visions you saw."

"You did? Where is it?"

"They seized it for evidence."

I can just imagine how the prosecution is going to use that against me.

Kyle lowers his voice. "Look, I don't know what kind of ideas you have about me."

"Right now, you don't want to know."

"But for what it's worth, I believe you." He sits up and leans toward me. "Now, you saw something that led us to Stacy. And after finding the name of Hank Jennings in your notebook . . . tell me again, why are you going to San Diego?"

God, help me pull this one off. Right, asking God to help me lie better. Brilliant, Xandra. "I'm going to visit my father."

"Now?"

"Well . . . yes." It's not working. Why am I lying to someone who believes me about the visions?

A man walking down the aisle in a navy raincoat accidentally bumps Kyle's shoulder with his briefcase. "Sorry about that. I'm feeling a bit dizzy sitting in the tail section." Pointing to the seat between Kyle and me: "Is that seat taken?"

Simultaneously we answer, "Yes."

The poor businessman pushes his glasses back up his nose and scratches the back of his head. "You sure?" His brow knits and . . . isn't that odd? Over his left eye, he's got a tiny scar running through the edge of his thick eyebrow. There's also something odd about his speech, but I can't put my finger on it.

"I'm sorry," Kyle says. "We're holding a confidential business meeting here."

"Thanks anyway." The guy goes forward and speaks to a flight attendant. He looks weary and almost reminds me of Dad. Guilt is not something I need right now.

"Okay, Kyle. If you really believe me, then you'll help me, right?"

"I've gone off the radar for this. My supervisor has ordered me back to Quantico and off this case. But I owe you—"

"Got that right."

"What's it going to take, Xandra? An apology? Is that how it's got to be? Well, okay then. I'm sorry. I've already told you so. I believe you about the visions and I never meant for this to happen. When are you going to believe that I'm on your side?"

This is perhaps the first time I've seen him get . . . not angered as much as exasperated. With a sigh, I glance at his distant eyes. "I suppose you deserve a little faith from me."

"You suppose?"

I'm going to risk it again and tell him everything. "All right, here goes . . ."

42

RICHARD COLSON

Of all the facilities across the country, my San Diego office is by far the most pleasant. Overlooking the tall palm trees and white waves of the La Jolla shores, I could simply step outside, walk five minutes, and become one with nature, if ever I need a quick de-stressing session.

The panoramic picture windows make walking outside hardly necessary, though. They almost compensate for this unscheduled but necessary detour in my campaign tour.

"Your ten a.m. is here," the receptionist announces through the intercom.

"Send him in." I smooth out my jacket and straighten my tie. It's been three years since we've met face-to-face. I'm actually anxious. Isn't that interesting?

The door buzzes and opens. Reaching out warmly with a hand of friendship, I step forward. "Peter! So good to see you." We shake hands with strength and enthusiasm clearly biased. Carrick makes this clear by withdrawing abruptly. Nevertheless, I will retain my charm. "Won't you have a seat?"

"So, instead of meetings on the shore, you can hold them from a distance and still capture their essence?" Carrick paces around my office for a while, gazing out at the view. "What's so urgent?"

I take a seat and light up a cigarette. There are only a couple of occasions when I smoke: under extreme stress, and celebrating a hard-earned victory. "So what's it been, two years, three?"

"Not long enough." A wry smirk. I would have expected nothing less.

"You're a hoot, Peter."

"I was thoroughly unimpressed with that kid you sent."

"Oh, Mark Collinsworth? He's brash. But you know these young hotshots. Come on, have a seat." I point to the chair facing my desk. "Italian leather, you've got to try it."

With unmistakable reluctance, Carrick relents and sits. "Only the best for you, eh?"

"You get used to it after a while." Manufacturing his most sincere expression of sympathy, he lets out a heavy breath. "I heard about Grace. You have my condolences."

"Save it."

"Oh, come now, Peter. We've known each other far too long to let a simple business arrangement impede our friendship."

"Friendship?" Carrick scoffs and reclines into the ebony leather. "I love the way you euphemize. You're a politician through and through." He runs his hand over the buttery leather arms of the chair. "You've done well for yourself, I see."

"Unlike some people, I wasn't born into money. I've earned everything through hard work and dedication. Fought my way to the top." Dear old Dad beat those values into me, ostensibly to toughen me up for the real world. But I suspect it was really to punish me for Deanna. The abuse continued until I was twelve, when armed robbers broke in and shot him in the back of the head, making off with forty-seven dollars in cash. From that point on, I was the man of the family, while Mom shuffled two or three jobs—it was difficult to tell exactly how many. I clawed my way through high school, college, the corps, and finally the senate with—as Winston Churchill put it—blood, sweat, and tears.

"My family's economic status never kept me from doing my absolute best," Carrick says sharply. "Why do you always bring that up, as if you had something to prove to me? Ever since Bình Son—"

"For pity's sake, Peter, once and for all, can we just leave the past in the past?"

He locks onto my eyes. "You tell *me*."

"I can and I have. Why haven't you? Look, there's no sense in destroying the future over things in the past you can't change."

"How do you sleep at night?"

"Sleep? Well . . ." I cleared my throat. "It's overrated, I'm told." Truth is, I avoid it as much as possible because it's the one place I can't exercise absolute control. Better to divert this conversation. "Now what's this I hear about your daughter's legal issues in New York?"

"A mistake." Folding his arms over his chest, Carrick scowls and stares out the window. "I was planning on flying out tonight to see her."

"I apologize for the inconvenience, but we needed to have this talk first." I fold my hands and rest them on the desk. "As always, if there's anything I or Suzanne can do. Anything at all."

"Magnanimous of you."

I smile, my palms open in genuine fellowship. "I can hire the best legal team on the Eastern seaboard. Just say the word, they're yours. Xandra's as good as exonerated."

"Thanks, but you've done so much already." Carrick gets up and goes to the display case by the window. There he examines the eight-by-ten sepia photo of me in fatigues with Echo Company. He'd taken that back in 1973. "You kept this?"

"I keep a copy in every office." I go over and look at it with him. "Reminds me of where it all started."

"Like a psychopath's souvenirs?"

"Said it before, I'll say it again: you're a hoot."

Carrick doesn't respond in kind to the grins, the brotherly slap on the back. "It was wrong, Rick. We all knew it."

I feel my shoulders rise and fall with a sigh. "Look, Peter. You're a decent man and I admire your conviction. But you've never had to carry the burden, the difficult choices that hover between the boundaries of what ordinary people call moral absolutes—as if such a thing existed in the real world."

"Haven't I? You've forced that burden upon me all these years. My only regret was not having the guts to—"

"Don't be so hard on yourself. You understood the importance of what we did."

"No, I allowed myself to believe a lie." He sets the picture down and turns to face me. "If the polls are correct, you're about to become the president of the United States. You can't keep this up forever. One day, when it comes out—"

"When?"

"If it comes out, it'll destroy your credibility, and the credibility of the country you swore to protect."

"Which is exactly why the terms of the NDA must be upheld." I smile, hoping my anxiety doesn't show. I'm holding to the illusion that we're on the same page.

"Ironic that you call it a nondisclosure *agreement*."

"Oh?"

"It's generally held that an agreement is arrived upon by choice."

"You had a choice."

A bitter laugh. "Right."

My already-perforated patience starts to come apart. Carrick's clearly not going to respond to the kid gloves. It's time to shed them and wield the iron fist. "Let's cut the crap, shall we?"

"About time."

"I remind you that if anything comes out, you'll be every bit as liable."

"There are worse fates."

Unable to restrain myself, I swear and stomp my foot. "Are you going to honor the terms or not!"

This brings out the first glimpse of a smile from Carrick since he stepped into the office. "Honor?" Nodding slightly yet triumphantly, he says, "What makes you think I'd change my mind after all this time?"

"I'm simply assessing the integrity of our arrangement." I say this dusting off my sleeve and trying to effect nonchalance.

"And integrity? Again with the euphemisms."

"Do we have an understanding?"

Carrick brushes past me and walks to the door. He opens it and says, "We've had the most perverse understanding for nearly forty years."

"These are the rare cases in which status quo is for the best."

"If you say so."

A minute after Carrick leaves I pick up my cell phone and dial Collinsworth. I'm shaking when he answers. "Mark, much as I hate to admit it, you were right. Carrick's going to be a problem."

43

XANDRA CARRICK

Patient, and without a trace of skepticism, Kyle awaits my confession. It still amazes me that he's taken me seriously from the start. He shows no sign of doubt as I begin. "It's not just in the darkroom now."

"What do you mean?"

"I saw one about my father in the mirror. Are there no boundaries?"

"And what exactly did you see?"

"I'm sorry, but I can't tell you. I have to talk to him about it first."

"So is that what you're planning to do when you see him?"

"I guess." All these years he has never been willing to talk about the war—what makes me think that's going to change now?

"I think we both need to speak with him."

"What do you mean, 'we'?"

"I dug up some information on Stacy Dellafina's father." From under his seat, he pulls out a laptop that he wakes from standby mode, and shows me a photo. "Did you know that during the Vietnam War, Tony Dellafina was a member of Echo Company, Third Platoon?"

The blood rushes from my face. "Isn't that the same—"

"Yes. Your father was an embedded photographer with them. Which explains why Stacy wanted to meet him."

"No, you don't get it."

Kyle leans in closer. "What?"

"There was another vision. This one was a magazine article about a soldier. You know, Corporal Hank Jennings? When I Googled his name, I found out that he served in that same platoon."

His fingers fly over the touchpad of his laptop, and he pulls up a spreadsheet. When he finishes moving the cursor, he lands on a name: "Corporal Henry 'Hank' Jennings, retired vet, lives in Alpine, California."

"Which is another reason I'm going to San Diego. Alpine's just forty minutes away."

"There's a reason for all this." He shuts his laptop, rubs his eyes, and yawns, which makes me follow in kind.

"For what?"

"The connections. Your visions are all somehow connected. Not sure how, but I feel it in my gut." He reaches behind his back, pulls out a pillow, and slips it behind his head. "However . . ."—another yawn—"research and keeping tabs on you is exhausting. Did *you* sleep last night?"

"Was it you who interrupted my internet connection?"

"No."

"How did you know I was taking this flight?"

"Red flags go up when defendants in a murder trial buy plane tickets. Now get some rest. We've got some time before we arrive."

Glad he said *defendant* and not *suspect*. I've yet to tell him about the vision of the mass graves in Bình Sơn. But for now, I think I'll take his cue and get some rest.

"Kyle?"

He grunts a little.

"I'm going to have to turn around and go back to New York, aren't I?"

"Eventually."

44

"Ladies and gentlemen, we're making our final approach to Lind-bergh Field. The temperature in San Diego is seventy-two degrees and it's partly cloudy with a seventy percent chance of thunder-storms. We're on storm watch for the next forty-eight hours. Drive carefully. Thanks for flying Southwest Airlines."

I'm amazed that I actually slept for the remainder of the flight. It must have been at least four hours. Instead of fast asleep, as I had expected he might be, Agent Kyle Matthews is awake and packing up his gear. I can't help but notice the gun and badge under his jacket as he stands up.

We're deplaning now and I have to squeeze under him to get my backpack from the overhead. I've brought the Graflex with me, just in case. "Excuse me."

"Do you have a rental car lined up?"

"No. Do you have the local police ready to arrest me?"

He grins. But doesn't say anything.

"Not funny."

"I might be able to pull a few more strings, just long enough for us to connect the dots, which might be the key to finding the real killer."

"And to my exoneration?"

"Of course."

It's unjustly sunny and bright outside on the tarmac of Lindbergh field. What about that 70 percent chance of rain? The workers outside are wearing shorts, for crying out loud. No wonder Mom and Dad kept telling me I should move out here.

As we exit the airport and walk toward the taxi stand, warm springlike air brushes against my face. The long pointed blades of palm fronds stretch out before me. All around me, I see something that in New York I can find only if I look straight up: the sky. No apartment buildings or skyscrapers impede my view.

Kyle slips on a pair of dark sunglasses. "Where are you staying?"

"Dad's, probably. He lives in Del Mar. But he doesn't know I'm coming. He'll be in for a surprise."

"Maybe we can go see him first."

"You keep saying 'we,' as if—" I'm interrupted by the sudden approach of a tall man in a black suit. Reacting, Kyle gets between us, his hand not so subtly placed near the gun behind his back.

"Alexandra Carrick?"

"Who are you?"

The black-suited man stands stiffly and produces a badge. "Special Agent Rolston, United States Secret Service, ma'am. We need to speak. In confidence."

"Hold on, just wait a second. Let me see that badge." Kyle takes it from his open hand and inspects it.

Rolston waits patiently until he gets his ID card and badge back. "And you are?"

"Special Agent Kyle Matthews, FBI." This display of IDs and badges is starting to resemble a cock fight. "Ms. Carrick is under my custody. Anything you need to—"

"I'm sorry, but she needs to come with me now. Ms. Carrick, if you would kindly follow me." He's got me by the arm now, and it actually hurts. Something's not right.

"Kyle?"

"Hey! You can't just take her like that."

Agent Rolston doesn't stop, just speaks coolly as we walk toward his car. "Ms. Carrick is a fugitive and under investigation by the Department of Homeland Security, Agent Matthews."

"I'm coming with you."

Now Rolston stops and shoves Kyle in the chest. "No. You're not."

"Where are you taking her?"

"One, that's classified. Two, I doubt someone like you has the clearance to know."

"Who's your supervisor?"

Rolston shakes his head, pulls his shades down just enough to look down over the rims. "If you have any questions, you can call to verify with the ECTF field office in Los Angeles."

"Count on it." Kyle is already dialing his cell phone and trailing us toward the center island where Rolston's black Lincoln is idling. "Don't say a word, Xandra. I'll get to the bottom of this!"

45

GRACE TH'AM AI LE

Saigon: April 29, 1975

Men and women, children and elders, all pushed in every direction, trying to free themselves from the crowd as more gunshots rang out over our heads.

"Get down! Get down!" shouted a soldier in Vietnamese. I could not see who he was, if he was one of ours or from the NLF. My only concern was finding Peter. But he was rushed into the embassy with the crowd, and the door had slammed shut.

Alone, despite the raging crowd, I dropped to the ground next to my suitcase and clung to it as though my life depended on it. For all I knew, it did. More shots rang out, this time a combination of automatic gunfire and heavy artillery. Would I die out here, without the chance to see Peter one last time?

The crowd barely thinned, and as quickly as the gunfire started, it ceased. How much time actually passed, I do not know. But it seemed an eternity. What caused me to lift my head was a shout from a woman behind me.

"They're taking off! My daughter is going to live, thank heaven!" Sure enough, the beating of the helicopter's rotors cut through the air and pummeled my eardrums.

From where I stood, the helicopter appeared full, and this time no one dared cling to the landing skids. I kept picturing Peter on board, banging against the window, trying to find me in a crowd of frantic people. How anxious he must be, wondering if and how he would ever find me again.

And I, too, wondered.

For a long while, I refused to move from my place at the gate. What if someone were to come out and give me instructions on how to find Peter? So I propped up my suitcase and sat on it, holding on to the bars like a prisoner.

An old Vietnamese man stood over me and held a letter through the bars. "I Tran Nguyen. I have paper! I have paper!"

"Sir, you need to wait right there," said the marine behind the gate.

"See this?" He pulled out a small metallic object that resembled a pair of wings. It was a pin or brooch of some sort. "Major Tom Bradley give me. I work for him, bartender in U.S. Air Force officers' club seven year!"

The marine took the letter and the pin and examined them both.

Mr. Nguyen smelled as if he hadn't bathed in weeks. I tried to move away from him, but he kept pressing in harder. Frantic and losing control, he shouted. "Major Bradley say, 'Just show letter, they let you go!' Please!"

"Sir, you need to stay calm and back away from the gate."

"No, please! I have paper!"

The marine tossed the letter and the pin back through the gate, sending the old bartender scrambling to the ground to retrieve them. The marine pointed his gun at the old man, just in case.

That was enough for me. I grabbed my suitcase and moved out of the way. But it wasn't necessary. Mr. Nguyen sat at my feet, weeping and holding his pin in one hand, the letter in his other.

I could not help but place a hand on his shoulder.

Without lifting his hands from his eyes, he showed me the letter and spoke in Vietnamese. "Seven years. I worked for Americans seven years!"

The letter read:

6 June 1967

Mr. Nguyen, the bearer of this letter, faithfully
served the cause of freedom in the Republic of
Vietnam.

Major Thomas Bradley
United States Air Force

"I am sure they will let you in," I said, more hopeful than certain. "I, too, am waiting." At this point, Mr. Nguyen looked up and noticed a space between the bars. As he was a very gaunt man, he stood up and slid through it.

But the marine caught him in the attempt and pushed him back out before he could get through. "For the last time, you cannot enter without proper authorization!"

"You don't understand!" Nguyen said. Of course he didn't—Mr. Nguyen was panicking and speaking in Vietnamese. "The Communists are going to torture us, kill us, cut out our brains, and run them under soap and water!"

His eyes were now like those of a madman. I feared for him and held his frail hand. "Mr. Nguyen, please. You'll get hurt."

"Vietcong kill us!" Once again, he pushed through the bars so fast, the marine could not stop him in time. A second marine hit him with the end of his rifle and shoved him out through the bars. He then threw the letter and pin out over the heads of the crowd.

I knelt down beside the old man, who wept pathetically. "My children and grandchildren. They have all left me here to die. Just like the Americans."

Left to die.

Nguyen was not the only one here in Saigon who shared this sentiment. Many who counted on the protection and provision of the United States felt the same. I, too, wondered if this would be my fate.

"Grace!"

I turned and there at the embassy building's door was Peter, running to the gate. As we called out to each other, another helicopter came to land on the roof where many more people climbed that ladder to the very top where it rested.

"Grace, are you all right?"

"Yes, what happened?"

The marine opened the gate slightly, pointed his rifle out as he allowed me to pass, then shut it again. "I just spent the last hour on the phone," Peter said, as we walked into the building. "They wouldn't take my word that we're engaged. We have no legal documents proving it. For all they know, you're a stranger I decided to help."

"But they're letting me in?"

"I've gotten a verbal confirmation that with the right signature, you can evacuate with me as my common-law wife." The paper was a letter stating our relationship and our intent to marry as soon as we found safe passage out of Saigon.

"Whose signature?"

"His."

A soldier in military uniform carrying a pistol at his side stepped forward and shook our hands, then spoke with Peter. Right away I recognized him as the officer in charge back in Bình Sơn two years ago, when I got shot in the crossfire of American and Vietcong fighting. This officer was responsible for seeing to it that I was rushed back to Saigon for medical treatment. I smiled, shook his hand, and thanked him briefly, though I didn't remember his name. It didn't matter, though. The soldiers hurried us to the elevators and finally to the rooftop, where we ascended the ladder to the helicopter.

As it lifted off, I looked down upon the spectacular view of the city that for the past three years had become my surrogate home. Fires, rising smoke, and flashes of weapons fire lit up various sections of Saigon. I wept for my fallen city, my fallen country, because I felt that I, too, was abandoning my people.

46

KYLE MATTHEWS

It's all happening so fast. Everything about Rolston—the badge, the fact that he knew where to find Xandra—seems legitimate. But the manner in which he took her doesn't.

A simple call will clarify this, but I can't just let them out of my sight. I set the Bluetooth into my ear.

Push to activate.

Two short beeps.

It's not connecting.

A dark car-service limo pulls up. I make eye contact with the driver while pairing my Bluetooth.

The driver, whose name—according to the prominently displayed license and certificate—is Srinivasu Venkatrarajan . . . something, speaks with an Indian accent. "Do you need a ride, sir?"

"Yes, but *I'm* driving." My cell phone won't connect. And just ahead, Xandra is stepping inside Rolston's car. She's got that look of fear that I'm going to let her down again.

The smooth tone in my ear tells me that the Bluetooth has finally connected with my BlackBerry.

"Sir, I cannot let you drive this vehicle. It's company policy, you know."

"You can, and you will." Judging by his trembling jaw, his eyes that are about to pop out of his head, and both of his hands raised up where I can see them, my badge alone would probably have done the trick. But I've pulled out my gun too. "Please, step out of the car."

"Yes sir. You don't need to point that weapon at me, sir. I am quite familiar with these procedures, you know."

"Sir, you are not being carjacked." Rolston's car is gone now. I jump in Srinivasu's seat and shut the door. As I pull away, he's scratching his head. If there were more time, I would feel bad about this. "You'll get your car back."

But in what condition, I can't predict.

"United States Secret Service, how may I direct your call?"

"This is Special Agent Kyle Matthews, FBI." I give her my ID number and wait in silence. "I'm calling to verify the identity of an Electronic Crime Task Force agent by the name of Rolston." He's a couple of cars ahead of me and unaware that I'm tailing him.

"I'll connect you with personnel, Agent Matthews."

We're stopped at a traffic light on Harbor Drive. A large city bus crosses the intersection and blocks my view. "Come on, come on . . ."

The receptionist doesn't reply immediately. "Sir, I'm working on it as—"

"Not you." The intersection is gridlocked, and Rolston's already out of visual. Sweat dampens my brow. More cars jam the path and join the chorus of impatient honking.

"Agent Matthews, regarding the name and identification number of this Special Agent Rolston . . ."

"Yes?"

"I've looked up the roster of the Los Angeles ECTF."

"And?" At last, the bus is clearing the intersection. The light's even turned green. Good.

But the next words I hear confirm my worst fears.

47

"I'm sorry, Agent Matthews, the information you requested is not available."

"He either works with the service or not, right?"

"That's all I can tell you."

"All right, can you at least tell me what the computer screen says?" The bus is clear. Just as I hit the accelerator, a courier on a bike zips past me. We almost collide, but instead of giving me the finger, he smiles, waves, and rides off.

"It's just an access message."

"Read the text aloud, please."

"It says: this file is restricted."

"Look, I just need to know if there is an Agent Rolston working for the Secret Service or Homeland."

"He's not on payroll, I can tell you that. Rolston's listed as a consultant. You can come into the office to discuss this with the assistant director if you like."

"Thanks, you've been helpful."

"Agent Matthews, who did you say your supervisor was?"

"Assistant Director Sharon Maguire, Quantico Field Office." With a sudden kick, the proverbial pedal hits the metal and I'm off. Whether or not this Rolston character knows I've regained a visual and am tailing him doesn't seem to make a difference. He's flooring it and getting onto the I-5 like his pants are on fire.

The sky's turned to molasses in a matter of minutes. First a trickle, then raindrops start to rap against the windshield, making an incessant sound like microwave popcorn. It's coming down so hard it's blurring my view.

As I follow Rolston, my cell buzzes. It's Maguire. I do not want to hear what she has to say now. So I hit the ignore button. This distraction continues a few more times until it's clear that she's not about to give up.

"Matthews."

"Where are you, Kyle?"

"Best if you don't ask."

"Best if you don't feed me any crap. Xandra Carrick's all over the media as a high-profile fugitive. She with you?"

"No. Look, Maguire, can we talk later, I'm—"

"You're off this case. You hear? Get back here right now."

A red Mustang convertible cuts across three lanes to get to the exit ramp. "Holy—!" In this weather, that ditzy blonde didn't even signal! Her tires skid, and for an instant, the thought of a multicar pileup in the rain comes to mind.

"I'm serious, Matthews. You need to report back to the office right now."

"No can do. The pieces are finally coming together. I'm on to something here, and I've got to see it through."

"Report back immediately, or the next time you do, you'll be turning in your badge, your gun—"

"Come on, Maguire. Threats? How effective have those ever been with me?"

The Secret Service impostor pulls his car in front of a couple of trucks and falls out of sight. "Dammit!"

"You don't seem to understand. I'm trying to save your— look, you know how this goes. The list is dragging on the floor. Obstruction, aiding and abetting, conspiracy. I could go on."

"I'm sure you could. Gotta go now. I'll call you—"

"You're coming in now, or I'll have no choice but to send out a team from the San Diego field office to bring you in! And according to our techs, you're driving east on the I-8 toward—"

Click.

Ending one call, I press my Bluetooth once more and announce, "Glen."

"Dialing . . ."

"Yo Kyle! What up? Man, you're up to your ears in it, homey!"

"Are you as good as you claim, flying under the radar?"

"Better."

"Can I trust you?"

"Duh."

"Trust you not to get yourself caught? Because if you do, we're both dead."

"I feel you, son. What do you need?"

I lay out what I need and keep him on the line for as long I can before either of us gets caught. Finally, he provides me with information on Xandra's location based on GPS tracking of her cell phone. I've got the general area within two thousand meters. Good thing this limo has a built-in GPS.

Glen, an unrepentant geek, suddenly speaks with uncharacteristic severity. "It's worse than you think, Kyle. I hear the orders to shut you down are coming from several levels above Maguire."

"That doesn't make sense. As far as she knows, this is just an interstate or a simple serial case."

"Just telling you what I heard, bro."

I'm wondering if there's a connection to that Rolston fake. "I need you to check one more thing for me. There's a man impersonating a Secret Serv—"

"Someone's coming, gotta go."

"Wait!"

"Watch your back, bro."

48

XANDRA CARRICK

He's already confiscated my cell phone and put my backpack with my Graflex in the front seat. I'm not sure what's going on, but it's not good. "What does Homeland Security want with me?"

"You're a bail jumper."

"Who's traveling with an FBI agent to investigate—"

"Let's not make this any harder than it needs to be." Beneath the harsh words, I sense something. Not sure, but it almost sounds like regret. There's that tingling in my fingers.

"At least tell me what to expect. You will let me call Agent Matthews, won't you?"

"I understand you're anxious. But not to worry, it shan't take long."

"Is it much farther?" I stifle a yawn. *Must stay awake.*

"The office is about twenty minutes from here." From this point on, he keeps silent. It's raining heavily now. He doesn't seem to take any driving precautions, even in this weather. Anyway, the main concern now is not getting shipped back to New York and spending the months leading up to my trial in jail. No matter what, I've got to speak with Dad, and that vet Hank Jennings. That's likely where I'll find my answers and get my name cleared from this nightmare.

Another yawn and a stretch. "Sleep, perchance to dream."

"*Hamlet*, act three."

"So you're a fan of Shakespeare."

"When I was younger, I fancied myself something of an expert." The English accent I suspected was lurking beneath has now risen to the surface. He pauses as though at the edge of a precipice. And the coldness returns. "That, however, was another life."

"Dare I ask?"

He doesn't answer, just keeps driving. After five minutes, the silence becomes less awkward and takes on a narcotic quality. I'm drifting . . .

I'm awakened by the *thunk* of the car door. Like rapid fire from a machine gun, drops of rain smack repeatedly against the roof and hood. I must have been really tired to have slept so deeply. The Homeland agent stands outside in the pouring rain with one hand on my door handle. But where is this?

Instead of a parking lot and office buildings, trees and brush surround us.

"Step out of the vehicle, Ms. Carrick."

I climb out, and he takes a step away from me. With one hand, he's holding one of my backpack's shoulder straps. It hangs and sways like a dead man in a noose.

"Where are we, Agent—?"

He pulls a gun from his jacket and points it right at my head. With a finger over his lips he hushes me. My hair is drenched now. Water rolls down my face like blood. His sunglasses are off, and now I can see the scar. He's the guy on the plane who bumped into Kyle. With a severe tone he says, "Don't struggle and we'll make it quick and painless."

49

GRACE TH'AM AI LE

Saigon: April 29, 1975

Crowded with dozens of people in the helicopter, I kept still in Peter's arms. When we'd flown off the coast, away from the land of my ancestors and over the water, I could not help but cry. Something told me that once I left, I would never return.

Peter held me tighter and kissed the top of my head. "It's going to be all right, Grace."

"Is it?"

"We're safe now. Keep all the good memories and leave the bad behind."

"I'm afraid."

"Of what?"

"I've never left Vietnam before. And in America, I won't know anyone."

"I'll take care of you, I promise. We'll start a family, make lots of new friends. You won't be alone."

But despite his assurances, that is just what I felt. As the cords that tied me to my people and heritage were severed, the void within my heart grew deeper. No amount of anticipation could compensate for the losses I'd suffered since the war began. I would have to live with that always.

Someone at the front of the helicopter called out, "Hold on, everyone!" Gasps and anxious murmurs rose up. "It's going to be a bit rough."

"Peter, what does he mean?"

He pointed out the window and braced me. "See that ship? It's a U.S. Navy ship called the USS *Blue Ridge*. That's where we're going to land."

"But there's no room!" Down on the ship's deck, scores of evacuees clutching suitcases poured out from a landed helicopter, whose blades were still spinning. Most of them were being inspected for weapons. After the last person left that helicopter, it flew up and passed us.

It was our turn to land on that tiny space on the deck. Off in the distance, a smaller helicopter hovered dangerously close to the water's surface. I pointed it out to Peter. "It's going to crash!"

Before Peter could respond, the pilot of that small craft jumped out and the helicopter hit the water. Its turning blades stopped suddenly and broke off, pieces flying in the air. "What are they doing?"

"I don't—wait! Hold on!" Our helicopter pitched sideways, sending people and luggage sliding. Then the front section dipped. Petrified, I could not even scream like the other women. I just shut my eyes and prayed.

A moment passed, and we landed.

A marine opened the door and lowered a set of steps for the passengers to climb down. "All right, people. We've got many more runs. Everyone out, let's go!"

It was hectic on the deck, and yet there seemed to be order in the chaos. An American man examined the paperwork Peter handed him, looked at us both, and nodded. "Welcome aboard. Please make your way starboard."

We found a spot to set down our luggage and wait. Peter took out his camera. He pointed to the very rear of the ship's deck and started walking. "Stay here. I need to get this."

Right away I saw what he was going to document. Seven or eight men put their hands on the sides of another one of those smaller helicopters. To my amazement, they lifted it from the bottom and tilted it over the edge of the ship. One man fell into a safety net on the edge of the deck as the helicopter fell into the water.

I understood now. After they had deposited their refugees on the *Blue Ridge*, they had to discard those smaller helicopters to make room for more people.

This happened a few more times. About sixty meters from the ship, a lone pilot would fly his helicopter and ditch it in the water. He either leapt out before it hit the water, or went down with it and climbed out. He would then swim to a rubber lifeboat and return to the ship.

It felt like the end of the world. I had never seen or imagined anything like this. And I suspected the same could be said for most people there. True to his vocation, Peter captured this historic event. I felt proud of him, but I wished he was with me at that moment. I couldn't bear all this by myself.

"Ma'am, are you all right?" A marine stood behind me with a green duffle bag.

"Is this what it has come to? How could this happen?" I said, too stunned to realize I was trembling.

He took out a thick wool blanket and put it around my shoulders. "I'm so sorry."

"Why are you sorry?"

"This is the first time we've ever walked away, left an ally to themselves. You know, I keep asking myself if there was more I could have done. Maybe if we had some more boats, helicopters, anything, maybe we could have . . ." He took a deep breath and turned away. "I feel like I've let them down. Like I'm just turning my back on them."

"You are a good man. Try to remember all you have helped. God knows your heart."

"Yes, ma'am."

USS Blue Ridge
South China Sea: April 30, 1975

Peter brought me to one of the meeting rooms on the ship where a TV crew and all the news correspondents gathered to discuss all that had happened in the past day.

An official-looking person stood up before the microphone and read from a paper: "At ten twenty-four this morning, President Duong Van Minh announced a surrender. He called for all South Vietnamese forces to cease hostilities and remain where they are. Minh then invited the Provisional Revolutionary Government to engage in a ceremony of orderly transfer of power so as to avoid any unnecessary bloodshed in the population.

"No such ceremony took place. At eleven thirty, PAVN tanks broke through and destroyed the gates of the Independence Palace, where they raised the flag of the National Liberation Front. Minh was arrested. At fifteen thirty hours, he broadcast over the radio and declared the Saigon government completely dissolved at all levels."

Clinging to whatever hope I could, I reached for Peter's hand. Saigon had fallen.

50

XANDRA CARRICK

Too many thoughts flying through my mind. All that rises out of the silent jumble is, *I'm going to die.*

"Hands on your head," Rolston orders. "Good. Now, on your knees."

"Please . . . don't do this."

"Shut up! I told you, quick and painless." He tosses my backpack on the grass. "Now, tell me the truth. How did you know about the Dellafina girl?"

"I don't know, lucky guess. What's that got to do with—?"

Rolston presses the point of his gun into the back of my head and with one hand pushes me to my knees. My hands squish into the mud, which splashes into my face. His grip is fierce. He could easily break my arm. "What do you know about the circumstances of her death?"

"Nothing!"

"Tell me what you *do* know."

"What are you talking about?"

"You bloody well know!" His breath is quivering now as he stands right behind me.

"I swear, I have no idea."

He clicks the safety off the gun. Presses into my head even harder. "Then you're truly of no use to me."

"Why are you doing this?"

"Should have known talking was a waste of time."

I can almost feel the tension of his trigger finger pulling back. Then the numbing pins and needles run down my scalp, down my spine, and into my hands and feet.

Faces.

Pale, vacuous eyes.

Death.

So many different bodies buried, submerged in the East River, incinerated . . . dismembered.

And then comfort, hope, acceptance. It's the face of a woman with auburn hair . . . Nicole . . . and a young boy, very sick, almost dead . . . Bobby.

In the span of a couple of seconds, I'm seeing what feels like years of memories. The gun is shaking as it presses into my scalp. "You don't have to do this."

"Lassie, you have no idea what I have to do, or why."

"Think of Nicole . . . of Bobby!"

"What?"

In a split second, fight or flight kicks in. I'm going to die anyway, might as well try what I can. With a feral shriek and all the might I can conjure, I launch an elbow up into his crotch.

Instead of seeing my brains splattering before my eyes, I blink and nothing happens. Only a heavy thud in the grass behind me and stifled groans.

I leap to my feet, whirl around, and find my assailant doubled over, still clutching his gun. Emboldened, I step over to kick it out of his hand. But he catches my ankle with his left hand. With one abrupt twist, he hurls me into a cold puddle.

He gets up and puts me in a choke hold, then drags me to the edge of an algae-covered pond. Splashing wildly, I struggle to break free. But it's no use. Even though he's groaning in pain from my well-placed strike, he's still too strong.

Then with alarming force, he thrusts my head face down into the water. His hands clutch my throat. His arms quiver with tension. I'm unable to lift my face out of the murky pond. Bubbles float up out of my mouth, tickling at my face. The tingling returns. I've been here before. At least, I've sensed this place before.

I can't breathe.

Can't breathe!

Can't shut my eyes either. They're about to pop out. Murky water stings so bad. My vision begins to darken. Is this what it was like for Stacy Dellafina?

51

So this is how it all ends.

Everything's vanished into the gloom of the inner mind. Mom's face appears, tears standing in her eyes. She's reaching out, not to embrace but to push me away.

It's too soon, Xandi.

Reach down, take hold!

Then, just as I'm about to pass out, a miracle happens. Heeding Mom's voice, I grope about the pond's miry bottom and touch something. Smooth. Hard. Heavy. I grasp it with my fingers, even as the final bubbles of life float by my eyes.

With all my strength I swing the rock out of the water and strike my attacker's head. He lets out a long grunt and staggers. His hands slide off my neck.

Water rushes away as he comes crashing down over me. I put my knee just between his legs. With all the force I can conjure, I ram my kneecap straight into his already-injured testicles. I can feel an awful crushing sensation. He lets out an agonized scream and wretches while hunched over on all fours, like a cat gagging on a hairball. It is now as I sit up, gasping for breath, that I realize the water is not more than two or three feet deep.

I slide out from under him, flail about, kicking at whatever I can. My heel makes contact with his face. He splashes onto his side, still holding his crotch.

I crawl out of the pond and grab my backpack.

Now I'm on my feet, sprinting away.

Can't look back.

My legs are so shaky, I stumble. Nearly fall on my face. A gunshot rips through the falling rain. I let out a shriek. But keep running.

And running.

The wet backpack straps dig into my shoulder. Right now, I'd love to just toss the Graflex into the middle of the freeway and be done with it forever.

Unable to overcome the burning in my legs and lungs, I press my back against the trunk of a tree and glance back over my shoulder, trying to catch my breath as quietly as possible.

No. He's not there.

Is that good or bad? At least if I could see him, I'd know to avoid him. But not knowing where he is fills every step, every breath with anxiety.

I'm frozen, trembling. If I move, step on a branch, splash into a puddle, I might give my position away. If I remain, he'll find me. Dammit, what should I do?

With great caution, I take a step back.

Softly.

Quietly.

All at once, every nerve ending in my body ignites. A pair of hands grab me like a boa constrictor, one of them covering my mouth.

I can't even scream.

52

Elbows swinging, feet kicking, I struggle to free myself. But the grip over my mouth suddenly gets tighter.

"Quiet!" he hisses. "Xandra, it's me."

At the sound of his voice, my arms relax. He senses this and loosens his grip, allowing me to turn around.

"Kyle?" It's him. It's him!

"Follow me, but stay close."

"He was going to kill me!"

"I'm not going to let that happen. Can you climb?"

I nod, wipe the water and mud from my face.

"Good, my car's up that embankment. On three, we make a run for it."

"Okay."

"One . . . Two . . ."

Before he reaches three, another series of shots slashes through the leaves. One of them hits the tree next to me.

"Three!" Kyle puts himself between me and Rolston's gunfire. "Go! Straight up, you'll see it parked. Careful, don't slip!" He puts the keys in my hands, pushes me forward, turns back, and returns fire.

A surge of adrenaline-induced energy propels me up the embankment at a surprising rate. Below, a fierce volley rings out.

Kyle is making his way up the hill now, both hands on his gun.

The car is parked at a frantic angle, its tail jutting slightly off the shoulder of the freeway. Its nose hangs over the edge of the embankment. At the edge of the road, a black Porsche hisses by and splashes a sheet of water at me. Misses me by inches.

Kyle calls up as he takes another shot. "Get in and go!"

I fumble with the keys now, trying to find the right one. My hands are shaking and too slick to get it into the door lock. But finally I do and leap into the driver's seat where I start the engine. Rolston climbs up to the roadside, swings around with his gun, then points it down and fires two shots in Kyle's direction. Through the rearview, I see Rolston turn around. He's spotted me and is approaching the car with his weapon trained.

A truck roars by at full speed and blasts its horns at my tail, which it nearly clips. Its wind tosses the car like a dinghy in a maelstrom.

I keep waiting for Kyle and an opportunity to speed out onto the road, but there's just too much oncoming traffic. Visibility is poor. All I can see are headlights, just seconds before they reach me. But I have nowhere else to go. The shoulder ends with a high dive over a ravine, just twenty feet ahead.

Alternately glancing over his shoulder and stepping purposefully toward me, Rolston lifts the muzzle of his gun and points it straight at the passenger window.

My gaze shoots back and forth between the rearview and the driver's-side mirrors. I race the engine. Don't dare shift into Drive. Not yet. Death by gunshot or vehicular suicide, what'll it be?

Then comes a bone-chilling tap on the passenger window. I scream and jump back against my door. My eyes zoom in on his trigger finger. He's just about to pull it.

Instead of glass shattering and a bullet lodging into my skull, a thud and a muffled grunt divert my eyes. Kyle has knocked Rolston to the ground.

From the edge of the passenger window, fist and limbs fly. The sounds of thumps and cracks join the cacophonous strains of horns and wheels zooming by.

I'm too afraid to unlock the door and let the wrong man in. But this doesn't stop me from leaning over to look. "Kyle, hurry!"

The side of Rolston's face slams up against the glass, which squeaks as he grits his teeth, snarls, then kicks backward. Kyle falls back, nearly toppling down the embankment. Rolston lunges at him, but Kyle swipes his feet out from under him. The fight draws them both toward the back of the car, where I can only see their legs through the passenger mirror.

Now Kyle is on his feet. A couple more swings and Rolston is down. Kyle rushes to the passenger door, which I unlock.

"Let's go!"

Just as I put the car in Drive, the loud squawk of a California Highway Police car makes me hesitate.

"Ignore it," Kyle says. "Just go!"

"Straight into that?" A double length UPS truck rolls past us. About three car lengths behind us, the CHP pulls over onto the shoulder, its blue and red beacons flashing.

"Remain inside your vehicle," the officer says over the bull-horn. Meanwhile his beige-clad partner steps out and notices Rolston lying at his feet.

"Now!" Before Kyle even says it, I seize the opportunity and blaze onto the freeway. The angry driver in the Benz I just cut off flashes angry high beams. I can't help but steal a glance back at Rolston.

In that split second, I almost wish I hadn't.

Rolston gets up, points his gun, and shoots the CHP officer point blank in the chest. And with cold precision, he turns and fires at the other officer who is standing on the opposite side of the squad car. "I can't believe it, he shot them!"

Kyle groans. "Get . . . to . . . the center lane!"

Within seconds I'm up to eighty miles per hour, weaving through cars that are now slowing down and moving to the right, as Rolston pursues us with the CHP's car, siren and lights blaring and flashing. "Rolston can't be working for the government."

Kyle grunts. "There is no Agent Rolston. Drive faster . . . will you?"

"Would you like to take the wheel? Stop barking at me."

"Trying to save your life."

"And I'm just playing around?" A bullet cracking the rear window interrupts our highly mature discussion. I let out a gasp. Rolston is right behind us now. "Can't you shoot at him or something?"

"Dropped my gun . . ." Kyle grimaces. His words trail off into a strained groan. He's holding his side with a hand soaked in blood.

"You're hurt. We've got to get you to a hospital."

"No! No hospitals or police stations . . . first place they'll check. Just . . . try to shake him." He forces a weak smile. "And find a place to hide."

"Where do you suppose we can do that?" Weaving through traffic, I discover there are now three police cars closing in on Rolston—or whatever his name is. "I think we might just have found some help."

The opportunity reveals itself now. I've got a clear path across two lanes to an exit into a town called Miranda Springs. The police cars have surrounded him. A vindictive grin tugs at the corner of my lip.

Off the exit ramp and driving down a quiet road now. Beyond the 7-Eleven and Chevron station, there's nothing but veined asphalt and verdant junipers. "Think we'll ever find out who that thug was?"

All I hear are the wheels rolling on the gravelly pavement.

"Kyle?"

He's leaning over against the door, his face pale and shining. His chest is rising and falling in short rapid breaths. His eyes are rolled back and white, eyelashes flitting like a moth's wings.

"Oh no. You can't leave me alone in this!" I think he's dying.

53

IAN MORTIMER

He was right. My heart's no longer in it. Hasn't been for ages. Yet somehow, he's managed to yank me back like a bleeding dog on a choke collar. I've gotten dreadfully sloppy. Xandra Carrick appears to have enlisted an ally from the Bureau, something that has slipped past my research. Bloody hell, she's managed to complicate things by not dying.

Carrick and Matthews are getting away. And if they do, TR will tighten that choke collar on my neck. If I'm lucky, that's all he'll do.

Flippin' CHPs are tailing me with backup now. I've no time for this!

"Come on, you buggering idiot!" I just cut off a truck driver, who flips me the bird. Three police cars are tailing me now. If I end up getting interrogated by any law-enforcement agency, TR might not kill me, but he will see to it that Bobby suffers. What kind of fouled-up country is this anyway, where someone like TR can literally get away with murder?

Focus.

For Bobby's sake.

It's no good. I have to get him to clear this obstacle. But that would mean admitting that Xandra's still alive. This mess grows increasingly difficult to clean.

Xandra and Agent Matthews are gone. But I've got the license-plate number memorized, and limo services usually install tracking devices in their cars.

When it seems inevitable, I pull over and wait for the police to approach. Two officers approach with guns aimed while another instructs me over the megaphone to come out with my hands visible.

I comply and set my hands on the roof of the squad car, while the officer with the name Dowler etched into his nameplate frisks me, takes my gun. "Special Agent Rolston, Department of Homeland Security. Badge is in my left breast pocket. The shooter's getting away."

"I've got two officers down back there, so you'll excuse me if I check your credentials." He takes out my badge and scrutinizes it. Hands it to his partner, who takes it back to their squad car. "What's the make and model of the perp's car?"

"Black sedan, I didn't get a good look. He's been shot. His accomplice is an Asian American woman, about twenty-seven, dark brown hair. She's driving."

"I'll put out an APB—"

"This is a Homeland Security case. Can't have anyone else interfere. Now release me so I can—"

"You're the only one seen leaving the scene of the crime, in the squad car of the downed officers."

"Mine was half a mile back! I pursued the suspect on foot until your men confronted him. Then he shot them!"

"I'm sorry, but I'm going to have to verify your identity. Should be quick."

"Look, I know you're just doing your job. But I've got to do mine. The guy who shot your men was a domestic terrorist. If we lose him, it's on you."

"I still gotta do this, Agent . . ."

"Rolston. Special Agent Rolston."

"Yeah, whatever." He cranes his neck back to his partner in their car. "Anderson, you get anything?"

Even though the rain is drizzling down on me out here on the shoulder of the freeway, I'm feeling hot, my collar's shrinking. Dowler's partner comes out of the car and hands my badge back to him. "Checks out. They said the information on him was non-transferable. What's that supposed to mean?"

I try to remain collected. "It means you boys are in over your heads."

"Actually, Agent Rolston"—Dowler pulls my hands down off the car, one at a time and cuffs them—"it means you're coming with us."

54

GRACE TH'AM AI LE

Brooklyn, New York: May 7, 1975

I was reminded of the opening of a book by Charles Dickens, one of my favorite English authors among the many that Peter has introduced me to since we met:

> It was the best of times, it was the worst of times; it was the age of wisdom, it was the age of foolishness; it was the epoch of belief, it was the epoch of incredulity; it was the season of Light, it was the season of Darkness.

This should have been the most joyous occasion of my life. Today, before God and before man, Peter and I were joined in marriage. Nothing could have diminished the joy of this occasion except for the news that came in a whisper from Juliana, Peter's sister, who served as my bridesmaid.

Because communication had been cut off since the Communists took over Saigon, I had no means of speaking or corresponding with any of my classmates or teachers who might still be there.

Footage of a big rally celebrating the new administration has been playing on all the television sets in department-store windows. We learned that Saigon would be renamed Ho Chi Minh City. But to me and all the other refugees here in the States, it will always be Saigon.

I determined not to let the news ruin our special day. In fact, I didn't even mention this to Peter until the wedding was over. We spent our wedding night at the Mayflower Hotel in Manhattan, but because of our limited budget, we will not be having a honeymoon.

I do not mind it as much as a girl who grew up in America might. My head was never filled with such dreams. It is enough for me to move into our apartment overlooking the trees and ponds of Prospect Park and begin our new life together.

Brooklyn, New York: August 15, 1977

I have been so busy with English classes, working as a cashier at Woolworths, doing community work at church, and taking care of the home that the past two years seem to have flown by and vanished before I knew it.

After hearing the harrowing stories of some of the Vietnamese and Cambodian refugees I have met through the Asian American Service Center, I realize how blessed I was to have arrived in America with relative ease.

However, Mother always said, "You cannot enjoy a durian without suffering its stink." In time, you learn to embrace it along with the sweetness of the fruit.

As for the sweetness, Peter and I had experienced the joy of expecting a child. We chose the name Philip—after Peter's father—and became deeply involved in matters such as purchasing a crib, a carriage, and many other things that a baby needs. Peter painted Philip's room light blue and even bought a baseball glove for him.

But around my third month, I began to experience bleeding and strange cramps. When I finally saw the doctor, it was too late. I had miscarried.

For two weeks, I shut myself in my room and cried. Peter did all he could to comfort me. In order to tend to me, he canceled his trip to England to shoot the launching of the HMS *Invincible* by Queen Elizabeth.

It is only now that I can even talk about it without breaking down. Our little Philip, whom we loved so dearly, represented my hopes and dreams in America.

Peter does not bare his sorrow for others to see. Not even me. I learned this one day when I confronted him about his lack of emotion. "You have not even shed a tear!"

Of course he was devastated, he said. But that just wasn't his way. I did not accept that. He took that as my calling him a liar. In my anger, I stormed out of the apartment and spent the rest of the afternoon in Prospect Park, watching mothers pushing baby carriages or holding their children's hands as they learned to walk.

When I came home, I did not see my husband. I called out to him, but he did not answer. The radio in the kitchen was on. "Peter, are you home?" Ordinarily he would answer. But his briefcase and jacket were still sitting on the living-room chair. He was not in our bedroom, nor the bathroom. Finally, I heard something coming from the baby's room. The door was half open. Without disturbing it, I looked inside.

There knelt Peter, his head draped over the crib. He was holding the baseball glove in one hand and covering his eyes with the other. I had never before seen him like this, weeping and broken as a man could be.

My own heart melted, and without another thought I went to him and knelt beside him. He looked at me with reddened eyes, tear-drenched cheeks, and a face crumpled with grief. He let out a wet sob. "My boy. My poor little boy!"

And now it was my time to hold him as he cried. How greatly I had misjudged him. If only I had believed him, respected his way of grieving. I might not have added to his pain. As he buried his face into my breast, I rocked him back and forth, caressed the back of his head. "Philip is with the Lord, Peter. He's in the best hands now."

That night, for the first time in months, I made love to my husband and he slept more soundly than ever before in our marriage.

Brooklyn, New York: May 16, 1980

I did not wish to say anything until it was confirmed. Peter has won the Pulitzer Prize for his never-before-seen photos, *Survivors of the Massacre at Huế*. Strangely enough, Peter was not happy when he found out. A friend of his had convinced him to submit his work and sponsored his entry. Peter never thought anything would come of it.

The subject matter opened up old wounds and caused quite a stir in sociopolitical circles. Most people wished to leave the past behind and not resurrect the atrocities of the Vietcong, or the failure of the United States.

But no one could dispute its importance. Nor could they deny the quality of the photos that captured so much more than the realism; they caught the emotion, the moment. Peter is widely acclaimed now and has become quite a celebrity. He deserves nothing less than this success, though he accepts it with reluctance.

Had this been the only event of the year, I would have been content. But one other competes with it. Something of greater significance than President Carter's grain embargo against the Soviet Union, Ayatollah Khomeini and the American hostages, or our boycott of the Summer Olympic Games in Moscow.

I am once again pregnant and am expecting in February next year. We have tried many times since Philip to get pregnant, but to no avail. Though Peter is not a believer, I am. So in secret, one night after we made love, I went into the living room, took out my Bible, and prayed the prayer of Hannah:

> O LORD of hosts, if You will indeed look on the affliction of Your maidservant and remember me, and not forget Your maidservant, but will give Your maidservant a male child, then I will give him to the LORD all the days of his life.

Peter thinks I should not write about this in my journal. "You'll jinx it," he always says. For a man who does not practice any particular religion, he certainly lives by faith. But I feel I must record this, even if I must do so in secret, lest one day I forget.

One night at a Wednesday-evening prayer meeting, the minister laid hands on my head and prophesied over me. "You will be gifted a child. Through her, many will be blessed and helped."

Her? I kept that in my heart and never mentioned it to Peter. He did not quite understand why I reacted with such excitement when the doctor confirmed that we would indeed be having a daughter.

Peter is nervous about this pregnancy and cannot fathom why I do not share his anxiety or partake in his odd precautions regarding bad luck and jinxes. I do not believe in luck. All things happen for a reason. Every event, no matter how random it appears, is connected by the hand of the Almighty. And I will have this child the good Lord gave me.

Brooklyn, New York: March 20, 1981

On February 23, 1981, at 6:35 a.m., Alexandra Phuong Carrick was born. She weighed in at seven and a half pounds and, to everyone's surprise, had the pinkest, clearest skin of any baby they'd ever seen. Labor had lasted only one hour, and Peter was amazed that I had not turned into what he called "a disheveled Medusa."

How rude.

But that was his way of complimenting me. He quickly explained, after I pinched his arm, that I looked radiant, not like a woman who had just gone through labor and childbirth.

We must have spent well over ten combined hours choosing a name for our daughter. But we both agreed Xandra would be more unique than the traditional spelling (Sandra), and more accurately derived—from Alexandra, which means *helper of mankind*. How appropriate, though I still have not told Peter of the prophecy spoken over me regarding our little gift from heaven. He would probably just laugh anyway.

I have just finished nursing my precious little Xandi, and she's sleeping soundly. I wish the same could be said for my husband. With the exception of a few nights, he always tosses and turns, having nightmares of which he claims no recollection the morning after.

55

XANDRA CARRICK

What will happen if he bleeds to death here in the car? I've parked right outside the first building I find in a small rural community, the name of which is lost on me because I didn't bother to look carefully at the wooden sign as I drove up the dusty path.

"Hang on, Kyle, okay?" He's breathing, thank God, but I don't know for how much longer. "I'm getting help right now."

Wind and dissipating rain blow through the trees over the valley below. I approach the brick building ahead. Dim light and shadows flicker in the windows. On the far left, a horse nickers and blows. Harnessed to a black carriage that looks like a stripped-down pickup without an engine, it eyes me with suspicion.

I knock on the door, but no one answers.

Again, I knock.

Still nothing. With my ear pressed to the door, I hear singing. Or maybe it's shouting, or crying. Whatever it is, someone's inside. This time I knock harder, repeatedly. "Hello! Please, we need help!"

The door opens, and I'm greeted by a smiling fair-haired man in blue overalls. He can't be more than a few years older than I. "Well, hello! Didn't hear you."

"Sorry to intrude." I point down to the car. The top of Kyle's head is pressed against the window where blood from his fingers smears three macabre lines. "My friend's been injured. We need your help."

The smile falls from Mr. Overalls' face as he jogs over to the car. "What happened?"

Keeping in step, I state what must be obvious—or perhaps not so obvious. "He's been shot."

Overalls stops momentarily, then calls back. "Ruth! Get Eli out here, right now!"

"Is Eli a doctor?"

"The only one in the colony." He reaches into one of his manifold pockets and gets a cell phone. "Good Lord, why didn't you take him to the ER?"

"I . . . I'm lost. Don't know the area."

"Okay, I'll call an ambulance."

"No, wait." I grab his hand. "Don't call anyone, please."

A puzzled look. "Why?"

"Please, just don't." How am I supposed to explain this? I'm just hoping this Eli person can help Kyle before it's too late. Overalls gives me a probing look. There's no deceiving him, it seems.

A frail-looking man comes running. Eli, I gather. The heavy-set woman behind him must be Ruth. Eli adjusts his wire-frame glasses and stares through the open door, where Overalls presses his ear to Kyle's chest.

"What's happened, Pastor Jacob?" says Eli. "Oh!" He puts his arm around Ruth, whose eyes are as wide as they are blue. The young pastor in overalls straightens and rolls up the sleeves of his plaid shirt. "This man's been shot."

Ruth gasps. "Oh, sweet Jesus."

Eli turns to me. "Have you called nine-one-one?"

"No, sir."

"Why in heaven not?"

"*We* need to help him," the pastor says.

Eli frowns. Leans in and checks on Kyle's pulse. "Ruth, fetch my bag from the wagon, please."

"Is he going to be okay?" I ask, wondering if by respecting Kyle's wishes, I've condemned him to death.

Eli lowers his glasses and peers over the rims. "This man needs to go to a hospital."

Pastor Jacob looks at me.

For a moment, I'm paralyzed. Kyle clearly said not to go. If we did, there would be some great danger for him, likely for us both. But what good will any of this be if he dies right here? How can I go through life with his blood on my hands?

Eli stamps his foot in the dirt. "Best hurry, he's not going to get better just lying here."

56

"He insisted." I take a deep breath. "No hospitals or police."

Eli nods. "No time anyway." He asks Pastor Jacob to help him lift Kyle out of the car. Ruth brings Eli's black medical bag. I follow as they carry him back into the building.

It's completely lit by candles inside. A handful of people look on as Eli and Jacob bring Kyle in and place him on a table. Ruth directs several youths to clear the chairs away and bring a cot to the center of the meeting room, while Eli washes his hands and prepares himself.

"Welcome." A little girl in a black cape dress and a soft white cap tied under her chin hands me a towel for my hair, which is still soaked. She smiles, pushes her glasses back up her nose. "I'm Rebecca."

"What a sweet name. Thank you."

With a slight bow of her head, she pulls the kerchief tighter around her shoulder and walks back to her mother.

Pastor Jacob comes over and gestures to the door. "Come, we'll wait in the office."

"Will Eli be able to help him?"

"In the end, life and death are in the Lord's hands. As for Eli, he has treated a man with gunshot wounds before."

"Did he live?"

"There were . . . complications."

We arrive at the office door. I stand at the threshold and hesitate. "Complications?"

"John had lost too much blood by the time they brought him to Eli. Please, come in. Would you like some tea?"

"No, thanks." I take a seat on the sofa facing his desk. He pours me a cup anyway.

"It's jasmine, from China."

"Despite my appearance, I'm not Chinese."

"Neither am I, I just like it. I have a feeling you will too. Here."

The mug is warm and soothing. I take a sip. Why haven't I tried this kind of tea before? Mom used to buy it from Ten Ren Tea House in Chinatown and brew it every weekend. "Mmm. Thank you, it *is* good."

He sits at his desk, sets his mug down, and folds his hands over his stomach. "You never told me your name."

"Xandra Carrick. Everything's happened so fast, I apologize."

"No need. Pleased to meet you. Now, I must ask—and forgive me if it seems intrusive, but—are you and your friend in some kind of trouble with the law?"

"You could say that." I take another sip. "But it's not what you might think."

"How do you know what I would think?"

"I mean, it's not what most people would think."

He spreads his hands and smiles. "Look around you. We're not like most people." His office is lit by a kerosene lamp, no lightbulbs, nothing electric. There's a distinct absence of things you'd find in a typical office: no computer, no printer, no fax machine, no telephone . . . "But you've got a cell phone."

"Yes, well . . ." The young pastor bows his head slightly. "For emergencies only. After John died in the hunting accident, I decided against the elders' counsel to get one. It's still a sore issue, modern technology and all. But they'll get used to it."

"So you're Amish?"

"Sure aren't. We're Old Colony Mennonites."

"Ah, Mennonites." I've heard but know very little about them.

I certainly don't want to trumpet my ignorance. "Pastor, sorry to be so direct, but are you going to call the police?"

"You *are* in trouble, aren't you? Why won't you just come out and say it?"

I'm in no mood to get into a debate with him. Either he's going to report us or not. Right? Yet, something in his eyes tells me he has no such intention. "Is it that obvious?"

"Besides the fact that you're avoiding the authorities," he slides the drawer out from his desk and places a copy of *USA Today* before me, "it's all over the news."

"Oh crap!" There's a huge, unflattering picture of my face on the front page, taken during my arraignment. "Pardon my French."

"Quite all right." His eyes narrow, but at the same time something of a smile emerges.

The headline reads:

Former NY Times Photographer Charged with Murder, Turns Fugitive

"Pastor Jacob—"

"Jake, please."

"You've got a good eye to recognize me from this picture, in my present condition." The newspaper is trembling in my hands.

"Would you like to tell me what happened?"

"Aren't you going to call the police and turn me in? I'm a murder suspect. For all you know, I'm dangerous."

Jake simply smiles and shakes his head. He opens a drawer and looks for something. While he does so, he continues to speak, though his eyes are involved with his search. "For all I know—and that's not really too much, in the grand scheme—you represent a danger to our entire colony, bringing in your worldliness and all."

"Oh thanks." I was shot at, beaten, and almost drowned. I'm dangerous? It takes all my self-control to bite my tongue.

"But I do know the truth. You're innocent."

"How do you know that?"

"Ah, there it goes." He places a black notebook on the desk

next to his Bible and thumbs through the pages. His eyes narrow in concentration. He stops on a page, then looks up a passage in the Bible. "Do you believe in God, Xandra?"

"Too deep for me right now."

"You do or you don't."

"Does it matter?"

"It will affect how you receive what I'm about to tell you."

"Can we check on Kyle first?"

"Don't worry; Eli will send for us."

"Fine." For a moment, neither of us speaks. I want to give Dad a call. But then it occurs to me: someone's trying to kill me. If I call Dad, I'll be dragging him into the crossfire. And though that Homeland Security agent was a fake, he had access to my credit-card activity and flight information. He's obviously someone with impressive resources. For now, I'd best sit tight and hope that Kyle will recover, and soon. He'll know what to do.

Jake is still waiting for my response. I glance at the worn edges of the leather Bible on his desk. "You know, back when I was thirteen, I stepped up in a youth-group service at church and—how did they put it?—gave my life to Jesus. But it's been so long since I've even thought about it. Since high school, I haven't even gone to an Easter or Christmas service. Can't remember the last time I prayed."

"But do you believe?" Something about Jake and this entire community that looks like a nineteenth-century time capsule puts me at ease.

"I suppose I'm sitting on the fence."

"Interesting."

"I mean, part of me thinks there's got to be more to existence than just being born, living seventy or eighty years, then dying. Of course, you try to do your part in making the world a better place before you go, but . . . you know? Something more."

Jake nods thoughtfully.

"But then, there are things that just make you wonder how there could be a God if there's so much evil in this world."

"Want to discuss that?"

"Not really." I set the tea down on the end table. "So, why do you ask?"

He sits up and leans toward me. "You see, depending on what you believe, my answer to your question—how I know you're innocent—will either make you believe in God more, or simply make you think I'm a liar with a hidden agenda."

"Let's say for argument's sake, I do believe in God."

"Well then, let's just say that the Holy Spirit told me you'd be coming here, in need of help."

If it had been just a couple of weeks ago, I would have laughed (silently, though). But after all the visions I've seen, this fascinates me. I reach over to take another sip, but my cup is now empty. I place it back down on the end table. "So what exactly did the Holy Spirit say?"

He gets up and pours me another cup of tea. "It wasn't an audible voice. More of a knowledge of something to come. But it feels like it already has."

"Like a premonition?"

"That'd be oversimplifying it a bit, but yes." He returns to his seat and gazes out the window, from which pale light fades in. The room has grown dim, save for the flickering glow of the lamp. Outside, night descends. "It was revealed to me that someone in great need would be coming to us, seeking help. And that she—*you* have been wrongly accused."

"You think God's willing to testify in court?"

"In a way, he's done far more than that for you and all of mankind. Anyway, great as that false accusation may be, it's not your biggest challenge."

"It isn't?" A chill slithers down my spine.

"When you showed up tonight, I recognized your face from the newspaper and knew you were the one the Holy Spirit meant. The one in great need."

A chill races through my body. My hair still feels wet and slimy as I twirl it between my fingers. But I'm too focused on what he's saying to care about pond sludge. "Do you know what just happened to me, to Kyle?"

"No." His eyes are back now, but with a more troubled expression. "But I do know you've got something very important to do, and that you're still in danger."

At this point, I feel compelled to share about my darkroom visions. It takes a good ten minutes, but finally I get through it all—the body in Central Park, the awful images of Vietnam, Dad, that soldier from Echo Company living in Alpine. "It feels like they're all connected. I just don't see how."

"Remarkable. But not unbelievable."

"What are *your* visions like, Jake?"

"They're spiritual gifts called 'words of knowledge' and 'words of wisdom.' I believe that's what you're manifesting."

"How is it that I just happen to run into someone like you, who just happens to—"

"Nothing *just* happens. Everything's connected. By a divine plan. What we humans perceive as infinite possibilities of events doesn't even come close to the infinite from God's point of view."

This is just a bit too bizarre. Should it not be comforting to know that I'm not the only person in the world who experiences these visions, or words of whatever? Instead, Pastor Jake's confirmation makes me even more anxious. Part of me would like to be told, "You're just imagining things," to be written a prescription and medicate it with some antipsychotic pills.

"Charles Spurgeon said, 'We must take care that we do not neglect heavenly monitions through fear of being considered visionary; we must not be staggered even by the dread of being styled fanatical, or out of our minds. For to stifle a thought from God is no small sin.'"

His words resound in my mind. It feels as though the floor beneath me has vanished.

"You okay, Xandra?"

"Hmm? Oh, yes. Fine."

"You seem upset."

"Why is all this happening? Why am I having these visions, being charged with murder, and why in the world is someone impersonating a Homeland Security Agent and trying to kill me?"

All at once, I'm aware of a hollowness within me. A void left in Mom's place when she passed away. She always had answers for me, could always make sense of things. It's now, as I lean over my knees and bury my tears in my hands, that I realize how much I've truly missed her.

Jake's voice is quiet and gentle but has an authority that speaks to my situation. "Your answers lie in finding the truth behind all those visions. Christ said, 'You shall know the truth, and the truth shall set you free.'"

"I don't know what's true anymore."

"Perhaps that's what you came out here to discover." Before he can say another word, a knock comes on the door.

It's Ruth. "Eli needs to speak with you, Miss. It's about your friend."

57

IAN MORTIMER

I've been waiting in a locked interrogation room in a suburban police station. All my personal effects have been confiscated. My badge, my gun, my cell phone.

Officer Dowler steps in and takes a seat facing me. "Here's the problem. Homeland refuses to give me the four-one-one on you, and it's nagging me like a pebble in my shoe."

Time to put on my public-service face. "One call. That'll assuage your doubts." Even though I'm projecting confidence, I dread calling TR. But if I'm to move on, I must.

Dowler brings in a Polycom phone from outside and sets it on the table. "One call."

In less than two minutes, Dowler is leaning over the speaker phone, listening to TR give him the entire rundown on national security and how any attempt to impede my investigation would result in severe consequences for him and his entire division. "Is that clear, Dowler?"

"Crystal, sir."

"The sooner you release Agent Rolston, the sooner we'll get the person who shot your men."

"Right away. We were just doing things by the book."

"Completely understandable, Lieutenant. Now, get Rolston out of there." TR hangs up.

Dowler barks at his subordinates. My gun, my BlackBerry, and badge are returned to me. A minute later my BlackBerry buzzes. It's TR again.

I motion for Dowler to leave the room. "Privacy, please." He nods and shuts the door behind him. My hand shakes as I press the cell phone to my ear. "Mortimer."

"What the hell's going on, Ian?"

"A minor inconvenience, that's all."

"You're supposed to keep a low profile."

"Not to worry, I'm playing my part perfectly. But this assignment has its hazards."

"So you've terminated the Carrick girl already?"

Uncertain how best to respond, I hesitate. If I become a liability, he'll have me terminated. The problem is, every time I try to carry out my assignment, I'm haunted by ghosts of my past. All the people I've killed before Nicole and Bobby came into my life. How naive I was to believe I could just walk away from it all. No, everyone pays for his sins. Everyone.

"Ian?"

"Right. Sorry, someone stepped into the room, and I had to send him off."

"So, is Xandra Carrick dead?"

"Yes. So is that FBI agent she traveled with." At the very least, I can buy some time to make it so retroactively and finish the job. Stupid of me to lie. But at the moment, it's the only thing I can do to keep myself and my family alive. I know what TR is capable of.

"Knew I could count on you, Ian."

"All right then. Our business is concluded." Just a bit earlier than delivered.

"Not quite. Your last assignment cast some doubt. I'm going to need proof she's really dead."

"Already thought of that," I lied.

"And there's one more assign—"

"Bloody hell!"

"There's one more assignment. Upon completion, barring unforeseen complications, that should conclude our association."

"I want this to be over with."

"As do I, believe me. This has been every bit as distasteful to me as—"

"Distasteful? Is that all this is to you? Of all the twisted, demented—"

"Oh don't start pontificating, you hypocrite. The very reason I'm working with you is because you're a cold-blooded, calculating killer who understands the necessary sacrifices for the greater good! At least, you used to understand."

The accusation cuts like barbed razor wire that surrounds the Supermax Prison that I'll likely end up in when this is over. He's right. I've killed so many, even after I stopped believing in the ideals that commanded such decisions. A deep breath. Mustn't let him rile me so. "You'll keep your word?"

"Lifetime supply. I will personally guarantee that Bobby will get the best treatment possible. Even experimental stem-cell research."

"Even when I'm dead."

"Even then. Come on, Ian. After all these years, you know me. I always keep my word."

True enough. That had been one of his greatest strengths. But now it's become his Achilles' heel as his integrity has been compromised by Machiavellian delusions. That he wields such power over me disgusts me profoundly. But most frightening is what will happen if he reaches his goals, which I'm helping him achieve.

"So what's this final assignment?"

TR explains, and I feel like vomiting, as I did the first time this operation began. "Another EC vet? You're sick, TR. Of all the persons—"

"Who are you to judge me? Anyway, he's never recovered. He's got no family, friends. Nine toes in the grave. If you ask me, we're doing him a favor."

"The favor is for you."

"And for Bobby, don't ever forget that."

"Swine." I should just blast the cover off this whole wretched thing. But TR's got the resources to silence and discredit me before

I could ever do him any harm. And in the end, Nicole and Bobby would pay.

For my sins.

"Again, details will be sent to your BlackBerry. Remember, I want proof of purchase for Xandra Carrick's termination."

"What did the lass ever do to you, anyway?" I let out a weary sigh. Dowler has returned and is standing outside with his back to the glass door. "Shouldn't I have been more concerned about her than you?"

"Doesn't matter now. She's all over the news as a fugitive. Let the media speculate on her disappearance. You've made sure there's nothing identifiable this time, right?"

"Of course." At least, when I find her, I'll make sure to do so. She can't have gotten too far, but if TR doesn't get off the phone soon, I might be too late. "I really need to get out of here. So I'll contact you tomorrow, when everything's completed. I'm going offline for twenty-four." Which means radio silence, or at the very least, cell phone, text message, and email silence for the next twenty-four hours.

"Be sure to complete your next assignment cleanly. I'm counting on you." A haughty scoff. "And if that doesn't move you, think of your boy."

I hang up, imagining that the End button I stab with my thumb is TR's windpipe. The urge rises up to hurl my BlackBerry at the wall and smash it to pieces.

I open the door; Dowler turns around. "All set?"

"Indeed."

He escorts me to my car, which his partner drove to the station while I sat in the back of their squad car. At the exit, he shakes my hand. "Sorry for the inconvenience, Agent Rolston. If there's anything you need, anything we can—"

"You've done quite enough, thank you." I shut the door and roll down the window.

"This cop killer's under my jurisdiction, remember."

"Maybe so, but Homeland Security's been after him well before he showed up here. So sit tight and keep this quiet until we contact you. There's a lot more at stake than the lives of two cops."

His brow crinkles. He inhales deeply but refrains from saying what's truly on his mind. "Yeah, whatever. You're not the one who has to tell their wives and kids."

Wives and kids. I have to focus on mine or I'll never get through this. "I don't envy you."

"Just find him, all right?"

"Trust me. I will."

58

XANDRA CARRICK

For some reason we're not walking back toward the meeting hall where Eli had been treating Kyle. Ruth hasn't said anything yet. She just presses forward with a concerned expression.

Finally, I have to ask. "Where are we going?"

"To the rectory, dear."

When we arrive, Kyle is lying on a bed in a small room toward the back of the apartment. It's dimly lit by oil lamps. He's unconscious and connected to an IV. The stand that holds the saline pouch looks like it came from a 1950s movie set.

Sitting bedside in a chair is Eli. He's patting Kyle's brow with a towel. "Didn't lose as much blood as I thought."

"How is he?" I step over and kneel to get a closer look.

"Came this close." Eli pinches his thumb and forefinger together. He points to Kyle's side. "Went in here, passed clean out there. Almost hit an artery, but didn't touch anything crucial. Quarter of an inch to the left and . . . Well, it's a miracle."

"That's luck for you."

"No. That's God's grace," says Ruth.

"Grace?" I let out an inadvertent chuckle.

"Something funny?" Eli asks, slightly annoyed.

"Oh, nothing. It's just that my mother . . ." I can't help it. I'm starting to cry. To hold it back, I put my hand over my mouth.

"My mother miraculously survived a gunshot wound during the Vietnam War. The bullet passed through her too."

Jake puts a hand on my shoulder as I wipe my eyes. I don't usually get so emotional, but the past couple of days have been too much.

"Mom's name is . . . her name was Grace." Gunshot wounds, miraculous survivals. Grace. God's grace.

"Well then," Eli says, standing and wringing the towel into the basin on the nightstand. "I'd say she was well named."

By her father, who became a Christian through a Jesuit missionary. With each realization, I'm starting to see what Jake meant when he said, *Everything's connected. By a divine plan.* "So is he going to be all right?"

"Trauma is trauma," says Eli. "He's going to need time to fully recover. But yes, he'll be fine." He reaches into his bag and takes out a rectangular case. With a small key, he unlocks and opens it to reveal several compartments of pills, each immaculately labeled. After he locates the ones he wants, he fills a small velvet pouch with them, pulls the drawstring tight, and hands them to me. "Three times a day with food. It's an antibiotic. Fever's gone down, but we'll need to keep an eye on him."

"I'll stay with him tonight," Jake says.

"No, we've put you out so much already. I'll stay. We have things to discuss when he wakes up."

"Sure?"

"Yes, Jake."

At this, Eli turns and scowls. "Getting a bit familiar, are we?" He peers disdainfully over his glasses at Jake, or me, or at both of us, I'm not sure.

"Oh, Eli," Ruth nudges him with her elbow. "You leave them be."

He packs everything into his bag and nods to me. "If you need anything, call on me. Ruth and I live just down the road from"— he scowls at the young pastor—"Jake."

"I'll do that."

With a final harrumph, he leaves with Ruth. A chilly draft blows into the room when they open the door.

I take the seat next to Kyle and touch his forehead. It's quite warm, so I wring the washcloth and apply it. "What was that all about?"

"Never mind them," Jake says. "Eli doesn't approve of my 'compromises' with the world. I'm too liberal for him."

"You?"

"Cell phone, TV, computer. Yes, liberal."

"Besides the cell phone, I haven't seen anything like that around here."

"Oh, I keep it hidden from those in the colony who are offended by it. Eli's like a father to me. I'm used to his indignant attitude."

"Ruth seems nice."

"Well, she's my aunt. Raised me since . . . I was only three months old."

Kyle takes a deep breath. He exhales slowly, and though he's asleep, pain twists his brow. Instinctively, I put a hand on his chest and he seems to relax.

"Jake, are your parents . . . ?"

He nods.

"I'm sorry."

"Don't be. I don't remember them. We have no photos here, so I don't even know what they looked like. Ruth and Eli raised me as their own. They couldn't have children, so they saw me as a blessing in the midst of tragedy. But you know, Ruth always says I'm just like my father. Headstrong, rebellious, I even have his chin. You can imagine how Eli felt when I became pastor for our colony and started challenging some of our Old Order practices."

"Like electricity?"

"Like electricity, yes."

"My mother passed away last year. All my life, I'd been close to her. So when she left us and I didn't cry much, I thought there was something really wrong with me. Guess I was too busy being strong for Dad, because it nearly destroyed him. Strange, I never felt the pain as much as I do these days. It's all coming at me at once."

He gestures to Kyle. "And now this."

"And more." I still don't know how Kyle found me back there in the woods. As far as I know, he hadn't followed us. But I'm glad he did, even though it nearly cost him his life. "I remember a verse they taught us back when Mom took me to Sunday school. Something about laying down your life for a friend."

" 'Greater love hath no man than this, that a man lay down his life for his friends.' John 15:13."

"That's it."

"So, he almost died protecting you."

"You have no idea." I notice a subtle smile on his face. "Or perhaps you do."

"I'm going to go back and finish our prayer vigil with the congregation, then home."

"This is a rectory, right? Aren't you supposed to live here?"

"The last pastor did."

"Oh? Where do you live then?"

"The house right behind this building." He opens the door and starts walking out.

"Why don't you live here?"

A boyish grin and a wink. "No electricity."

59

GRACE TH'AM AI LE

Brooklyn, New York: June 25, 1985

I have had enough! I know the Bible says that it is not right to divorce, but after tonight, I am beginning to wonder if I can be true to my faith. Peter has once again left on an unexpected business trip. When these trips first began, about a month after he was awarded the Pulitzer, I did not think much of it. Like a dutiful wife, I smiled, kissed him, and counted the days till he returned.

I did not even mind that he was unable to tell me about these trips due to the sensitive nature of the projects. But how can a photography assignment be "classified"?

Honestly, I have been more than patient with him. But this government work he's doing is affecting our family. Xandi is four now and too smart to accept anything less than a reasonable answer when she asks, "Why isn't Daddy home?"

"He's away on business" is always met with, "Why?"

Why indeed? Is any work so important that a man must leave his family, often with no prior warning, then come back and completely withdraw? He avoids us for days.

Today I did something I never dared before. I opened Peter's MasterCard bill. It was there I saw the airplane tickets he bought for the dates he's been away. I called the 800 number and learned that his flights were to Washington, D.C., and California. Why the secrecy? Could he not even tell me where he was going?

I began to think the worst. Maybe he's having an affair. The problem with belief is that it becomes faith. And faith, true faith, translates into action.

So when he came home tonight—late for dinner—I held up the credit-card bill with the mysterious charges circled in red. "Why have you been lying to me?"

He snatched the papers from my hand and stuffed them into his coat pocket. "Why did you do that? I told you not to pry!"

"It's not prying! I'm your wife. We should have no secrets."

"I told you, these are highly classified business trips. I can't talk to you—"

"That's right. You can't!" I was raising my voice, frustration threatening to erupt into rage. Xandi began to cry. Peter went over and picked her up, shielding her ears.

"What are you talking about?"

"Even when you're home, you are distant. You just go to your office to do God knows what. And when you do come out, it's just for a meal, or because you're feeling frisky and want to have—"

"Grace, please!" He pointed his eyes at our daughter whose ears he now cupped. "I'm sorry if I've been preoccupied."

"It's been four years like this! Four years of your sneaking out of the house like a criminal, four years of your missing your daughter's school plays, her first recital, our anniversaries, your own birthday . . ."

"I swear, I forgot about Xandi's recital; otherwise I would not have—"

"You have a photographic memory! You do not forget!"

"I don't get it. You never complained before. Why the hell are you whining about all this now?"

Never before had he used such language with me, never before had his eyes burned with such anger at me. I was afraid, for myself and my daughter. "Xandi, come to Mama."

He let her go, stepped into his office, and slammed the door shut.

The Phở Ga I had prepared for dinner was cold now. Not that either of us had any appetite left. When he returned, instead of appearing calmer, it seemed that his anger had only become more inflamed.

"You have no idea! The things I've had to—ugh!" He slammed his hand on the door so hard, Xandi began to cry.

"Wait in your room, baby. Okay?" She nodded and, staring at her father with eyes as big as a cow's, stepped around him and shut herself in.

I pointed a finger at him. "See what you've done?"

"What *I've* done? I come home and you've become a person I don't even know."

"That took four years to happen. You were too busy to notice!"

Peter almost slammed his hand on the wall but looked over to Xandi's room and stopped. He pulled his lips taut. "I'm doing my best to be a good father, a good provider. Just what do you want?"

"How about a good husband?"

Letting out a frustrated grunt, he clenched his fist. I drew back, but he was not going to hit me. I think I hurt him with that last remark, but I was too angry to care about his feelings. "Peter, I'm only going to ask you this once, because I expect only the truth. Your daughter deserves that. I deserve it."

"For heaven's sake, what?"

The words were so simple, yet so difficult to utter. But there was no turning back. I had to ask. "Are you having an affair?"

His upper lip twitched, as did the corner of his left eye. His eyes were red, but there would be no tears. And if there were, what would they indicate?

"Are you?"

Peter marched right up to me and glared down into my eyes. A single teardrop drew a moist line down his face. "No."

And with that, he walked out the door and shut it quietly.

Central Park West, New York: March 3, 1991

Looking back on the past six years, I am amazed at how so much has changed and yet how much has remained the same. Peter came home the next morning after that one huge fight in my last entry in 1985. Tearfully, we both came to what he called a cease-fire.

He pleaded with me to trust him, promised he had never been unfaithful. I wanted so much to believe him. But how could I know if he was telling me the truth when he continued with the secretive behavior?

To this day, he still goes to those classified business meetings. I came to the realization that my choices were clear. I could 1) continue to suspect he was having an affair and work toward proving him a liar; 2) take his word that he cannot tell me about these meetings for our own protection; or 3) divorce him and, for the second time in my life, start anew.

Since there was no way to know for sure without destroying my marriage, I prayed. The Holy Spirit brought a word to me from the Gospel of John, when doubting Thomas finally believed it was the risen Christ because he had seen and touched His wounded hands and side. And Jesus said: "Blessed are those who have not seen and yet have believed."

I had seen visions in the past, like the boy and his father trapped in the burning house in Cholon. I believed the vision was true, and because I acted in obedience, I was able to save their lives. I took this verse as another sign. Believe what you know in your heart, even though you don't have visible evidence.

The peace that filled my heart was enough to make me stop questioning my husband. I entrusted this matter to divine wisdom and justice. From that day on, we have lived in harmony. Not perfect harmony, for it still pained me that the Peter Carrick with whom I first fell in love had never quite returned to me emotionally.

We have since moved up to a vast apartment overlooking Central Park. Peter's career and fame have grown enough to make this economically possible.

I must confess to enjoying the benefits of being married to a celebrity. Aside from that part of Peter's life we will never share, and the distance that has grown between us, I am grateful for my life.

Xandi is ten years old now, and such a smart girl. I see a lot of Peter in her—his intense manner, that indomitable spirit, with a hint of self-righteousness. She has taken an interest in photography, but Peter is very cautious about it.

For a girl of her age, she's very insightful, oftentimes pointing out things that both her father and I may have overlooked. She's our official finder of missing keys and eyeglasses. Somehow, for no apparent reason, she knows where to find them.

Xandi's so pretty, but she has no idea that one day boys will all want to date her. Right now, she plays with insects and scrapes her knees with all the boys who treat her just like one of them. I thank God every day that she does not have to grow up in a country torn apart by war.

Peter left today on another of his business trips. There have not been many for the past two years—at the most, twice a year. After putting Xandi to bed tonight, while I was watching a rerun of *China Beach*, a news flash came across the screen.

The show was interrupted to report a plane crash in Colorado Springs killing all twenty-five passengers. Right away, I thought of Peter. Lord, please don't let it be his flight. When I found out that United Airlines flight 585 originated in Peoria, Illinois, I fell on my knees and thanked God. I realized then, for that torturous half a minute, just how much a part of me my husband was.

I stepped into his office, where his awards, trophies, and old camera from the war were displayed. There, the empty chair by his desk caused me to shudder.

Is this what it would be like walking into this room if he died? No.

He's alive, and well. He will come back to me.

I rested my hand on his antiquated camera and shut my eyes. "Peter, where are you?"

While I stood there, something happened within my mind's eye.

Peter as an older man sits curled up on the hard floor of a prison cell that can only be unlocked from the inside. Hideous creatures surround him, taunting, accusing, and tormenting him. Demons, I think. I want so much to go to him, but I cannot move.

Then a beautiful young woman appears—she reminds me a bit of myself, when I was that age, though she is not pure Vietnamese. Might this be a vision of the future, and the young woman, Xandra? But whenever she approaches the cell, Peter shrinks away, as if she means to harm him.

But she does not seem that way at all. In fact, she holds in her hand a key. But Peter does not see it.

"She has the key. Let her free you!" I shout, but not a sound comes out of my mouth.

When she approaches again, offering him the key, he cringes, covers his face, and backs deeper into the utter darkness of his cell.

Instantly, the entire vision vanished. I was filled with compassion, even a bit of pity for my husband. His secretive behavior, his nightmares that he refuses ever to speak about: they torment him.

From the day he brought me my brother's cross, and with it the news of his death, I have always felt that he was withholding something from me. If I am to be consistent with my faith in him, I should believe he is doing this to protect me.

Ironically, he has a photographic memory. After all he's seen as a war photographer, I can only wonder what demons have entrapped him in this prison of his soul.

60

XANDRA CARRICK

I'm jolted awake by the sound of cows mooing outside. For a moment, the darkness disorients me. The crick in my neck from sleeping in a padded chair does little to help.

The lamp has burned out, so I pull open the blinds behind me. Moonlight splashes over the bed. It's when Kyle stirs and groans that I remember where I am. He's sitting up and holding his side.

"Xandra?"

I hold my watch up into the moonlight. It's four forty-five. A rooster crows in the distance. "Morning."

"Where are we?"

"A place called Lucky to Be Alive. Don't try to get up just yet."

"I'm fine, really." He wraps the blanket over his shoulders and leans back against the headboard. From the tray on the nightstand he takes a buttermilk biscuit. Good, he's got an appetite.

"Sorry, I finished the egg sandwich."

"What is this place?"

"Mennonite Colony. Their doctor treated you. Can't believe I fell asleep."

Straining, he puts his hand on his wound and sucks in a sharp breath. "We've got to get out of here."

"Where do we go?"

"Give me a sec . . . head's spinning."

In the meantime, I pull out my cell phone. Risk or not, I have to call Dad. If he's in danger, I've got to warn him.

"Don't!" Kyle tries to get up, but the pain in his side stops him. "They'll track you down within a tight radius of the nearest cell tower."

"Don't worry." I get up and show him the phone. In bold letters, the screen displays: NO SERVICE. "I hate cellphones."

"Good. Man, I'm burning up!" Judging by the heat from his forehead against my hand, it seems he's got a temperature. There on the nightstand, next to the food and water, is the pouch of antibiotic medication Eli left.

"Okay, just relax. Take this; the doctor said it'd help."

Kyle takes the pill and swallows it without question. He makes a better patient than expected. "How far off the freeway did you drive?"

"About twenty minutes. Nothing but open fields and farms out here. That Homeland Security impersonator got pulled over by the cops long before I exited."

"Yeah, but if he's got the resources I think he has, he's probably out of their hands already. We're still in danger."

"Can't you get help from the FBI?"

"Yeah, right." He offers me a biscuit, but I decline. "I don't know who I can trust now. This whole thing's out of control."

"I'll say." Out the window, a bovine sea of white and black flows by. The sun hasn't yet peaked over the horizon, but a young man in dungarees and a thick wool sweater, very alert and very awake, urges the cattle on. "I could never live on a farm."

"Don't knock it till you've tried it."

"Hello? I'm here."

"For at least a year or two. You'd be surprised how it grows on you."

"Have you?"

"Till I went to college, yeah." He pours some water from the white-and-blue ceramic pitcher into his cup and takes a sip, then squints in pain. "Okay, priorities."

"First thing is to contact my father. He's probably worried sick."

"But we need to get to Hank Jennings before it's too late. I'm pretty sure he's in danger too."

"What makes you think so?"

"Sometimes, when a pattern reveals itself, you smack yourself for not seeing it earlier. It was under my nose all these years, but I didn't see it until that guy tried to kill you."

"What pattern?"

"Echo Company. Over the past four years, just about everyone who served in Echo Company has died, whether by natural causes or in some kind of accident. I've been watching this for a long time. Last December, two of them died in the same month."

"Last I checked, Jennings was still alive."

"Last you checked?"

"At least he sounded that way on his answering machine."

He tries to sit up but stops abruptly and clenches his teeth. "Okay, besides Jennings, there's only one other person from Echo Company who's still alive."

"And that is?"

"Senator Richard Colson."

I gasp. "I knew he fought in Vietnam, but he was in Echo Company too?" Dad never mentioned him, even now as Colson's running for president. "You don't think there might be an assassination attempt?"

"Every time I try to mention these potential connections and their implications, my supervisor dismisses it. So I've worked on this case entirely on my own time—in fact, when I met you, I was on paid leave. But they all think I'm paranoid, so forget any help from them."

"Dad was an embedded photographer with Echo Company. We've got to warn him." On my feet, I straighten out my clothes and ignore the fact that a shower would be in order right about now. "Can I use your phone?"

"Listen, Xandra. We can't—"

"Fine. I'll ask Jake, his works."

Now Kyle is on his feet, taking excruciating steps toward me as I pace on the rug. "If you call your father—"

"I can use a landline . . . at a gas station."

"No, that's too—"

"I saw one by the freeway. There's got to be—"

"All right, Xandra. Stop!" He grabs my shoulders.

But I pull free violently. "I am not going to sit around while that creep goes after my father!"

"Slow down for a moment, okay?" He reaches for his shirt. But it's been replaced with a new one Jake left him, as his own was ruined by the gunshot and blood. The mere act of buttoning it is painful for him. He grimaces. "You're working yourself up."

I didn't realize how frantic I'd gotten until I stopped and noticed my chest rising and falling, my heart pounding in my ears. "I'm fine . . . I'm fine." With my hand up deflecting any possible approach, I catch my breath and turn away from him. The cows have all gathered outside the doors of a tall barn. They're entering now in a steady stream.

"Take a deep breath. Good. Now, let's think this through."

"Okay." I turn around. I can't stand to see him struggling with the shirt, so I go over and help him. "All right. Based on your experience, what do you think we should do?" My eyes are fixed on his as I button his shirt. He's got to have some answers, a plan, a tiny reassurance that it's going to be all right. As he speaks, my fingers inadvertently wander into the groove between his pectorals. His skin is smooth, save for the subtle patch of hair that . . . "I'm sorry, I wasn't . . ."

"It's quite all right."

"I didn't mean anything."

"'Course not."

Quickly refocusing, I finish buttoning his shirt and step away. My instincts and burning ears tell me to look away. But I'm drawn to his eyes. They're so intense as the light from the oil lamp strikes his brow, casting a profound shadow over them. "You were saying?"

"We'll get some prepaid cell phones and calling cards. Can't contact your father by any traceable means. They'll be monitoring."

"They? You think someone in the government has been killing those vets?"

"I'm almost certain of it."

"But why?"

"The answer to that might just be our salvation. Those visions of yours have gotten us this far, but they've also put us in danger. Whatever this is about, someone really doesn't want you to learn the truth."

"Jake read me a verse from the Bible. 'The truth shall set you free.'"

"Who's Jake?"

The answer comes in a light rapping on the door. "Hello? I heard talking. Everything okay?"

I open the door and let Jake in. "You're an early bird, Pastor." He steps in and sees Kyle standing with one hand resting on the edge of the headboard. "Glad to see you up and running, Agent Matthews." He hands him his gun and wallet. "I'm Pastor Jacob Rittenhouse."

Kyle reaches to shake his hand. "I want to thank you for . . ." He places a hand over his wound.

"Glad it fits. But Eli's the doctor who patched you up. How're you feeling?"

"Tired."

While they talk, something tugs on my heart. It's not Jake or Kyle, personally—at least, I don't think so. It's more what they represent. Kyle is security, the one who believed me and risked himself to save me from certain death. And Jake is comfort, understanding, a connection on the spiritual level.

Have I lacked such things so much that I'm emotionally drawn to them now? Until middle school, Dad had always provided security and comfort. But understanding? Well, two out of three's not too shabby.

No. I am not a little girl seeking a paternal substitute. Am I? Jung and Freud would have a field day with me. I've got to focus on the matters at hand.

Unaware of my flight into oblivion all the time they've been speaking, Kyle turns to me. "We've got a plan."

61

The first thing we need to do, they tell me, is to remove and destroy the GPS tracking device attached to the car Kyle commandeered at the airport. It's something many car-service fleets install in their vehicles as an antitheft measure and to track their drivers.

Kyle's in no condition to crawl under a car right now, so Jake has offered to help me with that. We've parked the car in a barn for now and can only hope that the GPS transponder dome was too wet to transmit properly.

"I think it's that square thing right above the rear window."

"I'll get it." Jake unsheathes a hunting knife and digs under the cover. After a few attempts, the cover pops off. Using a screwdriver, he disconnects two wires. "We'll need to take the car to El Centro, reactivate the GPS for a few minutes, then disconnect and discard it."

"You think it'll work?"

"Agent Matthews seems to think it'll throw them off the scent."

"How far is El Centro?"

"About an hour and a half." He examines the wires on the bare transponder. "I haven't got a license."

"No, I couldn't ask you to do that. You've already done so much. And I wouldn't want to get you involved in this mess."

"Seems I already am." Jake picks up a paper bag and hands it to me. It's my clothes, washed and ironed. "Compliments of Ruth. She's such a mother hen."

"Would you thank her for me? This dress she lent me is nice, but it's really not my style."

"I think you look fetching in it."

"Thanks, but I prefer my Levi's." There's a clean and empty stable, and I'd like to get out of this stiff-collared and drab outfit. "Can I use that to change?"

"Sure, just make sure the door shuts tight. I'll replace this dome cover so it's not conspicuous."

As I disrobe and get into my own clothes, a thought comes to mind. "Jake," I call out over the open rafters, "do you think Kyle is well enough to take the trip with me to El Centro?"

"He's still drowsy from the medication. Eli says he needs another week or so to fully recover."

"Another week!"

"Though he tends to err on the side of extremely overcautious."

"That's okay, just wondering." After getting fully dressed, I step back out. The car is ready. And so is Jake, sitting in the driver's seat.

"What are you doing?"

"Taking the transponder and getting rid of it."

"But you don't have a driver's license."

He smiles like a cat with bright yellow feathers between its teeth.

"What?"

"Doesn't mean I've never driven."

Jake has pulled out of the barn with the nose of the car pointing down the dirt road, where puddles reflect blue sky and white clouds.

"Just don't tell Eli, all right?"

"I don't believe this. You want me to lie for you?"

Jake grins. "Try to avoid him so it doesn't become an issue."

"This is crazy. I should be the one going."

"Your face is all over the news. If you go into the city, you increase the chance of getting caught."

"I don't know."

"Hey, let's pray for success, okay?" He reaches out to me. Guess I'm supposed to hold hands with him while we pray. I don't mind. He's silent for a while, concentration pinching shut the corners of his eyes. "Mmmm . . . Mmm . . . Yes. Amen." He opens his eyes and smiles.

"That's it? Aren't you supposed to say something? Hail Mary full of grace, Our Father who art in heaven, or something like that?"

"Sometimes prayer is more about listening than speaking."

"Listening." That's something new to me. "And seeing?"

"On occasion."

"Did you just see something?"

"Kind of." He puts the transmission into drive and gets ready to drive off.

"Well?"

"I have a feeling our paths will cross again in the future." He dons a pair of sunglasses—coolest looking pastor I've ever seen—then waves and revs the engine. "Later!"

When not resting, Kyle has spent most of the day sitting up in bed, surrounded by papers and pencils, writing out plans and contingency plans. Each time I try to interrupt and inquire, he holds up a hand, "Uh-uh! Never disturb me when I'm planning."

"Fine."

I've followed Jake's advice about avoiding Eli. But in doing so, I've pretty much avoided everyone else here in the colony as well. They're not too nosy, though once in a while I catch a glimpse of some of the children. They take furtive glances at me, as if I were some new animal in a cage.

While I'm watching the ducks at a pond behind the barn, Rebecca, the girl who gave me a towel when I first arrived, comes to sit next to me on a log. "Hello, Rebecca."

She smiles and presses her face against her shoulder. "You can call me Becky if you like."

"Hi Becky. How old are you?"

"Seven. What's *your* name?"

"Xandra."

"That's a nice name."

"You can call me Xandi." I lean over and whisper in her ear. "Wanna hear something?" She nods. "It's Xandra, spelled with an X."

As if she'd been told the world's naughtiest secret, she puckers her lips and raises her eyebrows. "I thought it was spelled with an S."

"Xandra is short for Alexandra."

"I like that."

"So did my mom, apparently. It's Greek for 'defender of mankind' or 'warrior.' "

"Wow." From the look on her face, I'd say she believes that I really am those things.

"I don't know. I've never really been able to defend anyone because I'm always getting myself in trouble."

Rebecca giggles and puts her hand over her mouth. "Me too."

"And I'm no warrior."

"I am." She sits up tall, her chest proud.

"Really?"

"Oh yes. Come on, I'll show you." Rebecca pulls me by the hand and leads me to a clearing under the trees. "Watch me." She starts to sing a song about the armor of God and does these lively pantomimes to represent the helmet of salvation, the shield of faith, the breastplate of righteousness.

She finishes with a slashing motion with her imaginary sword of the Spirit. "Ta-da!"

"Very nice, Becky!" She takes a deep bow, then curtseys, fanning out the hem of her black skirt. Reveling in my praise, she smiles and skips off into the field where she starts picking dandelions.

Once upon a time, I was just like her. I was the apple of Dad's eye. Whether it was ballet, soccer, or cello, I lived for his praise. Funny how none of those hobbies lasted, not even cello playing. When I started to notice his pulling away from my life, I sought out things I knew interested him. Photography was to be my next conquest, and it proved serendipitous that I loved it enough to pursue a career in it. Just like Dad.

I really need to call him. He's probably going crazy with all the news reports and not being able to get in touch with me.

Becky returns and hands me a fistful of dandelions, their spores begging to be launched into flight. "Let's go." She pulls my hand into the field. There we blow them into the air. Tiny little parachutes liberated from the effects of gravity. But even they must fall to the ground and die, in order to fulfill their destiny and produce new life.

"Let's spin, Xandi!"

"Spin?"

"Yes, silly! Like this!" She points her face to the sky, shuts her eyes as warm sunlight bathes her cheeks, and twirls round and round. "Come on, Xandi. It's fun!"

Fun indeed. I haven't done anything this childish since . . . well, since I was a child. Oh, why not? Spreading my wings, I, too, lift my face to the sun, shut my eyes, and spin, while Becky sings an unintelligible song. The simplicity of a child's world. Unencumbered by the stress and responsibilities of life. All she needs is to be loved and cared for. For this moment alone, I permit myself to be such a child as I indulge in "spinning."

"Rebecca!"

Startled, we both stop. For the first time on her angelic face, I see fear. She's too petrified to answer Eli, who stands with one hand on a walking stick. The scowl is so deeply recessed into his face, it looks permanent.

"What are you doing, child?"

She hides behind my back as I greet him. "Eli, good morning."

"I am talking to her." He peers around me. "Answer me, Rebecca!"

"What's the matter?"

"Rebecca!"

"If you stopped shouting and scaring her, she might—"

"*You* . . . are a bad influence."

"Me? What did I do?"

"Child, I'll say it one more time. What are you doing?"

"She was just doing what a kid should do."

"Rebecca missed her morning devotions at school."

My throat parches. "It's my fault."

"It most certainly is!" He steps around me and takes Rebecca by the hand firmly. "Run along to your classroom."

"Yes, sir." Down the grassy hill she scampers off until she's out of view.

Eli mutters something and simply walks away.

"Eli, wait!"

"What is it?"

"I wanted to thank you for helping Kyle."

He tips his hat. " 'To the least of these,' saith the Lord," then continues hobbling down the path.

I match his gait, hold his elbow as we make our way down the wet grass. "We'll leave as soon as we can, I promise."

"You're welcome to stay long as you need, Ms. Carrick. Just remember, we Mennonites are in the world, not of it. You represent all the temptation we strive to avoid."

"How so?"

"Oh, your worldly ways, televisions that suck your brains and souls dry, your immodest clothes that cause men to falter, your violence and hate. For things such as these have we separated ourselves, lest we fall into temptation and sin."

I'm not offended personally, though sometimes I wonder if I do dress a certain way deliberately to get noticed. Mom never wanted me to do that when I began to blossom, and for the most part I was a good kid.

But during my decadent college years, and thanks to my wild roommates with whom I still have sushi once a week, I bought my first thong, Victoria's Secret Wonderbra, stilettos, and other Friday-night wear.

Except for the sexy underwear, I never actually wore any of those items to go out. And I never messed around with boys the way they did. Add to that the one and only time I got drunk and lost it all over Jenn's boyfriend's carpet, and you've got the full extent of my decadence. Right out of college, I devoted myself completely to my photography, with Ethan as my one and only mistake. A horrid mistake at that.

"Well, Eli, I'll try not to corrupt any of the good people here before we leave."

He lowers his glasses and stares at Jake's house. "Have you seen Jacob?"

62

The sun is setting and Jake's not back yet. Eventually I had to confess to Eli, who only scowled and walked back into his house. Hopefully Jake will forgive the betrayal. He was the one who told me, "The truth will set you free."

I'm sitting on the bench outside the congregational meeting hall. If only I could call his cell phone. If anything were to happen to him, I would feel terrible. And responsible. Even though it was his own idea to go into El Centro as a decoy.

"You look like the girl who got stood up on prom night." Kyle takes a seat next to me. The bench is narrow and we're shoulder to shoulder.

"I'm worried."

"You guys should've talked to me first. I wouldn't have let him do it. By now, we've probably got both Homeland and the FBI looking for us. Not to mention that psycho hitman pretending to be a Homeland agent."

"You think they got to Jake?"

"Hope not." Kyle ponders this and repositions himself by lifting his arm. Which he naturally puts to rest behind me on the back of the bench. If we were kids on a date, this would be known as the yawn-stretch move. I'm too worried about Jake to debate Kyle's intentions though. "What do we really know about him?"

"Why do you ask?"

"We just met him, you know. I just don't know what I think about your being so close—"

"Close?"

"That didn't come out right."

"Didn't it?"

"I'm just saying. He's on a critical mission, one that could put any or all of us in danger. And he's a minister for—for heaven's sake. What he's doing requires high-level field and surveillance training."

"I know, but . . . It was either he takes it, or I go alone. Even if he came with me, I'd be exposed. And after yesterday, well, it seemed like a good idea at the time."

"I get it." He lets out a long breath. "And no, I wouldn't have let you go out there either. I just wish you'd spoken with me. I might have been able to do it."

"You said we had to get rid of the GPS right away. And besides, you were recovering."

"Do you trust him, Xandra?"

That makes me stop and think. Strange, I never asked myself that question. I want to say yes, definitely. But I can't. "I don't know."

A pair of doves walk down the gravelly road. Their cooing fades as they vanish. Over the treetops, an amber veil casts itself over the sky, while the fingers of a gentle breeze run through my hair. The firmness against which my back leans is not the bench but Kyle's arm and shoulder. Exactly when we'd drawn so close eludes me. I must have felt his warmth, but it feels so intrinsical, I don't question it.

Kyle leans over. The warmth of his breath tickles my ear. "Do you trust me?"

I turn to face him, only to find his burnished eyes gazing intently into mine. I've heard somewhere that there are moments in life—rare moments—in which we make a spiritual connection with another human being. A connection so profound, so utterly real, that words cannot suffice in its description. It's a mutual recognition that something greater than either of you has ordained this very moment. This beautiful and yet infuriatingly enigmatic man has risked so much for me. And he asks if I trust him? "With my life."

With his hand resting warmly on my face, he presses his lips to my brow. Fearing this moment will atomize at the slightest disturbance, I dare not breathe. The warmth of his hand flows through my entire being. Through it, I sense the anguish of decades, a longing for truth and meaning, a thirst for culmination.

Our lips touch, like a spark igniting a long fuse. I cannot help but fall into his embrace as we kiss like lovers reunited. I have needed him.

My arms entwine his sturdy body. Gasping between kisses, I open my lips to say his name. Nothing but short breaths come forth. Finally, "I do, Kyle. I do trust you."

"You're safe with me. I promise."

"I know." A pang of dread pierces my heart. "I know." Soon I'm trembling, trying not to cry.

"What's the matter?" Tenderly, he wipes my tears with his thumb.

"I'm just so . . ."

Holding my gaze, his own eyes shimmer, reflecting the twilight sky.

"Everything. I'm happy, I'm grateful . . ."

"But?"

"But I'm scared. Kyle, I'm scared."

He holds me tight, reassures me that everything is going to be all right. "I'm not going to let anything happen to you, don't worry."

"No, it's not that." I touch his face. "I don't think I've ever known such joy, such understanding. I'm so afraid of losing you!"

"You won't. Not if I have anything to say about it."

One of the doves flies out from behind the shrubs and sings a doleful dirge as it ascends the heavens alone. Until the sun has completely expired, and the moon and stars have taken their places in the firmament, I remain nestled in Kyle's protecting arms, the occasional sighing and cooing floating up with the steam of my breath. Oh, that this moment would last.

But it never does.

63

Jake returns, the headlights of the car reminiscent of a panther's feral eyes. It's about seven forty-five. He climbs out, looking worn.

Filled with relief, and a bit of annoyance, I run to him. "What took you so long?" I almost scold him the way Mom would scold me as a teenager for staying out past my curfew—which only happened once or twice.

Maybe three times.

"I might have erred on the side of extremely overcautious," Jake says and hands me the keys. Kyle limps over. "But I reconnected the transceiver in a parking deck in downtown El Centro, left it on for about half an hour. I'll tell you, every car that passed by scared the daylights out of me. I thought for sure I'd be arrested."

"What about the transponder?" Kyle says.

"I disconnected it and tossed it in a pond fifty miles east of El Centro. They'll think you've gone to Arizona."

Kyle sucks his teeth. "Not that simple."

"But thank you." I give Jake's hand a squeeze, discreetly.

"We've got a long day tomorrow, Xandra. Lots to do." Kyle starts back to the rectory. "We should get an early start."

"Are you up to it?" Jake asks him.

"I'm just fine, thanks."

"Because if you're feeling too weak, you can stay and rest up as long as you—"

"I said I'm fine!"

I turn to Kyle and pat his chest, the way I'd pat Oscar, our old Labrador, whenever he'd bark aggressively at visitors to the house. "Hey, take it easy."

Kyle turns and walks back into the rectory. "Early start in the morning. That's when we'll be leaving, Pastor."

Oh, we will? I'm tempted to make a snappy comeback and say something to the effect of having to consult with me before trying to dictate my schedule. But he's right. We've lost precious time and must get going.

Jake looks at me. "What's gotten into him?"

"Never mind him. Thank you so much for helping us with the transponder."

"Glad to be of service."

"There's one last thing."

"Yes?"

"Eli wants to speak with you."

64

Kyle had hoped to avoid seeing people when we left, but in the end everyone came out to say good-bye. Even Eli. Kyle thanked him for saving his life. Eli even came to me and said in a conciliatory voice, "You're a good girl. Be careful out there. Don't let the darkness overtake you."

Whatever had been troubling Kyle last night didn't seem like much of an issue this morning. He shook hands and patted backs with Jake like a good sport.

When it was time for me to bid Jake farewell, I felt my face heat up. We shook hands, but soon thought it silly and hugged instead. "You're a godsend, Jake. I can't believe how lucky we were to meet you."

"Not luck. Everything's connected, remember."

"Of course."

"See you soon, Xandra."

Just as I was about to get into the car, Rebecca came running. She held a rag doll up to my face. "Xandi, this is Dolly."

"Hello, Dolly."

"I told her she needs to go with you."

"Are you sure?"

"Uh huh." She puts Dolly in my hands. "Whenever I get scared at night, I just hold her, and we pray together."

"Well, thank you Becky. I'll take good care of her."

"And remember to spin a little, every day." With a wide grin, sans front teeth, she curtseys.

After winding through manifold unnamed roads some twenty miles from the colony, the nearest 7-Eleven stands like an oasis. No cell phones on our persons: they were turned off long ago and buried in the barn where the morning cows went to get milked. It's all part of the plan.

We're discreet, Kyle in sunglasses and baseball cap courtesy of Pastor Jake, and I hiding in the restroom while he makes his purchases. I'll confess, his confidence and skill are as attractive as his chiseled features.

Three minutes later we're driving into Nowheresville with breakfast burritos, coffee, and a white, green, and red plastic bag full of prepaid cell phones and calling cards.

I reach for a bacon-and-cheese burrito and cup of coffee, the aroma of which wafts up into my nose and makes my mouth water. "How much did all that cost?"

"Most of my cash. We'll have to be careful how we spend from now on."

"My credit cards are maxed, and I've got less than a hundred dollars on my debit card, not that I can use it anyway." Not with my every financial transaction being tracked.

It's the first cup of coffee I've had in what feels like years. It might as well be a magical elixir, judging by the way my entire body awakens to the mere scent of it. While I drink and nibble on my breakfast, Kyle makes a call on one of the new phones. All the technical jargon he employs discourages me from eavesdropping, so I just tune him out for the duration of the call.

"Thanks, Glen, I owe you." Kyle ends the call and hands me the cell phone. "Communications are set."

"Great. Who's Glen?"

"An IT-Telecom engineer back at the field office. I've worked with him for years. He's helped me on more cases than I'd like to remember, or admit."

"How is he going to help us?"

"By getting a prepaid cell phone, calling cards, and dialing instructions to your father so we can reduce the chances of detection when we communicate."

"Isn't your friend in Virginia?"

"One of the advantages of knowing a guy who spends his whole life on the internet: he's got friends all over the world."

"You think his Facebook buddies are reliable?"

"Facebook?"

I let out a frustrated grunt. "You *know* what I mean."

"If Glen says his friend will do it . . ." But Kyle doesn't finish his sentence, and the half he did speak lacked conviction. "It'll happen."

"How can you be certain?"

"Because if he lets me down, he's a dead man."

I roll my eyes. "Lovely."

He shrugs, and after a few minutes of neither of us speaking, he turns on the radio. A sleazy talk-show host is yelling.

"What do you expect? I'm telling you, this Carrick chick is guilty as sin! She's probably doing that FBI agent and running off to South America with a boatload of embezzled money. But hey! I say, if you can get away with it, rock on! Run, baby. Run like the wind!"

"That's not particularly helpful." I smack the dial and shut off the radio.

"Hey, I was listening to that." Kyle turns it back on.

"Try a less trashy station."

Through the dark lenses of his shades, he glares at me and then turns the dial. This time he stops on NPR. The announcer goes on to speak about the elections.

". . . and today, on the eve of the election, Independent presidential candidate Richard Colson has the analysts on the edge of their seats. Most predict that he will win."

"At least there's some good news there."

Kyle scoffs. "You can't be serious. Colson?"

"Yeah. He's got my vote. What about you?"

"Not."

"Oh let me guess, you're a Republican."

"What if I were?"

"Are you kidding? Haven't you had enough of the current re-gime?"

"He isn't on the ticket. And I don't trust Colson. Something about him."

"It's not in your nature to trust, is it? Anyway, Colson reminds me of my father."

With a smirk Kyle says, "Oh so that's it. He reminds you of Daddy?"

"Quiet, you." Disarmed by his attempt at ribbing me, I jab him with my elbow. At which he lets out a hissing groan.

"Ow! Watch it!" It was his wound.

"Sorry."

"Yeah, sure."

We've kept clear of the freeway and taken many a back road. After forty-five minutes of driving, we arrive at Larry's Preowned Cars. By some strange maneuvering, Kyle has persuaded Larry to lend us a car. I use the terms "persuade" and "lend" in their broadest sense.

"So you'll take this Camry that Larry has so graciously loaned us, and I'll take Srinivasu's limo," Kyle says, holding the door open for me. I slide into the driver's seat and adjust the seat.

"Are we going to split up?"

"No. We're going to drive together to a lake five miles from here and sink Sri's car. From there, we'll take the Camry. And go straight to Hank Jennings—"

"No. I told you, we go to my father first."

"He's in Del Mar, Xandra. Alpine's the opposite way. If there's any chance of stopping these people, we're going to have to find out if anyone unusual has contacted Jennings."

"I will not put a stranger before my family."

We're raising our voices now. Kyle sees that and comes to the window, leans on it, and calms himself. In a patronizing tone that irritates me to no end, he says: "I don't think you understand."

"Don't I?"

"This conspiracy goes beyond any one government agency. I've put everything on the line to expose it."

My jaw falls open. "So you want me to put my father on the line for one of your cases! I should have known. That's all that matters, your investigation. You betrayed me in New York, and you're doing it again now!"

"Look, that wasn't supposed to happen."

"But it did!"

"How many times do I need to apologize for that? I'll say it again if it makes you feel better: I'm sorry, all right? But right now—"

"This is not just some pet case of yours, Kyle! It's my father's life. It's my life!"

He lets out a long breath and speaks slowly, as if by doing so, I will understand better. "You really don't understand, Xandra. The first—"

"Save it!" Furious, I shift the car into drive.

"Where do you think you're going?"

"If you'd been paying any attention, you wouldn't have to ask."

"You don't know what you're doing!"

Final straw. "No, *you* don't know!" Before he can say another word, I kick the accelerator and speed off.

65

KYLE MATTHEWS

Standing in the dust cloud Xandra kicked up as she sped away, I'm trying to comprehend how she could act so recklessly. Of course her father is her priority, but allowing emotions to determine one's course of action is the surest way to failure.

Peter Carrick may very well become a target. And we do need to arrange a meeting with him, as he could provide more information. But it all needs to be done under the radar.

Speaking with Hank Jennings is the first thing we must do, because he's the next probable target. And he's probably the best bet for clues as to the killer's identity.

From Xandra's point of view, though, I'm unreasonably consumed with solving this case. What she doesn't know is that it's not just a professional obsession.

In 1988, Lieutenant Raymond O'Neil was the second Vietnam veteran from Echo Company to die prematurely. Local authorities officially filed his death as a suicide brought on by posttraumatic stress disorder, but I knew better. Raymond O'Neil was my uncle.

My father passed away when I was about three years old, so Uncle Ray, Momma's older brother, was the father figure in my life. Yes, he had been treated for PTSD. But it was his faith and the loving support of his family and friends that helped him overcome the nightmares and relapses.

He and I were close enough for me to know to an absolute certainty that he would never have killed himself. I'd sooner believe it if he were to be struck by lightning three times in a row, hit by a truck, then mauled by a polar bear. Not only was suicide against his beliefs, he just had too much joy and gratitude at that point in his life.

"I've found my peace and forgiveness in Jesus," he'd tell me. "I'm a new creation. The old is gone and the new has come."

I was only twelve when they came to his house and wheeled his body away under a white sheet. I can remember the shock on Momma's face, her hand holding back a scream of terror. I ran over shouting, "Uncle Ray, Uncle Ray!"

For weeks, Momma kept telling me to be at peace. He was with the Lord now, and all things work for the good of those who love God, etcetera, etcetera. But I always knew there was something suspicious about his death. And that is what drove me to a degree in law-enforcement investigation, then directly to the FBI Academy.

In my nine years of service I've been honored three times for investigative excellence by the Bureau. But none of that means a thing to me. Not while Uncle Ray's killer—or killers—continues to go unchecked.

So, while I'm not about to admit it to her just yet, Xandra is not the only one taking this personally.

I enter the car, slam the door shut, and start the ignition. *Why does she have to complicate things? Why now, when we're so close to the key that will lead me to the case that has haunted me for twenty years?* The voice of that twelve-year-old boy whose uncle, the closest thing he ever had to a father, was murdered, cries out for justice. *Forget Xandra, follow your head, not your heart.*

Another voice urges me to go after her. It's the voice of that part of me that longs to stop hunting and find peace with the woman who, despite her emotionalism, makes me feel whole. She might very well be walking into the lions' den.

Pulling up to the intersection, the proverbial fork in the road confronts me like Cerberus at the gates of Hades. To the east, Jennings's house. To the west, Peter Carrick's.

66

XANDRA CARRICK

I really ought not to be here like this. But Dad has not answered any of my calls on his cell, nor in his house. There are no cars parked along the long road leading to his house on the hill, so I can assume that he has no visitors. But even as I pull up into the fountain rotary, a sense of dread courses through my blood.

This place has never truly been home. Mom and Dad moved out here during my first semester at Princeton. And during the few holidays that brought me back, I felt like a guest, even though they had set up a guest room for my exclusive use.

Don't get me wrong; it's a splendid house. High vaulted ceilings, chandeliers that sparkle with refracted rainbows, rococo crown molding that frames every room and door. The photographic art that adorns the walls tells a story. This house is Dad's personal gallery.

The baby grand Steinway—which many a pianist had played, accompanying me for rehearsals and recitals at home—brings nothing but emptiness, disillusionment. Still, Mom insisted on bringing it all the way from New York.

The security key code still lingers in my mind from the months I spent living with Dad last year. I punch the numbers into the keypad and open the door. The alarm beeps twice. It's already been disarmed. "Dad?"

The lime alarm console LCD reads:

WATCHPOINT 14 DEN

He must be in his study with the window open to the coastal view he enjoys so much. "Dad?"

Bringing the Graflex back here reminds me of a salmon fighting all kinds of turbulent conditions to return to the spawning ground of its birth. As I step through the threshold and enter the wide open foyer, that inner rumbling alerts me. The tingling radiates from my heart to my hands and feet.

I reach into my backpack and take hold of the Graflex. Before I even take it out, several images flash into my mind.

An elderly Vietnamese man, on his knees, squinting in anticipation of something truly terrible.

Two Vietnamese girls, sisters—twelve and fourteen years of age—curled on a straw mat. Blood stains their torn white shirts. They're shrieking, eyes wide with trauma.

This is not a full-on vision, as I'm still aware of my surroundings. But the images flash quick and clear.

I don't want to see this, because I'm starting to recognize the dread I felt at the door. Quickly, I shake it off. Pull my hand from the backpack.

Again, I call out to Dad. My voice echoes through the marble-lined hallways. *Please be home. I need to speak with you about these visions.* A door opens upstairs. Any second now I expect he'll show up, take me in his arms, and make sure I'm all right. I make my way up the winding staircase and turn toward the den.

More images assail my inner mind:

Corporal Hank Jennings.

A ditch with bodies. It's Bình Sơn. The Mekong Delta!

There's Dad, taking pictures with the Graflex!

My knees buckle. I grasp the balustrade. "Dad, where are you?" Though it cannot possibly be, it feels as though these images come from within my memory.

But if these visions persist, I think I'll be ill. When they come in such rapid succession, the nausea is almost too much. Straining, I pull myself up.

The alarm system beeps.

Which means another window or door has opened.

It's not the front door, I can see from up here.

"Dad?" I whimper, not realizing until now how frightened I've grown. His den is just ahead. The door is open. God, please let him be there.

But he's not. I gasp as I behold the sight. Papers strewn all over the floor, blowing in the wind of the open window. Desk drawers ripped out and overturned, their contents strewn all over the floor. Locked file cabinets pried open. Who's been here? Why is the den the only room that seems to have been touched?

A casualty of this pillaging, an old photo of Dad with the soldiers of Echo Company in Vietnam lies on the floor, the glass shattered. I should get out, but I cannot help but examine it closely. While gazing carefully at each face in the black-and-white photo, I lift my hand and touch the frame.

Without warning, a vision grips my mind.

Dad!

Someone takes him at gunpoint and forces him into a car. It's not a vision of the past. Dad's hair is gray, and he's wearing the jacket I bought him last month.

Suddenly, I'm falling. I catch hold of the back of a chair and brace myself. *Breathe . . . don't pass out!* My entire body has gone pins and needles now. The images become more insistent. I almost feel like I'm being pushed into doing something. Dad's safe. The panic room. *Get out!*

The next alarm system beep confirms my fears. I'm not alone! With labored steps, I stagger into Dad's bedroom.

It's untouched.

Letting out a strained grunt, I pull on the headboard of his king-size, four-poster bed and slide it away from the wall. There, built into the wall is a safe, the combination of which Dad insisted Mom and I memorize:

5-7-7-5

Their wedding anniversary.

Not the most secure passcode, but easy enough to remember when under duress. Out in the halls of this five-thousand-square-foot house, someone opens and closes a door. *Hurry.* My fingers slip, and the dial spins the wrong way.

"Come on!"

Again, I dial the combination.

Footsteps come thumping up the stairs to the second floor.

The safety box opens. There, like a perfectly preserved artifact, lies a handgun, which I take with my jittery hands. They're so slick with perspiration, I'm afraid the gun will slide out.

A blast of amber sunlight hits me in the eyes as I pass the open window. For a moment I'm blinded. The only thing I hear is the sound of the ocean, door hinges in the distance, and the percussion of my own heart.

From the sound of the rushing footfalls, there's more than one person in the house—no fewer than two. Furtive murmuring, irregular movement patterns. They're looking for something, or someone.

Should I call the police? I'm a fugitive, hunted by God knows how many law enforcement agencies—probably not. The panic room! That's why I saw it. I'll hide there until they leave.

Regardless, I can't just stand around here. The master bedroom has a door leading directly to the media room. From there I can exit to the back stairs and go directly to the panic room. Or continue downstairs past the mud room, then the garage.

I open the door, steal inside, and shut the door behind me.

Pitch black. Of course.

There are no windows in the home theater room. If only I could remember where those light switches are. The farther in I walk, the shakier my breath gets. It's still as death in here. The acoustic insulation and heavy curtains dampen any sound that might escape.

But sounds in the room can be heard. Such as someone taking a step onto the carpet before me.

Someone's in here with me.

If I could find the door, I would turn and run. But any move I make will give my position away. Silent as I can, I bring the gun up in front with both hands.

Cock the hammer.

Within a fraction of a second, another gun hammer clicks right in front of me.

"DROP IT!" he hisses.

"YOU drop it!"

In an instant, I thrust my hands forward. The muzzle of my gun presses against something. It moves at first then freezes in place. Then something cold and metallic presses against my forehead.

There's going to be blood.

67

GRACE TH'AM AI LE

Del Mar, California: December 31, 1999

Sitting on the deck of our beautiful house overlooking the Pacific Ocean, I now see what Peter meant over twenty years ago when he described the beauty of a Pacific sunset. Life has been wonderful since we've moved out to San Diego, Peter's birthplace. Del Mar is such a beautiful place. So quiet, so serene, and the ocean view is spectacular.

Peter has not had any secret meetings for six years now, and I am happy to say that he is becoming more and more like the man who loved Phở Ga and proposed to me not once but twice.

Xandra has been accepted to Princeton on a full scholarship. She has grown into a fine, trustworthy young woman. Serious about her work and studies, not like those loose girls you hear about who think only about parties, sex, and drugs. No, Xandra has taken after her father and become an award-winning photographer in her own right. Peter doesn't show it, but we both know that deep inside he's proud. As a graduation present, he gave her his Graflex camera, the one that helped him win the Pulitzer.

The stocks Peter's invested in, once fledgling internet companies, have returned over four million dollars in gains. Financially, we are set for life. And yet I am troubled by dreams and visions concerning Peter and now Xandra. The images seem random, and I cannot discern their meanings as clearly as I could when I was younger. Perhaps it is my advancing age.

Del Mar, California: September 11, 2001

We were awakened by a phone call from Peter's colleague in New York. Right away, while still on the phone, he tossed me the remote and motioned for me to turn on the TV.

On every channel, the most horrific, surreal scene imaginable filled the screen. Over and over again, the footage of a huge airliner crashing into the Twin Towers played.

But what really made me cry out loud was when one of the towers just crumbled like sand. If you have never stood on the sidewalk and tried to look up to the top of the Twin Towers, you would have no idea of just how immense those buildings were.

It was like a scene from a high-budget Hollywood disaster movie. But it was real. And that is what put me in a state of shock, my hand over my open mouth the entire time I watched.

"Dammit!" Peter had been trying to make a call on his cell phone, then on the landline. "I can't get through."

That's when I remembered. Xandi had taken a semester off to work an internship for a law firm located in the World Trade Center towers. "Oh Peter, you have to call her!"

"That's all I've been doing, but the circuits are busy."

Then came the footage of people leaping from burning offices. How awful it must have been for them to choose to die by jumping to their deaths. A dark voice in the back of my mind said, *That could be her.*

"No!"

"Grace, what are you—?"

Right away, I grabbed my Bible, clutched it to my chest, and prayed. I didn't care that Peter shook his head, or that he of all people thought I was being superstitious. I just prayed. And a verse came to my mind.

A more familiar voice spoke to me in my spirit. Not the dark one, but the bright, comforting one. *Proclaim it.*

Proclaim what?

The Word.

I opened my Bible without thinking. There under my fingertip was a verse I had never read before. From Psalm 118.

Proclaim it for her.

And I read it aloud. Repeated it again. Because it was for my Xandi's sake, I continued to repeat it.

"I shall not die, but live, and declare the works of the LORD."

Del Mar, California: September 12, 2001

Peter did not sleep at all last night. He kept trying to call Xandra, kept watching the nonstop news reports. Only once did he attempt to lie down, and that was at my insistence.

Finally, around nine forty-five a.m., we got the call.

It was Xandi!

She was all right. Yes, she was in the South Tower before it went down. Her entire law firm had a good lead and began to evacuate together down a stairwell.

But she heard the voice of an elderly woman across the hall. It was one of those women who pushed a cart around selling bagels and coffee every day. She had tripped, and her cart had fallen and pinned her leg to the ground.

Xandi watched as every one of her coworkers rushed for the stairs. But she could not just leave the old lady there. So, despite the urging of her friends not to, she went down the hall to help the bagel lady.

Xandra and the lady ended up going down a different stairwell and eventually made it out alive, thank God.

"But Mom, that's not the most incredible thing of all this."

Xandi was crying when she told me this. "No one else from my of-fice made it out."

That day, Peter even said to me, "Maybe there *is* a God."

Del Mar, California: July 4, 2007

I cannot sleep tonight. The fireworks have stopped, the people have gone home after a wonderful barbecue that Peter arranged with our neighbors and my friends from church. I am awake at two thirty in the morning because of three things.

For one, Peter's nightmares have returned. And when he ex-periences them, I am the one who is kept up.

Another reason is that I am so worried about Xandi, who right now is on assignment in Iraq, doing a feature on female sui-cide bombers.

Peter forbade her to go, which of course only goaded her fur-ther. He thinks she's trying to outdo him, though he denies any sense of competition. I honestly think she's trying to prove some-thing, to win his approval.

"It just takes a couple of words," I always tell him. "You can speak life into her by just telling her how proud you are of her."

"Oh, come on," he'll say, brushing it off. "She knows."

But I don't think she does. Since she was twelve, she's been trying to win his affection. By the time she turned sixteen, it was apparent she would just settle for any attention, positive or nega-tive. She still does, in my opinion. Which is one reason I believe she dated that terrible young man, Ethan. He was everything her father wasn't. Negative attention.

But instead of dealing with it, Peter asked me to talk with her. Of course, Peter has started again with those secret meetings. Where are those visions now? Perhaps it's best if I don't know about those meetings. Perhaps I truly am being protected. At least he is not flying away for days at a time now. But the very memory of those days early in our marriage causes me to feel ill.

And that brings me to the third reason I can't sleep. I've been suffering from severe migraines. Peter has taken me to some specialists, but so far none of the medications they've prescribed has helped. Putting a bright face on it all, I keep my family from worry. But I fear it may be worse than anyone imagines.

68

KYLE MATTHEWS

We were shouting simultaneously. All I can tell is that it's a woman. No time to speculate, she's got her weapon pressed into my chest. What was I thinking coming after Xandra like this? It goes completely against protocol. This is what I get for following my heart.

We're both breathing heavily. I've got to take control of this situation. "All right," I whisper. "We're both going to have to—"

"*Kyle?*"

"Xandra, is that you?" The gun lifts away from my chest. I lower mine as well.

"Yes. Where are the lights?"

"What are you doing sneaking around in my father's house? I almost killed you!"

Reaching out, I find her hand. It's clammy and shaking. The thought that I almost put a bullet through her head horrifies me. Thank God I didn't. "I decided, against my better judgment, to come after you. Where's your father?"

"I don't know. But whoever ransacked his office—they're still here."

Someone's rummaging around behind the door to Carrick's bedroom. "We have to get out of here."

"Back stairs," Xandra says. "We can get to the garage."

"I just came up that way. The back door was unlocked.

Caught a glimpse. Three men. They look like Secret Service agents."

"Real ones?"

"Hard to tell. But they're armed." The person stalking about Carrick's bedroom is stepping toward the door. "We have to go back down." I take Xandra's hand and lead her in the dark toward the rear door.

Groping in the dark, I find the wall, and finally the doorknob. The bedroom door opens behind us.

A shot rings out. "Get down!" The bullet whisks over us. I fire two shots into the dark. I feel under my feet the heavy thud of a body hitting the ground. Taking Xandra's hand, I lead her to the exit.

Someone else pushes against the bedroom entrance to the media room, but the body of their fallen colleague blocks it. Xandra aims her gun back at them and pulls the trigger.

Nothing but an empty click. She forgot to insert the clip.

Blindly, I fire two more shots in their direction and push Xandra through the exit door. But two agents force their way into the media room. They fire several shots, a couple of which hit the exit door.

Just in time, we escape into the long hallway that leads to the back stairs. But the door jams as I try to shut it. It must have been damaged by the bullets. "Can't close it," I whisper.

"Wait," Xandra whispers and pulls my arm back.

"What is it?"

"Don't move."

Her whims are getting on my nerves, especially now, with a dangerous situation bursting at the seams. "We don't have time for—" Right when I take a step forward, the hallway lights—which I now realize are controlled by a motion sensor—activate.

Xandra whispers something not particularly nice.

One glance back tells me that the bright lights I just turned on are now streaming through the crack I left in the doorway. The footfalls in the home theater rushing toward us confirm this. "We've got her," the voice of our pursuer says after a walkie-talkie beep.

To make matters worse, another set of footsteps pound up the back staircase, converging on our position. "We're trapped."

Xandra takes me by the arm and leads me through the hallway. "Maybe not." Running her hand along the wall, she stops at a picture frame. She slips her hand behind the picture. Suddenly, a panel in the wall recesses and slides to the left. A hidden door appears. "Panic room."

69

XANDRA CARRICK

The panel slides open. I pull Kyle into the panic room and shut the door.

He jiggles the doorknob. "There's no lock!"

"It's all electronic," I tell him, fumbling with the keypad on this side of the panic room. The first combination yields a rude beep.

"Doesn't matter, they'll wait us out. Or burn the house down."

Two words enter my mind: *auxiliary exit*. That's right. I almost forgot. Dad told me about it during the orientation held by the company that installed the panic room. The auxiliary exit was designed as a last-measure fail-safe if the panic room is breached.

I punch in the correct sequence and enter my security code. "Follow me." I take Kyle's hand and lead him past the bathroom and kitchenette to the back of the room. "Check for another control panel door hidden in the wall."

"Got it!"

"Two-two-three-eight-one!"

He enters it and another door opens. We get inside and the door slides shut. On the monochrome monitor screen, two men in black suits rush into the panic room. Their guns are held out ready to shoot.

I hit the red button with an octagonal icon. The entire panic room goes pitch black. A heavy slam confirms what is now displayed on the monitor:

PANIC ROOM SEALED

"Let's go."

Kyle follows me, his eyes still drawn to the monitor. "I assume the room is lined to—"

"Block cell phone signals, yes. At least, that's what they told Dad. Only the right access code can remove the shield." For all intents and purposes those men are trapped inside until we let them out.

The auxiliary exit leads us to a tunnel that ends at a ladder stretching up to a hatch door. We climb out and find ourselves standing on a hill overlooking the road leading up to Dad's house. Wincing from his wound, Kyle points to his car parked outside the gate; we make haste to get in and drive off.

"Your father's got the cell phone and calling cards. He's gone dark until he can contact us safely."

"I am such an idiot. Should have known they'd come here."

"Your father's clearly a target now."

I'm not concerned with the thugs locked in the panic room—there's enough food and water to sustain a family of five for two weeks. The real question lies with Kyle. "Why did you come?"

"Following my heart, for a change." He puts his gun down on the center console and turns to me. "Still, you should have discussed this carefully before storming off like that."

"What would you have said?"

"Besides waiting until we make a plan with your father, that it was too dangerous to go to his house." He strains and puts his hand over his wound. "By the way, why does a photographer need a panic room?"

"Doesn't every public figure have one?"

"No."

"Dad always told us that public figures—wealthy ones in particular—are always potential targets of crime. That's why he made sure we knew about the room, the gun, how to use it. My mother wouldn't even look at the gun."

"Well, all I can say is, I'm glad I came."

Grateful that this was the closest he came to saying "I told you so," I redirect the conversation to something that I've wanted to ask since Kyle showed up on my flight to San Diego. "Just what is it about this case that's got you so obsessed? You're as driven as I am, but what's your motivation?"

He presses his lips into a tight line. Finally, after some deliberation, he speaks. "My father died in a mining accident when I was three. So I was raised by a single mother. But I had a strong father figure up until I was twelve. My uncle Ray. You might be familiar with his name."

"Can't say I—"

"He was a member of Echo Company."

"Oh!" It doesn't take a vision now to know what he's getting at. "Lieutenant Raymond O'Neil."

"That's right."

"Didn't he take his own life?"

"Absolutely not. And trust me, I'm not exaggerating when I say his murder was what drove me into a career with the FBI. For twenty years, I've hunted his killer."

It all makes sense now. Caressing his hand, I let out a long breath. "Kyle, if my mistake costs us the chance to find out who's been killing the Echo Company vets, your uncle . . ."

"There's still a chance. I spoke with Jennings earlier. He's expecting us." Gradually, his fingers intertwine with mine. His warmth infuses me from my hand to the center of my being. For the next couple of miles we're silent.

"Since we're being so open here, there's another question I've been meaning to ask."

"Shoot."

I'm not particularly fond of that phrase at the moment. "How is it you never questioned my ability to see visions? I think I've had more doubt than you."

He considers the question. Rubs the back of his neck—which I continue for him—and then answers. "For one thing, I know you're sincere."

"But it's so bizarre. Makes no sense scientifically."

"One thing Uncle Ray taught me that I've never forgotten: things that can't be explained by science are in themselves evidence of its limitations."

It takes a few seconds to sink in. "So you don't think science can explain everything."

"If I did, I wouldn't have solved half of my cases."

"So, how many psychics have you consulted with over the years?"

"None."

"Really? I'm the first?"

"You're no psychic."

"How exactly has Uncle Ray's wisdom guided you then?"

"It's just thinking outside the box. I took this with me to the Academy where Professor Blake Danielson refined my thinking. Believe it or not, the way I approach my cases, as well as my choice to believe in your abilities, has its roots in mathematical concepts."

This turns my head and causes me to stop massaging his neck. "Mathematical concepts?"

"Are you familiar with decision theory?"

"I studied it in college. Briefly." He can tell I'm lying.

"All right, how about probability theory?"

"Something about finding patterns in rolling dice?"

"Oh, and finally, there's Pascal's Wager."

I sit up, galvanized, because this is one I actually remember from high school. "If reason can't be relied upon, it's a better bet to believe in God than not to."

"I'm not saying that every paranormal event I encounter is about God. But I don't automatically dismiss it as nonsense either. Based on the events that brought us together, and the flawless accuracy of your visions, it seems the better bet to believe your abilities are real than not to."

"Even if you can't explain them rationally."

"Right."

Though it's a bit of a stretch, I lean over and kiss him on the cheek. "Thank you."

"For what?"

"For believing me." I put my hand in his. "And coming for me."

70

We're pulling up to a secluded property, where a dirt road stretches out for at least a quarter of a mile before we see anything that resembles a house. At the top of a hill, tall palms glower down upon the sun-scorched grass, most of which is golden, save for the lawn areas surrounding Jennings's ranch house.

Dusty clouds rise up behind the car, and tiny stones grind under the wheels as we arrive. Judging by the cobwebs in the wheel wells of the white Dodge Ram parked on the side of the house, I'd guess old Hank hasn't driven it in years.

Toward the back of the property, a black horse grazing in a pen lifts its head and stares at us with ears perked. After a while it blows, shakes its mane, and resumes grazing.

"It's quiet out here." A cool breeze runs through my hair, tickles my neck, and makes me shudder. "Bit too quiet."

"I like it that way." He gives me a peculiar look and pats the backpack I've brought with me. "What's that for?"

"The Graflex. Just in case. You never know."

We approach the porch, and before he knocks on the screen door's frame, a loud squawk from directly above makes me jump. "Holy—! What in the world?" Kyle just chuckles and points up. Perched on the rain gutter is a huge black bird. "That's one honkin' crow."

"Raven. You city chicks don't know jack."

"Quoth the farmboy, 'Nevermore.' "

"What?"

"Who doesn't know jack? Or in this case, Edgar."

"You're weird." The stupid raven doesn't budge even when Kyle waves his hand to shoo it away. Once again, he knocks on the flimsy door frame.

No response.

He knocks again. "Hello? Mr. Jennings?"

But still there is no answer. The raven caws once again and this time spreads its wings—which, up close, are surprisingly large—and flies away. One of its black feathers alights on the shoulder strap of my backpack.

"Not going to break down the door, are you?"

He opens the screen door and tries the doorknob. To my surprise, the door is unlocked. He steps inside and says, "You watch too much TV."

Immediately, a stench of something like months-old food you discover in the back of the refrigerator wages an olfactory assault. Trash bags, newspapers, garbage, and magazines cover the floor like a carpet.

"Anyone home?"

"Mr. Jennings?"

We've knocked on and opened every door, but there's no sign of him. With great care, I wade through the trash and follow Kyle into a den on the second floor.

After a quick look, Kyle steps out. "I'll check the bedrooms."

Something on the far side of the room catches my eye. In a glass display case on the wall are war medals. Next to them, old sepia-tone pictures of young soldiers.

He's got a Purple Heart and a letter from the White House in a nice frame. There's something here, I sense it. But not in the natural realm. So I unzip my backpack and snap off two pictures with the Graflex.

The medals, the framed pictures, and then . . .

A low-pitched rumbling like thunder fills my ears. Everything around me fades into shadows. Extremities go cold and tingly. *Here we go.* The images from that one photo, with the soldiers standing in front of a jeep in the rice fields of Vietnam, float up from the frame.

Before I realize what's happened, I'm transported into another realm. Everything exists in monochrome, sepia tones. Different images, like movie clips flash before me. Only it's real.

Machine-gun rapid fire, mortar shells, white hospital beds, Jennings's wife who has left with their baby boy in her arms.

Now it's Hank Jennings. His hair white, his blue eyes faded and wide open, not blinking. All around the back of his head, a crown of dry hay. A single ribbon of sunlight cuts through the musty air.

Because I've experienced it before, I know what's happening. And though I can't break out of this state, I call out, in case Kyle can hear me.

"I know where he is!"

Then a heartbeat.

Pounding, pounding, pounding. It stops, and for some reason, so does my own breathing. I can't adequately describe this sensation—it's cold, it's lonely, it's dark.

It's death.

71

"He's in the stable, Kyle!" Black and golden curtains of light fall, tearing the vision away. I'm left gripping the Graflex so hard the loose parts are rattling.

"What was that?" Kyle steps into the den, concern scrawled across his face. "You okay?"

"I'm fine. Just had another vision. He's in the stable." My head is spinning, but I have enough presence of mind to start for the door. But along the way, I trip. My knee hits the floor, and I let out a pained grunt.

Kyle stops, turns back, and as he stoops to help me up, grits his teeth and strains. His wound might be reopening.

I wave him off. "Don't worry about me, just hurry. I'll catch up." He puts his hands around my waist anyway and pulls me to my feet.

A minute later, we're in the stable. It takes a few seconds before my eyes adjust to the sudden darkness. Still out in the pen, the horse whinnies and grunts and paces around in large circles as we call out to Jennings. Except for the hay, none of this looks like my vision.

Rubbing his chin, Kyle eyes the entire stable in a slow three-sixty. "You sure?"

"I know what I saw."

"Can you give me some details? Otherwise, I'll just grab that pitchfork and start—"

A sharp gasp whisks through my lips. "There!"

"What?" He has no idea what I mean because I'm not pointing. To him, I'm merely staring into the air.

Just a few steps ahead, through a small crack in the splintery boards that make up the wall, a lone strip of sunlight stretches down at an acute angle. Flecks of dust fashion it into a golden laser beam pointing to a spot in the hay.

My breath is shallow, tremulous. Two false starts, and I realize what I'll find if I run over and start digging in the hay. "Under there, Kyle." Now I point. "He's there."

"All right, stay here." His steps are padded by a thick carpet of sawdust. Slowly, Kyle kneels by the pinpoint of light and reaches into the hay.

I'm terrified. That same sense of death fills my heart like India ink. Once again the images flash before me. I've still got the Graflex strapped around my neck. It feels like a noose.

Kyle pulls up a fistful of hay and tosses it aside. "I don't see anything . . ." Another bunch. "Here!"

From beneath the pile of hay, a bony hand claws blindly. Grabs at Kyle's arm. Kyle swears and pulls the old man up, props him against the wall. "Hank Jennings?"

But the old soldier clutches at his own chest, his throat. Like an extradited fish, his mouth gapes open then shuts. His eyes roll back. It takes all my willpower to go over to him.

"Hang on, Mr. Jennings. I'll call for help."

"Xandra, don't," Kyle calls out.

"We can't just let him die!"

Jennings reaches out and touches my arm before I can reach for my cell phone. His fingers dig into my sleeve and then go slack. With eyes and mouth still wide open, he slumps back against the wall. Not so much as a breath.

"Oh no. Come on, don't—!" Kyle starts performing CPR, but

it's no use. After a few minutes it's clear that Jennings is gone. What good are these visions if I'm always too late? But Kyle continues to try to revive him.

"Kyle . . ."

"No, wait." His efforts grow more desperate. "Come on, Hank, come on!"

"Kyle, please. It's too late."

"You don't understand. We need him. I need him. He's got the answers . . ." Eventually Kyle sees the futility of his efforts. He stops and wipes his brow. Then he lets out a grunt and punches the thin plywood wall repeatedly, snarling in frustration.

For the first time, I perceive despair in his eyes. Had I not been so stubborn, so prideful, we might have come here first, arrived in time to prevent this, and found answers that could bring us closer to uncovering the truth.

"He was the last of Echo Company."

"I'm sorry." I reach over and touch his hand. I sense his pain. He's wondering if he'll ever find his uncle's killers. "What about Colson?"

"Didn't you hear? He won the election by a landslide."

"That's great. Why don't we—"

"If we try to contact him or get anywhere near him, we'll be arrested. Every law-enforcement agency is looking for us. It's too late."

We seemed to have passed "too late" sometime ago. I'm so tired of this, the stress, the anxiety, I almost want to give up. But I can't.

"I can't believe we can't get any help. It's not just us, not just my father. There could be an assassination attempt on Colson!"

"Don't worry about him, he's got the entire Secret Service and Homeland Security. Right now our priority is staying alive, under the radar."

"My father might have some information." Though what he knows is quite different from what he's willing to discuss. It's all I can offer, and it's not enough to express my regret.

Kyle gently sets the old man down in the hay. "We've stumbled upon something serious enough that someone's willing to kill for it, three decades after the fact. We've got to get out of here."

"What's the next step?"

"Hank's got to have a gun somewhere in his house. Let's go."

It seems wrong somehow to just leave Jennings's body there. But Kyle's right. There's likely a high price on our heads now. We can't risk getting caught. As we return to the house, I wonder aloud, "How did he kill Jennings?"

"No blood, visible wounds. Looked like he was having a seizure or asphyxiating. I'm sure the ME will deem it a natural death."

"Natural?"

"Like the others."

In the den once again, a cold drop of perspiration rolls down the middle of my back. Kyle rifles through every drawer, every cabinet. There's that tingling sensation in my extremities. It's about to happen again.

From the back of a desk drawer he pulls out a handgun, holds it up to the light, and checks it. "That's better."

I, however, am preoccupied with the sensations of a forthcoming vision. So I quickly pick up the Graflex and start snapping off pictures of anything and everything that might possibly be relevant to our search for answers.

As I take a picture of the gun, it happens. Kyle's voice fades into a wash of white noise. The spinning in my head isn't so disorienting this time. And the rush of wind doesn't make me tense up as much. Instead of simply seeing images now, I'm now standing in them.

I'm in a carpeted hallway with dim sconce lights on the walls that are lined with textured wallpaper and fleur de lis accents and borders. The carpet smells like cigarette smoke. The hallway is cavernous and silent.

Save for the sound of murmurs behind closed doors.

It's coming from the one at the end of the hall. In an instant, without opening the door, I'm in the room. The murmurs are now clear as glass. Someone's shouting in the inner room. I step into the foyer and let out a terrified cry.

On the ground, a body lies in an expanding pool of blood by my feet. I don't know who it is, and yet it feels like I do.

A shout comes from the next room, "No!" It's a familiar voice, so I rush over to see. Again, no need to open the door to the suite; I'm already in. I blink repeatedly, certain that my eyes are deceiving me.

But they're not.

Gripped by shock and confusion, I struggle to suck in a breath. This can't be!

Standing in the middle of the room is a woman—it's me— pointing a gun at . . . How could it be me? It doesn't make sense! I'm pointing a gun at him!

Then I pull the trigger.

72

"Come on, Xandra. Snap out of it!"

The entire hotel room dissolves around me.

Kyle shakes me out of my trance, his face lit with concern. I've not been breathing, though in my head I've been screaming. A deep, wheezing gasp—hyperventilation.

"No! No, no, no!" I'm shaking my head so hard, involuntarily tempting whiplash.

"What did you see?"

"It's me! I'm the one who's going to kill him!"

"What are you talking about?"

"I saw it all, the body, the blood, the gun. The *gun*! I was pointing the gun right at him. I pulled the trigger!"

Kyle's grip loosens. He backs away. From the look on his face, you'd think that I'd suddenly been replaced with a stranger. "Who did you—who *are* you going to kill?"

"And someone else was dead, on the floor. I couldn't see who it was." I reach up and cling to his jacket. "I think it was someone I care about—oh God, why would I do that?"

"Who did you shoot?"

"Don't you get it? I'm the assassin. I'm going to kill Richard Colson!" I expect him to say something to make sense of it all, but he's just as confused.

"Are you sure?"

"My visions haven't been wrong yet." Now comes the dizziness. My head feels as though it's filled with helium. My eyelids flutter. Even though I catch a glimpse of the lightbulb glaring down from the ceiling, everything begins to dim. "I'm going to do it, that's what it means. I'm going to hold him at gunpoint. I'm going to pull the trigger. I'm going to . . ."

73

KYLE MATTHEWS

"Xandra!" She's barely conscious. I'm not sure why this particular vision has affected her like this. But there's no time to waste. With her arm slung over my shoulder, and through the excruciating pain of my GSW about to tear open, I walk her to the car and lay her down in the backseat where she finally drifts off.

As I speed down the freeway, my cell phone rings. Only one of two people could be calling. Leaning my head over, I activate the Bluetooth by clicking it against my shoulder.

It's Glen. "You stepped into a pile of it, Kyle. Do you have any idea what kind of trouble you're in?"

"An inkling. What's our status?"

"My guys have arranged everything. Peter Carrick's agreed to meet you."

"Good."

"No, wait. It's worse than you imagined."

"What are you talking about?"

"You always said conspiracies are always found where you never expect, right? Well, I took that principle and looked exactly where I would never think of looking."

"And?"

"You're not going to like this."

"I already don't."

"It's your boss."

"Maguire? She's sending someone to bring me back in, I know."

"You don't get it! She's in on it!" In a brief moment, that statement goes from making no sense to complete sense. "Whatever it is you're looking for, she totally doesn't want you sticking your nose in it."

It takes a moment to sink in. The signs were all there: her tension at the mere mention of my investigations into the Echo Company murders, the adamant insistence that they weren't connected. "Do you have any proof?"

"It's all here on my flash drive. Voice mails, emails, memos."

"Did you make backups?"

"What are you, my mother? I just got this stuff today and rushed home to call you."

"Fine. But you need to make multiple copies and—"

"Hold on, someone's at the door."

"Glen, wait!" Before I can say another word, he's put the receiver down. In the background, his door opens. A low murmuring of dialogue exchanges.

The door slams shut.

He lets out a cry, but it's cut off quickly. "Glen!"

A horrible gurgling. Someone's just slit his throat.

Immediately I disconnect the call. But it's too late. They'll be able to track me down. Sure enough, my phone rings. It's Glen's number. I roll down the window and toss the phone out into the freeway.

Slamming my hand on the steering wheel, I swear silently, cursing myself. I shouldn't have gotten him involved. He didn't deserve this!

More than ever, I've got to find the person or people responsible. I owe it to Uncle Ray and, now, Glen.

Carrick's our last hope.

74

XANDRA CARRICK

A gentle nudge wakes me. "We're here."

I'm lying down in the backseat of the car. It's dark outside. We're in a parking lot with dim, jaundiced lights. Looks like a mall, with people walking back and forth.

"What happened? Where are we?"

"You fainted. Come on, let's go." Kyle takes my hand and pulls me up. I step outside, and a cold breeze sends a shiver through me. In reaction, I rub the back of my arms. Kyle removes his jacket and drapes it over my shoulders. His warmth still lingers in the sleeves as I pull it around me.

By the time we walk past the tour buses and into the lobby, I can tell by the choking cigarette fumes that the not-so-subtle "Welcome to Comanche" sign is for a casino.

"I don't want to go in there. All that smoke."

"We'll just pass by, then take the elevators up to the hotel room."

"What are we doing here?"

He takes my hand and starts walking. I'm jolted by the touch of his fingers. So warm and at the same time toughened like old leather. "We're meeting your father."

"When did he contact you?"

"He got the message to Glen before . . ." For a moment, his countenance darkens.

"What is it?"

"They killed him. We're completely in the dark now." Suddenly, he affects a smile, puts his hand around my waist, looks around. "It's a surprise, honey. Happy anniversary!" He leans and whispers into my ear, "In case we're being watched. Follow my lead."

Which, I suppose, is to impersonate a married couple, celebrating their—what, first anniversary? "I hate surprises, sweetie." A forced grin.

"Trust me, you're going to love this. I got us the honeymoon suite."

A simulated smile and we're off to walk through the throngs of people in the casino lobby and into an elevator. Shielding myself from the toxic nicotine fumes, I cover my nose and mouth. But it doesn't help much.

Kyle casts a furtive glance around, seems glad we're alone, then presses the button for the fifteenth floor.

For some odd reason, it's moving from floor to floor really slowly.

"You can take your hand off my waist now. No need to pretend in here."

"Surveillance cameras," he whispers and nods to the black dome in the corner above us. I would guess that he's enjoying this charade, but his tone is completely businesslike. "Keep up the act."

Act?

"Fine." Then for reasons I hope one day to fathom, I turn and grab the back of his head, pull him down toward me forcefully, and begin kissing him. Several times he tries to say something, but the best he can manage is, "Xan—wait—"

What I'm trying to prove eludes me. Perhaps that I can be just as unemotional as he is. Or that he shouldn't have to work so hard at pretending.

After a few long seconds, our bodies relax. His arms are no longer stiff. I don't have to hold him to my lips anymore.

My backpack falls and hits the floor. The otherwise nauseating crack of vintage equipment doesn't faze me in the least. I'm too busy getting lost in Kyle's thawing embrace. Like a bridge, erected from both sides, we converge. At once, I sense the little boy in him that fought so hard to overcome loss and fear to become the man that he is. I'm sure he senses something similar flowing through me as well.

"Kyle . . ."

"Shh . . ." His fingertips glide over my face, touch my lips; then as he replaces them with his own lips, he runs those fingers through my hair, down the back of my neck. Pulls me into a deeper kiss.

Blissful confusion.

We separate slightly to breathe. Heavily. Hearts pounding to the point of exhaustion. Or relief. Or both. "I'm sorry, Kyle. I don't know what . . . I was just—"

"You think too much." Those intense eyes, unyielding, so profound with unspoken pain, joy, all the things that I want desperately to know about him. He lets up and says, "You know what you need?"

"I've got a pretty good idea." I cup his face in my hands and kiss him again.

"You need to have some faith."

"Not what I had in mind." This time when I kiss him, he kisses back with equal intensity. We grip into a tighter embrace.

Whereas before, our tension was as opposing forces, we're now pulling together against something else. Something so inevitable that it both frightens and excites me. He desires me. And I him. I think I always have. "What would be so wrong if—"

The bell chimes, and the elevator door slides open. A geriatric couple stands before us like nocturnal frogs stunned by a flashlight. A white-haired granny in a gaudy warmup suit starts and puts her hand over her mouth. Gramps just grins and gawks, until his wife slaps the back of his head with her little pink, bling-studded clutch. "Harold!"

"What? What?"

"Excuse us," Kyle says as he leads me by the hand down the hall. As the elevator doors close, Harold continues to smile stupidly.

What just happened between us? Perhaps it's all the stress, but all I can think of is Kyle pulling that key card out of his pocket, sliding it into the slot, and opening the door to the honeymoon suite.

He does, with more haste than I expect. He slams the door shut, and we don't even make it to the bedroom.

"We've got an hour."

"Till?"

"Your dad."

I've liberated myself of the jacket and simultaneously, as I lie back on the sofa, he's on top of me. Gazing into my eyes. Never before has anyone looked at me this way. I can't possibly allow this moment to slip.

He kisses my forehead. "I never thought—"

I silence him with a kiss. "Now who's thinking too much?"

A boyish grin stretches across his features. He slips his arm under my back and leans in close. My face against his. It's as though we've been together for years. I trust him.

Despite what happened in New York, I trust him. Because he's trustworthy, though a bit dangerous. Transparent, though somewhat enigmatic. When I'm with him—and not just now, in the throes of passion—I feel secure.

"You might not believe this," I say, as I begin unbuttoning his shirt. "But I've never . . ."

"I believe it."

I thump his shoulder. "Want me to get Harold's wife and make her slap you with her bling-bling purse?"

His shirt falls half open now. But I'm going to resist the temptation to feel his sinewy chest again. He's got to make a move.

And he does, but it takes me by surprise. Instead of raw animal passion, he touches my face tenderly. "I have no idea how this is going to end, Xandra. But from the moment I saw you, I knew . . . I mean, I knew that . . ."

"What?"

"I knew that you were a person I had to know better. Someone I could open up to."

"I thought you were going to say you knew I was a psycho."

"That, and that you really needed help."

"As in psycho."

"No." He laughs, in spite of himself. "I mean, you're gorgeous, you're smart—"

"I've got a cute tuckus. Don't forget that."

"Yeah, and a weird sense of humor."

Right now, I'm wondering at what point he's going to rip my clothes off. But something above and beyond my raging hormones rises to the surface. It's almost frightening. Kyle isn't simply physically attracted to me. It's deeper than that.

Still, I'm not letting this moment escape us. "Let's talk later, okay?" I slip my hand into his shirt, caress the firm lines of his shoulder muscles, his chest, his back.

Now he's reaching for my buttons.

One.

Two. *Keep going, don't stop there.*

He doesn't.

Our eyes meet. There's a mutual sense of recognition. It doesn't take long before we both realize it. I take his hands. "Kyle, I'm sorry. Maybe we shouldn't."

Shaking it out of his head, he blinks. "I'm the one who should apologize." He gets up and starts buttoning his shirt. Again, a tender touch to my face, a kiss on my head.

My head is clearing now. Catching my breath. All my adult life I've focused on—all right—*hidden* behind my work, my goals. I've found some guys attractive, but my one and only foray into the strongholds of romance ended badly. I'd concluded that relationships simply weren't worth the trouble. Since then, I've never allowed myself the time to meet anyone, to date, or otherwise. Could it be that in the back of my mind, I sense that my days are numbered? And for that reason, I'm permitting myself to have passion, to be passionate? It's intoxicating. It's dangerous.

"Look, just so you know, I'm not the kind of girl who just—"

"Of course not. And I've just had so many so-called relationships that went bad because . . . well, let's just say I promised myself I'd never do this again unless it was for keeps."

"Honorable." A smirk twists my lips.

He leans in close and takes my hand. "But when this is all over, I'll give anything to spend time with you, get to know you. Under normal circumstances."

"Hello? It's me, Xandra Carrick, psycho seer. I don't do normal. Why would you want to know me?"

"Because I . . . I really—oh, I stink at this!"

He turns and stares into the kitchenette. Recomposed and sitting shoulder to shoulder on the sofa, I lean against him like a cat. That I'm so comfortable confuses me. I can't remember the last time a man made me feel this way. "Don't keep me in suspense."

He takes my hand again. "All right, listen. You are the most beautiful, fascinating, weird, annoying—"

"Hey!" I punch his shoulder.

"I've never wanted to connect with anyone like I do with you. It's deeper than physical. When you look at me, I feel like you're looking into my soul."

"I haven't had a vision about you yet."

He brushes my hair away from my face and kisses me. "I'd sure like to know if you see a future for us."

"I prefer living in the present."

"Carpe diem." As he wraps his arms around me, I lean into his chest, relieved that our heads came out victorious over our hormones. For a few minutes, neither of us speaks. I'm content knowing I'm not alone in this world. I sense it's mutual. Just for this moment, when all the world is quiet—no visions, no one trying to kill us, no mysterious murders to connect—it's sufficient.

The exhaustion of the past couple of days weighs down my eyelids. Just for an hour, I'd like to disappear. Exist in another world where Kyle and I can be free. *The truth shall set you free.* "You know what would be nice, Kyle?"

"Quitting the FBI. Going somewhere nice together."

"Venice."

"I was thinking Maui, but sure, that'd be—" He stops abruptly at the sound of someone jiggling the door. He checks his watch, swears, and gets up. "Quick, get in the bedroom, out of sight."

"Who is that?"

"I don't know. We're supposed to meet your father later in the bar."

"But what if—?"

"Hide in the bedroom. I'll try to draw them away from the door. If you see an opportunity, get out and run. Take the car." He puts the keys in my hand, pulls the gun out, and kneels behind the arm of the sofa, his gun aimed at the door. "Go."

75

It's difficult to hear what's going on through the closet and bathroom doors. Could anything other than a gunshot be heard from here?

I've got to know what's going on. Waiting in here could cost me precious seconds. Quietly, I turn the doorknob and crack open the bathroom door. Outside of the bedroom door a volley of muffled shouts erupts.

Then it's quiet.

What's happened? I put my ear up against the bedroom door.

Before I reach it, it clicks open.

Startled, I freeze in place.

Kyle comes in. "It's okay."

I peer through the door, and the first thing I see is my backpack lying on the floor. Then a pair of shoes. Then further up, my heart just about stops. "Dad!"

I can't tell how long we've been gazing at each other. Countless emotions rage like a Class VI rapid. Finally, he comes to me and gathers me in his arms.

I begin to sob. "Daddy, I can't believe . . ."

"It's going to be all right, sweetie."

"We just scattered Mom's ashes. How did it come to this?"

"Are you hurt, Xandi?"

"I'm okay. Thanks to Kyle."

"I know." He pats him on the shoulder. "Do you know what a pain it was following the instructions that friend of yours sent? Prepaid cell phones, setting up call-forwarding, and then destroying one—"

"Necessary precautions, Mr. Carrick." Kyle motions for him to take a seat on the sofa. I, too, sit, with Dad's arm around me.

"Agent Matthews, could I have a moment with my daughter?"

"I'll be in the bedroom." He shuts the door, and awkward silence seeps into the room like household methane. In and of itself, it won't poison you. But it's highly combustible, and if enough of it fills a closed area, it will suffocate you. All the joy of reuniting and finally seeing Dad has ebbed, leaving those haunting images behind.

"I can't believe the trouble you've gotten yourself into, Xandi."

The entire mood shifts. Relieved smiles pull into taut frowns. Glad eyes narrow as the decade-old floodgates give way. "I'm not a murderer. And I don't have anything to hide."

"Says the fugitive."

"I thought you were on my side." I push his arm off and slide away from him.

"I am on your side! Always have been."

"You've got a strange way of showing it."

"And you've been clueless. It's not just murder charges, it's not just fleeing the jurisdiction. Every law-enforcement agency's going to be hunting you down after that news release tonight."

"Whatever."

"You listen to me, young lady! The Department of Homeland Security's flagged you as a domestic terrorist. In addition to that Dellafina girl, they're holding you responsible for the deaths of Mitchell Cooper, George Kimble, and . . . what are you doing, Xandra?"

"You think I killed them?" I launch to my feet, put my shoes on, ready to walk out and slam the door. "It's just like you! You assume, assign blame without even bothering to hear my side of the story!"

"You have no idea what you're—"

"No, *you* have no idea!" I slam my hand on the counter so hard that the glasses in the cupboard rattle. Dad blinks in surprise. I've never shown him the full extent of my emotions before. But now, I'm not holding back. Never again. "You're the one they should interrogate. You're the one who's been hiding behind some stoic wall of silence. You, the great Peter Carrick, Pulitzer Prize-winning monolith! You think you can hide? I know, Dad. I know about Bình Sơn!"

Kyle opens the bedroom door and sticks his head out. "Problem here?"

"Family matter, Agent Matthews." Dad controls his voice. Barely. "Give us a few."

"Try to keep it down." He looks over at me. I nod and wave him off. He shuts the door. If Dad's eyes were flamethrowers, I'd be lit up by napalm. His jaw is set, his lips curl. "I will not have my little girl talk to me that way!"

"I am *not* your little girl!"

Now he's on his feet, stabbing his finger in my face. "You're acting like a pubescent teenager, shacking up with Secret Agent Man back there. Meanwhile the whole stinking world is going to hell in a handbasket!"

"Oh yeah, that's right. You know everything even without asking, without seeing, without knowing! That's why I ran off with him. Right."

"Listen, Xandra—"

"*You* listen! You talk big, but you don't know, you don't see. But guess what? I can see. And I have. And you're going to tell me the truth about Bình Sơn."

"What are you yammering about?"

"I saw you back there. Not last week, thirty-seven years ago. The bodies, the ashes, the graves!"

"I don't—how could you possibly . . . ?" His face has turned paper white. "Nobody knows about that except . . ." He takes an absentminded step back and stumbles into the sofa.

"What are you so afraid of?"

"Who told you?"

"Nobody. I saw it. I saw you."

"How?"

As I explain all the visions, how every one of them proved true, how each brought me step by step to where we are now, he listens without question, without doubt.

But there's such fear in his eyes. He's more vulnerable than I've ever known him to be. Overtaken by compassion, I sit next to him and hold his hands. "Daddy, please. Tell me what happened in Bình Sơn."

76

"Why couldn't it just stay put?" Dad buries his face in his hands.

"If this is at all connected with the murders, you've got to tell me."

He sits up, grits his teeth. "Agent Matthews!"

The door opens. "Sir?"

"Take notes, you'll need to hear this."

Kyle takes a seat at the bar, ready with pen and paper. "Go ahead, sir."

Dad takes a deep breath and steadies himself on the arm of the sofa. "Anything in the wet bar?"

"High octane or regular?" Kyle says.

"Diesel."

Kyle pulls out a small bottle of Absolut, pours it into a glass, and hands it to him. "Best I could find."

Dad nods his thanks, downs a gulp, and sighs. All the fire in his eyes has been smothered, replaced with fear, regret. "You have to understand. Your mother didn't even know. I had to protect her, protect you both." He takes another swig. "It happened before I met her."

How must it feel to keep a secret like this for thirty-three years? I feel more pathos for him than anger now. "Go on, Dad. It's all right."

"I've never told anyone this story before, and with good reason . . ."

77

PETER CARRICK

Back in '73 while I worked as a war photographer with Echo Company, all kinds of crazy stuff went on in the hills of Nam. You have to understand, those boys started out all right.

Lieutenant Colonel Richard "Thundering Rick" Colson, Echo Company's commanding officer, sent Privates Cooper and Ross on a reconnaissance mission to check out this one village in Bình Sơn, the village your mother was raised in, Xandi. He believed that the VC had infiltrated it and set up a guerrilla-warfare base amongst the population.

A day late for his expected return, Private Ross just barely made it back to report. He and Cooper had been discovered lurking in the bush by some of the villagers. They looked friendly enough and welcomed them in for a meal. Many seemed happy to see American soldiers. The privates learned otherwise, only too late.

Ross escaped, but he had multiple stab wounds and had been stripped down to his skivvies. The skin on his back had been ripped to shreds by God only knows what kind of torture devices. Apparently, there were two or three VCs living in that village. And they still had Cooper.

Ross didn't make it through the night.

Colson treated his men like they were his brothers, and this affected him profoundly. But the soldiers under his command took it far worse. At first they wanted to light up the village, smoke out the damn Charlies, and do to them what they did to Ross. But he calmed them down, told them their first priority was to rescue Private Cooper.

By then, everyone in the world knew about the Mai Lai massacre. I feared we might be standing at the brink of another such atrocity. But Colson kept a level head.

At least, initially.

Days went by as he made multiple plans and contingency plans, and backup plans for those contingency plans. But the soldiers were starting to talk. Some of them even questioned their CO's ability to lead, since he appeared to be stalling.

The tension was palpable. At any moment, I might be sent away so as not to witness the breakdown of a United States military unit. But they didn't send me away. Instead, Colson confided in me. Probably because I was the only objective party around. That, and later I learned that there was no safe way to get me out of there without giving up our position.

Tempers flared, fuses grew short. Lieutenant Marks stepped forward one day and got right in Colson's face. "Sir, if you're not going to lead, I'm going to have to find you unfit and relieve you of duty."

To my surprise, Colson remained calm. "Command decisions are not to be made in haste."

"Four days squatting in the bamboo is not my idea of haste; it's indecision."

"Are you questioning my authority?"

"I'm questioning your ability, or your willingness to make the tough decisions. Now, give us our orders, or step aside and let someone with a backbone do it!"

A dark cloud had rolled over into the mountains, and in the distance, the rumble of thunder reverberated under our feet. I started taking pictures, but Lieutenant Marks shoved me aside. I don't think he realized his strength relative to that of a young civilian. I fell and landed on my camera. Thankfully, the damage was not serious. To my utter disbelief, Marks pulled out a pistol and aimed it right at me. "What do you think you're doing?"

But at this, Colson stepped between us. "Stand down, Lieutenant."

"Do my ears deceive me, or did you actually issue an order?"

"Stand down and take ten to cool off."

Marks scoffed. "We're done here." He pointed at four other soldiers, and they all came to his side. "Anyone who wants to do something better than sitting on your hands should come with us."

"Stay where you are, men." Colson's poker face could freeze molten lava.

But Marks smirked, shrugged, and turned his back on him.

"This is desertion. Stay where you are, that's an order!" Which was followed by the clicking off of his gun's safety and the pointing of the muzzle in the back of Marks's head.

"Oh, look who's grown himself a fresh pair," Marks said, stopping in his tracks.

I could not believe my eyes. What happened next could not have taken more than half a second. Marks swung around, pointed his gun right at Colson's chest. A gunshot went off. I ducked, covered my head, and remained that way until the echoing of the round dissipated, blending with the approaching thunder.

A cold, wet drop hit my neck. It wasn't blood. It was rain. Within seconds, the entire area was engulfed in a thunderstorm. I lifted my head and saw a scarlet stream of blood flowing past my foot. At the top of this stream was Lieutenant Marks's head, or what was left of it. He lay dead on the ground, his men gawking in wonder.

By the next morning, Colson got the would-be deserters to cooperate. Seems they didn't have much of a spine after Marks was executed, which by law, he had earned. Until then, I hadn't yet seen a drop of blood spilled. I wanted to take pictures, but Lieutenant Colonel Colson, who seemed depressed, said, "Trust me, Carrick, the world will be better off not having to see this. It'll do for me to write the report. Dammit, what am I going to tell Larry's old man?"

I was young and impressionable. What he said seemed to make sense. So I let it go. Wasn't sure I wanted pictures of American mutiny in my portfolio, anyway. Little did I know, the Graflex would capture things unimaginably worse.

By the time the rain stopped, even I was getting cabin fever. You can't imagine how awful it was, trying to sleep under a make-shift tent in the rain. The soldiers didn't dare complain to Colson, but he knew they were murmuring behind his back. He also knew if he didn't do something soon, they'd all turn on him. And this time, he would be the one on the ground.

That night, when the sun went down over the hills of Bình Sơn, he laid out his plan to rescue Private Cooper. It was to be a quick, two-pronged attack. A diversionary strike on the eastern outskirts of the village and a quick raid with minimal collateral damage in the village itself. Get Cooper, blast their way out, and fall back into the depths of the Mekong Delta. There, they would rendezvous with Delta Company, which had arranged for a mede-vac to take their wounded back to Saigon.

As dawn broke, I stayed behind in a hidden trench a couple of hundred meters away from the village. From there, I could remain unseen and wait.

The first prong worked like a charm. Within five minutes, Echo Company surrounded and captured a couple of villagers who looked too untrained and scared to be actual Vietcong. They surrendered readily.

What surprised me most was how quickly the second prong succeeded. We'd taken control of the village in less than thirty minutes. I was given the green light to come out.

Apparently, there were only three Vietcong hiding in the vil-lage. The people seemed more frightened of them than they were of us. Private Cooper was in bad shape when they found him. But he had survived.

The first Vietcong refused to surrender and came out wielding an AK-47 and swearing at our soldiers. They put him down with three quick rounds.

The other came out with his hands up and was taken for questioning. I don't know what exactly they did to him behind the doors of that hut, but from his screams, I imagined an eye-for-an-eye applied.

"What manner of evil have they brought upon us?" a toothless man said, holding his hands over his five-year-old granddaughter's ears, trying to block out the tormented cries. The screaming ended with a single gunshot, followed by deathly stillness all around the village. The eyes of the women, children, and elderly grew wide with fear.

When Colson stepped out of the hut, he holstered his gun and wiped the sweat from his brow. He addressed the village while one of them translated: "There is one more of you in this village who is a Vietcong! Hand him over and the rest of you will be shown civility."

The entire village population, which numbered about twenty-five, gathered around and stared in disbelief. A boy whom I later learned was my wife's brother called out, "Just those two! They came and took over, forced us to hide them!"

Colson spoke like Moses holding the two stone tablets. "You must cooperate in order for us to protect you. You know who he is. Hand him over."

The interrogations continued for the next two days, but to no avail. You could see the frustration mounting on the soldiers' faces, even on their COs. More than anything, they had to find that last VC, make him pay for what they'd done to Cooper and Ross.

But life just went on in the village as though nothing unusual had transpired. What else could those people do? They were innocent. It was a couple of Vietcongs who tried to set up a guerrilla base in their homes. Now the VCs were dead, and for all anyone knew at the time, there were only two of them. But Colson and his men did not believe that to be the case, which only added to their frustration when they could not find the third VC.

Finally, Colson approached me in confidence. "Carrick, I'm going to have to send you to meet Delta Company tomorrow without us. If I don't get some kind of resolution for my men . . . It's safer if you go."

"All right," I said, having grown weary of sitting around taking pictures of soldiers giving me the finger and villagers carrying about their business. Frankly, I wanted to go home.

Later that afternoon, Colson walked me out to the woods. His eyes darted around as he spoke cautiously. "I have good reason to believe that this area is about to heat up. VCs from the north will be here soon, and unless Delta Company gets here first, we're sitting ducks."

Frightening, but this was just the kind of event I came here to photograph. "I can take cover somewhere until it's safe."

"You should get closer to the rendezvous point. On the other hand—" Gunshots and the sound of women screaming interrupted.

With my camera ready, I turned and started for the village.

"No!" The CO gripped my arm so hard I gasped, had to bite my lip not to cry out like a child. "Whatever you do, stay out. You hear? Wait for my signal that it's safe."

I nodded, and he ran back into the village. He turned and pointed over me into the woods. "Take cover!"

78

Of course, no self-respecting photojournalist would allow personal peril to deter him. With my Graflex strapped and prepped, I waited until the CO entered the village. Then I followed.

I stood behind a thicket of tall grass and peered into the village through the viewfinder. What I saw went beyond horrifying, but what I heard was worse.

Pop after *pop*, men young and old fell to the ground, their heads ruptured, their brains splattered red and gray against the wooden plank walls and on the ground. The soldiers of Echo Company were lining them up and executing them.

Some of the soldiers even held crying children's faces and forced them to watch their parents meet their bloody demise. One little toddler screamed as the blood of his father splashed over his face.

I wanted to shout, "Stop it!" but I froze, trembling with outrage and, I'm ashamed to admit, fear. Then they lined the children up and gunned them down.

These were my fellow Americans! Once men of honor fighting for a cause, now soulless barbarians bent on vengeance. I snapped off as many pictures as my shaky hands could manage, though I thought I'd never want to look at them again.

But I hadn't yet seen the worst. I heard women and girls

screaming, some behind the doors of the wooden huts, some of them out in the open. They were begging, pleading.

"Please!" one said, "take me, she's only ten!"

How could this be happening? It was Mai Lai all over again. Where was Colson? What was he doing about this? Surely he'd stop these cowards who dared to wear the uniform of the United States Marines. I wanted to call out for him but knew I'd be shot on the spot if one of them found me.

Then I saw him.

Lieutenant Colonel Colson, Echo Company's commanding officer, stood in the middle of the village, his hands on his hips, gun in his hand. Instantly, hope rose. Surely he'd put an end to this madness.

But when he removed his sunglasses and looked at one of the soldiers who dragged a young girl, kicking, screaming, with blood streaming down her bare thigh, I saw for that fateful instant something in Colson I could never have imagined: approval.

The soldier flipped off a smug salute and dragged the girl into a hut.

A scream. Then muffled.

The screaming stopped.

Disconcerting silence.

Then a gunshot.

Colson stood there, surveying the havoc wreaked by the soldiers under his command. Another one stopped by, removed his shirt, and flung it into a pile of blood-stained uniform shirts. Barely looking through the corner of his eye, Colson nodded, and the soldier ran off whooping like a banshee, ready to shoot or rape his next victim.

If ever hell had spilled over onto the earth, it was now. I stood there unable to do anything about it. Sinking to the ground, I covered my face and wept bitterly.

I nearly jumped when a young black man, Corporal Wilkins, barely out of high school by the looks of him, collapsed next to me, clutching his rifle to his chest. "Oh, dear Jesus!" He grabbed my arm and shook it desperately. "Tell me!"

"What?"

"Just tell me!"

"Tell you what, soldier?"

"Tell me I'm dreaming, man. Please, tell me this is just a nightmare!"

I couldn't. If only it were.

Eventually, after an hour or so, all the screaming and crying and shooting stopped. Amidst the morbid quiet, bird songs returned, the sun shone warmly on my shoulders. I lifted my eyes to the hills, where palm fronds stretched out like a mother's soft fingers touching clear skies.

Echo Company vacated the village, though only momentarily, as I would soon discover. That's when I started taking the pictures of the bodies. Discreetly, while no living soul was around. Horrible as it was, this must not be forgotten.

The pictures I took of that massacre refused to leave my memory. The images of the children's broken and violated bodies, the gaunt, white-haired elders on the ground, their dead eyes wide in disbelief, they have haunted me every night since this happened.

I finished the film roll and switched it out for a new one. Who would have thought that roll of film in my vest would alter my life forever?

"I thought I told you to keep out!" Colson's thundering voice startled me out of my stupor. I turned and found him standing, his face haggard, but tall and dignified. His entire demeanor exuded absolute justification and self-righteousness.

"You just stood by."

"There was no stopping them, Carrick."

"You stopped Lieutenant Marks. For simply walking away."

"That was different."

"How?"

He put a heavy hand on my shoulder. "I don't expect you to understand the intricacies, the psychology of war. But I'll tell you this, these men are on the brink. If they fall apart before Delta Company arrives, we'll all die out here when the VCs attack."

"You can't possibly believe—"

"This goes beyond personal beliefs and comfort. You see what those pinko dogs did to Ross? There's not enough of him left to send back to his family for a funeral."

"But still . . ."

"Want to tell a story? Take some pictures of his remains! Show the world what those animals did to him!" He sniffed and wiped his brow. "These boys are tighter than family. They need closure."

It seemed Colson spoke from his true convictions. I felt nauseous. "Killing innocent women and children, old men and women, raping ten-year-old girls, you call that closure?"

"It's barbaric, I know. And for the record, I never touched one of them." He paused and squinted as he stared out at the blood-covered ground. Then in a calm voice: "It was for the greater good, don't you get it?"

I didn't. But he spoke with such sincerity, I actually started to wonder if my objections were naive. After all, I was a recent college graduate who'd barely experienced life as a civilian. What did I know of war and human nature?

He put his arm around my shoulders and led me away from the center of the village. As we continued, the soldiers of Echo Company began piling the bodies in a trench at the edge of the community.

"It's tragic what's happened here, Carrick. It truly is. But this is war. Soldiers get a little lost when they can't see their enemy. When a good man, a brave soldier, is caught off guard because these damned Commies dress like rice farmers and shred his body into minced meat—it's enough to make the toughest marine crack!

"If I don't allow them to release some of that stress, we risk losing ground. And if that happens, everything we've fought for, all the lives of brave men like Private Ross, will have been lost in vain. I'm sure you can understand that."

Disputing his argument would have made me feel stupid. "I don't know."

"You're an American, dammit, think like one! We don't claim to be perfect, we're only human, all of us. But one thing we do—we put our country and her interests first. And you're going to do the same."

"What do you mean?"

He nodded toward my camera. "Take the film out."

"What?"

"You heard me. No one must ever know about this. Give me the film."

I couldn't even think of a reply. It was like asking a priest to destroy a sacred scroll. This was the physical manifestation of my entire purpose as a photojournalist: to bring the truth in pictures to the world in a way that words alone could never do.

I knew where this was going, though, and feigned compliance. With the film full of photos of the mass grave actually resting in my pocket, I removed the unexposed roll from the Graflex.

He snatched it out of my hands. "I'm sorry to do this, but it's our duty to protect the honor of our nation." With that, he tossed it into a wood-burning stove.

At the edge of the filling trench, one particularly enraged soldier howled and tossed the body of a small boy into the pile. I swear, if my camera were a bayonet, I would have given that soldier the business end of it.

Colson cleared his throat, stared down at the dirt. "I know what you're thinking. But understand this. This was one of those tough choices someone in my position must make. I pray you never have to find yourself—"

"Condoning rape and murder? Destroying the evidence?" As far as he knew, anyway. "The choice isn't that difficult."

"From your perspective, no. But you're only responsible for your own life and well-being. When you've got the interests of your entire nation in your hands, everything changes."

"The important things don't."

"I get it, son. You're young, idealistic. But if this war can teach you anything it's this: it's time for you to grow up. America can't have another Mai Lai dangling from her neck, you hear? When news of it broke out, the Ruskies equated us to the stinking Nazis. Can you imagine what it would do to our credibility in the global community if *this* came out?"

"God help us all."

He sighed and rubbed his eyes. "God will judge each of us accordingly. But I don't serve God; I serve my country. And if He damns me to hell for protecting the honor of my nation, then so be it." He stood tall now, his chest high and his voice deepening. "Now, can I count on you never to so much as whisper a word of this to anyone?"

"You're insane."

"Not for me, Carrick. For your country."

I didn't feel it in my heart, but on many levels, he made sense. I felt a part of me gravitating toward his rationalizations. Perhaps that part felt complicit and sought any form of absolution. It troubled me that I actually felt the pull. But in truth, I was a man sentenced to death by having his limbs tied to two horses, poised to run off in opposite directions.

79

XANDRA CARRICK

I'm trembling, holding back tears. "Daddy, how could you?"

"You don't understand. This whole time—"

"You participated in the cover-up. All those people in Bình Sơn, Mom's brother. That's what you've been hiding from us all these years!"

"Don't you see? Her brother was that third Vietcong! I didn't know at the time, but right after I saved your mother, she asked me to go back and find him. She'd just come back from Saigon and didn't know what had happened in her village. But I knew. Nobody survived.

"I went back to look for the gold cross he was wearing, just before Echo Company incinerated all the bodies. There was a tattoo on his arm identical to those of the other two VCs they caught. He was the reason the Vietcong set up shop in your mother's village. I couldn't tell her that."

Kyle quietly remarks, "The official report stated that the entire village was destroyed when Vietcong soldiers took it as a strong-hold."

"That's what Colson wrote."

The floor has vanished beneath me, and I'm falling endlessly into a dark pit. I pull away from Dad, revulsion rising up from my belly.

"He convinced you it was in the best interest of the United States to keep quiet?"

"It was more than that."

"You've been living a lie since you met Mom. How can I believe anything you say?"

"I had to protect you both."

"By lying to us? Who *are* you?" I'm pacing around the room. Every now and then, Kyle tries to calm me down, but I just walk right past him.

"You think it was easy for me? I haven't slept peacefully since. Their ghosts still haunt me every night."

"Why didn't you ever talk to us? Ever since we moved to Manhattan, you just pulled away. We thought—I thought it was me. That you were disappointed, that maybe you wanted a son instead."

"It wasn't anything like that. You have no idea what I had to do."

"You didn't have the guts to come forward, so you shrunk away. All my life, I just wanted . . . but you just . . . You thought giving me this stupid camera could compensate?"

Dad slams his fist on the end table. The little vodka bottle tips over, but it's empty. "Don't you see? It's all connected; the atrocities, the murders of those vets. And now it's falling apart, kicked up to the next level, because of you."

"Oh, so I'm to blame!" My furious steps stop short when my foot hits my backpack. That accursed camera. I reach down and pull it out, pieces rattling, and thrust it at him. "You know, maybe there's a reason I've been given this ability to see visions. Maybe there's a reason this camera ended up in my hands."

Without the usual warning, a sudden rush of heat runs through my body like electricity. I fall forward into Dad's arms.

"Xandra!"

A sudden detonation of light, sweeping wind, and the images obliterate the walls.

Dad and I float in a sea of temporal vignettes. His eyes are squeezed shut, and I can't seem to get through to him. We're watching a young

Peter Carrick carrying my mother through gunfire in Bình Sơn.

Next, in a New York apartment, they're doting on a baby girl—me.

And then, on the vast shore of a beach, Dad is speaking furtively with an older man. He's got white hair, stands about the same height as Dad. I can't see his face, but I'm aware of what they're saying.

"I can't live with this anymore," Dad says.

"You'd do more harm to our nation than good, Peter. These are the sacrifices we've all had to make. The demons we'll have to abide."

"They're not my demons."

"Sure they are, don't be naive. This has always been bigger than you or me. You're going to keep quiet."

"If they knew the truth about what you've done—"

"Don't, Pete." The white-haired man grabs Dad's arm violently. "How old is that beautiful little girl of yours? Seventeen? You'd give anything to see her grow up, achieve greatness, live a full, long life. Wouldn't you?"

Dad pulls free.

"Oh, and how is that lovely wife of yours—Grace, is it? After all she's been through, it'd be such a shame for it to end prematurely, now that she's living the American dream with you."

"Sonofa—"

"Such language. I should be hurt, after all I've done for you, for Grace. Why, if it weren't for me, she'd have been stuck at the embassy. Clearly, you're ungrateful."

"So that's how it's going to be? Thundering Rick, the twice-decorated war hero resorts to cowardly threats?"

"I'm a man of my word. That's my reputation, isn't it? Whole country knows it. You'd do well to bear that in mind."

A blinding flash, and we're back in the hotel room. Dad staggers, braces himself against the door frame. He can only muster a weak murmur. "Colson."

Just as I stumble Kyle catches me. "A vision?"

"How long was I out?"

"Five or six seconds."

"Feels like I've lived thirty years of his life. Dad, you okay?"

His chest quivers in tiny convulsions. "This is what you've been experiencing?"

"That was by far the most graphic vision ever. And the first I've shared." Nearly falling, I sit down. The sensory overload is draining from me. "It's Colson."

Dad exhales slowly. "The only reason he's let me live is because he can't be sure what'll happen with the evidence if he does anything to me. But he's held your lives over my head ever since I once threatened him with the photos I took of the massacre." With his hand over his eyes, gritting his teeth, and restraining himself from breaking down, he holds the Graflex. "Three decades of hell. Every day, trying to look normal, happy, all the while wondering if today was the day he'd change his mind and have the three of us killed. If you or your mother had even the slightest hint . . ."

I'm only beginning to comprehend, but I know enough. "You have to come forward."

"I know." Dad regains some of his composure and pulls himself off the door frame. "It's more than our lives at stake now. Agent Matthews, how do you think this will play out if I turn myself in?"

"If we can build a solid enough case against Colson, we might be able to bring it before the Supreme Court. At the very least, I'm going to prove he's responsible for the deaths of all those Echo Company vets. We might even bring this straight to the ICC, where he could be tried as a war criminal."

"What about Dad?"

"With his cooperation, they might grant him immunity. Some statutes of limitation could apply."

Dad scoffs. "Doubt it."

"Wait. You could go to prison?"

Dad's eyes are clearer than I've ever seen them. "I've been a prisoner for over thirty years. If speaking the truth means doing time, losing my good name, it's worth it, because I'll finally be free."

"That's what he said."

"Who?"

"Something a pastor quoted from the Bible. The truth will set you free."

"Your mother whispered those exact words to me just before she died."

"She never knew about Colson?"

"All she knew was that he signed the papers that let her out of Saigon." His countenance softened, Dad regards me poignantly. "Thank you, Xandi."

"For what?"

"Confirming what I need to do." He reaches into his coat pocket and pulls out a small Manila envelope. He pours the contents of the envelope out on the coffee table: large-format negs wrapped in onionskin, a USB thumb drive, and a worn notebook. He hands me the book. "That's for you. It's your mother's journal. I can't read it because it's all in Vietnamese." He gives me a weak grin. "Maybe you'll translate it for me one day."

"What are you planning on doing with all this?"

"When Agent Matthews's contacts told me about the danger you're in, I knew it was time." He picks up the thumb drive. "It's been my only trump card, all these years. Now it's time to play it. It's the only way to deal with Thundering Rick."

"So you're going to strike a bargain with him?"

"No."

"He can't be allowed to run this country," Kyle says.

Dad points to the evidence on the table. "I'm going to put him away."

Kyle turns and walks quietly toward the door, pulls out his gun. After a tense few seconds he presses his ear against the door, and then staring through the eyehole, he relaxes. "Thought I heard something." Then to Dad: "With all due respect, I don't think Colson will let you just walk away."

"I thought of that for a long time. At first, I considered handing these over to him. Maybe the nightmares would stop, maybe he'd leave us alone. But I know him. It'll never be enough."

"I don't want to lose you, Dad." Not when it feels like he's finally returned to me.

"Prison can't be any worse than the pit I dug myself into." He kisses my head. "I brought Mom's journal tonight, thinking it might be my last chance to do so."

"But, Dad—"

"You and your mother deserved better."

"We just wanted you in our lives. I still do."

"A bit late now." He holds me tight. "But I'm here. And thanks to you, I'm not going to back down from Colson. Matthews, we have a case to build. Do you know anyone in the attorney general's office?"

"Assuming I can dig myself out."

Confidence that I haven't seen in years infuses Dad's demeanor. "Let's get started."

Kyle steps over and hands me the gun. "Would you mind?"

"I don't like guns."

"Nothing to be afraid of." He grabs a pen and paper and sits opposite Dad. "Let's start with the massacre."

With Mom's journal and the gun Kyle placed in my hands, I walk to the bedroom. "My head hurts. I'm going to lie down." As soon as I sit on the bed, a loud snap jolts me back up. I turn my head and look out to the foyer. The outer door to the hotel room flies open and slams against the wall.

The intruder kicks the door shut and pulls out a gun with a long silencer on its muzzle.

"Dad!"

Kyle leaps to his feet and rushes the intruder, but I've got his gun. I recognize him; he's the one who tried to kill me. The realization freezes me in my tracks. It's all I can do to aim the gun at him and tremble.

Kyle tackles and wrestles him to the floor, while Dad gathers himself and gets up to help him. Grasping the gunman's wrists, Kyle points the gun up toward the ceiling. A round discharges.

The gunman thrusts his knee into Kyle's stomach and rolls over, pinning him to the floor. Dad steps toward them, but with the gun waving in every direction, he's unable to get close enough to help.

By the time I take the four steps into the living room of our suite, the sound of a muffled gunshot cracks in my ears.

"Kyle!"

Facedown in a slowly expanding pool of blood that sinks into the carpet, Kyle lies writhing. On his feet, the assailant sees me and points his gun at Dad's head. I aim my weapon with one shaking hand, the other wiping the tears from my face. Kyle's been shot. I've got to do something!

"Why couldn't you just keep out of this, lassie?" the gunman says.

Dad tries to step over to me, but the killer orders him to stay in place and turn over the envelope with the photos. Dad reaches down to the coffee table and gathers the evidence, then holds it out to him.

"Keep your hands up in plain view and give those to me!"

Dad does so while glancing over at me. To the killer: "If you're working for Colson, trust me, it'll never end." Dad struggles, but the gunman presses the gun deeper into his temple.

"Bleedin' fool." He stuffs the evidence into his coat pocket and takes a hard look at Dad. "You made yourself far too easy to track."

"Don't move!" I'm gritting my teeth, snarling, and praying I won't have to pull this trigger. With great care, I kneel at Kyle's side. He's not moving. With one hand, I point the gun at the attacker; with the other, I touch Kyle's face. "Oh, Kyle."

"Don't worry about me," he whispers. "Take him out."

"I can't do it."

The gunman ignores me and murmurs through his surveillance earpiece, then speaks *sotto voce* to Dad. "You are going to walk out with me slowly and not make a scene. I have full authorization to shoot and kill. Do I make myself clear?"

Dad nods. They start for the door.

"Stop!" I take a step forward and cock the hammer.

Dad's eyes widen. "Xandi, no."

"Please . . ." I stumble forward, still aiming the gun. "Just leave us alone."

He turns Dad toward the door, opens it, and as he steps out, he turns back. "I can't."

The door swings shut. I squeeze the trigger and scream. Two rounds explode like cannons in the hotel room. Glass from the light fixture, chunks of drywall crumble down in a powdery cloud.

The room goes dark.

The door clicks shut.

80

Go after him!

I've got a gun. What am I waiting for? But Kyle's hurt. I've got to get help. Dim light from the bedroom spills into the living area, just enough to illuminate Kyle's face.

I drop the gun, reach for my cell phone, and try dialing with one hand. I feel for a pulse with the other. It's useless. Can't manage both. And then, a fleeting moment of hope. He squeezes my hand. "Hang on, Kyle. Please. You're going to be all right."

A hissing sound passes through his lips. It's now I see it. He's been shot in the chest. With a weak tug, he beckons me. I lean down to him, and he brushes my earlobe with his lips.

Barely audible: "Hurry."

"I'm not leaving you."

With whatever strength he has left, Kyle lifts his eyes, touches my face with cold fingertips. "Would've given anything . . ."

My tears run down his hand. I force a smile. "You're taking me to Maui when this is all over, remember?"

"You're weird." He smiles, winces, coughs weakly. "That's why I love . . ." A deep gasp, and his eyes shut. Those beautiful hazel eyes, which once peered into my soul. Connected with my innermost being.

Tears stream down my face. Blood stains my clothes as I hold him to my chest. Rocking him gently, I weep. "We're going to Maui." The words seep through the vice grip on my throat. "To Maui, Kyle."

Images flash: Kyle smiling with a frothy latte mustache, kissing at twilight, snow-white beaches to which we'll never go. He's slipping away.

I barely notice the footfalls entering the room. Absently, I reach for the gun, but someone kicks it away. Then something hard presses into the back of my head. "FBI. Don't move, Ms. Carrick."

Gently, I set Kyle's head down in my lap. His life pulses weakly under my fingertips.

"Put your hands behind your head, stand, and turn around slowly."

"He needs help."

"Xandra Carrick, you're under arrest for the murders of—"

"Call an ambulance, you idiot!"

A female agent steps in and mumbles something to the one Mirandizing me. He pulls me to my feet and directs me to the bedroom door while she looks down and sighs. "Dammit, Kyle, what have you gotten yourself into? Burrell, shut the door."

He does, but not before I catch a glimpse of the female agent attaching a silencer to her gun and pointing it down at Kyle.

"No, no, no! You can't do this!" Thrashing wildly, I inadvertently hit Agent Burrell in the face.

"I'm warning you, Ms. Carrick. Keep still." He pulls me back into the bathroom. For a few horrendous minutes I hear nothing outside in the living area but the low murmuring of the female agent and the voice of another man that's come into the room.

Beyond the door, a loud but muffled pop rings out. It jolts me. I pull free, the threat of a bullet notwithstanding, and elbow him in the gut so hard he doubles over. Before he can reach me, I shut the bathroom door and prop a chair against the door knob.

Cautiously, I peek through the crack in the bedroom door. Out in the living area, Kyle lies completely motionless, his face covered with a pillow, a single wisp of smoke rising from a black spot in its center.

Serpentine dread coils around my chest, making it difficult to breathe. That woman is with the FBI, and she just executed Kyle in cold blood.

The tall man who entered the room speaks with the female agent, detached and cold. Shadows obscure his face as she replies.

"It's done, sir."

"Thank you, Assistant Director."

Burrell starts banging on the bathroom door. I bolt into the living area, reach over to the bar, grab the gun that Burrell kicked away. Swifter than I've ever reacted before, I point it at this tall man whose identity is somehow clear to me, though I've yet to see his face. "You murderous freak!"

Every single hammer in the room cocks. The tall man turns to face me.

"Colson!"

"That's *President Colson*, sweetheart."

"Not until January." It's clear he's seen more than his share of weapons pointed at him. He doesn't even blink, just looks down at me with an arrogant smirk.

"Put that down, young lady. You might hurt someone."

I refuse to turn. From the corner of my eye, I see Kyle, put down like an animal. I almost forget that I'm pointing my gun at the newly elected president of the United States, who happens to be a war criminal.

"Stuck your nose where you shouldn't have." Colson steps forward, not even holding his hands up. "Though I must admit, it's great to finally meet the daughter of the illustrious Peter Carrick."

"Not another step or I swear I'll shoot!" This doesn't deter him in the least. He's right in front of me, chest pressed up against my gun.

"Sometimes you have to choose the lesser of two evils, knowing someone will die in either case."

"Is that all Bình Sơn was? A choice?"

He turns to the agents. "Burrell, Maguire, would you step outside, please?"

Burrell looks on with concern as he follows Maguire to the door. "Are you sure, sir?"

Colson nods. They shut the door. "You know, Xandra, you shouldn't speak so strongly against things about which you have no clue."

"I know more than you can imagine."

A thoughtful pause. "Which means your father—"

"Shut up!" Dad's gone. Kyle's gone. I'm certainly not getting out of this alive. So what's to stop me right now from putting a bullet right between Colson's eyes? He more than deserves it.

"What now? You think you're going to shoot me?"

"I said, shut up!"

"Like a cold-blooded killer? Oh, there's irony for you. Well go ahead! Surprise me!"

· My hand is shaking so hard the gun rattles. I bring it up to his forehead.

"DO IT!"

I pull back on the trigger. Just a bit more and it'll fire. This is right. I'm doing the nation—no, the world—a great favor. I want so badly to deliver the justice he deserves. When will there ever be another opportunity like this?

But then I hear Mom's voice, "*Your gifts are to help others.*" Just a little farther on the trigger. A little more and . . . "No! I'm not going to sink to your level!" I shove him back and lower the gun.

Tremorous breaths.

Racing pulse.

I nearly killed the president-elect.

He scoffs. "Just as I thought. You're weak, indecisive, and easily manipulated. Just like your father. What a disappointment!"

I point the gun at him again. But he just laughs.

"Rotten apples don't fall far from the tree, do they? I bet your mother was glad to die knowing—"

I let out a feral shriek and jam the gun into his chest. This time, Colson's eyes widen in surprise. Murder or not, there's no turning back. "You need to die. Right now!"

And with that, in the absence of the slightest hesitation, I pull the trigger.

81

IAN MORTIMER

"One sound and I'll see to it that your daughter is returned to you in four easy installments." I slam the trunk shut and climb into the passenger seat. Though bound and gagged, Carrick might just be foolish enough to test my resolve.

Mark Collinsworth gets in the driver's seat and starts the ignition. "He specifically said he wanted both of them dead."

"Slight change of plan. Didn't TR tell you?"

"No."

Peter Carrick is more trouble than he's worth, but I've got to keep him alive. No doubt, when TR learns that Xandra is alive, I'll need to use her father as a bargaining chip. "I take it you didn't get the message about the change of checkpoints?"

"Guess not."

I hope my lying skills haven't waned. "Right. Well, we're going to pull over to an alternate checkpoint where I've got another car waiting. We'll split up there, and I'll dispose of Carrick alone. This will minimize your chance of exposure."

"That's a bit odd, isn't it?"

"He calls the shots. We follow to the letter, you know that. Would you like to call and ask him if he's certain?"

Mark smirks and drives up the road away from the freeway. I'm less than pleased that TR's assigned me a partner at this late stage. Especially Mark Collinsworth, of all people. After years under my supervision, he's almost as good at this as I am. Or once was, as it were. The lad's learned well and managed to rise up as PM in Colson's special projects team.

As for my predicament, I suppose I ought to appreciate the fact that TR hasn't yet demanded proof of Xandra's execution. "We'll turn left and take SR-5 for about two miles."

Mark turns off the main road into a wooded area. His cell phone chimes. One touch of the Bluetooth earpiece and he's connected. "Yes . . . no . . . right. Sure. You got it." As if nothing just happened, he ends the call and continues driving.

"Who was that?"

"Len, my golfing buddy. We're going tomorrow. Want to join us?"

"Don't be daft. In seven years have I ever said yes?"

"Just give it a try. You'll be hooked, I promise."

"No thanks."

"Whatever. We'll get you one day."

It's been a while since we've worked a project together, and I'm wondering how he's changed over the years.

"Pull over here." I point to a wood off this remote road. It's the perfect spot. Carrick's been quiet. Smart man. Mark is accepting my fabrications, which is exceedingly good luck for me. I'm glad he hasn't permitted the promotion to inflate his ego, as many less-seasoned professionals do. "I'll transfer Carrick to the Benz behind those trees; you wait here."

"Got it."

"When I give the signal, drive south. I'll wait five minutes and go north." I shut the door and Mark opens the trunk. With my gun pointed, I pull Carrick up by his collar. The hood is still on his head and he's not struggling. The duct tape over his mouth is doing a fine job keeping him quiet. "All right, I'm going to remove this hood and have you step out of the trunk. If you try to run or do anything other than what I tell you, I will shoot you. Nod if you understand."

Carrick nods.

When I pull the hood off, I hear another door open. It's Mark. I turn around only to find his gun aimed at my forehead. "What's this?"

"Like you said, TR calls the shots. We follow to the letter. Except this time, you didn't."

"You're mistaken. Just listen—"

"Xandra Carrick's still alive. You failed your mission. Colson wants you and Peter Carrick dead. Now."

Carrick tenses up, but with his feet and ankles bound and his mouth sealed with duct tape, he's not in a position to do anything about it. "You're in over your head, Mark. Once TR's got his hooks into you, you'll never break free. He'll hold everyone you care about as collateral."

"What do you know, old man?"

"You think you can just make a pile of money off him, then quit and settle down somewhere nice with a girl and start a new life? You can't. Trust me, I tried."

"What makes you think I want to settle down?" He cocks the hammer. "Sorry, Ian, but you of all people know that I have to."

Before he can pull the trigger, I duck and ram my head into his gut—a hit worthy of a championship rugby tackle. I may no longer be as spry as I once was, but I'm still every bit as strong.

He's winded. Gasping. I've got him pinned down with my knee on his chest. Mark fires a shot into the night.

From the corner of my eye, I catch Carrick hopping away, his hands tied behind his back. Any other time, it might be comical. But Mark strikes me in the head with his gun. For a moment, everything goes black, except for the floating flecks of light.

I've only got a second to act. So I grab at his gun. Thrust it high into the air. He fires another round. Tries to pull it down.

Another shot.

With all my weight, I ram my elbow down into his neck. I feel the sickening collapse of his windpipe. In this tiny window of opportunity, I twist his wrist and he drops the gun without a struggle.

At last, my vision clears.

Mark's eyes bulge. He's holding his throat and unable to breathe. Our eyes meet. For a moment, he silently pleads with me. *What have you done?* Then his eyes fill with hate. If he could, he'd kill me with his bare hands right now.

But he hasn't got the strength. If I simply walk away, he'll asphyxiate in a few minutes. But what a horrible couple of minutes that shall be.

He squeezes his eyes shut and his body jerks subtly. Tears draw wet lines down to his ears. He can't be more than thirty years old. My thoughts turn to Bobby. On those painful nights when he can barely move, he's so brave, tries not to cry out loud. Tears draw the same lines down his face.

I can no longer stand to see this. I've already caused so much suffering. Might as well, I'm a murderer and going to hell anyway. Mark opens his eyes. He's scared.

I reach for the gun that's fallen to his side. Press it into the middle of his forehead—Mark shuts his eyes.

Then I end his torment.

82

XANDRA CARRICK

The greatest shock after squeezing the trigger of the gun pointed at Colson is the hollow *click*. No explosion, no recoil, just a void click under my index finger. I open my eyes, and there is President-elect Richard Colson, his mouth pulled into a tight line, more disappointed than ever.

"Didn't bother checking, did you?" In one seamless move, he twists the gun out of my hand, flips it over, shoves in the missing clip, and aims it right at my face.

I step back, but it's no use. He twists my arm behind my back. "You've earned a distinct honor, sweetheart. I'm going to make an example of you."

Agent Burrell and Assistant Director Maguire return. Three other black-suited men arrive as well. Colson hands the gun to one of them.

A second agent speaks into his headset and covers Kyle's body with a sheet. I can't believe he's dead. Numbing trepidation cauterizes the sorrow and outrage. I'm feeling faint. Agent Burrell reads me my rights and straps my wrists behind me with plastic tie wraps, while the exchange between Maguire and Colson fades into white noise.

"Was it really necessary, sir?" Maguire says.

"Agent Matthews was your responsibility. You failed to contain."

"I'd feel more comfortable if I knew exactly—"

"That's beyond the scope of your position." Colson leans over and murmurs something to one of the Secret Service agents, then straightens up and adjusts his tie. "Assistant Direct Maguire, you have the thanks of my office for your cooperation in apprehending Ms. Carrick. Agent Russell will take it from here." Colson pats Russell on the back and leaves with the other two Secret Service men.

Maguire speaks to Russell quietly. "Where are you taking her?"

"An FDC. After processing, she'll be transferred to a NAV-CONBRIG."

"But this is a federal case."

"Homeland's got a list as long as the Verrazano Bridge on this one. Her anti-American activities go back almost ten years. The terrorism and attempted assassination charges supersede, but don't worry. The murder charges you're concerned about will also be brought up."

I probably shouldn't speak, I can't help myself. "I haven't killed anyone. It's Colson. He's the one you should be investigating!"

"You'll want to keep quiet until you have an attorney," Maguire advises. But keeping quiet is what precipitated this nightmare in the first place.

83

IAN MORTIMER

It's come to a head, all this damned killing. I've had enough. TR's made it exceedingly clear that he's cutting all ties now that he's been elected president of this screwed-up country.

Carrick has tripped over a rock and lies facedown in the grass, thrashing and turning. I pull Mark's BlackBerry from his belt. The next move is absolute. "Settle down, Peter. I'm coming." I turn him over and sit him up. With my gun pointed, I squat down to meet his gaze. He squints as I pull the duct tape off of his mouth.

A text message from TR pops up on Mark's BlackBerry.

TR: Status?

Mustn't hesitate. But I've got to stall him. On Mark's behalf, I text back:

MARK: Mortimer and Carrick Dead. Possible exposure.

TR: local police?

MARK: Y

TR: Go offline 72 hours. Upload proof of purchase then.

MARK: Offline 72 hours. Confirmed.

That ought to buy me some time. TR believes Mark's killed

me. The lad was talented, well trained, but ultimately inexperienced. If not for this final betrayal—though, given his situation, I could expect nothing else—we might have gone on to become friends.

Perhaps not, but a twinge of regret grips me nevertheless as I stare at his lifeless form.

"Are you going to kill me now?" Carrick asks.

"I'm done."

"Pardon me if I don't take your word." He stares over at Mark's dead body. "Aren't you working for Colson?"

I nod and spit out some blood. "Collinsworth would have ended up dead in a few years at the rate he was going. I just saved him a lot of heartbreak. And the lives of God only knows how many."

"Yeah. You're a real humanitarian."

"Let me remind you that I'm the one holding the gun. Don't you dare judge me. You haven't the foggiest what it's been like. The constant fear for my family because of that monster."

"I've got more than an idea. I've suffered thirty-five years of it. And that monster is now the president-elect of the United States. What's he got on you, anyway?"

"Everything! And now that I've failed to . . . Look, I was assigned to take your daughter out—"

"So you're the one who tried to kill her!" Carrick shouts and lunges at me. "I'll tear your guts out!" But his limbs are still bound and he just falls on his side.

"Easy now." I back up and wait for him to right himself. He's snarling like a rabid wolf. "The important thing is that she's still alive—"

"No thanks to you, you piece of—!"

"As are you! What you're failing to grasp is that I've been out of this business for a while. It was only a couple of years ago that Colson reinstated me—against my will, I might add. You want to know what he's got on me? I'll tell you."

For the next few minutes I tell him about Colson's deathgrip on my life, how he's got Bobby's in the palm of his hand. How every night, I pray for forgiveness for the lives I've had to take. "Now Bobby's got this incurable disease. And it's through Colson that we've been able to get access to experimental treatment, albeit illegally."

"Sorry about your boy," Carrick says, calmer. "But that doesn't excuse what you've done."

"No. It doesn't. Not a night passes that I'm not haunted by the faces of those I've killed. You'd think that twenty years of clean living might mitigate some of that, but it doesn't. But why is God punishing my little boy? It's the sins of the father revisiting the son, I tell you."

Carrick is suddenly quiet. I didn't expect it, but something's changed in his demeanor. The rage has been replaced with—I don't know—resignation. "Some sins are unforgivable, aren't they?"

"Indeed."

"And everything you've done for Colson, you did to protect your family."

"Precisely."

"Dammit, Mortimer, that's what it was like for me too."

"What are you on about?"

Carrick tells me about Colson's blackmail for the past three decades. As he does this, a bridge of solidarity forms over the gulf of suffering each of us has experienced and caused. A perverse solidarity at that.

"In a strange way," says Carrick, "if one could remove the emotions, I'd say you and I have more that unites us than divides."

"I've nothing against you or your daughter personally. And if it makes any difference whatsoever, I am sorry." I pull a hunting knife from the sheath on my belt. This makes him back away abruptly. "I'm going to release you now."

Confused, he blinks. "How do you know I'm not going to turn around and kill you?"

"I don't." He cuts the plastic tie wraps from my wrists. Then the duct tape strapped around my ankles. "But I trust you won't."

We eye each other with suspicion, but at the same time, we're two lost soldiers, once opponents, now facing a common enemy.

Rubbing his wrists, Carrick doesn't attempt to hurt me. Nor does he flee. "My wife used to quote this verse from the Bible: 'For we wrestle not against flesh and blood, but against principalities, against powers, against the rulers of the darkness of this world, against spiritual wickedness in high places.' "

"What's that supposed to mean?"

"That's the problem with eidetic memory. I can recall perfectly all the images I see, all the words I hear, but not necessarily their meaning. She quoted that verse every time we got in an argument. I think she was reminding herself not to get into personal conflicts. But to do battle with her own personal demons."

"A wise woman." I offer him a cigarette, which he declines.

"Beyond her years."

"Listen, Peter. Right now, I daresay we share similar goals. If Colson's willing to kill me, and anyone who could possibly expose him, there's nothing to stop him from going after Nicole and Bobby. He's already after your daughter. No matter what happens to you and me, we must protect them."

"Agreed. But how do you stop the most powerful man in the world?"

"There is a way. But it's going to cost us."

84

CNN.com
AP Press Release

The nation witnessed a landmark event in American history yesterday as Independent candidate Richard Colson won the election for president of the United States. History will mark him as the first Independent Party candidate elected since George Washington.

Coast to coast, victory parties ran straight through the morning, hailing the man everyone believes will lead the nation out of these troubled times of economic, military, and cultural decline.

President Bush called President-elect Colson this morning to congratulate him and offer the cooperation of his office for a smooth transition until his swearing-in on January 20, next year.

The mood around the country is one of excitement. Young and old, people of diverse cultures all have expressed great expectations for Colson, who has been called "the California Maverick," and still remembered by Vietnam veterans as "Thundering Rick."

85

GRACE TH'AM AI LE

My doctor has found a massive tumor in my brain. It is malignant and inoperable. They are amazed at my strength, considering the pain.

All I can say is "His grace is sufficient for me." But I know my time draws near. I have already exceeded my predicted survival period. I believe this is because I have unsettled business to attend to.

I have come to realize that the spiritual gifts that were given me were for one reason: to help others. For some time, I believed they were mostly for personal benefit—wisdom, comfort, direction, reassurance. Until now, what I failed to see was that these gifts were also there to reveal truth to me.

One of the greatest truths I have come to understand is that I must forgive Peter. Even now, he has not told me what he holds in his heart—or perhaps what in his heart holds him.

I suppose I rationalized, thinking, *How can I forgive him for something he doesn't admit?* It is not just the classified business meetings, but the choices he made. The distancing from his family. For this, I must forgive him.

And I do.

If there is one thing I can impart to my beloved husband and daughter it is this: Seek the truth. It will set you free.

I have.

I have requested that a letter I wrote to Xandi several years ago be sealed and given to her only after my death, along with this journal. Perhaps when the time is right, my exhortation will shed more light for both her and Peter.

I pray they will find both truth and freedom.

I had one last vision, lying here in my bed, while my husband finally fell asleep in the chair by my bed. It was a glorious vision, too beautiful for words. It's Peter's Pacific sunset, the open window to the eternal.

No longer afraid.

I am coming home.

86

AP Press Release
COLSON ADMINISTRATION'S PLAN FOR
GITMO CLOSURE

An unofficial leak from the Colson team indicates
that the closing of the Guantanamo Bay Detention
Camp will be high on the list of executive orders
under his new administration.

In his proposed plan, some of the suspected
terrorist detainees will be released, while the
majority of those remaining will be tried in
United States criminal courts.

Denouncing the idea of creating a new court
to handle the cases most entangled in highly
classified information, the Colson administration
will provide added information-security measures
and safeguards for detainees, to prevent any
abuse endemic to closed and anonymous military
tribunals.

At the same time, the plan is said to ensure the
security of classified information pertaining to
national security. Advisers directly involved

with this plan spoke on condition of anonymity because it has not yet been finalized.

This plan rides on the heels of the recent arrest of domestic terror suspect Xandra Carrick. Daughter of famed photojournalist Peter Carrick, Ms. Carrick has been charged with conspiracy and an assassination attempt on President-elect Colson. In addition, she has been charged with the murders of at least two veterans who served with Colson during the Vietnam War.

Carrick is also accused of murdering her father. Details have yet to be released, but a spokesperson for the prosecution speculates that the murder charges will be accompanied by terrorism charges.

Colson's plan to transition away from military tribunals will not take effect until the order is signed after his inauguration in January.

87

XANDRA COLSON

Naval Consolidated Brig
Marine Corps Air Station, San Diego, California

It's been about a week since I was transferred to the Marine Corps Air Station's Brig. I've heard people here refer to this place as NAV-CONBRIG. According to the staff, it's home to the Department of Defense Women's Correctional Facility, the only one in the military that is designated for female offenders.

I'm dazed, uncertain of what to do. Everything's happening so fast. I can only imagine that Dad is gone. God only knows what kind of evidence Colson has manufactured to pin his death, and the deaths of the other vets, on me.

Colson's managed to keep his atrocities hidden for thirty-five years, and with all his political power, virtually limitless personal resources, and an unprecedented approval rating as a senator that's sure to transfer over to his presidency, there's no way I'm going to beat the charges.

I've been here overnight in a six-by-twelve cell with a tiny window in the door and another on the outer wall. I wasn't permitted a phone call. I was told it is a privilege, not a right. Who would I call, anyway? Even if I knew lawyers on the West Coast, I'm broke. I've declined counsel by a military defense lawyer, but I shudder to think what kind I'll get from the list of civilian criminal defense attorneys.

The cell door opens, causing my heart to climb into my throat.

A pair of armed guards stands at the door as the female uniformed staff steps in. "You have a visitor."

The chains on my feet scrape the ground as we walk through the hall and arrive at the door to a conference room. I've never had my hands cuffed before, and when I see the young man seated at the desk, I make a pathetic attempt to hide them. These chains make me feel like an animal.

He stands, nearly trips in his haste to meet me at the door. "Ah, Ms. Carrick! John Morgenstern." He extends his hand to shake, but because of the manacles, all I can offer are my fingertips.

Which he actually takes and wiggles. "Pleased to meet you. I'm your appointed counsel for the tribunal next week."

"Next week? How's that possible?"

"Yeah, I tried to get a continuance, due to the ridiculously short discovery period. But look who we're up against. Doesn't work that way."

"Figures." I'm led to a table where I sit, with my chains fastened to an eye screw in the floor.

John Morgenstern rubs the bristles on his unshaved face and rolls his eyes. "I'm going to let you know this up front. I'm a first-year associate at my firm, and my boss, a senior partner, threw me into the lions' den because no one else would touch this case. And I—being at the portion of the totem pole where the sun don't shine—was handed the short straw in this month's *pro bono* lot."

"I would think they'd be happy to sink their teeth into a high profile case like this."

"You would think. But the fact is, Lawrence S. Goldman, president of the National Association of Criminal Defense Lawyers, has advised its eleven thousand members not to act as civilian counsel for tribunals like this."

"Why?"

"For one thing, there's no way I can guarantee attorney-client privilege. Everything you and I discuss is monitored by the government for intelligence purposes. On top of that, I can't say a word to the press without permission from the DOD. Not exactly a gag order, but it covers more than just classified information that might be involved in the trial."

"And yet, here you are."

"While my hands are tied—and most would argue that I can't provide a zealous or ethical defense under tribunal rules—with me, you have one thing going for you."

"Your charm? Don't tell me. You could sell the Brooklyn Bridge to the pope, and he'd buy the extended warranty with it."

"You're something." He chuckles and wags a finger at me. "I was going to say that the advantage of having me as your attorney is that I hate to lose."

"As opposed to being represented by someone who loves to?"

"I've never lost a criminal case yet."

"How many have you won?"

"Did I mention that I graduated with honors, top of my class at Cornell Law?"

"John, please tell me you've won all your cases."

"Okay, look. I second chaired for Jody Bauer of Bauer & Associates for all but one of them. So in a way, they weren't all my losses. And our clients got significantly reduced sentences because they pled out."

"Somehow, you're not inspiring a great deal of confidence."

"But I won my first case just last month. It was a capital, and I got my client a full acquittal. Made one heck of a closing argument. I can do this."

Sitting silent, staring into his sea-green eyes, I'm at a total loss. I don't know if asking for a more experienced attorney will do much good, even if I were allowed. But he's representing me for free, and that's all I can afford. It's John Morgenstern or an appointed military attorney.

88

I'm going crazy in here. For the past three days, I haven't spoken to anyone but interrogators about the most insane charges imaginable. "When did you first make contact with al-Qaeda?" "Who was your cell leader in Iraq?" "Where did you get the materials for the dirty bomb you intended for the presidential inauguration?"

These are the charges.

The imagination behind the elaborate fabrication of evidence is worthy of a Tom Clancy thriller. Nothing I've said seems to help. What good is it for a suspected terrorist to explain that the president-elect is a mass murderer? The truth is doing anything but setting me free.

My first hearing is today. I'm frustrated to no end that I've been able to speak with John Morgenstern only twice. He says he's trying to limit our communication due to the monitoring. I've told him my side of the story, even the visions I've had. But I can't tell if he believes me or not. He just takes notes and once in a while says, "Hmmm . . ."

I've just finished breakfast. Eggs and a biscuit served on a plastic tray. So far, life as a detainee isn't as bad as one might imagine. By far the worst part is the anxiety, the isolation. Plenty of time for my thoughts and feelings and imagination to get well acquainted. That isn't a good thing.

I miss Dad. Did we ever reconcile? Everything happened so quickly, and now he's gone. I never got to tell him how much I really do love him, despite the troubles we had. But now that I understand why he had to distance himself, all those years of resentment seem to wash away, leaving regret in their wake. How awful it must have been for him to carry around that kind of guilt all those years. And with his photographic memory, it's no wonder he couldn't sleep. All those horrific memories from Bình Sơn, alive in his head. He never got to redeem himself.

And what about Kyle? We came so close to a true connection. Only to have it ripped away. I'm sure they'll spin up some kind of bunk about him as a rogue agent helping the infamous terrorist who almost murdered the president and a million onlookers at his inauguration. Every day, anger competes with grief. Today, grief has the upper hand.

The door locks click open, the highlight of my day. It's Corporal Davis. She flashes a brief smile. "You have a visitor."

"I can't believe it."

Sure enough, when I arrive at the conference room, there with my attorney is Pastor Jake, dressed in a charcoal suit and a red tie. "Hello, Xandra."

"I almost didn't recognize you."

"Mr. Morgenstern told me you wanted to see me. I'm here in a clerical capacity."

"Don't perform my last rites just yet, I just . . ." I slump into my chair at the table. The guard secures my chains as they clatter. My cheeks burn, and tears fill my eyes as I behold my closest approximation to a friend. "John, could we have a moment?"

He looks at the guard, who nods. "Don't talk about the case," John says and points to his ear. All but Jake leave the room, though armed guards stand outside.

Jake takes a seat opposite me. "Are you all right?"

"No." I sniff and wipe my nose on the sleeve of my orange

prison uniform. "I'm sorry. You would not believe what I've been through."

"I can only imagine. But you're being held in a military prison as an enemy combatant. Have they—?"

"No. No, it's not like Abu Ghraib. I saw some brigs while on assignment in Iraq. This one isn't so bad."

He takes my hands in his. A pained expression comes over him. "Your courage is inspiring." Jake's the first ray of sunlight, breaking through the dark clouds. I glance into his eyes for a moment, then look down at the table for fear I might start crying.

"Have you had any more visions?"

"The Graflex is gone. I don't think I'll have any more visions. Maybe it's for the best." I tell him about everything else that's transpired since I left the colony. And then about that last vision, the one that uncovered Dad's past.

A knowing look comes upon him. "They're saying you killed your father."

"Oh, sure. I'm sure Colson's already scripted my motive, means, and opportunity. Does no one in this entire nation know what a danger their new president is? It's hopeless."

"It's never hopeless, Xandra."

"Wish I had your faith."

Jake leans forward, holds my gaze intently. "It's been said that you only need faith the size of a mustard seed. And with it, you can speak to a mountain, tell it to be cast into the sea. And it will."

"I'm facing Everest. And it shows no sign of budging."

His eyes brighten. Like he's got a secret but wants me to figure it out. "What would your mother have done at a time like this?"

"Well, I guess she'd pray. I don't know, I always thought it was just kind of superstitious, you know? Like a rabbit's foot, a placebo to get you through the tough times."

"Maybe it's more than that. Want to give it a try?"

He's right. Mom would have done just that. Pray, when things were looking their worst. It couldn't hurt. "All right. I could use all the help I can get."

Jake begins, "Father God, I thank You and praise You that You alone are sovereign, and You alone have established all authority in heaven and earth . . ."

My head is bowed, eyes shut. I'm actually hoping that another vision will come and reveal what is to come. But the words flowing from Jake's lips grow quiet. Now speaking in a strange language. I know I shouldn't, but I open my eyes—I can just hear Mom scolding me for doing that—and gaze, fascinated. He's deep in prayer, and it evokes a memory that I'd long forgotten until now.

I'm about three or four years old. At the time I don't know that I've got a high fever that isn't responding to medications. Mom is by my bed, praying just like Jake is. She has called her pastor over to lay hands on me and pray for healing. He, too, is speaking the same strange prayer language.

"You shall not die, but live, and declare the works of the LORD."

And at the same moment as this heretofore-forgotten memory comes to me, Jakes declares, "Xandra Phuong Carrick, you shall not die, but live, and declare the works of the LORD." His hand is on my head now. A warm tingle flows through me down to my feet like an anointing of light.

When he finishes, he looks up. "Another word. The Lord wants you to know. You're not alone."

89

AP Press Release
CARRICK'S REMAINS FOUND

FBI officials announced last night that the charred remains of Pulitzer Prize-winning photojournalist Peter Carrick were found in a remote wooded area three miles from the California Interstate-8 freeway. Forensics experts identified the body by dental records. Carrick's body was found in a car that had been set on fire, but the cause of death was a single gunshot wound to the head.

Carrick's daughter, Xandra Carrick, a former photojournalist for the *New York Times*, has been charged with his murder. Ms. Carrick, who is best known for her work on the plight of female suicide bombers, spent six months on assignment in Iraq. She has been named by the Department of Homeland Security as an enemy combatant and charged with multiple counts of murder, domestic terrorism, and the attempted assassination of President-elect Richard Colson. Carrick is currently being detained at the Naval Consolidated Brig in San Diego, awaiting a military tribunal.

Staff members for Colson, who, shortly after the election, had announced his intention to resign as the chairman of the Investigative Branch of the Senate Oversight Committee on Homeland Security by December, spoke on the condition of anonymity. The Department of Defense has approved a request to expedite the tribunal so that sentencing and security matters can be resolved well before Colson's inauguration in January.

In related news, the St. Deicolus Children's Foundation in New York announced today that its CEO, Ian Mortimer, is missing and presumed dead. Mortimer, a longtime supporter and personal friend of President-elect Colson, was sailing with Terrance Finley, a business associate, on Tuesday afternoon when the boat capsized. The Coast Guard continues to search for Mortimer and Finley's bodies, but after forty-eight hours, given the depths and temperature of the water and the distance from land, it is improbable that anyone could survive this long.

Mortimer is survived by his wife, Nicole, and son, Robert. They could not be reached for comment. Of Mortimer, Colson remarked, "He was a magnanimous man, devoted to the betterment of children with terminal illnesses. In the twenty-five years of our association and friendship, I have yet to meet someone with his level of integrity and competence."

90

XANDRA CARRICK

It takes a great deal of faith to believe that, as Jake prophesied, I'm not alone. Standing before a jury of uniformed officers and a judge who reminds me of General Patton, I couldn't feel more alone than I do right now.

It's difficult to concentrate during the opening statements. My thoughts are weighed down with grief. Dad, Kyle, Mom. They're all dead. Does it really matter what happens to me?

If God gave me a gift of clairvoyance, then I have to ask, to what end? All it did was get people I cared about killed. The truth has not set me free at all. On the contrary, it's imprisoned me and condemned me to death, and all the while the perpetrator of mass murders and the deception of our nation creates his version of the facts surrounding my arrest.

The list of charges is absurd. When Lieutenant Colonel Nevins, the prosecutor, gets to the portion of his opening that asserts that he will prove to the court that I spent a year in Iraq establishing connections with al-Qaeda, I can't help but laugh aloud.

Colonel Hardings, the judge, scowls. "Mr. Morgenstern, you will advise the defendant to refrain from disruptive outbursts."

"I apologize, Your Honor."

Morgenstern chastises me, but only in a written note: *Watch it!*

The prosecution calls a telecom expert from Homeland Security to testify about my so-called communications with terror cells in Iraq. While he speaks, the browser screen on Morgenstern's cell phone draws my attention. It's CNN.com. The headlines mention that Dad's body has been found. It's finally confirmed. I want to cry out, weep, scream. But I have to cover my open mouth, trying to control myself from another disruptive outburst.

At some point, the telecom expert concludes his testimony. I haven't heard a word he said.

Colonel Hardings addresses Morgenstern. "Counsel, would you like to cross-examine the witness?"

"No, thank you, Your Honor." A quiet stir can be felt throughout the room. He's still thumbing through his notes. I'm so numb, it doesn't bother me like it should. I really have lost hope.

Hardings: "Lieutenant Colonel, your next witness?"

Nevins: "The prosecution calls FBI Assistant Director Sharon Maguire." She's sworn in and takes a seat. Our eyes meet briefly, and she seems a bit reticent. But I'm glaring at her, as if the scorn in my eyes could strip her bare before the tribunal so that all can see her for what she is. A murdering, traitorous thug! *You killed Kyle . . . you killed him!*

Nevins walks up to her. "Ms. Maguire, would you describe for the court the conditions under which you found the defendant on that night in question at the Comanche Hotel?"

"We were following a tip on Kyle Matthews, one of my field agents who at the time had gone AWOL and was traveling incognito with Ms. Carrick. Upon arrival at the hotel room, I found Ms. Carrick standing over Agent Matthews's body. She'd shot him in the head point blank."

This launches me to my feet. "That's a lie! *She's* the one that—"

"The defendant will remain seated and quiet, or be removed!"

John pulls me back down into my chair. "Yes, Your Honor." He puts a finger as a bookmark in his notes. "My client apologizes." I did no such a thing.

"The witness will continue," says Colonel Hardings.

"Shortly after, President-elect Colson and a Secret Service detail arrived. It is my belief that he wished to interrogate the defendant. Before I could secure her, Ms. Carrick got a hold of my gun—"

Nevins looks surprised. "Your gun?"

"I'll admit it. I was distraught to see one of my top agents, a person I considered a friend, dead on the floor of that hotel room. My professionalism slipped for just a moment, and . . . I suppose when someone is as desperate as Ms. Carrick—"

John objects.

Hardings sustains the objection. "Move on, Ms. Maguire."

"The defendant pointed the gun at the president. She was swearing and threatening to shoot him. But President Colson—likely because of his military experience—remained calm and disarmed her."

Nevins returns to his chair. "Nothing further."

Finally, John decides to do his job and cross-examine a witness. He looks at his watch, then gets up and approaches the stand. "Ms. Maguire, at what point did my client become a suspect for the FBI?"

"The moment she fled the jurisdiction of her original incarceration."

"Meaning New York. The Dellafina case."

"Yes. Agent Matthews had been working on a case involving the deaths of several veterans of the Vietnam War. A connection to the defendant was found and he . . . As Agent Matthews had an outstanding record, I am loathe to say anything that would dishonor his nine years of service."

Colonel Hardings nods to her from the bench. "Noted. Please continue, Ms. Maguire."

"Matthews had been working on a case in which various Vietnam veterans of the same unit were dying. He believed there was a pattern to these seemingly natural deaths, or accidents. The connection led him to the defendant. It came to my attention at some point that he had become romantically involved with her. That was his mistake, and he paid for it."

"I see. Thank you, Ms. Maguire."

So far, I'm not terribly impressed by Morgenstern's cross-examination. Judging by the faces of the uniformed officers in the jury box, neither are they.

"Is it true, Ms. Maguire, that Agent Matthews was shot and killed with a twenty-two caliber round from a Beretta Bobcat?" He picks up the gun from the other exhibits on the table. "This very gun?"

"Yes. And I'd like to add that this gun had been registered to retired Corporal Hank Jennings, whom the defendant also killed."

"Allegedly."

Morgenstern returns to the desk and picks up a large Manila envelope. From it, he pulls out a photograph, a close-up of the gunshot wound to Kyle's forehead, and clips it on the whiteboard just left of the witness stand. It takes a good deal of willpower not to react. "Defense enters this photograph subpoenaed from the FBI forensics laboratory as exhibit four. Ms. Maguire, take a good look at this picture. Do you recognize it?"

"Of course, it's the gunshot wound to Agent Matthews's forehead."

"Do you notice anything unusual about it?"

"Nothing."

"Are you sure?"

"Anything else would take a trained medical examiner or ballistics expert."

Morgenstern takes the photo down and hands it to Maguire. "Sure you don't need another look?"

"I'm sure."

"You went on record stating that the gun was fired near point-blank. Didn't you?"

"Yes."

"Sure you don't need another look?"

Nevins objects. "Asked and answered."

She glances down and back up. "I don't see anything unusual."

"Well, I'm not so sure. You see, at so close a range, there should be some gunpowder residue, don't you think?"

"Academically, yes."

"I'm not seeing any dark stains that resemble gunpowder residue around the wound. And there's no explanation offered in the ballistics report as to its absence. Ms. Maguire, isn't it true that such an absence of residue is consistent with the use of a silencer?"

"I don't know."

"Isn't it true that the FBI uses silencers, or more accurately, suppressors?"

"Objection. The Federal Bureau of Investigation is not on trial here."

"But the veracity of the evidence is crucial to my case." Morgenstern faces Maguire. "Doesn't this report raise more questions than it answers?"

She puts the photo down and gives him a patronizing smile. "You'll have to take that up with the pathologist who wrote the report."

Without taking his eyes from her, he takes three steps back and reaches over the rail to retrieve a stack of papers from the desk. "You mean this report?" He enters it into evidence and hands it to her.

"This is the report."

"Please tell the court who prepared it."

She cranes her neck a bit to examine the cover. "It says Avijit Singh."

Morgenstern rests his hand on the rail of the witness stand. "Are you aware that Mr. Singh resigned from his position the day after this report was filed?"

"I don't keep track of anyone's career outside of my own direct reports."

"Why do you think he'd do that, after working in the Bureau for fifteen years?"

"Objection," Nevins says. "Relevance."

"Sustained."

A stir rises up from the jury.

"If I were to call him as a witness, Ms. Maguire, what do you think Mr. Singh would say, under oath, about this report that fails to mention the lack of gunpowder residue?"

"Objection!"

Before Hardings can rule, Morgenstern plows through the next set of questions. "Isn't it true that this report has been falsified and that the actual murder weapon was a Glock twenty-two, standard FBI issue?"

Maguire's eyes dart quickly between the jury and Nevins. She's unaware of her appearance until she notices the report shaking in her hands and puts it down.

"A Glock twenty-two with a suppressor, Ms. Maguire. Standard issue for the FBI, isn't that true?"

Nevins: "Your Honor!"

Hardings: "That's enough, counsel."

"Isn't it true, Sharon Maguire, that you did in fact shoot and kill Special Agent Kyle Matthews?"

"Counsel, you're to stop this line of—"

"And that you're part of an elaborate—"

"Mr. Morgenstern! Chambers!" Hardings is pounding his gavel repeatedly now; each rap rings in my head like a gunshot. John finally stops. Maguire's eyes are blazing, her teeth clenched. For a moment, it seems no one dares breathe. Then the judge addresses the courtroom. "We'll reconvene tomorrow morning at 0-eight-hundred hours."

91

"You're insane." Which is a bit easier to say to John when I'm locked in a guarded conference room in the brig. "What were you thinking?"

"Desperate times."

"I didn't think you'd go on the offensive like that."

"Reasonable doubt. That's the strategy. I saw an opportunity." John shrugs. "Colonel Hardings chewed me out real good in his chambers. He's under the impression that I got my law degree from FoxTV University."

"Can't say I blame him."

"We need to stay focused. This is just day one. Tomorrow Nevins will call Loran Stevenson, Homeland's National Cyber Security Director. I have to tell you, the evidence they've prepared—"

"Concocted."

"It's pretty tight."

"Is there any hope?"

"I believe so."

"I'm having a hard time believing in anything now."

"Even with that pastor's pep talks?"

I put my head down and let the grief and frustration pour out onto my sleeve. My words evaporate into a whimper. "I don't know."

Warm sunlight pours in from the window and bathes my shoulders. Small comfort, but I'll take what I can get. Reflecting on the past few days in prison, I realize that I haven't had any appetite, can't sleep well, and I'm probably losing weight.

John has been thumbing through pages upon pages—no doubt briefs, affidavits, and evidentiary documents. Then the rustling of paper stops. All is silent save for the soft buzzing of the white flourescents overhead. "Hey."

I barely answer with a soft grunt.

"It's not over till G. Gordon Liddy sings. And even then, it ain't."

"You're naive."

"And you need to have some faith."

"You've been talking to Pastor Jake, I see."

"What?"

"I just can't make any sense of it. If there really is a God, a God who gave me those visions, then He's either incompetent or He's a sadist."

John puts his papers down and sits up, his eyes a bit wider. "I once saw a bumper sticker that said: *If you're an atheist, you'd better pray that you're right.* Couldn't help but laugh. But you know, we often laugh at things that make us uncomfortable."

"Are you an atheist?"

"Always thought I was. Then I realized that it takes the same kind of faith *not* to believe, you know?"

"Never thought of it that way."

"People always say, 'I'll believe it when I see it,' right? But I'm starting to think that faith isn't about seeing. It's counterintuitive because, well, it goes beyond human perception."

"As in supernatural?"

"Possibly. The way I see it, faith says: *I'll see it when I believe it.* And true faith is something you're willing to act upon, especially when under stress."

That makes me lift my head. "Wow. This from an atheist."

"I think we atheists have to have the strongest faith of all. Because if we're wrong . . ." He smiles and points a thumb at the ground. "Look, I don't know about these visions you've had, whether they're some kind of psychic phenomenon or a supernatural gift. All I know is that you're innocent until proven guilty. And I'm having a hard time believing in the evidence the prosecution's presenting."

"That's because it's all fabricated." I pick up a bunch of papers and start looking through them. "These so-called facts about me are unbelievable when you know the truth. But if you don't, it actually looks credible."

He tries to take the papers from my hand, but I'm still reading them and grip them tighter. I motion for him to come close, so I can whisper in his ear. It's risky, because I know we're being monitored, but it's the only chance I have to speak with John about the case. "Look at this one. This is evidence that I had conspired to assassinate Colson in January at his inauguration with a dirty bomb. Look at these receipts—I can't even tell you what these items are."

"It's difficult to prove these documents are fakes. I've checked them thoroughly and their purported sources all corroborate them. You know, you don't get the same stringent chain of custody for evidence in a tribunal as you would in a civilian criminal case."

"There's got to be a weak link in Colson's machine, someone who'll bring the truth to light about the atrocities in Vietnam, the cover-up, the murders. Someone who'll testify."

"Would you?"

"Would I what?"

"Testify against him, if you worked for him?"

I let that question sink in as I flip through to the final page of this dirty-bomb brief. It looks so official that even I'm almost convinced. "I see your point. Anyone who was that involved would know the dangers of speaking out."

"It's an unholy matrimony."

"Till death do you part."

"Yeah." Now, in a normal voice, John says, "Hey, you mind?" He tries again to take the document I wouldn't relinquish. "I need that."

"Oh, right. Sorry."

John takes a deep breath and gathers his things. "Well, anyway. I just thought I'd fill you in on what happened today."

"Going after the prosecution's witness like that? I wonder how Nevins took it."

"Oh, he's ticked. But these military lawyers like a good fight. I was just doing a little punching below the belt. He'll get over it."

"Hope you haven't flushed your career down the toilet."

A shrug, and he stands. "If I have, it's okay. I'm just placating my parents. They put me through school and hoped I'd come back to the East Coast and become a partner in my father's firm. But truth be told? My real passion is surfing."

"Hold fast to dreams."

"Right on." He knocks on the door, and the guard lets him out.

Not a lot accomplished in this meeting. Because of the strict intelligence monitoring and lack of attorney-client confidentiality, John can't really tell me much about strategy. He's asking me to put a lot of faith in him.

He's crazy.

But it just might be a lunatic I'm looking for.

92

Day two of the tribunal.

I'm disturbed by the similarities between my case and that of José Padilla, who was arrested by federal agents at Chicago's O'Hare Airport in 2002 on terrorism charges and subsequently declared an enemy combatant working to construct a radioactive dirty bomb. Only, his case was eventually moved to a civilian court. With all Colson has at stake, it's impossible he'll permit that to happen with me. After all, if the truth ever came out, what kind of faith could our nation ever have in our governing leaders again?

We all looked to Colson as the hope of the nation after eight years under the Bush regime. God only knows where Colson will lead the country after he's sworn in.

These are the thoughts that run through my mind while Loran Stevenson of Homeland Security is sworn in. He's a formidable man with a silver crest who looks like he could have been an NFL linebacker in his prime. Even now, he's not the kind of person with whom I'd get into a disagreement. When he speaks, his voice booms throughout the courtroom.

Intimidation incarnate.

Nevins dives right in with his testimony, all of which, when bolstered by the ostensive evidence, seems compelling. So compelling, in fact, I can't even think of a way to refute it.

What's our defense? "They're lying." Is that all we've got? Oh, we've got my testimony. My visions, my version of what happened when I pulled a gun on Colson.

All of Stevenson's testimony atomizes into distant words. The portrait they've painted of me shocks me to the point of numbness. I'm really quite dangerous, apparently.

Nevins sits down. "No further questions."

Before John approaches the witness, Judge Hardings points a finger. "Careful, Mr. Morgenstern."

"Sir." He's a lot tamer on today's cross, which makes me feel both relieved and somewhat peeved. Stevenson is a much heavier hitter than Maguire, the assistant director of the FBI serial-crimes unit. He's the one John should pummel, isn't he? But no. It's almost like he's throwing the fight. A chill creeps up my back. Could my attorney be on Colson's payroll as well? Colson's corrupted power stretches out deeper and wider than imaginable. He's obviously controlling the media now. Did he get to John too?

"Mr. Stevenson, can you state to an absolute certainty that none of these documents and records entered by the prosecution into evidence have been tampered with, or even fabricated?"

"Yes."

"Let me remind you that you're under oath, sir."

Stevenson smiles at John as though he were a five-year-old. "Which part of my answer did you fail to understand?" Subdued laughter erupts from the jury box and even from the judge himself. What are you doing, John?

John grins, but his ears and face flush crimson. "Nothing further."

"Call your next witness, Lieutenant Colonel Nevins."

"Yes, Your Honor. Please the court, the prosecution has just acquired new evidence in regard to the defendant's assassination attempt."

"Objection." John hasn't even returned to his seat, and he turns back to the bench. "I should have been informed."

"I wasn't at liberty to do so without compromising classified information."

"Your Honor, this is unfair surprise. At least grant me a continuance to review."

Hardings shakes his head. "You're not in civil court defending the indigent, counsel. This is a military tribunal. You need to be prepared for anything. I'll not lower the bar for you."

"With all due respect, Your Honor, what in the name of—"

"Call your witness, Mr. Nevins."

He nods to the guards in the back of the courtroom, and they open the double doors. "Your Honor, the prosecution calls President-elect Richard Colson."

93

It's an eerie portent. President-elect Richard "Thundering Rick" Colson stands ramrod straight with his right hand raised as the sergeant at arms swears him in.

Is this how they imagined it at the inauguration, where supposedly I planned to plant a suitcase-size nuclear bomb? To kill him and the faithful multitudes out by the Lincoln Memorial? The initial detonation would have killed him in the blast, along with the vice president and other dignitaries on the stage. The radiation would contaminate everyone in a five-block radius.

Excepting the thousands of innocent people who could get cancer from the radioactive spread, I almost wish it were true. This man is evil. And what makes him so frightening, besides the fact that he has so much control over this nation's perceptions, is that he's so debonair, so well liked, and perceived as such a hero.

Colson doesn't make eye contact or even glance my way. But my hands are cold and damp anyway. The thought of his ordering the deaths of countless individuals and walking away with absolute impunity sickens me.

John leans against my shoulder. "You okay?"

"I think I'm going to be ill."

"Can you wait until afterward?"

"How can you make light?"

He shrugs and points his chin at the witness stand. Nevins's obsequious posture is almost laughable. "I would like to remind the court that President-elect Colson testifies today in his capacity as chairman of the Senate Oversight Committee on Homeland Security. I am deeply grateful for his taking time out of his busy schedule to be here."

Judge Hardings nods. "Thank you, Lieutenant Colonel."

"Mister President-elect, how long has the defendant been a subject of interest for the Department of Homeland Security?"

"I was not made aware of Homeland's interest until she was arrested in New York for the murder of Stacy Dellafina. According to my staff, Homeland's been eyeing her carefully since the summer of 2007, when she went on assignment to Iraq."

"Is it there that she first made contact with al-Qaeda?"

John stands. "Objection, there is no evidence—"

"Overruled." Hardings waves a dismissive hand. "Sit down, son."

Colson continues. "We believe she had made initial contact in Iraq, yes. But the actual interest arose when the FBI began investigating the deaths of the Vietnam veterans who served under me during the war."

"Did you fear for your life?"

"Son, I faced down the Vietcong in the Mekong Delta."

"Of course, sir. Allow me to rephrase. When did you become concerned for your safety?"

Colson leans back in the chair, his hands folded neatly over his belt buckle, not a care in the world. "I had a campaign to run, an election to win. I let the Secret Service handle those concerns. But to answer your question, I would say sometime around August. They never used the term 'assassination,' but I knew they had their concerns."

"Tell us about what happened the night that Xandra Carrick was arrested."

"Following a lead by Assistant Director Maguire, I came to the Comanche Hotel."

"The casino hotel? How did you fare?"

"I resisted the temptation." A collective laugh rises from the old boys' club. They're all cronies here, and their next commander in chief is cracking jokes. "But seriously, when I came to the room where they had found Ms. Carrick, she seemed distraught that she'd shot Agent Matthews.

"I had planned on interrogating her, but she managed to grab Maguire's weapon and pointed it at me."

"Do you believe she would have killed you?"

"I believe she would have tried her best. But compared to some of the people who've aimed a gun at me, she wasn't that bad."

"Still, an attempted assassination."

"Don't get me wrong, I don't minimize the gravity of such actions. Homeland's since explained to me her plans to detonate a dirty bomb on January twentieth at the Mall in Washington D.C. during the inauguration. I suppose she grew impatient and decided to step up the assassination date."

"How many people are projected to attend the inauguration?"

"Experts estimate the turnout will reach upwards of two million."

Nevins lets out a low whistle. "Two million people. That's quite a large target."

"I doubt she'd have gotten very close. Nevertheless, conspiracy to commit acts of mass terrorism is a serious offense. And she's killed many people on her long road to infamy."

Biting my lip, I nudge John. "Now might be a good time to object."

But he doesn't respond. His eyes are stuck on his watch, then his cell phone, which has been buzzing in his jacket with text messages. How can he act so cavalier? Is he tanking my case?

"Thank you, Mr. President," Nevins says. "Mr. Morgenstern, your witness."

John fumbles his cell phone, drops it on the floor, and apologizes. I'm face palming now.

"Counsel, would you like to cross-examine the witness?"

"No, thank you, Your Honor." He peers directly at Colson.

"The witness is dismissed," Hardings says. "The court wishes to thank the president-elect."

Colson gives Hardings a winning smile and a thumbs-up.

"However," says John, "at this time, I would like to call a rebuttal witness."

"Objection," Nevins calls out. "He's trying to make a mockery of these proceedings." Colson pauses and stands next to him, awaiting the result of John's latest antic.

"May it please the court, I never had a chance to depose the prosecution's surprise witness."

"Depose the president-elect?" Nevins scoffs.

"The prosecution's case in chief is not over yet," says Judge Hardings. "And even if it were, what basis do you have for a rebuttal?

"*United States versus Grintjes*, 2001, Seventh Circuit."

Nevins stands, clears his throat. "This is improper use of a rebuttal, Your Honor."

"And *Peal versus Terre Haute PD*, August 2008. The Seventh Circuit stated, and I quote: 'The proper function of rebuttal evidence is to contradict, impeach, or defuse the impact of the evidence offered by an adverse party.' "

Hardings thinks hard on this. For all of two seconds. "Counsel, I can't allow this."

To everyone's surprise, not the least mine, John walks up the center aisle back toward the double doors. "But Your Honor, if you'll just—"

"The defense will be afforded the opportunity to make its case at the appropriate time."

"Your Honor, I must insist you give me that opportunity now."

Hardings stands and points a finger at him. "Keep this up, Morgenstern, and I'll—"

"It's all right, Your Honor." He calmly pushes against the doors with both hands. "Just let me introduce them."

"I'll hold you in contempt!"

Ignoring him, John announces, "Officers of the court, the defense calls Ian Mortimer and Peter Carrick."

The entire room erupts with confusion. Quicker than ever seen in this courtroom, everyone stands and turns to the doors. Not even when the sergeant at arms calls out "All rise" do they get up so suddenly. A clamorous wave sweeps through the courtroom. Nevins is objecting all over the place. Hardings pounds his gavel for order.

I can't see past all the standing people, so I, too, get up. I can't believe my ears, much less my eyes. Dad, dressed in a dark suit, walks down the center aisle; his abductor, my would-be killer, Ian Mortimer, follows behind him.

It's him. It really is him. "Daddy!" I shout, unable to contain my joy and tears. But an armed guard stands in my way. My father meets my eye with a reassuring look that says, *I'm here now. It's going to be all right.*

Oddly enough, before Ian Mortimer takes a seat in the gallery, he and Dad exchange a glance of camaraderie.

I turn to John Morgenstern. "What's going on?"

"All hell."

"Why didn't you tell me?"

"Big Brother was watching. Had to be done under the radar."

Dad is sworn in and steps into the witness stand. And as he begins his testimony, I can see the future. I don't even need my Graflex to know.

THE PACIFIC LAW JOURNAL
AP Press Release
San Diego, CA
STUNNING TURN IN CARRICK TRIBUNAL--COLSON
UNDER INVESTIGATION

A dramatic turn of events threw the case against
Xandra Carrick into disarray yesterday at San
Diego's Naval Consolidated Brig. The entire
tribunal looked on with perplexed wonder when
freshman attorney John H. Morgenstern of the
San Diego firm Bauer & Associates pulled not one
but two rabbits out of his legal hat.

Reported dead, both Peter Carrick and Ian
Mortimer showed up alive and well as surprise
witnesses for the defense. Both gave testimonies
that not only impeached the prosecution's
evidence, but launched grave accusations against
its star witness, President-elect Richard Colson.

Peter Carrick testified against him and
provided evidence of his involvement in a
massacre of innocent village inhabitants in Binh

Son, during the Vietnam War. Carrick served as a photojournalist embedded with Echo Company, a Marine Corps unit under the command of then Lieutenant Colonel Richard "Thundering Rick" (or TR) Colson. Carrick witnessed and photographed the brutalities, which included the raping of young girls and the torture of children and the elderly. But under threat of retribution, the photojournalist buried this evidence. Until yesterday.

Fully aware of the self-incriminating nature of his testimony, Carrick went on record as saying, "My silence made me an accessory to the cover-up. And to the good people of Binh Son, home of my departed wife, Grace, I offer my deepest regrets and ask forgiveness."

Asked if he thinks he'll get immunity, or at least a lightened prison sentence for coming forward, Carrick said, "I'm ready to pay my debts."

The most damaging testimony against Colson came from Ian Mortimer, who confessed to serving as the president-elect's chief assassin for nearly twenty-five years. Mortimer confessed to a long list of murders he committed in compliance with Colson's demands. This list includes Stacy Dellafina, Colonel Hank Jennings, and several other retired Echo Company veterans whom Colson allegedly wished to silence.

The details are classified, but the *Pacific Law Journal* has been informed by an anonymous source that Mortimer had been granted special access to many of the resources of the Secret Service and the Department of Homeland Security in order to cover his tracks—tracks that might have led back to Richard Colson.

Ironically, these very resources and connections

helped provide records and other forms of inculpatory evidence against Colson. A spokesperson for the Federal Ethics and Anti-Corruption Commission stated, "It's too early to determine the scope of Colson's influence throughout the conspiracy. But it is believed that several agencies, including the FBI, Homeland Security, and the Secret Service, have been compromised."

A probe has been launched to investigate. Currently, Richard Colson is under house arrest while Jennifer Bradley, the vice president-elect, prepares for the most unexpected event in her life: becoming the first female president of the United States.

Xandra Carrick has been released and exonerated of all charges in light of the exculpatory evidence provided by her father and the man who was hired to kill them both, Ian Mortimer.

96

PETER CARRICK

Bright orange isn't my favorite color, but I suppose I'll have to get used to it. For at least ten more years. That's what I'm facing when I enter my plea next week in federal court.

Seated in a tiny booth with a telephone and thick glass between us, Xandra waves hello. The prison guard leads me to my seat where I pick up the handset. "Hi, sweetie."

"Daddy." She wipes her eyes, smiles courageously. "I can't stand to see you like this."

"I'm all right, Xandi. Don't cry."

"You know, when Mortimer took you, I thought God wouldn't take you away from me, not when you finally faced down your demons and returned to me. But when the news came out that your body was found, burned beyond—" She covers her eyes and sobs.

"Colson leaked that story to plug the hole on my disappearance. By the time he found out Ian had tricked him, it was too late."

"I can't believe you came back to confess like that."

"I'd do anything for you, Xandi. It hasn't shown for years, I know. But to me, you'll always be that precious little girl I held in my arms the day you were born. Did you know that was the first, perhaps the only, time I ever prayed?"

"Really?"

"I promised God I'd do anything to protect you, even lay down my own life."

She just smiles a wet smile and places her hand up against the glass. I put mine up to meet hers. "I love you, Daddy."

"I love you too. Maybe it's a side of me you don't know because—"

"I've always known. You're a great man, a great father."

"You've got more faith than I."

"It takes just as much faith not to believe. I just made the better choice."

I don't think I can come up with the right words to express how much I love her. After all these years, my expressive skills have atrophied. But I'll have plenty of time to practice and write her from prison.

"Daddy, I don't know how to thank you."

"I did it for myself as well."

"But twenty years."

"Morgenstern says the AG's office is willing to reduce it to ten if I plead out."

"It's not fair. You helped expose a murderous war criminal and they're taking away your freedom."

"No one's taking it from me, Xandi. I'm giving it up. There's no prison wall that can ever take the freedom I've gained." For the first time, I can look my daughter in the eye, unashamed. As she says good-bye and leaves, I'm comforted by the knowledge that tonight, the faces of Bình Sơn will no longer haunt me.

And I will sleep.

97

RICHARD COLSON

I can only laugh at the irony.

They think they've taken down a war criminal, saved their nation from an unspeakable evil. All they've done is signed their own death sentence.

If they can't understand that everything I've done, from the moment I joined the Marines until my election as president of the United States, has been to protect this country, then they deserve what's coming to them.

Look at this mess they've gotten themselves into: Iraq, Afghanistan, the collapse of the American economy, threat of shifting superpowers. Who's going to make the tough choices, the ugly ones? Neither my Republican nor my Democratic opponents had the balls for that, and now this country is going to be handed over to a president with no biological balls.

Life is war—when are those idiots going to face it? For those who stand in the way, indecisive, hesitant, legislating the future away, I say, get out of the way and let someone who can lead get the job done. True leaders are above the rules and codes that apply to the ordinary people we fight for and sacrifice to protect. You do whatever you can to gain the upper hand, and you get out. Face it. Some people are going to die. I learned that the hard way in Nam.

Tragic, but that's just the way it goes, no need to cry about it. Crying weakens you.

That's something I've told my boys since they were little. Ingrates won't talk to me now. Suzie is filing for divorce. After all I've done for her, all I've sacrificed.

Dammit, now I'm crying.

There's nothing left. It's just me and this empty house, guarded by the very men once sworn to protect me. All I've got left is my pride and my love for my country, which I'd gladly die for. And now, with the muzzle of my classic Winchester 1895 tucked under my chin, I will.

This is my rifle. There are many like it, but this one is mine.
My rifle is my best friend. It is my life.
I must master it as I must master my life . . .
Before God, I swear this creed. My rifle and myself are the
defenders of my country. We are the masters of our enemy.
We are the saviors of . . .

98

IAN MORTIMER

"Bloody hell, Nikki, why did you bring him?"

"He's your son." Even though Nicole has shielded him from the media, there's no escaping the truth. His father is a murderer. Nevertheless, I cannot bear to have him see me this way, in manacles and prison garb. "Please, Ian. He'll start to worry out there, waiting with the guard."

"Mightn't we have a moment alone first?"

"I'm here now."

Truly, the most amazing thing about this entire debacle is that when I had confessed all to Nicole, after the initial shock and anger and a sense of betrayal, she decided to forgive me.

"In a way I'm relieved." She glances over her shoulder to see if Bobby is watching. "All those secretive phone calls, all those out-of-town trips you wouldn't talk about. I thought you were having an affair."

"I had no choice. Colson would have come after you and Bobby. Confessing was the only way to stop him."

"Please, Ian, let Bobby come and say good-bye before they transfer you."

"I'm not quite ready, love." A sob catches in my throat. "What have I done? How's he going to go on, knowing his father's a monster? And worse still, I can't get any more meds for him now."

"You really think drugs will save him?"

"It helps with the pain."

"He needs a miracle. How much can we hope or pray for, as long as what we give him results from ill-gotten gain?"

"I'm going to hell, Nicky. All those people I killed. I deserve the death penalty, I do."

"We won't leave your side." She's been uncommonly strong through this entire ordeal. But now, despite the smile, tears pool in her eyes.

If only this blasted window weren't in the way. I'd gather her up in my arms, hold her forever. I may die by lethal injection, or at best live out the rest of my life in prison, but never shall I have to kill or do anything for Colson again. An unexpected wet sniffle. I blow a kiss to the beloved mother of my son. "Would you bring Bobby in now? I'm ready."

99

SEALED LETTER ADDRESSED TO XANDRA CARRICK

19 December 2003

My Dearest Xandra,

If you are reading this letter, then I have already gone home to my Lord. Do not be overcome with grief, but look forward to the day when we meet again.

If you have read my journal, then you know that there are some matters of significance I have never spoken with you about. I am referring to the visions I have had in my life.

Today, I experienced one of the most real, most frightening, and most wonderful visions in my forty-eight years. Afterward, I felt compelled to write this letter and put it in my will that you only read it after my death. Which may come sooner than expected.

I have seen symbolic images of your future. And while I cannot discern what each of them means specifically, I believe I understand their meanings. Please consider what I am about to say, and see if it verifies what you may be sensing in your spirit today.

If you have followed the path for which you have been ordained, you will have helped free your father of whatever bondage he suffers from all these years. It will come at a

great personal cost for both of you. But what you will gain
will be beyond measurable worth.

My daughter, I saw that you will be given spiritual gifts
even greater than mine. Do not fear them, though they cost
you your comfort, your preconceptions of reality, and even
your mortal life. You should not keep these gifts to yourself.
They are imparted for the benefit of all God's children.

And finally, my dear Xandi, accept who you are without
the need for the approval of anyone on earth. You are a
child of the Almighty, and that is what matters most. You
have a calling, a purpose. And as Jesus Christ told His
followers regarding the miracles He performed, "You shall
do these works and even greater works."

I am so proud of you, and I know at this point, your
father is as well.

I love you always,
Mom

100

XANDRA CARRICK

For to one is given the word of wisdom through the Spirit, to
another the word of knowledge through the same Spirit . . .
to another the working of miracles, to another prophecy . . .
But the manifestation of the Spirit is given to each one for
the profit of all.

—1 Corinthians 12:8–11

For the profit of all. Mom would tell me this, whenever she talked
to me about how gifted I was. Along with these verses, she would
tell me that old Vietnamese *Tiger's Throne* fable. I'm beginning to
understand the truth she meant to convey.

She used to tell me I had many gifts, that one day I would
do great things. That I was extraordinary. But I stopped believing it.

I see the truth about my gift, now that it's gone. Had the
truth set me free? Had anyone profited from it? One thing is certain: the change in Dad's life. His very countenance radiates the
joy of a resurrected spirit. Come what may, he no longer needs
to hide in the darkness. Even in prison, he stands tall in the
light, no longer a captive to the deceptions that held him in

chains for half his life. Inmates look to him as a beacon, and he gladly accepts that role.

Dad's not the only one. I, too, have been set free. Like that old hymn says: *I once was lost, but now am found, was blind but now I see.*

Since I began seeing visions, I questioned the purpose of this ostensible gift. Why would anyone want to see or know the details about horrific murders? Of what use were they? All they seemed to do was bring me to a life-threatening precipice and demand I take a leap of faith. Until now, I truly believed that some things were not meant to be seen, to be known.

But I see now that these visions are gifts, given for the sake of truth. Hidden truth. Truth that brought closure to the Dellafina family, that brought justice to a forgotten farming village in Vietnam. That exposed Richard Colson for what he really was. Truth that brought light to the darkness.

The manifestation of the Spirit is given to each one for the profit of all.

If given another opportunity, I wonder if I'd embrace that gift and the responsibility that comes with it. It doesn't matter now. The Graflex is gone. I don't even care about the Marbury now.

In a way, I'm glad. I've had enough and am perfectly happy never to see another vision again. No more negatives, chemicals, or darkrooms. I've decided to start playing the cello again. Perhaps I'll start with a recital in a retirement home.

I'm content viewing some pictures as a slideshow on the computer monitor in Dad's house. I took some great shots at Del Mar beach yesterday using my Nikon digital SLR. With a click of the mouse, I pause the slideshow on this one, my favorite: An expiring sun infuses the firmament with its essence. Broad scarlet strokes form a celestial fresco. There's nothing quite like a Pacific sunset.

The shore reflects like a mirage, except here, the water is real.

Everything on this unadulterated canvas is real: sand, sea, and the light. Edouard Manet said: "The most important person in any picture is the light." Nothing disturbs this image.

Except . . .

The sound of rushing wind, the numb tingling in my body I am perceiving. The salty breeze, the sand between my toes. Without the Graflex or darkroom, I can see it's something that had not been there when I took this picture.

I'm on the shore, suspended in that state of existence where past, present, and future coexist in perfect unity.

The waves ebb.

From beneath the glassy surface of the ground, it emerges.

The body of a missing person.

And with it, a new story.

The truth.

Acknowledgments

The conception of this book was very much like that of a child. I had just lost my job of nine years and decided to take advantage of the free time to concentrate on my passion for writing. After discussing what we felt makes a great novel, my wife and I sat in the living room for several hours thinking up ideas for the central character (Xandra Carrick) and a plot we felt we'd love to read.

From that point on, *Darkroom* flowed from my mind without pause until it was completed. I'd like to call it divine inspiration, but that would be oversimplifying things. Suffice it to say, this book was founded on love and faith, themes that weigh heavily in this work.

But it's not enough to simply say that *I* wrote this book. No man is an island, and contrary to what some may say, neither is any successful author. There are so many people I wish to thank and honor, and I'll have to beg forgiveness from those I was not able to mention by name.

First, I wish to acknowledge my editor Holly Halverson, who helped bring this book to the polished quality expected of Howard Books. I'd also like to thank Jessica Wong for her tireless help coordinating the manifold logistics involved in the production of a book. I am deeply grateful for all the effort and support of the entire *Darkroom* team. Of course, I must mention Becky Nesbitt, who in her extremely busy role as vice president took the time and believed in my work enough to acquire it.

I would also like to thank my Online Writing Trio members, Susan Wingate, and Michael Bellomo for all their encouragement throughout my career. I've learned so much from them both. A special thanks to Khanh Nguyen for helping me with authentic Vietnamese-American cultural questions. I would also like to thank Dean Wesley Smith (my first editor ever) and Kristine Kathryn Rush, my mentors in writing and the publishing business for years. The effects of their generosity and wisdom will remain with me always, and I can only hope to pay forward as much as they have poured into me. And, of course, my fellow Fall 2009 Master Class alums, who have given me invaluable feedback and cheered me on as I embarked on this journey of writing.

I would be remiss if I neglected to honor the people from The City Church San Diego, my second family. Pastors Jerry and Tami McKinney, the Business Owners Prayer Group, Tom and Christy Giangreco, Patrick and Connie Montoya, Chris and Carol Essex, Kerry Layton, and my connect-group members: Brandt and Jennifer Strieby, Reza and Kathy Namvar, Ken and Lisa Lako, Cary and Tammie Gilmore, Tom and Trish Vesneski, and Farshid and Marisol Farokhi. Also, my very close friends and relatives William and Ckristina Sutjiadi, Michael and Patricia Goh, Stephen and Vivien Tseng. Thank you all for your fervent prayers through some of the most challenging times of my life.

In all my books I wish to honor the memory of my mother, Anna, as well as my father, Paul, who at the time of this note continues to race across the planet preaching and teaching the good news of Christ at the age of eighty-three! God bless you always.

Of course, I must save the best for last. I want to thank and honor my beautiful wife, Katie, for standing by me all these years, from my first short-story sale to the publication of this book. You are my muse, my best friend, and my wonderful helper in life.

Reading Group Guide

Discussion Questions

1. In *Darkroom* Peter Carrick withholds the truth in order to protect his family—a lie of omission. Do you think it's ever moral or acceptable to lie? Why or why not?

2. Xandra Carrick is a strong individual but vulnerable when it comes to her relationship with her father. How much does your relationship with your father (or other paternal figure) affect your view of yourself?

3. Xandra's visions bring her knowledge that put a burden of responsibility on her shoulders. Have you ever become privy to something that you struggled with, wondering whether you should turn a blind eye or bring it out into the open? How difficult was that decision?

4. Peter Carrick was not a religious person, yet he was married to Grace, a deeply spiritual woman from a different culture and ethnicity. How do you think their differences affected their marriage and life? Have you ever had to overcome such vast differences?

5. How were the following characters imprisoned by the lies and secrets they kept? Peter Carrick, Ian Mortimer, Richard Colson.

6. Have you ever kept a secret that ate away at you? How did it feel when you finally came clean with it, if you did so?

7. When Pastor Jake speaks to Xandra about faith and his views on life, he says: *"Nothing* just *happens. Everything's connected. By a divine plan. What we humans perceive as infinite possibilities of events doesn't even come close to the infinite from God's point of view."* Do you agree or disagree? Explain.

8. When Kyle explains why he never questioned Xandra's ability to see visions, he cites Pascal's Wager, which states: "Though the existence of God cannot be determined through reason, a person should wager as though God exists, because living life accordingly has everything to gain, and nothing to lose." What do you think of this?

9. Xandra actually pulled the trigger when pointing the gun at President-elect Colson. Was this from vengeance, self-protection, or to rid the world of an evil man who abused power? If you were in Xandra's position, would you have done the same?

10. John Morgenstern, Xandra's defense attorney, said, "I think we atheists have to have the strongest faith of all. Because if we're wrong . . ." Do you think it takes faith to believe there is no God? Explain.

11. After testifying and confessing his own lies, Peter Carrick goes to prison where he says: " 'There's no prison wall that can ever take the freedom I've gained.' For the first time, I can look my daughter in the eye, unashamed." Can you think of a time when a lie has imprisoned you? And a time that the truth set you free?

Author Q&A

1. You mention in the acknowledgments of *Darkroom* that you began pursuing your passion for writing after losing your previous job of nine years. What kind of work were you involved in before? How does it affect what you write about today?

In the past I worked as a professional musician (I'm a cellist) and professor of music. I hold a bachelor's and master's degree from Juilliard and a doctorate from Johns Hopkins University. I performed internationally and in the United States as a cello soloist and as principal cellist of various professional orchestras and taught on several music faculties including Shepherd College, Western Maryland College, Columbia Union College, and Brooklyn College. My most recent prior line of work was information technology. When my entire department was outsourced in 2008, I found myself facing some very difficult decisions especially in the face of the economic downturn. But it was the greatest thing that ever happened to me in many ways. I believe it was a God-ordained plan to use a bad situation to pave the way for me to become a full-time writer.

My past experiences help add some flavor (seasoning, if you will) to my books. Because I have so much of it in me, it is natural to incorporate classical music (Xandra Carrick is a cellist—coincidence?), computers, and my faith into the books I write. Write what you know, as the saying goes.

2. What role does your personal faith play in writing novels? What kind of messages are you trying to convey to readers?

I cannot begin to express how important a role my faith in Jesus Christ plays in my novel writing. Without reservation, I always tell people that all of my success has come through divine inspiration. I know that might sound cliché, but it's completely true. Before Darkroom, *my book* Beyond Justice *hit #1 on three different Barnes & Noble Bestseller lists and #3 on Amazon.com. It also won the 2011 International Book Award. But that book came as a result of deep soul searching and prayer. The message I am trying to convey in all of my books is not one that preaches and/or tells a reader what to think or believe. I want to show my readers a side of Christianity that is rarely portrayed in the media and to present controversial issues with fairness. To that end, I don't portray nonbelievers in a bad light, nor do I portray believers as perfect. And as for the questions about God and faith, I present both sides as unbiased as I can and let the reader draw their own conclusions. I am grateful that, based on all the positive feedback for* Beyond Justice, *many readers who are not "religious" appreciated my approach and were given a chance to glimpse this faith in a way they might not otherwise have done. As for the message, it varies from book to book and I try to write what I feel God has given me to write. That's not as lofty as it sounds. After all, we all have divine purposes and assignments (according to Ephesians 2:10) and it is God's plan that we should walk in those callings.*

3. How did you develop Xandra's character?
It was just a few months after my mother-in-law had passed away. I began to ask my wife (an avid reader) what she felt made a great novel. We started brainstorming about Xandra and to make a long story short, I borrowed many ideas and character traits, and angst, from my wife. Some of them were her suggestions; others just grew as I wrote. I wanted to write Xandra as a real person with whom everyone can identify. She's smart, she's capable, but she knows she's flawed. She has identity issues that are very common with women that resonate well, so I'm told.

4. What did you enjoy most about the writing of *Darkroom*?
The research was one of the highlights. I learned a lot writing this book, not just the historical facts, but the spirit of the time/place. Much of my research came from the firsthand accounts of Vietnam War photojournalists and correspondents.

I also enjoyed weaving in the twists and turns, as well as the character interactions. My favorites are the tension between Xandra and Kyle. But I also loved it when Peter Carrick confronted Mark Collinsworth.

5. How and why did you choose not to include Jake as one of the narrators in *Darkroom*?
None of the scenes featured him as the person with the most at stake. That is how I decide in whose point of view I will write a scene; the one to whom the most significant things happen.

6. It's very interesting that Colson took his own life—an act that feels more complex than just an "easy way out." What were you trying to illustrate with his choice to commit suicide?
Ah, yes. Definitely not an easy way out. Colson firmly believed that what he did was right. To the very end he kept that "You can't handle the truth!" attitude (to borrow from the Tom Cruise/Jack Nicholson movie, A Few

Good Men), *even as he lost everything. But deep down, I see Colson as analogous to Lucifer. He deluded himself to believe that he has the right to take Machiavellian actions, that he is above the law because of his power. But at the heart of his actions and attitudes is the sin God hates most (according to Scriptures): pride.*

So to the very end, unrepentant, Colson shakes an angry fist at eternity, at God even. He will not let anyone punish him for his crimes. He would rather take his own life than allow anyone to bring him to "justice."

7. Colson is clearly an advocate of "the end justifies the means," but this is clearly a flawed philosophy. Did you intend for this story to serve as an allusion to current governmental practices? What can readers take away from Colson's demise?

I had no designs on drawing an allegory to our current government. Regardless of my agreement or disagreement with my authorities, I honor and respect them. The Scriptures say that all authority is given by God. Colson's practices are fictional, and while similar actions may have occurred in our world, I was not drawing any known parallels. That said, I've always been a conspiracy theorist when it comes to writing fiction, be it a national cover-up, or a murder mystery.

Colson's demise will hopefully resonate with those most difficult parts of our human nature: pride and self-righteousness. Pride masks fear, but manifests itself in many ways, from outright rebellion or arrogance to passive-aggressiveness. But as humans, we all have to deal with it. We all have a little bit of Colson in us, though we don't want to admit it. Colson dealt with it by using all his resources, drive, and passion to do things his way, unrepentant to the bitter end. My hope is that as I recognize my own pride and self-righteousness, I will turn from it, repent, and be set free like Peter Carrick at the end of this book.

8. How did you imagine the process through which Xandra has visions? Have you ever known anyone who experiences similar visions the way Xandra does?

When I was a teenager, my older brother studied photography. Someone gave him all the equipment needed to set up a darkroom at home and I developed many photos with my brother. It always gave me the chills as the ghostly images came up under the developing solution. So when I imagined Xandra's capabilities, these experiences were very prominent in my memory.

I have known several people who have experienced visions, though not exactly as Xandra did. But these visions were ones which told of the future (a spiritual gift called "Word of Wisdom") as well as visions of past/present things ("Word of Knowledge") which the person experiencing the vision could have no way of knowing outside of the vision. One thing they have had in common was that they benefit, edify, and encourage those whom the visions were about. While some consider such things esoteric and "supernatural," for those who believe in the power of the Holy Spirit, they are quite common and familiar, though life-altering.

9. How does *Darkroom* compare to *Beyond Justice*?
I wrote Darkroom *shortly after I completed* Beyond Justice. *There are similarities, such as the supernatural visions, the Christian undertones, and the legal drama, but* Darkroom's *stakes are global, whereas the stakes in* Beyond Justice *are deeply personal.* Darkroom *takes on multiple time lines and delves into a moment in history, whereas* Beyond Justice *is a huge journey of faith and redemption. While both books incorporate multiple points of view,* Darkroom's *main protagonist is female, while* Beyond Justice's *is male. Neither books are heavily gender-weighted in content, and there's plenty of action and suspense, as well as some romance intertwined in both books.*

10. Xandra Carrick's character had a wide-open ending. Are you considering including her in an upcoming story? Are you currently working or planning on another novel?
This book was meant to be the first in a long series of Xandra Carrick books. I plan to write more Xandra Carrick books and stories in the near future.

11. If you weren't writing, what else would you be doing? What else are you passionate about?
It's amazing how much time this writer spends on things other than writing. I love spending time with my family, traveling, and going to activities. I am passionate about my church, The City Church, and the small group that I and my wife lead (the members of which are mentioned in the acknowledgments).

I also enjoy playing the cello, reading, watching movies, dining, and playing Texas Hold 'em with my good friends. I am so blessed with friends and loved ones. Truly, my cup runneth over.